THE CURSE OF THE
HOUSE OF FOSKETT

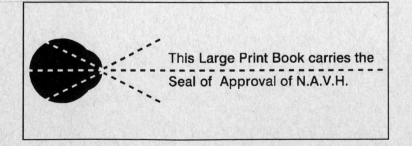

This Large Print Book carries the
Seal of Approval of N.A.V.H.

THE GOWER STREET DETECTIVE

THE CURSE OF THE HOUSE OF FOSKETT

M. R. C. KASASIAN

THORNDIKE PRESS
A part of Gale, Cengage Learning

GALE
CENGAGE Learning·

Farmington Hills, Mich • San Francisco • New York • Waterville, Maine
Meriden, Conn • Mason, Ohio • Chicago

GALE
CENGAGE Learning

LIBRARY OF CONGRESS CATALOGING-IN-PUBLICATION DATA

Kasasian, M. R. C. (Martin R. C.)
  The curse of the House of Foskett / by M.R.C. Kasasian. — Large print
edition.
    pages cm. — (The Gower Street Detective) (Thorndike Press large print
mystery)
  ISBN 978-1-4104-8038-5 (hardcover) — ISBN 1-4104-8038-0 (hardcover)
  1. Private investigators—England—London—Fiction. 2. England—Social
life and customs—19th century—Fiction. 3. Large type books. I. Title.
PR6111.A77C87 2015
823'.92—dc23   2015010174

Published in 2015 by arrangement with Pegasus Books LLC

Printed in Mexico
1 2 3 4 5 6 7 19 18 17 16 15

For Robert, with love.

INTRODUCTION

It is almost a year since I wrote the introduction to my first memoir of my guardian, Sidney Grice — *The Mangle Street Murders* — and its modest success in these days of paper shortages has encouraged me to give an account of our next major case, the terrible series of events in the autumn of 1882.

When I last wrote I was sheltering in the cellar of 125 Gower Street with Hitler's bombs pulverizing London. The Blitz continues, though with less ferocity, and the Nazis have learned the folly of conducting raids in daylight hours. The threat of invasion still hangs over us, though, and the sight of old men and skinny youths training for the Home Guard is a touching reminder of our determination not to be conquered.

This case of which I now write nearly destroyed my guardian, but it marked an important shift in our relationship. Until then I had been present only under sufferance. When Sidney Grice began these investigations, however, we both acted under the assumption that I should accompany him. This I continued to do whenever possible, apart from our great rift, until the day he died.

M.M. 3 September 1942

1
THE CURSE OF THE FOSKETTS

Legend had it there was a curse on the House of Foskett. Giles, the first Baron Foskett, it was said, had been present in 1417 at the siege of Bowfield during the long Wars of the Roses and led the second wave of attackers through the breached walls. The defenders had placed their wives and children in the Church of St Oswald for sanctuary but a bloodlust was upon the attackers and they forced their way into the building, slaughtering everybody who sheltered there.

As if this were not outrage enough, Baron Giles, upon discovering a young nun hiding in a chapel dedicated to the Virgin Mary, ravished and slew her upon the side altar. With her dying breath the nun put a curse upon him and his descendants, and the moment Baron Giles left St Oswald's he was attacked by a pack of rabid dogs and torn to pieces in the street.

Baron Giles's son and heir was by all accounts a good man. He gave generously to the poor and paid for St Oswald's to be refurbished and a memorial built for his father's victims. His pious life did not save him, however. He had no sooner rededicated the chapel than the statue of Mary came crashing down, splitting his skull open so that he died in agony ten days later.

And so the catalogue continued — hangings, impalements, disembowelments — as various members of the Foskett family met untimely and violent ends. Sometimes the curse skipped generations and was consigned to family history, but sooner or later it reappeared. Nor was the curse confined to the male side of the family. Baroness Agatha drowned in a rain cistern at the age of ninety-five and Lady Matilda, the daughter of Baron Alfred, was decapitated on Brighton beach.

In 1724, following the incineration of Baron Colin in Mount Vesuvius, the Foskett title fell vacant and so it remained until 1861 when Reginald, tenuously descended from a nephew of Baron Giles, successfully applied for the right to adopt it. Little good did the honour do him. Within six years of being admitted to the peerage he was pierced through the eye, into his brain, by a stair rod. The wound became purulent and he died, raving in torment.

Shortly after this *The Times* announced that his heir, Rupert, had predeceased him on a South Sea island, so it was Reginald's widow, the dowager Baroness, Lady Parthena Foskett, over whose head the curse hung menacingly now.

2
THE DUST AND THE DREAM

The dust had still not settled from the Ashby case, the general opinion being that Sidney Grice had sent one of his own clients, an innocent man, to the gallows. This was not good for business, so much so that when the Prince of Wales lost his signet ring in a house of ill-repute, it was Charlemagne Cochran and not Sidney Grice who was called upon to retrieve it. And the fact that he managed to do this quickly and discreetly only served to deepen my guardian's depression.

A couple of cases came his way — rescuing a wealthy northern industrialist's daughter mysteriously afflicted with blue carbuncles and exposing a fraudulent society for men with ginger hair — but my guardian's workload was light that summer and, as the days shortened and the leaves fell in the windswept London parks, it all but dried up.

He took to lying in his bath for hours, clambering out in the evenings for a little dry toast and a lot of tea before limping wordlessly upstairs to lock himself in his bedroom. He did not bother to put his glass eye in but wore a black patch all the time. He was usually a voracious reader but now he would not open a book or even pick up any of his five daily newspapers. However, that was probably for the best. My guardian never took well to adverse criticism and there was no shortage of that in the press or the many abusive letters that were delivered several times a day.

My mother had died giving birth to me and my father had joined her in the summer of '81, leaving me the Grange, our family estate in Parbold, but not the means to maintain it. I had never heard of my god-father, Sidney Grice, but my lawyers assured me that he was a gentleman of the highest repute and so his offer to take me under his wing had seemed like a gift from heaven six months ago. But now I was beginning to wonder if I should have struggled harder to stay at home.

Many evenings I dined alone, forking a reheated vegetable stew around my plate and nibbling chalky bread. Afterwards I would go into the tiny courtyard garden to smoke two Turkish cigarettes under the twisted cherry tree and then upstairs to write my journals. And after that I went to my writing box and pressed the button under the inkwell to open the secret compartment and untie the ribbon around my precious bundle.

Your letters are so few and I know them by heart but your dear hands held them as mine hold them now.

I dreamed of you that night. We were drifting in a rowing boat down a holly green river, the sun blazing in the indigo sky and the herons scudding raggedly over us. We had a picnic basket at our feet and a bottle of Champagne hanging into the water and we lay back just holding hands and happy. It was all so lovely until the end. I can never change that.

I destroyed the last letter you wrote.

On the first Tuesday of September, however, my guardian came down for breakfast and graced me with a grunt. We sat at opposite ends of the table, me looking at him with his unopened copy of *Simpkin's Diseases of the Human Foot.*

'I need a big case,' he said suddenly, 'or my brain shall become as stagnant as yours.'

14

'Something will turn up,' I said, but he shook his head.

'Who will employ my services now? I cannot even show my face without being ridiculed and abused.'

I cracked open my egg and pushed it hastily aside. The smell of sulphur was nauseating. 'Perhaps you need to get away for a bit.'

'A bit of what?' He picked up a slice of toast, crustless and charcoaled just as he liked it.

'Why don't we take a holiday?'

'What an absurd idea. Can you imagine me in a striped blazer ambling along gaudy promenades and eating cockles from a paper cone?'

I had to admit that I could not, but I was delighted to see him so suddenly animated. He leaned over and stretched across to slide my eggcup towards him with his Grice Patent Extendable Fly Swat, and smelled it appreciatively, though he was still very snuffly from a cold.

'Why not visit a friend,' I suggested.

'A *friend*?' He recoiled in disgust. 'I have no *friend* and what on earth would I want one for?' He shuddered. 'Really, March, it is quite bad enough suffering your shrill gibberish day and night, week after week, without taking on a *friend*.' Sidney Grice

15

tucked into the egg with relish.

I threw down my napkin. 'I have lived among what most Englishmen would describe as ignorant savages and met with more courtesy than you are capable of.'

'What is courtesy?' My guardian dabbed his lips. 'It is deceit bursting with lies. If I were courteous I should have to tell you that you look nice when to the best of my knowledge you never have and I do not suppose that you ever will.'

'You are the rudest man I have ever met.'

'I hope so for your sake,' he retorted. 'A ruder man might express his opinions on your low intelligence or ungainly deportment.'

'Most girls glide about like statues on casters,' you told me, 'but you sway and move like a woman. You have blood in your veins, not weak tea.'

I toyed with the idea of throwing my plate at him, but I was hungry and there was little enough to eat in his house as it was.

'I think I preferred it when you were silent.'

'So did I.' Sidney Grice ground his burnt toast into a powder and sprinkled it into his bowl of prune juice.

16

Far away and below us the doorbell rang.

'Molly has forgotten something.' He scrunched his napkin on to the tablecloth.

'How do you know that?'

'Because I do what I am unable to persuade you to do — use my ears. She is answering the door in her heavy outdoor boots. Therefore she must be planning on going out for an essential supply.'

I listened but I could hear nothing until our maid began to mount the stairs to the first-floor dining room.

'You have a caller, sir, a gent.' Her ginger hair was escaping either side of her white starched cap. 'He said he must see you on . . .' she screwed up her face in an effort to remember '. . . a matter of the outmost importance.'

'Did he give you a card?'

'Yes, sir.' And, as my guardian had deduced, Molly had her outside boots on.

'Where is it?'

'In my pocket.'

'Why not on a tray? Never mind. Just give it to me.'

Molly held out the card and her employer snatched it away.

'Mr Horatio Green.' He shivered. 'What a revoltingly bucolic surname. Where is he now?'

17

'Outside, sir. You told me to admit no one without your premission.'

Sidney Grice stood up. 'Then show him to my study at once.' He untied his patch. 'Idiotic girl. You never obey my instructions when I want you to.' He took a steely-blue glass eye from the velvet pouch in his waistcoat pocket, pulled his lids apart and pressed it into his right socket, checked his cravat in the mantel mirror and pushed back his thick black hair with his hand. 'You had better come too, March. All this moping about has made you even more irritable and irritating than usual.'

3
THE VISITOR
AND PARTY TRICKS

I followed him down the stairs into his study, his shoulder dipping jerkily with his left leg. A plump, middle-aged man in a navy-blue coat and charcoal trousers was already seated to the right of the fireplace, his hand to his cheek. This was my usual chair but Molly would never have dared allow him to sit in her employer's. The moment we appeared our visitor jumped up and grasped my guardian's hand.

'Mr Grice. It is such a thrill to meet you. I have read so much about you in the newspapers.'

'You will have been hard pressed to find an accurate fact then,' Sidney Grice told him.

'And you must be Miss Middleton.' Mr Green compressed my hand in his. 'I believe you helped Mr Grice solve the Ashby stabbing case.'

My guardian adjusted his eye. 'She may

have accompanied me on that case,' he said, 'but I can assure you she was nothing but a hindrance. Ring for tea, Miss Middleton.'

'I shall try my idiotic best.' I pulled the bell rope twice as the two of them sat facing each other, then got myself an upright chair from the round central table.

'Go on then.' Mr Green flushed with excitement and Sidney Grice blinked.

'What?'

'Make a series of ingenious observations about me.'

My guardian stretched languidly. 'I do not perform party tricks.'

But our visitor leaned forward and urged, 'Oh, come on. Tell me something about myself.'

Sidney Grice waved a bored hand. 'Apart from the fact that you are a pharmacist . . .'

Mr Green touched his cheek. 'How the blazes . . . ? It is almost supernatural. Do I have faint stains of chemicals on my hands?' He scrutinized his fingers. 'I cannot see any.'

'It is written on your calling card,' my guardian said.

'Well, that is not much of a trick then, is it?' Mr Green said. 'Do another one.'

'You are suffering with an earache,' Sidney Grice told him, 'though not as much as I might wish.'

Mr Green stroked his left ear in confirmation. 'I have been a martyr to it since my eardrum was burst by an earwig when I was fourteen.'

I laughed. 'But surely the belief that earwigs burrow into one's ear is an old wives' tale?'

Mr Green became sorrowful. 'I am living proof that it is not.' He put his fingertips to his left temple. 'But a child could have worked that out from the cotton wool in it. Say something cleverer.'

Sidney Grice scratched his head in exasperation. 'How am I supposed to know what is or is not obvious to a man of your mean acumen when everything about you is obvious to me? For instance, you are clearly a bachelor.'

Mr Green thought about this and said at last, 'Very well. I give up. How did you work that one out?'

'Three reasons,' my guardian explained. 'First, the button stitching on your waistcoat is at least four years out of style — five, if you live in one of the better squares, which you do not — and no wife would allow her husband to be abroad so unfashionably attired. Second —'

'Yes, but what if I choose to ignore sartorial trends and my wife is too meek to prevent me?'

Sidney Grice gave a clipped laugh. 'Yet more proof that you are unmarried. You must have been reading the small-brained scribblings of Mr Dickens if you believe that such a thing as a meek wife exists outside the bindings of one of his tawdry novels. To proceed, you do not wear a wedding band — which many men do not — but since you are a Roman Catholic —'

'Can you smell incense on me?'

'I can smell something,' I said, but both men ignored me.

'Your rosary is hanging out of your coat pocket,' Sidney Grice observed. 'Third, and most conclusively, you are such an insufferable man that no sane woman would ever consent to be your wife and an insane woman is barred by law from entering into the marriage contract.'

Mr Green clenched his jaw and half stood. His mouth worked itself into forming a reply but then he beamed and fell back, laughing heartily. 'Capital. Capital. Your rudeness is as famous as you are, Mr Grice, and now I shall be able to tell all my customers that I have been a recipient of it.'

'I can give you much more than that to report,' my guardian said. 'I could discourse at length upon your imbecilic grin, for

22

example.'

Mr Green blushed. 'I can take a joke as well as any man but —'

'So how was your trip to the dentist?' I asked, and my guardian glanced at me.

'But —' Mr Green said again.

'I can smell it on you,' I explained, 'and you keep touching your right cheek.'

Mr Green clapped his hands. 'Why, you will be putting your guardian out of work. I —'

'Perhaps you could tell me why you are taking up my time,' Sidney Grice broke in, and our visitor's smile vanished.

'It is a bad business, Mr Grice,' he said as Molly came coughing in with the tea.

4
THE SOCIETY OF FOOLS

'A very bad business,' Mr Green said when Molly had gone. 'Have you ever heard of final death societies, Mr Grice?'

'I have three such societies in my files,' Sidney Grice said, 'and in all of them some of the members were murdered or died in extremely dubious circumstances, but, as I was not called upon to assist in any of the cases, they remain unsolved.'

I poured three cups of tea and asked, 'What exactly is a final death society?'

'It is an association of fools,' my guardian said, 'with large estates and microscopic traces of common sense.'

Our caller straightened indignantly. 'Let me describe it in less emotional terms,' he began.

But it was Sidney Grice's turn to bridle. 'The whole world knows I have no emotions,' he said, 'other than my twin loves — of possessions and the truth.'

'Milk and sugar?' I offered and Mr Green nodded.

'The societies are groups of men,' he explained, 'though in our case we have two lady members — who either have no heirs or have heirs that they do not care for. They make wills for a sum of money usually based upon the total assets of the poorest member, all of them being independently audited. These testaments are put into the hands of a mutually employed solicitor who will collect and manage their estates as they die and release the total funds to the final surviving member. For his services he takes a twenty per cent share of any increase in the value of the fund. The —'

'In other words,' Sidney Grice interrupted, 'all the members have a vested interest in ensuring the prior demise of their fellows.'

'Which is why I am approaching you.' Horatio Green raised his teacup carefully with both hands. 'You see, seven of us formed the club and we lodged a promise of eleven thousand pounds each into the fund, the surviving member to receive the grand sum of seventy thousand pounds plus any interest that has accrued in the meantime.'

'And who gets the remaining seven thousand pounds?' my guardian enquired.

'Why, you do, Mr Grice,' our visitor said.

Sidney Grice checked his watch. 'Explain.'

Mr Green sipped his tea. 'We are not so reckless as you suppose, Mr Grice. First, we allowed only those of the highest character to join our society and, second, we hit upon the stratagem of investigating the death of every member no matter how natural their passing may seem. For this, we agreed to engage the skills of the finest independent detective in the empire.'

'Then you have come to the right address,' my guardian said.

'However,' Mr Green continued, 'Mr Cochran was unwilling to take up the challenge and so I have come to you.'

Sidney Grice shot a hand to his eye. 'Am I a pigeon to peck at that vain imposter's crumbs?'

Mr Green put down his cup and chuckled. 'Got you there, Mr Grice. You see, you are not the only one who can be rude. You are, of course, our first and only choice.'

'I still consider it a great impertinence that I was not approached before now.' My guardian eyed him icily and considered the matter. 'If I accept your brief, Mr Green' — he tapped his watch and edged the minute hand forward — 'it will only be because the

26

prospect of investigating your death will bring me boundless joy. Let us hope I shall not have to wait too long.'

Mr Green put his thumbs in his waistcoat pockets and drummed his fingers. 'Well, come what may,' he said, 'I shall not be the first. We have only been constituted for a week and we have already lost one member.'

'I am so deeply sorry,' my guardian said.

'Well, thank you, but —'

'That I ever employed that useless lumpen serving wench,' Sidney Grice continued. 'This tea is as weak as a Frenchman, and why is she creeping about in the hall?'

'I cannot hear her,' I said.

Mr Green cocked his head. 'Nor I.'

'Dull minds have dull senses,' my guardian told us and tugged the bell rope sharply twice. 'I suppose I had better take the details.'

'His name was Edwin Slab,' Mr Green began, but my guardian raised a hand to silence him.

'You will provide the information as and when I ask for it. Now . . .' He took a small, red leather-bound notebook from the table by his chair and his silver-plated Mordan mechanical pencil from his inside coat pocket. 'What is the name of your ridiculous society?'

27

'We called it the Last Death Club.'

'Ingenious,' Sidney Grice murmured. 'And who are the other members?'

'I have made out a list with all our members' names, addresses, occupations and ages.' Mr Green proffered a folded piece of paper, but Sidney Grice sat back, closed his eyes and said, 'Read it to me. Just the names and ages for now.'

Our visitor unfolded the sheet, hooked a pair of horn-rimmed spectacles over his ears and began, 'Edwin Slab, aged eighty-one.'

My guardian raised his eyebrow. 'An unlikely winner then.' But Mr Green demurred.

'We tried to organize our club so that all members had similar life expectancies. The Slabs have a long history of centenarians and until yesterday Edwin Slab was in perfect health.'

'You were friends?'

'The best of. I introduced him to the society.'

'So how did Mr Slab end up on one?'

There was a clatter and Sidney Grice spun round. 'Filthy footling tykes,' he said. 'Why have those street urchins nothing better to do than throw stones at my windows? There is no shortage of blocked drains they could be sent down.'

'And no shortage of rats and disease to attack them there,' I objected. But my guardian was unmoved.

'No harm done this time,' Mr Green observed. 'You should have seen what they did to my pharmacy last night. I was just about to shut up shop when a group of boys burst in and started throwing stock off the shelves. I tried to stop them and got knocked over for my troubles. If a vicar had not turned up with his daughter and frightened them away, I dread to think what they might have done.'

'Did they steal anything?' I asked.

'They did not get the chance,' he said. 'There were a few breakages but nothing too serious. The vicar picked most of the things up and I put them back on the shelf whilst his daughter composed herself. Ladies do not cope well with excitement.'

'They so rarely get any,' I informed them.

Sidney Grice, who had been leaning back with his eyes closed, opened them and asked, 'How many children?'

'Six or seven.'

'Which?'

'Does it matter?'

'If it came to trial it would matter enormously to the seventh urchin who was or was not there. Had you met this vicar before?'

Mr Green winced and put his hand to his face. 'I know him from a previous visit — a Reverend Golding from St Agatha's. He suffers with his ears too and asked what I could recommend.'

'That is the most intriguing petty crime I have come across in four years.' My guardian waved a hand. 'Proceed.'

'Well, I told him that after breakfast —'

'Not with that twaddle.' Sidney Grice gesticulated. 'Tell me about Mr Slab.'

Mr Green puffed up but only for a moment. 'The doctor put it down to a seizure.'

'You have your doubts?'

Mr Green spread his hands as if to demonstrate that they were empty. 'I have no opinion on the matter, Mr Grice, but the rules of the society oblige me to ask you to investigate his passing.'

My guardian yawned. 'I am rather swamped by work at the moment.'

'It is a thousand pounds a time, Mr Grice, with a two thousand pound bonus should you be able to prove that any member was murdered by another.'

'To be paid when?'

'After the death of the last member.'

'And what if I predecease you? Does the

30

money stay in the society's fund? If so, I am laying myself open to the same risks of murder as you so blockheadedly are.'

'We thought of that,' Mr Green said. 'If you should die before all of us, the money for each case you have investigated will be left to whosoever you desire.'

'But there is nobody to whom I would wish to leave money. I have not been cursed by children.'

'You have a mother,' I said and he shrugged.

'A few thousand pounds would be nothing to her. She probably spends that much every month, purloining lumps of chipped stone from that old temple in Athens.'

'Another relative or friend or somebody you are fond of,' Mr Green suggested, but my guardian frowned.

'There is no one.'

'What about Miss Middleton?'

'She does not enter any of those categories.'

Molly came in with a fresh pot.

'Perhaps you could have the money buried with you.' I poured our teas, pleased to see them actually steaming for once, as Molly tried an elaborate curtsy and stumbled out of the room.

'That is the first sensible thing you have

said,' my guardian told me, 'especially as I intend to be cremated.'

Mr Green laughed uncertainly, but Sidney Grice held out his hand and said, 'Give me the roster.'

Mr Green passed it across and my guardian perched his pince-nez on the bridge of his long, thin nose to study it with interest.

'Horatio Green,' he read out, as if the name had a new meaning for him. 'Edwin Slab, Gentleman; Primrose McKay — an unsavoury lady if a small proportion of the stories are to be believed.'

'Is she connected to McKay's Sausages?' I asked and he nodded.

'One account has it that her father took her to the abattoir on her tenth birthday and that she found the experience highly entertaining. Her greatest joy was to be allowed to cut a sow's throat.'

'How horrible.' I fought down the nausea.

Sidney Grice blew his nose. 'And by no means the worst I have heard of her.' He scratched his scarred ear. 'She is very young.'

'Twenty-nine,' Mr Green confirmed, 'but none of her female antecedents has lived beyond the age of thirty-five since records began. In fact —'

'The splendidly equestrian-sounding

Warrington Gallop of Gallop's Snuff Emporium,' my guardian continued. 'The Reverend Enoch Jackaman, rector of St Jerome's Church — I met his brother on the crossing to Calais once; the eccentrically named Prometheus Piggety, self-proclaimed entrepreneur.' His voice had dropped soothingly but it suddenly rose. 'Baroness Foskett,' he said loudly and Mr Green sat up.

'You know the baroness?'

'Nobody has known her for over one and a half decades now. My father was a great friend of the late Baron Reginald and as a child I often played at Mordent House, the family home in Kew, with their late son, the Honourable Rupert. What is so amusing, Miss Middleton?'

I covered my mouth. 'I am sorry. It is just the thought of you playing.'

My guardian scowled. 'I was a perfectly normal boy and Rupert was only thirteen years older. Many were the boisterous games we enjoyed . . .' a slightly wistful look drifted across his face '. . . of chess, or, in more frivolous moods, we would set each other mathematical or syllogistic problems.'

Mr Green winked at me. 'Quite a jack-the-lad then.'

Sidney Grice grunted and said, 'I am

nonplussed that Baroness Foskett engages in such a frivolous and foolhardy enterprise.'

'Why, she is very enthusiastic.' Mr Green helped himself to the sugar and I added his milk. 'She told me so herself.'

'I understood that she is still in deep mourning and receives no one.' My guardian leaned forward. 'You have met her?'

Mr Green sipped his tea. 'Well, sort of,' he said and pulled a wry face. 'This tea tastes very odd.'

My guardian tried his. 'A touch flowery perhaps, but we are sampling a new blend from the lower eastern slopes of the Himalayas.'

'Very odd,' Mr Green said again and took another mouthful. He winced. 'So hot.'

Sidney Grice wrinkled his nose, looked briefly puzzled and, throwing his cup and saucer down, leaped up. 'Stop!' He flung the table between them towards the hearth, smashing the china and spraying my dress with hot water. 'Spit it out, man. Spit it out.'

Our visitor looked about him.

'Anywhere! On the floor!' my guardian shouted.

Mr Green gulped. 'I couldn't do that.' He smacked his lips sourly and screwed up his face. 'Goodness, it burns.'

'You stupid man.' Sidney Grice prodded

his lapel. 'That was —'

'Prussic acid,' Mr Green whispered in confused wonder, letting the cup fall empty into his lap. He blanched and countless tiny beads of sweat broke out on his brow. His head jerked back and his mouth opened wide as he clutched the arms of the chair, raising his shoulders and expanding his chest to take a deep breath.

I rushed over, loosened his cravat and undid the stud of his shirt collar. The sweat was trickling down his temples now. Mr Green exhaled heavily and took another shuddering breath, his face blood-red and his eyelids pulled back in terror.

'Save me.' The words came out half-strangled. 'Please.'

'Do something,' my guardian barked. 'You are the one with the medical experience.'

Mr Green's hands clutched at his neck. He was panting quickly and I could hear his lungs starting to fill with water. His complexion turned dark blue.

'Lean forward.' I felt as if somebody else were giving the instructions. 'And try to breathe slowly.' But I knew that whatever I said was useless.

Horatio Green's face was black now as he fought to take in air.

'Do *not* die in my house,' Sidney Grice

said. 'I absolutely forbid it.'

Horatio Green doubled up, the fluid gurgling in his chest. With one gigantic effort he struggled to his feet. His left hand went down but missed the arm of the chair and he slipped sideways. I caught his arm and he gripped the sleeve on my dress, pinching my skin so hard that I cried out.

'Stay conscious,' my guardian commanded.

'It is all right,' I said as he swayed towards me. I steadied myself. 'It is all right,' I said again slowly. 'I have got you and I shall not let you go.'

Those eyes locked on mine in helpless desperation. I had seen that look before and I had hoped not to see it again.

'God bless you,' I said as his knees sagged under him. I held on, but he was too heavy for me as he slumped.

My guardian grabbed him under the shoulders and tried to take his weight, but he was a big man and we were off-balance. Horatio Green made one last shallow gurgling suck of air before it was flooded out of him, and toppled backwards into his chair. I felt for his pulse but there was none to detect. I put my ear to his nose and listened for what I had no hope of hearing.

'Blast and blazes.' Sidney Grice put his

hand to his forehead. 'I have lost another client.'

5
THE DANCING SKULL

I took a step back, and breathed deeply in and out slowly to try to calm myself. 'You have lost a client? Is that all he was?'

'To me, yes.'

'And do you only care about the money?'

Sidney Grice returned my gaze coolly. 'From a financial point of view — as you well know — the sooner they all die the better,' he said. 'But my reputation hangs in tatters already and this will fray it to threads.'

I worked my way round the toppled table and the debris of our tea tray and pulled the bell rope, the ivory skull dancing obscenely. My guardian looked back. 'What are you doing?'

'Summoning Molly.' Something sharp caught in my chest. 'We must call the police.'

'No.' Sidney Grice raked his hair back and hesitated. 'Yes, of course.' He crouched to peer into Horatio Green's bulging eyes. 'But how did you get the poison?' he asked. 'It was not in the teapot and you had nothing to eat.' He coughed.

The smell of bitter almonds was filling the room. I went over and pulled up a sash window. It was stiff and probably had not been opened in years and the hubbub of Gower Street with all its clattering hooves and rattling wheels flooded in.

'It was not in the milk or sugar either. He and I both had those,' I recalled. 'And he did not take any pills, unless he slipped one in his mouth while we were not looking.'

'I would have noticed.'

Molly came in, carrying a feather duster over her shoulder like a parasol. She stopped and opened her mouth.

Sidney Grice pointed at her. 'Do *not* screech.'

She closed her mouth, took one nervous step forward and peered over. 'Is he' — she pushed a lock of hair up under her hat — 'dead?'

'I am afraid he is,' I told her and she bent to pick up the sugar bowl which had rolled into the middle of the room.

Sidney Grice picked up our visitor's shattered cup and held it to his nose. 'No prussic acid here.' He put it down and inspected the soles of Mr Green's boots.

Molly looked puzzled. 'Did you want some, sir?'

'No, Molly,' I explained. 'It is a poison.'

'Oh, sir' — Molly's hair escaped again — 'when I accidentally listened at the door and overheard you telling your visitor you hoped he died soon, I didn't think you meant to murder him here and now.'

Her employer's eye fell out. He caught it deftly and dropped it into his waistcoat pocket. 'I did *not* kill Mr Green.'

He was holding Horatio Green's right hand, turning the palm up and then down, and scrutinizing the fingernails. He held it under his nose, as one might capture the fragrance of a flower, and let it fall back on to the dead man's leg.

'If you say so, sir.'

Sidney Grice straightened up. 'Why am I always beset by dead men and imbeciles?' He went to his desk.

'Dead men are your profession,' I reminded him. 'And if there are any imbeciles in this room, you brought them here.'

But my guardian was not listening. He was bent over with his Grice Self-Filling Fountain Pen, scratching a letter.

'Now, Molly, I am probably asking too much, but listen carefully.' He blotted his note, folded it and screwed the nib back into his pen. 'You will go into the hall and run up the flag. When a hansom comes, go straight to Marylebone Police Station.' He slipped the letter into a white envelope, dipped a brush into a pot of glue and gummed down the flap. 'Do not stop to gawk in shop windows or chatter with your grubby scullion friends. Go to the desk and ask for Inspector Pound. You are *not* to give this letter to anyone else. Have you got that?'

'What if he ain't there?'

'Then come straight home with the letter and tell me. Here is two shillings and four pence. That is one shilling for the fare and tuppence for the tip each way.' My guardian dropped the change into the sugar bowl. 'Go.'

'They ain't grubby,' Molly muttered to herself as she left. 'Well, not very.'

I righted the table. 'Perhaps the poison was already in his mouth,' I suggested. 'Maybe he was sucking on something for his toothache.'

Sidney Grice snapped his fingers. 'Baumgartner,' he said.

'What is Baumgartner?'

My guardian strode past his desk to the row of oak cabinets on the right-hand wall, pulling the lowest drawer of one halfway open. His fingers ran over the top of the tightly crammed brown envelopes as his lips moved silently through the titles.

'Here we are.' He whipped up a file and opened it to bring out a sheaf of handwritten notes and cuttings. 'Not *what, who.*' He passed me a yellowed copy of a newspaper, *Wiener Zeitun.* 'Otto Baumgartner was an Austrian dentist who counted several members of the Habsburgs amongst his clientele. In the summer of '54 a number of his patients died suddenly within days, hours or, in one case, minutes of attending his surgery. But it was only after the archbishop of Vienna fell dead at the high altar of the cathedral that Emperor Franz Joseph himself ordered an investigation.' The paper was dry and crackled as I opened it. 'Even then it was some months and several deaths later before the police made the connection to the victims' recent dental treatments,' Sidney Grice continued. 'A search of Baumgartner's surgery revealed a nearly full bottle of strychnine powder — sufficient to wipe out half the city. Confronted with this, Baumgartner confessed. He had been lining his patients' cavities with the powder and weakening his restorations so that they disintegrated when the patient had a meal or even a hot drink.' I surveyed an artist's

42

impression of the murderer, a rotund, jolly-looking chap with mutton-chop whiskers. 'It was estimated that Otto Baumgartner killed over forty of his patients.' He took the newspaper back. 'But the true figure and his motive may never be known as he had managed to destroy his records before the arresting officers arrived at his house, and self-administered his own medicine in the middle of the trial.' Sidney Grice dumped the file on his desk. 'Come, March. Help me to put him on the floor.'

'Should we be interfering with evidence?'

'Wherever the crime took place,' my guardian said, 'it was not in this house. Now, if I take the corpse under the arms . . .'

'He had a name.'

'And lift it like so . . .'

I pulled the chair away. For a small man, Sidney Grice was surprisingly strong and he lowered Horatio Green on to the floor with hardly a bump. 'Turn the gas up.'

The white flames high on the wall made little difference to the day-shadows as my guardian put on his pince-nez, kneeled beside Mr Green's head and prised his jaws apart, twisting the head from side to side to catch the light. He produced a white hand-kerchief and wiped round the open mouth, glancing at the bloodied linen before tossing it into the unlit fire.

'What do you make of this, March?'

I kneeled on the other side and took a closer look, the sharp fumes stinging my eyes and making my head spin.

'He has bitten his tongue quite badly and his throat is very ulcerated. He has' — I counted — 'seven teeth missing. The two molars on the lower left have been filled recently with silver amalgam and there are three older fillings on his top teeth, but they all look intact.' I twisted round to look at him from the other side. 'There is a large cavity in the back of his upper-right canine. Perhaps he had a dressing in that.'

'Possibly.' My guardian sounded unconvinced. 'Let us take a look in his jacket.'

In the left inner pocket was a pair of spectacles and in the right a calfskin wallet with two compartments. One contained three one-pound notes neatly folded and six of Mr Green's calling cards. The other side bulged with different cards and Sidney Grice read them out as he dealt them on to the floor.

'Auctioneer. Wine merchant and — here we are — Mr Silas Braithwaite, dental surgeon, 4 Tavistock Square. I think Mr Braithwaite might be worth a visit.' He stuffed the cards back into the wallet and

44

slipped it back inside the coat pocket. He scrambled to his feet and dusted his trousers down. 'In the meantime I must have some quiet while I think.'

My guardian went back to his armchair and sat on the edge of the seat, looking intently at the body in front of him. He brought out two halfpennies from his waistcoat and flipped them about in his left hand. I heard a banjo strumming and went to look out. A young man stood on the pavement, singing in a fine tenor voice to the tune of 'My Bonny'.

'I had a small problem on Monday
So I went to see Sidney Grice
He said, "Don't you worry. Just pay me.
I'll have you strung up in a trice." '

A few pedestrians stopped to listen and his body swayed as he went into the chorus.

'Strung up, strung up, I'll have you strung
    up in a trice, a trice.'

Two young ladies giggled behind their white gloves and a little girl with them broke into a waltz. And all the while, behind me, the coins clicked and Sidney Grice sat staring, seemingly oblivious.

'Strung up, strung up, I'll have you strung up in a trice.'

I slid the casement down and muffled the street again, and thought how strange that a sheet of glass could isolate us so effectively from the world.

From the hall I heard the front door open and the tumult of traffic swell before it was cut off again. My guardian looked up, as if out of a pleasant dream, and got to his feet.

'Do you trust me, March?' He straightened his shirt cuffs.

'Sometimes,' I said.

'Then I would ask you to make this one of the occasions that you do.' He ran tidying fingers through his hair.

'Inspector Pound,' Molly announced, 'ain't —'

'That is one shilling off your wages,' her employer snapped. 'I have warned you before about saying *ain't.*'

'Oh, but I ain't done nothing wrong.' Molly fiddled with her apron. 'I only tried to tell you —'

'Two shillings.'

'But —'

'No *buts.*' He sliced the air. 'If I were not so famously soft-hearted I should dismiss you without a reference on the spot,' he

46

said. 'I shall be out in a moment . . . Go away.' He turned back to me, his voice low and urgent. 'This is very important, March. There is no need to mention the dentist. That is not evidence, just what we have surmised. We must allow Pound to draw his own conclusions. Do you understand?'

'Yes, but —'

'I do not tell lies and I am not asking you to, only not to disagree with him.' My guardian slotted his glass eye back into its socket. 'Please, March.' I had never heard him say *please* before and there was something almost childlike in the way he looked at me now.

I tried to smarten my dress but there were tea stains down the front and sides.

'Very well.'

Thank you would have been nice, but Sidney Grice was never overly concerned with being nice. He strode straight to the door without another word and threw it open.

6
THE CRACKPOTS OF WAPPING

The man who stood in the hallway was not Inspector Pound. This was a shorter, older, clean-shaven but vaguely frowsy man.

'Tried to tell you.' Molly slunk away.

'Are you a servant?' the stranger asked.

'No,' I replied. 'Are you?'

He straightened his straight back. 'No, miss. I am a detective.'

'So am I,' I said.

'But you are a girl.' His voice was low but clear and his fingernails, I noticed, were cropped back by chewing.

'What a fine detective you must be to observe that,' I said, at which my guardian stepped forward, holding out his hand.

'Inspector Quigley,' he said. 'Don't mind Miss Middleton. She has a sense of humour.'

'Never saw the point of one myself,' the inspector said as they shook hands, and Sidney Grice grunted.

'It is just a passing phase, like a bicycle or the electrical telephone. Is Inspector Pound not available?'

'His mother is ill.'

'But his —' I began, and my guardian shushed me with a finger to his lips.

'Then I must thank you for coming in his place.'

Inspector Quigley brought out a notebook. 'If that maid of yours is to be believed, you have threatened and murdered your client. I suppose at least you have saved the hangman the trouble this time.'

'When I sent Ashby to the gallows' — Sidney Grice put a finger to his glass eye — 'it was with your force's enthusiastic collaboration, Inspector. Fortunately for both of us, I was able to prove twice that he was guilty as Cain.'

'I only wish the public shared your opinion,' Inspector Quigley said. 'But I have plenty of other fish to fry at present. Perhaps you would like to tell me what the trouble is here.'

Sidney Grice led the way into the study where Horatio Green lay untidily on his back beside his pulled-away chair. The inspector walked over and looked down at the body.

'Well, he's dead all right.' He toed an

49

upturned saucer on the rug.

'Yes.' My guardian blew his nose.

'Prussic acid,' the inspector said. 'I can still smell it. Now where would he have got that from?'

'He was a chemist,' I said and the inspector twisted towards me.

'Did you see him take it?'

'No. And his name, if you are interested, was Mr Horatio Green.'

Inspector Quigley crouched to smell half the broken cup. 'Well, it wasn't in his tea. Did he have anything to eat?'

'Nothing.'

He replaced the cup and got to his feet.

'Seems straightforward enough,' he pronounced. 'Man dies of poisoning. You didn't give it to him either deliberately or by mistake. Nobody else was here. Therefore he took it himself.' He inspected himself in the mantel mirror. 'No doubt about it. Suicide.'

My lips parted but I forced myself to stay silent.

'Your note said something about a society,' Inspector Quigley recalled.

'One of those final death clubs,' Sidney Grice said. 'He came to see me because he was concerned that the members might murder each other.'

The inspector faced me again. 'Did he seem very agitated?'

'No,' I said and Inspector Quigley inclined his head wisely.

'There you have it.' He clicked his fingers. 'Nine out of ten of these cases come as a complete shock to the suicide's family and friends. The criminal —'

'Criminal?' I interrupted and the inspector frowned.

'Suicide, as you are probably aware, Miss Middleton, is an offence in law.'

'Punishable by what?' I asked. 'A fine? Imprisonment with hard labour? Death?'

Inspector Quigley smirked at my simplicity. 'By the stigma it casts upon him and his family and by being excluded from a burial in a Christian cemetery.'

'But why would a man who was worried about being murdered kill himself?'

My guardian shot me a glance.

'Men who fear death most are often the ones who will try to preempt it,' the inspector explained patiently. 'I have lost count of the number of men who will take their own lives rather than face the gallows.'

'Usually by hanging themselves,' Sidney Grice said and the inspector cackled.

'Quite so,' he concurred. 'This Mr Green had got himself so terrified with the thought of what might happen to him that he decided to end it all here and now rather than await some grislier fate.'

'I had not realized quite how crass men could be until now,' I said, and Inspector Quigley patted the air where my shoulder had been before I stepped smartly away.

'Not all men are as wise as me and Mr Grice. But as a matter of fact I come across far more female suicides than male in the course of my work — cheap girls usually, who have seduced gullible men and then failed to entrap them. I am sorry if this shocks you, Miss Middleton.'

'The hypocrisy of men will never fail to appal me,' I said. 'Have you never heard of men seducing women or even forcing themselves upon them?'

'Steady on.' It may have been the shadows but I could almost swear the inspector blushed. He rubbed the back of his neck. 'There will have to be an inquest,' he said.

'Without a doubt.' Sidney Grice ushered him back into the hall and I followed. 'But you can leave that to me.'

'I hope so. I have more than enough on my plate at the moment with those damned — excuse my language, miss — so-called New Chartists.'

'But surely Chartism died out thirty years

ago,' I said.

'As a mass movement,' the inspector agreed, taking his long overcoat off the stand where Molly had hung it. 'But there is a fanatical core still all too active at the moment.'

'But what have they done?' I asked.

My guardian blew his nose and told me, 'Their very existence is an affront to civilization.'

'What is wrong with wanting universal male suffrage?'

Sidney Grice flushed indignantly. 'The word *universal* is what is wrong.' He gestured towards Gower Street. 'If you followed that view to its lunatic conclusion, why the potman and the wretch who sifts through the sewers for trinkets would have the same voice in choosing a member of Her Majesty's government as I do. A minister of the Crown would have to court popularity with the vagrant and the rag-and-bone man. Can you conceive it? The whole structure of society, the monarchy and the empire itself would collapse into a hideous heap of . . .' his lips curled, *'democracy.'*

'Is it not their country too?' I asked and Sidney Grice rolled his eye.

'The privilege of voting has to be earned,' he told me. 'You cannot hand it out like stale bread at a soup kitchen.'

'And before you knew it, we would be giving the vote to *women.*' Quigley chortled and my guardian groaned.

'Do not put that thought in her head,' Sidney Grice told him. 'Miss Middleton has enough eccentric ideas as it is.'

'I see nothing wrong with some women having the vote,' I said. 'Not all of them, of course. But I still do not see what the problem is.'

'This is strictly between ourselves.' The inspector put on his bowler hat. 'Recent intelligence suggests that they are planning to assassinate Her Majesty and set up a revolutionary council in Wapping. Crackpots, needless to say, but in the meantime I have been deployed to round up suspects.'

'Then we shall leave you to it.' My guardian opened the front door and closed it behind the inspector. 'You promised not to argue with him.'

'I promised not to argue with Inspector Pound,' I said and an unborn smile fleeted across his face.

'After the impression you made, he would probably have been suspicious if you *had* agreed with him.' His voice rose. 'Come out, Molly.' And she appeared sheepishly from behind the stairs.

'I was just —'

'Do not bore me with any more lies. You were eavesdropping.'

'I —'

He blotted her words out with the palm of his hand. 'Why did you give that letter to Inspector Quigley after my strict instructions?'

Molly twisted her fingers. 'Oh but, sir, but he made me.'

'Did he knock you unconscious and wrench it from your bleeding fingers? If so, you have made a remarkable recovery. If not, you should have returned the letter to me.'

'No, sir. It was worserer than that. He said as he would tell you about my abdominable past if I didn't. So I did.'

Her employer groaned. 'Molly, has your brain been completely vulcanized?'

Molly considered the question. 'I like to think so, sir.'

'The only thing Inspector Quigley knows about your past is that, like everybody else, you have one, whereas I know more about it than you do.' He pointed the way she had come. 'Go down and ask Cook to broil your head.'

'Boil, sir?'

'Broil.'

'Thank you, sir.' Molly dipped lopsidedly.

'And I have warned you before about trying to curtsy.' He looked at his hair in the mirror. 'Stop it or I shall replace you with the jackdaw you so closely resemble.'

'Very good, sir.' She scuttled away.

Sidney Grice straightened his sticks in the hallstand. There were eight of them, all of which looked identical to me.

'Anyway,' I said, 'Inspector Pound's parents are both dead. He told me so himself.'

'I know.' He ran his finger under the hall table. 'If he is taking time off work he must have a very good reason.' He held up his finger coated with dust. 'Now I must write a note for the undertakers to come and remove the body. Then Molly can tidy up and everything will be back to normal.'

'Normal?' I echoed. 'A man has just died.'

'And what' — Sidney Grice selected a cane — 'could be more normal than that?'

I went to my room to change my dress, then sat at my dressing table tidying my hair as I prayed for the soul of Horatio Green and for the strength to continue. *And I wondered if that strength was making me ugly and whether you would recognize that woman in the mirror.*

7
THE DENTIST AND THE MILLER'S DAUGHTER

We could easily have walked to Tavistock Square but my guardian rarely rubbed shoulders with his fellow man if he could avoid it. Had he consented to go on foot it would have been a great deal quicker since a collapsed sewer had closed the road at Byng Place and half the traffic of Bloomsbury was being diverted.

A sizeable crowd had gathered in the central gardens of Russell Square and, as our cab halted yet again, I stood to get a better view. The centre of their attention was a man holding a black bear by a chain around its neck. He was trying to make the bear stand on an upturned tub but the bear swiped it over with one giant paw and sat on the grass. The onlookers jeered and the man lashed at his animal with a broom handle. Half a dozen times his stick rained down, while the crowd hooted and clapped and I heard the bear bark and saw its toothless mouth roar impotently.

'We should stop him,' I said and my guardian looked grim.

'I thrashed a man once with the whip he was using to flay a donkey. I thought I had saved the creature from its suffering but I found out later that the man sold his animal to the abattoir, having mutilated it first in revenge.'

'We should call a —' But even as I spoke I saw two constables push their way to the front. There they stopped and applauded as the bear stumbled blindly on to the tub. I fell back into my seat as we lurched forward.

The hatch opened as we turned down Bedford Way. 'T' ain't right to 'it a bear wiv a stick,' our cabby called down.

'I am glad you think so too,' I replied.

'Well, it's obvious.' He appeared to be searching for something in his armpit. 'You need an iron bar for a savage beast like that.'

'The only savage beast I saw had a stick in his hand,' I called up.

'Women.' He slid the hatch shut.

We stopped on the right-hand side of the square outside a row of Georgian houses and walked along until we came to one with a tarnished brass plaque inscribed:

S. G. BRATHWAITE ESQ, LICENSIATE OF DENTAL SURGERY, ROYAL COLLEGE OF SURGEONS, DENTAL PHYSISIAN AND SURGEON.

'I hope his work is better than his spelling,' I commented as Sidney Grice sounded the bell.

'The trouble is no man with an education would waste it on becoming a sign writer.' He blew his nose. 'You would not credit the number of ways Gower can be spelt by card printers touting for business.'

A very smart young maid answered our summons and my guardian gave her his card. She had blonde hair clipped under a crisply starched hat and wore a spotless white apron over a simple black dress.

'How was your departed father's flour mill destroyed?' Sidney Grice asked as she admitted us to the hall and the maid started in astonishment.

'Why it was burnt down, sir. But how do you know about that?' She took our hats and overcoats.

'Millers test their stones every morning with a pinch of grain, do they not?' my guardian enquired.

'Yes, sir, but —'

'The daily abrasion leads to a wearing and

eventual thickening of the digital dermis,' he pronounced, 'a condition most imaginatively known as *miller's thumb.*'

The maid looked at her right hand as if seeing the hard pad for the first time.

'Why, sir,' she said, 'you should be on the stage.' She led us to the waiting room — five baggily upholstered armchairs and a mahogany table piled with old copies of *Household Management.* 'I shall let Mr Braithwaite know you are here.'

'I thought you did not do party tricks,' I said when she had gone, and Sidney Grice pulled the net curtain aside to look on to the square.

'Nor do I,' he confirmed, 'but that girl could be a witness and it is important to assess her reliability. If she had been what the vermin of Fleet Street refer to as *on the run* she would have been flustered at having her past life exposed.'

A wasp was crawling over the mantelpiece and I flattened it with a copy of *The Strand.*

'How lightly girls kill,' my guardian observed.

'But how did you know it was her father's mill?' I asked.

'Flour mills are invariably a family concern,' he explained, 'and it would have taken many years of work there to develop that condition, so she could not have married recently into the business.'

I picked up another magazine and the middle fell out of the cover. 'And you knew he was dead because . . . ?'

'No prosperous father would allow his daughter to go into service while he was alive.'

'How do you know their mill was prosperous?'

He prodded a cigar butt on the floor with his cane. 'Cuban,' he postulated before replying. 'Her speech is well modulated for a southwest Shropshire girl. She has had elocution lessons, which are not cheap. A struggling miller would not bother with such things.'

'And the destruction?'

'If the mill were viable she would be running it. She carries herself with a pride and dignity that you would do well to imitate, March.'

I flung the torn journal down and asked, 'Do you never get tired of being right?' Sidney Grice opened his mouth. 'Do not answer that,' I said.

'Note the smell of nitrous oxide.'

'Which I noticed on Mr Green,' I pointed out.

'I have a slight case of Molly's cold.' He

coughed as footsteps came down the hallway towards us.

'Mr Braithwaite will see you now.' The maid turned and led us to the back of the house and into another room.

The surgery was small and cluttered. A complicated anaesthetic machine stood with its twin gas cylinders, dials, taps and rubber tubing, at the head of a brown-leather and iron chair with its foot pump and dumbbell-shaped headrest. The work surfaces were covered with glass bottles and pottery jars. A stainless-steel tray was piled high with forceps. A small man, with unnaturally sable hair dragged sideways and plastered in oiled strings over his peeling dome, was slouched on a wooden stool browsing through a catalogue. He did not look up or offer his hand and, remembering that he spent the day with his fingers in saliva, I did not offer mine.

'Take a seat, Mr Grease.' He pointed without raising his head.

'Grice . . . and I have come on a business matter.'

'Quite so, but we might as well give the old grinders a quick survey while you're here.' He indicated the chair again but Sidney Grice remained resolutely standing.

'I have come about a Mr Horatio Green,' he said.

'Oh yes? Recommended me to you, did he? Well, don't you fret, Mr Grease, I can see from here what the problem is. You have effeminate teeth.'

'The name is *Grice* and I most certainly —'

'And are embarrassed to show them,' our host pressed on smoothly. His shoulder was littered with flakes of dead scalp. 'Does your husband ever smile, madam?'

'I have never known him to.'

Sidney Grice huffed. 'There would be precious little to smile about if you *were* my wife.'

Silas Braithwaite closed a drawer. 'Or laugh?'

'Never,' I said.

The dentist got up in an oddly mechanical manner, as if he were hinged.

'This is all most amusing,' Sidney Grice said, 'but to return to the subject of Mr Green —'

'The trouble, Mr Grease, is that your teeth are too small, but don't you worry about that.' He took a dental mirror from his breast pocket. 'We can soon whip them out under a whiff of gas and fit you with a lovely set of walrus ivory dentures, so natural that no one could ever tell.'

'Except perhaps another walrus,' I put in and Mr Braithwaite tittered uncertainly. His teeth, I noticed, were crumbled and black, and I was about to ask why he had not filled his own mouth with carved tusks but my guardian had had enough.

'Mr Horatio Green,' he said firmly. 'How long has he been a patient of yours?'

Silas Braithwaite inserted his middle finger into his right ear. 'Such information is confidential.' He puggled about in his ear hole.

'If you had the intellectual capacity to decipher the Roman alphabetical symbols on my calling card you would have deduced that I am a personal detective,' Sidney Grice said. 'Any information you give me will be treated with the utmost discretion.'

'Why not ask him yourself?' He inspected his fingertip. 'Or is he in some sort of trouble?'

'Why would he be?' I asked.

Silas Braithwaite sniggered. 'Bit of a card, Horatio. Always playing practical jokes. Pretended to be blind once at King's Cross Station and got someone to walk him to St Pancras. Then he got somebody else to guide him back again. They bumped into the first man on the return and Horatio had to pretend to be' — he could hardly get the words out now — 'his own . . . identical . . . twin.'

'How intensely irritating,' Sidney Grice said.

'A group of us followed at a distance to witness the jest. We were utterly incapacitated with mirth.'

'I am sorry to hear that,' my guardian said. 'Now —'

'A great character,' Silas Braithwaite chuckled. 'But we always said he would get into trouble one day. What is he up to now?'

'He —' I began.

'Nothing,' Sidney Grice interrupted.

'Has he sent you to dispute his bill? He did that once to embarrass his doctor. I know my charges lean towards the high end of the scale but, in light of my overheads, they are hardly criminal. Why are you looking through my appointment book, madam?'

I closed the book. It had very few entries. 'To see if Lady Constance has made an appointment yet.'

Silas Braithwaite dropped his mirror on the floor. 'Lady Constance?'

'You are too clever for us, Mr Braithwaite,' I said.

'I have met cleverer cadavers,' Sidney

Grice muttered but I pressed on. 'You have seen through our subterfuge, haven't you?'

'Well, of course.' Silas Braithwaite shifted his feet.

'Mr Green did not recommend you to us, but to Lady Constance who asked us to check your professional standards first. She requires a great deal of extremely expensive work on her teeth.'

Sidney Grice cocked his head as if listening to something else and brought out his watch.

Silas Braithwaite kicked the mirror under a cabinet. 'Then she will be coming to the right man. My standards are, as you can see' — his arms encompassed the chaos of his surgery — 'of the very highest.'

My guardian crouched, his knees clicking in unison. 'The spoor of *Mus Musculus*,' he pronounced as he clipped on his pince-nez. 'House-mouse droppings.'

'Lady Constance's greatest concern is for her privacy,' I said as Sidney Grice dropped on to all fours. 'You have already allayed her first concern, that you might divulge information about a patient to a third party.'

My guardian was snuffling along the floor like a beagle. 'You have rising damp,' he said, 'and *Lepisma saccharina*.' He took what looked like a gold cigarette case from his inside pocket and flipped it open but, instead of Virginians, a variety of keys and lockpicks were fixed inside. 'Silverfish infestations to you.' He scratched at the side of the dentist's trousers with a fine pick, holding the open lid to catch his scrapings.

Silas Braithwaite pulled his leg away. 'What are you doing?'

'My job. Hold still.' Two more scrapes and he slipped his pick away.

I struggled to carry on. 'Her second concern is that you might be writing information of a personal nature in your patients' notes. She is most concerned that, when she recommends you to her wealthy and titled friends, they might glimpse some intimate details of her life in your records.'

Silas Braithwaite scratched his nose and straightened indignantly.

'My interest in my patients is purely clinical and financial.' He stepped over Sidney Grice's leg to his filing cabinet, which was almost empty. 'I am sure Horatio will not mind. There you are — nothing but the bare essentials.' He thrust a white card at me.

'She will also be pleased to know that you write in a code,' I said and Silas Braithwaite looked baffled.

My guardian shut his case, got up, laid the case on a shelf and peered over my shoulder. 'I have written an unpublished paper on the handwriting of dentists, physicians, surgeons and veterinary practitioners,' he said. 'Let me see. Ah yes. Two fillings. Two guineas. Dated today.' He let the card drop on to the desk. 'What poisons do you stock?'

'Several.' Silas Braithwaite opened a drawer of stoppered bottles, many of them leaking into sticky rings on the brown paper lining. 'We use arsenic to kill the nerves in teeth; sulphuric acid to whiten them — the ladies like me to apply that before their weddings. Tincture of aconite — now there is a deadly one — we use that for inflamed wisdom teeth. Let me think —'

'I do not expect to live long enough for that process to begin,' Sidney Grice said.

'Well, of all the . . .' Silas Braithwaite was lost for words.

'What about prussic acid?' I enquired and Silas Braithwaite stuck a yellowed finger out at me.

'Oh, I wouldn't advise the use of that.' He scraped under his thumbnail with a sickle-shaped scaler. 'Your husband would smell it. No, I should stick to aconite if I were you. It has a bitter taste which is difficult to mask but its effects are immediate and irreversible.'

'Do you stock prussic acid?' I asked.

Sidney Grice picked up a glass jar full of extracted teeth, lifted the lid and closed it promptly.

'I have no need for it.' Silas Braithwaite chucked the scaler back into a drawer. 'Why are we talking about poisons?'

My guardian put down the jar and wiped his hands on a white handkerchief. 'Are you in the habit of murdering your patients, Mr Braithwaite?' He snatched up the catalogue and thumbed through it.

Silas Braithwaite sniggered again. 'You might think so from the fuss some of them make . . . Oh, you are not joking . . . But why . . .'

'Because Horatio Green was poisoned this morning,' I told him.

'Oh.' Silas Braithwaite sat heavily on the arm of his chair. He rubbed the back of his head. 'Poor Horatio. Is he very ill?'

'Dead.' Sidney Grice slapped the catalogue down on the stool.

'Oh.' Silas Braithwaite blinked several times rapidly. 'A joke gone wrong?'

'I do not think so,' I said and Silas Braithwaite pinched the end of his nose. 'It would seem I have lost a friend and a patient in one fell swoop, and I am not sure which I have the fewer of now.'

My guardian looked at him severely. 'A man has died, Mr Braithwaite. He will never see the sun set or pat an infant on the head again. Is that all you care about — your profits?'

The word *hypocrite* came to mind as Mr Braithwaite rocked backwards. 'No,' he whispered. 'But it is difficult not to worry with my low returns. All the servants have left except Jenny, the maid, and she has not been paid for three months.'

'Which might explain why she left the house' — Sidney Grice produced his watch — 'six and a half minutes ago.'

Silas Braithwaite's eyes flickered. 'She probably went to fetch something.'

'She was dragging a leather suitcase.'

'How do you know it was leather?'

'I heard it creak and I am able to distinguish twenty-four different types of creak with complete confidence — over a hundred with slightly less than absolute certainty.'

'So you are investigating Horatio's murder?' Silas Braithwaite asked.

My guardian stepped towards him. 'Who said it was murder?'

'Why, you did.'

'I said he was poisoned.'

'Then I jumped to that conclusion.' Silas Braithwaite coiled a length of catgut thread round his forefinger.

'What do you know of the Last Death Club?' Sidney Grice challenged.

'Nothing.' A strand of Silas Braithwaite's hair swung down over his eye. 'What is it?'

'You are hiding something from me.' My guardian clambered on to a wooden chair and tapped the ceiling with the ferrule of his cane. A lonely shaving of plaster drifted away.

Silas Braithwaite wound the catgut round his hand. 'I hope you are not going to pry into my tax affairs — not that there is anything amiss with my accounts. It is just I am a year or two behind in completing them.'

'Be quiet.' Sidney Grice climbed down, retrieved his cigarette case, licked his first fingertip and picked something out. 'What is this?'

The dentist screwed up his eyes. 'It looks like a dog hair.'

'Do you keep a dog?' I asked.

'No, I hate them.'

'That is something in your favour.' Sidney Grice kept his eyes fixed on Silas Braithwaite. 'What do you think, Miss Middleton?'

'I do not know. It is very coarse and speckled, more like a bristle.'

My guardian brought out an envelope. 'I

found it embedded in your right trouser leg at about ankle height, and it does not appear that you can give me a satisfactory explanation of what it is, nor where, how or when you acquired it.' He dropped the bristle into an envelope.

'It is only a hair.'

'Nothing is *only* a hair,' Sidney Grice barked and folded the envelope over. 'Have no fear, Mr Silas Joseph Anthony Braithwaite. I shall find the answer to all those questions and I have small doubt and every hope that it will prove you guilty of something.'

The dentist turned to me. 'What is he talking about?'

'I do not know.'

'Neither do I,' my guardian admitted blithely. 'But I do know a clue when I see one, though it may be a clue about something entirely irrelevant.' He clipped his satchel shut and began to hum loudly.

'So Lady Constance was just a pretext to gain information,' Silas Braithwaite said.

'I am afraid so,' I told him.

'She will not like it when she learns how you bandied her name about.'

I looked at his crestfallen face. 'I am sorry to tell you she is a fiction.'

He tied his first three fingers together with

an injured air. 'That was unkind to give me false hope.'

'I am sorry. I did not realize things were so bad.' I felt as if I had kicked a lost child. 'I think we had better go.'

My guardian broke off from his humming. 'I think so too. It is almost three hours since I last had a proper cup of tea.'

We left Silas Braithwaite trying to untangle the thread.

The maid's hat and apron were neatly folded on the hall table when we took our hats and coats off the stand as we saw ourselves out.

An omnibus went by, the five passengers on the roof pulling collars up and hats down against the chill breeze.

8
CHELSEA BUNS AND THE SOLES OF MEN

There was a cosy cafe just round the corner, which I had walked by before and hardly noticed, but Sidney Grice was clearly a regular customer for the waitress, in response to his hand raised like a papal blessing, brought a tray with a large, freshly steaming pot of tea almost before we had time to settle ourselves at a square table by the window.

'Will you be indulging today, sir?' she enquired.

'We will both be indulging,' he said.

'In what?' I asked and my guardian looked almost embarrassed.

'I have a secret vice,' he said and my mind raced. Was this what Molly had once referred to? Was there an opium den at the back of the building? I hoped so. He continued. 'A weakness for Chelsea buns.'

'How decadent.'

'I am not proud of myself,' he said, 'but

sometimes a craving comes upon me, especially when I am upset. And the manner of Mr Green's death has affected me more than I like to admit.'

'It *was* horrible,' I agreed and he grimaced.

'That rug was from Marie Antoinette's anteroom in Versailles and a present to me from Emperor Napoleon III himself. I fear it is forever stained.'

The waitress marched smartly back with two white plates. Each had a square spiral of dough dotted with raisins and glazed with sugar.

'My father brought me here once,' he said dreamily.

'And did he buy you a bun?'

Sidney Grice blinked and his eyes misted over. 'Of course not,' he said. 'This was a land agent's office at the time. He had come to evict some tenants who were too idle to pay their rents.'

I poured us both some tea. 'Is your father still alive?'

'Sadly . . .' my guardian's face clouded, 'he is.' He sliced his bun carefully into ten exactly equal pieces. 'So what did you make of our trip to the dentist?'

'I did not care for him,' I said, 'but I do not think he killed Horatio Green.'

'For once' — my guardian picked up a stray morsel of his bun and wafted it under his nose as a French chef might a truffle — 'we are in complete accord. On what do you base your presumption of innocence?'

'Well, he was obviously taken aback by the news of Mr Green's death.'

Sidney Grice carefully replaced his piece of bun as if trying to reassemble it.

'Oh, March,' he said wearily. 'March, March, March. When will you begin to activate that lump of gristle in your head? In the short time I have so selflessly mollycoddled you I could name a brace of killers who you believed to be as blameless as suckling babes because they *seemed* nice. I could take you down Drury Lane and show you a man on stage who manages to convince hundreds of people that he is Othello, six nights a week and twice on Saturdays, but I assure you he is not. Nobody is *ever* clearly *anything* on the basis of their demeanour.'

I put my knife down and said, 'Very well. Why have you decided he is not guilty?'

'The evidence,' my guardian said, rolling a raisin around his plate with the tip of his first finger, 'was under your very nose. Why do you think I took such an interest in Mr Braithwaite's floor?'

I covered my mouth to hide the large piece I had pushed into it. 'Because you are eccentric,' I said.

'I hope I am.' He blew his nose. 'A centric mind spins on the spot, going nowhere and only succeeding in making itself dizzy. The eccentric travels unpredictably but often towards the inspired. No, March, I got down on the floor to smell it. The room is poorly ventilated — hence the damp I detected. And hydrogen cyanide — to give prussic acid its chemical nomenclature — is heavier than air. If Silas Braithwaite had been using it in his surgery that morning there would have been a lingering odour on or just above the floor, and the linoleum would have prevented the gas from seeping through the boards. Even with my nasal congestion I would have detected it. There was no such aroma. And since Mr Braithwaite had not left his surgery the entire day . . .'

I swallowed the cake. It was very good, sweet and moist. 'How on earth can you know that?'

'By scrutinizing' — Sidney Grice had a crumb on his upper lip — 'the soles of his shoes.' The tip of his tongue darted out to dab the crumb away.

I waited for him to eat another piece and

said, 'Please elucidate, dear guardian.'

He picked up his napkin. 'I am in the process of writing a study entitled *A Brief Introduction to the Basic Elements of the Study of the Undersurfaces of European Footwear.* It will be published in three volumes over the next five years.'

'Just what every child will want for Christmas,' I said.

'It is not primarily aimed at juveniles,' Sidney Grice said, 'but they could do a great deal worse. There is a serious dearth of improving material in the nonsense peddled by publishers these days.'

'And what did you discover under Mr Braithwaite's boots?'

'The floor, as even your untrained eyes will have noticed, was covered in . . . ?' He looked at me over his teacup.

'Dirt,' I said.

'What sort of dirt?'

'Just dirt.' I had another piece of sugary dough.

'There is no such thing as just dirt,' he told me, 'any more than there is just a leaf or a stain, and I have devoted most of one volume to the topic. Dirt consists of innumerable things: mud, of which there are several types; hair, both human and animal; excrement; squashed insects with and without wings; particles of food, et cetera, et cetera. The dirt on the floor of a dentist's surgery — to which I have set aside a particularly entertaining chapter — is unique. It contains substances in combinations and proportions not to be found elsewhere — plaster of Paris, tooth fragments, blood, mercury and its amalgamations, and porcelain, to name but a few of its ingredients. Vulcanite dust is becoming more prevalent.'

My guardian sneezed and I dived into the pause. 'So how did this help you to reach your conclusion?'

'Because,' he informed me, 'Silas Braithwaite's soles were thick with this dirt and no other — plus there were faint footprints of it in the hall but none matching the shape of his boots. Ergo he had not left his surgery and, since no prussic acid had been used in the surgery that morning, he did not kill Horatio Green and we shall have to enjoy our decadent repast without the happy anticipation of sending him to the gallows.'

'What will we do next then?' I asked and Sidney Grice let his napkin fall to the floor.

'Even the simplest of crimes is a labyrinth,' he told me. 'There are so many routes which lead nowhere and we must be careful not to follow too many of them. We shall go home and I shall look through my files. There are aspects of this case which I believe to be unique.'

'And what shall I do?'

'You can be of incalculable help to me.'

A butcher's boy ran past, waving a hockey stick, his blue-and-white striped apron flapping around his legs.

'By keeping quiet and intermittently ringing for tea.' He jumped up like a jack-in-the-box. 'Come, March. We have work to do.'

'The very thought of it exhausts me,' I muttered as he paid the bill.

A wooden foot-ramp had been erected in Byng Place and the traffic was still bad, so we decided to walk. But we had got no further than re-entering Tavistock Square when a young woman came rushing out of the dental practice and straight towards us. Even without her uniform it was easy to recognize her as Jenny, the maid who had admitted us less than two hours ago. She was in a simple black dress and her hair was still tied back.

'Oh, sir, I hoped it was you.' She was red-faced and panting. 'Come quickly, please. Something awful has happened.'

'To your employer, I hope,' my guardian said.

She tugged at her sleeves in agitation. 'Please, sir.'

The front door was wide open and Sidney Grice paused to examine the lintel.

'There is a very strong smell of nitrous oxide,' I said.

'Why, March' — he tapped the wainscoting with his cane — 'you are turning into a veritable bloodhound.'

'Oh, miss, please make him come quickly.'

'If, as I suspect, your employer is dead, there is no hurry whatsoever,' he told her as he ambled down the hallway. He stopped and crouched, then ran his fingers over the parquet.

'Oh, please,' she said.

'Interesting.' He jumped up to look at the unlit gas mantle before following a distraught Jenny towards the surgery.

The smell of gas was very strong by now and almost overpowering as we entered the room. Silas Braithwaite was slumped in his patients' chair. The anaesthetic mask lay upturned in his left hand on his lap. I felt for a pulse.

'I found him like this, sir,' Jenny said and my guardian turned to me.

'Looks dead to me,' he commented. 'What

do you think?'

'I think we should open the window,' I replied and Jenny rushed over to do so. There was a welcome gust of cold air but whatever view there might have been was obscured by a mulberry bush thick with creepers.

Sidney Grice was looking at a framed sepia photograph.

I tapped the gas cylinder with a mirror handle and felt it with the back of my fingers. 'It is ice-cold and empty,' I said and examined the other cylinder. 'But the oxygen is warm and almost full.'

Sidney Grice went to the other side. 'He who lives by the gas . . .' He lifted Silas Braithwaite's right hand, holding it like a fortune-teller, wiggled the fingers and replaced it on the arm of the chair. 'Stupid man.' And after a while he said to himself, 'But who is doing this to me?'

9
EAGLE BEAKS AND OPIUM

Jenny was sent to fetch a policeman and found one almost immediately. He was a sturdy middle-aged man who I had seen before, clearing vagrants from the square. It was an offence to sleep out at night and so they were forced to walk the streets in darkness and sleep all day instead.

The constable took one look and marched off to summon help.

'Well, Miss Middleton, we might as well sit in the waiting room,' my guardian said.

'Are you not going to examine him?'

Sidney Grice looked at me as if I were simple. 'What on earth for?'

'To find out how he died?'

'I know how he died and so do you, unless you have one of your bizarre theories,' my guardian said.

'But who do you think killed him?' I asked.

My guardian blinked. 'I know I did not do it and I am confident that you did not.

Possibly this maid did.'

And Jenny jumped. 'Not me, sir, honest. I just found him like this.'

Sidney Grice waved an uninterested hand.

'Mr Grice is not accusing you of anything, Jenny,' I said. 'But why did you come back?'

Jenny's eyes jumped about as if she were searching for an escape route. 'He owed me four months' wages and I came back to ask him for them. I thought if he realized he had no servants at all he might come to his senses. And I was going to threaten him . . .'

My guardian put on his pince-nez and scrutinized a pair of eagle-beaked forceps.

'Kindly do not make a confession,' he told her. 'I have better things to do than be called as a witness at your trial.'

'What trial?' Jenny reddened. 'Why aren't you looking for clues? I thought you was supposed to be a detective.' And Sidney Grice piffed a little air between his lips.

'I am not *supposed* to be a detective; I *am* the foremost detective in the British Empire. But I am a personal detective and not a public lackey. Your ex-employer was not a client of mine and so his death is no more than an inconvenience for me.'

'Have you no heart?' she asked.

'Certainly.' He prodded his chest with the forceps. 'And it pumps blood to my unequalled brain but does not rule it.'

I touched her shoulder. 'How were you going to threaten him, Jenny?'

She started to sniff. 'Just with being blacklisted by the employment agencies. That's all. You can't expect a girl to work and play games for free.'

'Note how she regresses into her native dialect when she is distressed,' Sidney Grice said. 'The elongated vowels and the burred *r*. I would place it somewhere between Craven Arms and Clun.'

'Are you going to hang her for that?' I asked and my guardian tapped a barometer on the wall.

'It is a small point in her favour,' he said.

'Why?' I demanded. 'Do they not murder people in that part of Shropshire? Have you no cases in your files?'

Sidney Grice ran his finger under the edge of a shelf but did not examine it.

'Several, including one of a wonderfully colourful nature involving a Serbian engineer.' He wiped his hands on his handkerchief. 'But in my experience people who are lying become more — and not less — careful about how they speak.'

Jenny was crying now. 'I didn't do him no harm.'

'*Any* harm,' he corrected her absently as

he opened and closed the forceps.

'Could he really not pay you or was he just being mean?' I asked.

'He couldn't pay no one for he never had no — any patients.' She blew her nose. 'The butcher wouldn't give him any meat. Even the laundry wouldn't let him have his clothes back 'cause he owed them six months.'

'These forceps were designed with an almost complete ignorance of mechanics and human anatomy,' Sidney Grice said. 'The fulcrum is too high and the points are designed more to destroy the jawbone than cleanly extract a tooth. When I have the time I shall design a better pair. You,' he told Jenny, 'will sit in the hallway.' He carefully replaced the forceps, turning them so as to lie exactly as they had before he picked them up. 'Come, March.'

I looked at Silas Braithwaite. His skin was blue.

'There is a red mark on his wrist,' I observed.

'No, there is not,' my guardian called over his shoulder. 'There are three such marks and not one of them is any of our concern.'

I sat in the waiting room in a sagging armchair and Sidney Grice stood with his back to me, staring out of the window, hum-

86

ming the same tuneless few notes over and over again and tapping an erratic beat on the floorboards with his cane. I could see Jenny's feet. They were motionless.

'Stay there,' he snapped without taking his eye off his view. 'You do not work here now.'

The bell rang. 'See to it, Miss Middleton,' he said without turning.

I thought of telling him to do it himself, but it did not seem right to bicker when there was a dead man lying in the next room.

'I see that girl detectives greet callers.' Inspector Quigley stepped inside, leaving his constable to guard the step.

'And I see your powers of observation have not deserted you — yet,' I told him as my guardian came into the hall.

'Well, Mr Grice,' the inspector said, 'I am beginning to think the papers are right. Death follows you like a shadow, according to last night's *Evening News*.'

'If the press are to be believed man will fly in an engine-powered machine one day,' my guardian retorted. 'No, Inspector, I follow death. I learn his secrets; I sometimes forestall him but even my brilliant powers cannot thwart him for ever.'

'So what happened here then?'

'We were called in by this servant.' Sidney Grice indicated Jenny, now on her feet and smoothing down her dress. 'And came in to find her ex-employer, Mr Silas Braithwaite, dead in his dental chair and his surgery filled with nitrous oxide.'

'Laughing gas?' Inspector Quigley asked.

'Quite so.'

'Well, let's take a look then.' The inspector held up his hand in a halt sign to Jenny, who was still standing beside her chair. 'Wait there.'

'I haven't done anything wrong,' she protested and the inspector smiled bleakly.

'If I say you have, you have. If I say you haven't, you haven't,' he said. 'I will let you know in five minutes. In the meantime sit there.' Quigley marched on past me. The smell of nitrous oxide was fainter but still strong. 'I hate dentists,' he said as he stepped into the surgery.

'Well, here is one fewer for you to loathe,' Sidney Grice said as the inspector stood at the foot of the chair.

'Any theories, Mr Grice?'

My guardian opened the filing cabinet and rifled through its contents.

'None whatsoever.' He picked the husk of a spider out by one leg. '*Pardosa amentata* or the spotted wolf spider, so named because it does not build a web but tracks its prey and hunts it down.' He let it fall. 'I am sure you have a solution already, Inspector.'

'Indeed I have,' Quigley said. 'No point in dawdling over these things. Accidental death.'

'How have you decided that?' I asked and Sidney Grice groaned.

'I shall keep this simple for you,' the inspector promised.

'And please try to speak slowly,' I entreated, and he gazed at me as one might a dead rodent.

'Have you ever heard of laughing-gas parties?'

I had attended one in Cabool but I said, 'I think so.' And Inspector Quigley put his hands together and explained, 'Degenerate people, particularly university undergraduates, artists who can't paint and poets who won't rhyme sometimes gather secretly for the purposes of inhaling nitrogen oxide, which by all accounts has a stimulating and intoxicating effect.'

I resisted the urge to ask him to explain what *intoxicating* meant and said, 'I think I understand.'

'What these allegedly intelligent people do not realize is that all drugs can lead to an irresistible hunger for more, what we professionals call an *addiction.*'

'Does that include opium?' I asked.

'Even opium,' the inspector told me. 'There is a dark and terrible underworld based around that seemingly harmless household medicine, which I trust you will never encounter. But, to continue, these misguided youths soon find themselves unable to resist its effects. They start to crave it but their cravings can never be satisfied. This man may have gone to such parties but more likely the amount of gas he inhaled in the course of his work turned him into a laughing-gas fiend. He administered the gas to himself and, in his confused state, forgot to turn on the oxygen. The gas filled his lungs and so he had no air and suffocated himself to death.'

'A neat theory.' Sidney Grice clapped his hands together. 'Now, Inspector, if you have no further need for us we will be about our business.'

Jenny looked up anxiously as we came back into the hall.

'Prepare your soul to meet its maker,' my guardian told her as he passed by.

I turned back to reassure her but she had fainted on to the floor.

'I suppose you think that was funny,' I said as I waved my blue vial of sal volatile under her nose, and her eyelids fluttered.

Sidney Grice considered the matter. 'Do you know, March,' he said, 'I do not believe it was.'

10
FRENCH POLISH AND THE SECOND-BEST TEAPOT

The study at 125 Gower Street had been tidied while we were away and Horatio Green's body had been removed, as had the rug. The chair he had died in — my usual chair — had been pushed back into place. The smashed crockery was gone and the table wiped clean.

My guardian sighed. 'It will have to be French polished.'

He pulled on the bell rope and sat down but I hovered. 'It does not seem right to use the chair after what has happened.'

Sidney Grice skimmed his hand over the armrest and said, 'Molly clearly thinks like you. Female brains are simple mechanisms but surprisingly often attuned. She has swapped the chairs round.'

'Are you sure?'

'You think I do not know my own chair?'

I sat gingerly and said, 'Inspector Quigley seems very quick to form a conclusion.'

He picked a copy of *The Lancet* from the satinwood lowboy at his side. 'One of the best minds in the force,' he said. 'Not that he has much competition.'

'But in both cases today he has reached the wrong conclusion.'

Sidney Grice leafed through his magazine. 'In seven weeks' time Chief Inspector Newburgh will be retiring. He is going to breed cattle in the desolate hinterlands of Surrey, I believe. The post will fall vacant and our friend Quigley is hotly tipped to fill it, but he is unlikely to gain promotion if, over the next few weeks, he has a string of unsolved murders on his books.'

Molly came in with a tray. 'Cook says begging your pardon, sir, but this is her second-best teapot and please can you not break it.'

'Tell Cook I shall try to restrain myself.' Her employer went back to his journal but I could not let the matter rest.

'So anyone may commit any crime with impunity for the next two months if Inspector Quigley is on the case,' I said.

'Unless he can make an arrest on the spot.' He flipped a page impatiently. 'Obviously, solving cases instantly improves his career prospects.'

'Even if he gets the wrong person?'

'As long as he gets a conviction . . .'

Sidney Grice flapped a hand and went back to his reading.

I poured the tea. 'What about Inspector Pound?' It was a lovely Regency tea set — fine white china with rosy periwinkles and a deep-pink scalloped border on the rims of the cups.

My guardian closed the cover wearily. 'A man would get more peace in Billingsgate Fish Market on a Friday morning,' he said. 'If you want to know whether Pound would let a guilty man go or convict the wrong one to enhance his career prospects, the answer is *no*. Pound has as good a mind as Quigley, if not better, but he lacks that ruthless streak which lifts the scum from the dregs.'

'How cynical you are.'

'If you mean I am sceptical of other people's motives, I would be foolish not to be, in my profession.'

He turned back to his journal but I pressed on. 'Do you have any more theories about how Horatio Green was poisoned?'

My guardian tested the teapot with the back of his fingers and something like approval flashed over his face.

'Not yet,' he said, 'and please do not annoy me with any of yours.'

'I have one thought,' I said and he dropped

his *Lancet* into his lap. 'What if Mr Green was sucking on a lozenge?'

'He was not. I would have observed it in the way he spoke.'

'He could have had it in his cheek pouch.'

'Prussic acid, as the name might suggest even to your sluggish mental processes, is an acid. It would have burnt the cheek membranes. I did not observe any ulceration anterior to the oropharynx and, if I do not observe something, it is not there to be observed.'

My guardian popped his eye out and massaged around his socket vigorously.

'Does your eye hurt?'

'My eye is buried in Charlottenburg Cemetery.'

I put the upright chair back at the round table in the middle of the room. 'You had a funeral service for your eye?'

He slid open a drawer and took out a rosewood box. 'The eye was in the throat of a Prussian colonel. He choked to death on it.' He produced a green bottle, clearly not interested in pursuing the subject.

'What do you suppose has happened to Inspector Pound?'

'I do not suppose anything has happened to him that is any of our concern.' Sidney Grice pulled out the cork. 'If anything had he would have told me.' He upended the bottle in a ball of cotton wool.

'Perhaps he cannot. Perhaps he has been hurt or —'

'What? He has been kidnapped by fairies or press-ganged by pirates?' He put the wad to his socket and winced. 'Really, March, you should write shilling shockers for a living. They would sell like saints' fingers in a Roman bazaar.'

'But he is your friend. Are you not even a little concerned?'

'As we have already established, I have no friends.' The cotton wool was stained blue. 'And I doubt that he has either.' It turned red around the edges. 'The life of a criminologist is a lonely one — thank heavens.' Sidney Grice deposited the cotton wool into his wastepaper bin. 'I hope you have a more presentable dress than any I have seen you in so far.' He recorked the bottle. 'We have an appointment tomorrow morning in Kew.'

'Baroness Foskett?'

He wiped his hands with a stained cloth. 'None other.'

From somewhere in the house there was a scream. For a moment I hoped I had imagined it but then there was a second scream, louder and longer and higher.

'If one of the servants is being murdered,

I do hope it is Cook,' my guardian said.

Far away there was a crash followed by footsteps rushing up the hallway. I grabbed the coal tongs and raised them over my head as the door flew open. It was Molly — no hat, no apron, hair hanging loose and wild — with a look of utter terror.

'Oh, sir, come quickly!' She struggled for air. 'It's 'orrible.' She forced herself to say the words. 'That dratted cat from number 123 has brought an alive rat in.' She looked at me, the tongs still raised high. 'Oh, miss, if you wanted the fire made up you should've rung.'

'Why am I troubled with these domestic matters? Call the rat catcher immediately.' Sidney Grice touched his cheek and a thin violet tear trickled from his empty eye.

I said my prayers, as always, that night, wrote in my journals and opened my writing case. The scent of the sandalwood lining filled my senses and transported me once more.

We rarely visited the city but, when my father had to go for supplies, it was too good an opportunity to miss. And, after he had finished his official duties, we had two spare hours before the train. My father took me to Caldebank's cafe — a little piece of England tucked down a side street — for high tea: four different kinds of sandwiches and two of cake, fruit scones with butter and strawberry jam, though we decided not to risk the clotted cream. And afterwards we walked by the shops. It was a happy day. I admired the fabrics and my father invested in a new meerschaum pipe. And then I saw it — a writing box. We went in and had a look.

The box was beautifully made, polished oak with a lovely grain and brass fittings and inlays, opening out to reveal the compartments for correspondence, stationery and pens. It had a folding-out, green leather writing slope with feathered gold edging and, of course, a 'secret' compartment.

The shopkeeper was a little Frenchman with luxuriant moustaches. He raised his eyebrows politely when I pointed out how easy the compartment was to find. 'Now find zee ozzer one,' he challenged. I pressed every section with no success. My father tried too, turning it upside down and tapping it to no avail. The owner smiled. 'Shall I show mademoiselle?' He pressed the inkwell down and rotated it a quarter-turn, then there was a click and a drawer slid out from the side.

I laughed. 'I shall take it.'

'You already have a serviceable one,' my father pointed out.

'Just as you have a dozen meer- schaums,' I countered. 'Besides, it is not for me. It is Edward's birthday next month.'

My father frowned. 'But can you afford it?'

'Of course I can.' I slipped my arm through his. 'With a little help.'

11
THE SPIKE AND THE CORPULENT KING

We crossed the Thames but the narrow bridge was so chock-a-block that I could hardly see anything other than the railway bridge to one side and the slow-swaying masts of a clipper disappearing behind the smoking stacks of a paddle steamer on the other. Now and then I glimpsed the red-sailed barges scattered like rose petals on the water. It had been an early start and a long journey.

The Prince of Wales was visiting the Royal Botanical Gardens at Kew and the roads were blocked with the carriages of the gentry. Landaus and barouches converged, while curious onlookers milled around the main entrance, queuing at a coffee stall or chewing ham sandwiches, and bunches of ragged children shouted ironic comments at the visitors making their way to the gate.

We quit our hansom on Lichfield Road and pressed our way through. The royal coach was visible inside the grounds.

'Oh, but we have missed him,' I said.

'We have missed nothing,' Sidney Grice told me, 'but a dull-witted, corpulent, ill-tempered libertine.'

'You do not approve of him?'

'I dislike him intensely.' My guardian barged his way through a group of laundry women and I followed in his wake, trying to ignore their indignant glares. 'And he sometimes treats me as if I were the royal dust collector. But he will make an excellent king if he outlives his bovine mother. Hold on to your impractical bag, March. Where there are crowds there are pickpockets.'

The mass of people thinned out and we saw a tiny boy in a yellow jacket hold out his cap to a young man resplendent in a frock coat and highly brushed beaver-skin top hat. The young man ignored him but when the boy darted in front of him, he raised his cane without warning and whipped it across the child's face. The boy yelped and fell to his knees. I ran over and crouched to look at him. A red weal ran from his mouth to his eye. I looked up.

'If you were a man I would thrash you for that,' I said and the man pulled his lips down.

'I *am* a man.' His voice was as high and thin as his aristocratic nose. 'A gentleman.'

'No,' I said and got to my feet. 'You are a sort of vermin.'

He screwed a monocle into his eye to inspect me. 'Have you any idea whom you are addwessing?'

'Yes,' I said. 'A preening popinjay with the manners of a slattern. I hope your mother never gets to hear of your behaviour.'

The young man inspected me with utter scorn. 'My mother would not have you emptying her bedpan. She —' He stopped abruptly, his face contorted, his monocle fell out and he screeched.

'You will apologize to the lady,' my guardian said as the young man screwed up his face in pain.

'I see no lady.'

'This instant will do.'

I looked down and saw that Sidney Grice was grinding the end of his cane into the top of the young man's highly polished soft shoe.

'I am sowwy.' The tears were rolling from his eyes.

'Will that suffice?' my guardian asked me.

'I accept your apology,' I said. 'On condition that you give that child a sovereign.'

'Anything.' He reached into his trouser

pocket. 'But please stop.'

'No need for the money,' Sidney Grice said. There was blood oozing from the young man's shoe. 'That grubby rascal made off with your wallet nearly two minutes ago.'

I laughed.

'And your purse,' Sidney Grice told me, and I looked in my bag to find it gone.

My guardian removed his cane and I saw it had a sharp metal tip on the end. He retracted it by screwing the handle. 'The Grice Patent Spike Stick,' he announced as the young man hopped to a nearby plane tree to support himself and inspect his foot.

'The child has more need of the money than I,' I said and my guardian frowned.

'It is a short tumbril ride from that philosophy to a guillotine in Trafalgar Square.'

We walked away.

'I will wememba you,' the young man yelled. 'Both of you.'

'If there *is* a revolution it is men like him who will ignite it,' I said.

'I recoil from your mixed metaphor,' Sidney Grice told me. The crowd died out as we emerged slightly crumpled into a quiet side street. 'We have made a powerful enemy today.'

'I would not want him for a fwend,' I said

and his mouth twitched faintly.

'Nor I, but you must learn to stop interfering.'

'What would Christ have done?' I asked.

'I dread to think.' He gestured to a street sign. 'Not far now.'

The roads of Kew were wide and leafy and the air had lost the stench of factory fumes, though the sky was still strewn with ribbons of smoke from the city. Sidney Grice stopped and pointed with his cane. Through the treetops and a hundred yards away I could just make out a weathervane and the tip of a lead-sheeted turret.

'There it is.' His face fired with excitement.

12
CUTTERIDGE AND THE KEY

Mordent House stood on the corner enclosed by a high brick wall. We passed a rotting once-solid wooden gate.

'That used to be for the gardeners, but Rupert and I used it once without permission,' my guardian told me.

'You devils,' I said.

'But it is sealed now. They welded a grid behind it after Rupert's grandfather nearly escaped.'

'Escaped?'

But Sidney Grice was looking up beyond the rusting criss-crossed spikes that topped the wall. He stopped and pointed to a high chestnut tree overhanging the pavement.

'I climbed that once,' he said, 'to check the accuracy of our trigonometrical calculations of its height.'

'What larks.'

We walked on and he flipped a twig on to the road with his cane. 'We had underestimated by five eighths of an inch.'

The wall stretched round another corner.

'The extra climb must have been exhausting,' I said and he stopped abruptly.

'Why must you inject levity into every conversation?'

I kept walking and called over my shoulder, 'Why does everything have to be so serious?' The brickwork was bulging quite badly here and supported by five S-shaped iron plates. 'I am only trying to make life pleasant.'

My guardian caught up with me. 'You can try to mask the taste of a lemon' — he sneezed — 'but it will always be sour.' We came to a break in the wall and a pair of tall wrought-iron gates. The pillars were topped by heraldic animals so eroded that I could not tell exactly what they represented. 'The family crest,' my guardian explained as he wrenched on a bell chain.

'How sweet,' I murmured.

On either side stood a small lodge, both of which appeared to be deserted. The roof of one had collapsed and the other was missing several slates, with a sycamore escaping through its sloping hole.

We waited. A robin hopped on the arrowhead tops of the gate. Through the bars I could just make out a gravel driveway thick with tall grass and dandelions. My guardian tutted. 'These grounds were laid out by Simeon Gunwale.'

'I have seen tidier jungles,' I said as a skeletal grey-striped cat wandered across the path, followed by three kittens. 'Shall I ring the bell again? It might not be working.'

'It has worked.' He touched a corroded point with his thumb. 'Somebody will come.' He put out his arm to hold me back. 'Interesting.'

'What is?'

'The condition of these leaves.'

'Fascinating,' I said.

The sun was high but it could not cast light into the garden. Copper beeches and silver birches battled each other for space.

Perhaps five minutes passed.

'Look.' He pointed into the undergrowth but I could see nothing. 'Follow my finger.'

'I am trying.'

'Use your tobacco-damped senses.'

I screwed up my eyes and far away through the mass of vegetation something moved.

'What is it?'

A blackbird sang.

'Cutteridge,' Sidney Grice said, 'the major-domo.'

I watched intently, and the black shape grew and became a man walking slowly but steadily towards us. He disappeared behind a bush but reappeared a moment later, a tall man, shoulders curved by the mould of time, with a mass of white hair trained back behind his ears and a clean-shaven elongated face. He came to the gate carrying a hoop of keys.

'Mr Grice.' His voice rustled drily. 'How nice to see you again.' His manner was dignified and imposing but his eyes were crinkled with kindness.

'I trust you have the dogs under control.'

'Your trust is not misplaced, sir.' Cutteridge selected a large intricate key, straining to turn it as the lock brattled stiffly back. He grasped the octagonal handle, twisted it and heaved, and the high gate squealed jerkily open.

13
AQUINAS AND THE VIPER

The moment we entered what used to be the front garden the blackbird's song changed to an urgent scolding clatter.

'The cats or us?' I wondered.

'Neither.' Sidney Grice directed my gaze to where a green-brown line was sliding along the trunk of a fallen ash tree. I saw the black zigzag on its back as the tongue whisked out from under its raised snout.

'A viper,' I said.

'I saw an injured female blackbird this morning,' Cutteridge told me. 'The snake is probably after that, miss.'

I watched it slide smoothly over the trunk as the alarm cries of the male grew increasingly urgent, while from the undergrowth came a weaker alarm call and some scuttling.

'Nature red in tooth and claw,' I quoted.

'Why, March' — my guardian brushed a leaf from his shoulder — 'that was almost poetical.'

We wound our way through a thicket of rampant rhododendrons, Cutteridge first and Sidney Grice following, slashing some nettles to widen the path for me.

'I refuted every one of Aquinas's seven proofs under that mulberry tree,' my guardian recalled proudly.

'And Master Rupert was chastised for encouraging you as I recall,' Cutteridge chipped in.

'At twenty-two?' My puzzlement went unremarked.

The shrill cries of the blackbirds became frantic, then fell silent, and a flock of crows rose suddenly from a spinney, flapping blackly across our path. Sidney Grice crossed his arms over his head, his cane raised like a sword about him. He darted towards the mulberry and the crows disappeared.

'They will not harm you, sir.' Cutteridge held back a long bramble for us to pass.

'Their very existence harms me.' My guardian put a hand to his right eye and shuddered. 'No wonder they are called *a murder.*'

'Now who is being poetic?' I asked as we rounded a clump of skyward-straining bamboo, the stems as thick as pine trees, and found ourselves in a clearing. The gravel was still tangled with creepers and thistles, but the canopy was gone and ahead of us stood a massive edifice of grey stones. Amongst the confusion of soaring towers and angular turrets were domes and spires, closed balconies and empty niches, jutting ledges, crenelated walls and windows of every shape high overhead — arches rounded and pointed; circular and oval; square and rectangular; many with stained glass, some unglazed, some with panes smashed, some no more than archers' slits. The walls were strewn with ivy, all but obscuring many of the openings.

A clock tower leaned to the right of us, the time fixed at eleven fifty-nine.

'One minute to midnight,' Sidney Grice observed.

'Or noon,' I said.

'Midnight,' he insisted.

There was a dead pigeon under a dock leaf, its breast bursting with wiry red worms.

'The locals call this the Madhouse,' Cutteridge told me. 'They say the architect lost his mind after he built it.'

'After?' I queried and he smiled crookedly.

'Part of the trouble is that every Baron Foskett had his own ideas on remodelling the house, but all of them died before they could realize their intentions. Please follow me, sir, miss.'

We went up the wide marble steps — tilted and cracked, slippery green with algae — that led to massive bleached oak doors, the right-hand one being already open, and into a great hall, lit only by the entrance, the windows being heavily curtained and the central lantern skylight being boarded over from the outside.

'I shall inform the baroness that you have arrived,' Cutteridge said and made his way up the cantilevered stairs, surprisingly strongly for a man of his age, while we stood under the high ribbed ceiling, the plaster blistered and fissured, and looked about us. The walls were grey and tidemarks had crept up and down the sides. The smell of damp and mould was almost suffocating. I pointed to the floor, broad planks with a threadbare Persian rug thrown over, in front of a huge, cobwebbed marble fireplace and littered with droppings.

'Rat?' I suggested.

'And bat.' My guardian's eye was misty. 'I remember liveried footmen on duty night and day, ostlers holding magnificent black horses on the driveway, gold and green coaches with coachmen uniformed to

112

match, French maids dusting these mirrors, and valets bustling with their masters' wardrobes. This hall was filled with flowers — roses from the garden in summer and rare orchids from the hothouse in winter. There was an ornamented spruce in every room at Christmas.'

I had never heard him so lyrical about anything before, not even murder.

'So what happened?'

'Death and decay,' he said. 'When society rots, it rots from the top. The greatest of our families are in decline now — loss of land and power — wealth squandered and bloodstock contaminated by marriages to peasants and Americans, which amount to the same thing.' He lifted back a curtain and a dull rhombus of day fell down the wall and over the floor. 'Look.' The windows were scratched, every pane of glass being filled with columns of numbers — thousands upon thousands of tiny digits in neat rows disappearing behind the cobwebs. 'Rupert loved numbers. He would cram his journals with them. Sometimes he only spoke in equations.'

'How entertaining,' I said.

'Indeed.' He put on his pince-nez and said excitedly, 'What an unusual web. Clearly the spider has a damaged front right leg.'

He took out his notebook to sketch an outline of it.

'A useful clue' — I took a look — 'if you wish to track down the killer of that lacewing.'

He let the curtain drop and the daylight scrambled away.

There were panelled doors ajar on the right-hand side of the hall. I wandered over and pushed them apart, the cream paint peeling like birch bark to my touch. They led into a long wide gallery, the full-length windows covered by frayed satin curtains, the walls draped with faded tapestries, the chandeliers bagged in cotton sheets and the floor patterned with snail tracks.

A tall frame hung on the left-hand wall with a clean white sheet over it. I lifted the cloth aside and saw a full-length portrait — a slender, elegant woman in an ivory and silver-threaded gown, with one hand resting lightly on the head of an Afghan hound.

There was an enormous mirror, fixed floor to ceiling and bordered by dull gold ferns. The glass was covered by a dust sheet. I wiped the surface through a triangular rip and something moved, ghost-like, deep behind the tarnished backing.

'Is she not lovely?' Cutteridge said so suddenly behind me that I jumped.

'Quite beautiful,' I said. 'Is that Baroness Foskett?'

'In the first year of her marriage.' He cleared his throat. 'Ah, the balls we had here, the glittering ladies, the aristocratic men, the sparkling conversation, the baths of iced champagne, the music, the laughter . . . Oh, miss, if you could have been here . . .' He drifted through his memories for a moment. 'But that was all so very long ago.'

'What happened?' I asked.

'All life is dust, miss.' Cutteridge wheezed long and wearily. 'Dust and vipers.' He straightened his cuff. 'Her ladyship will see you now.'

The three of us ascended the staircase. I refrained from observing that most of life's dust appeared to have settled in that house, for there was not a surface that was not encrusted in it.

'Mind the banister rail.' My guardian reached over and demonstrated how easily it wobbled. I stuck close to the wall, the steps bowing and creaking under our feet as we climbed.

'I expect you used to slide down these,' I said to my guardian.

'That would have been frivolous,' he said.

'I did once,' Cutteridge declared. 'When I

115

was the under-butler, the late Baron Reginald bet me a month's wages to a hundred guineas I could not do it carrying a tray of sherry glasses. I slipped off at the first turn and broke both arms. So I lost six months' wages anyway.' His shoulders quaked in remembered mirth.

'How jolly,' I said.

'Happy times,' Cutteridge agreed as we paused on a half-landing. 'Master Rupert made an attempt as well, but he was disadvantaged by his thumb.'

'The Foskett males had an extra spur of bone . . .' Sidney Grice explained.

'Is that what he scratched the window with?' I whispered.

'Which made it difficult for them to grip things tightly,' my guardian continued flatly.

'Master Rupert broke his ankle and it never really healed,' Cutteridge continued. 'The game was banned after that.'

'What a shame,' I commented. 'How many servants work here now?'

'I am the last, I fear.'

Sidney Grice was quiet, seemingly lost in wonder at his surroundings. A portrait hung lopsidedly, so darkened that all I could make out was part of an ear and two eyes gaping from the grime. I peered gingerly over the banister. We must have been thirty feet up by the time we reached the first floor.

The stairs wound upwards and a corridor disappeared into the darkness on either side. Here the windows were all shuttered, the light creeping between warped slats, weak and grey on to the bare boards. Even the dust specks floating in numberless argent stars only served to add to the gloom.

My guardian sniffed. *'Serpula lacrymans,'* he said. 'Dry rot.'

'The whole House of Foskett is rotten now, sir.' He led us a few more paces. 'Here we are.' Cutteridge stopped and put a hand on my guardian's arm in an oddly familiar fashion at which he appeared to take no offence whatsoever. 'I must warn you, sir, that the baroness has changed greatly. She has not been well for many years and is unused to visitors now. Even I see her but rarely. Also, she tires very easily so I shall presume upon your good nature not to overtax her.'

'You may rely on it.' Sidney Grice put a finger to his eye, ran a hand through his hair, plumped up his cravat and shone his shoes on the back of his trousers as Cutteridge pushed open the door.

14
WHISPERS IN THE DARK

The room we entered was in complete darkness. From the dim corridor I could see nothing at all, but Cutteridge strode confidently in and almost immediately disappeared.

'Mr Sidney Grice and Miss March Middleton,' he announced from nowhere into nowhere.

There followed a silence, the distant groan of disturbed floorboards re-settling and then a shallow rasp: 'Light the candle, Cutteridge' — a whisper but louder than any whisper should be and curiously remote and metallic. I looked at my guardian. He was staring intently in the direction of the sound and I thought a shiver rippled over him, but it was not one of fear.

There was a scratching noise and a hiss, and a sudden flare of light as Cutteridge struck a Lucifer and put it to the wick of a half-burnt candle in a frosted glass bowl on an otherwise empty scalloped oval table. He blew the match out and there was only the yellow flame, sinking, then rising fitfully, wavering in the globe, a dull halo fading into nothing. We walked towards it and Cutteridge directed us to two low chairs.

Gradually, my eyes made out the shape of a box on the far side of the room. It was about the size of a four-poster bed and draped in what reminded me of mosquito netting, but was more of a heavy black gauze, hanging from top to floor, so that it was impossible to see the person inside.

'Good afternoon, Lady Foskett,' Sidney Grice said. 'I trust I find you well.'

The same breath and tin voice: 'You will never find me *that,* Sidney. What time has passed until this day?'

'Twenty-nine years, ten months and four days,' he said.

'So brief a span? It seemed to touch eternity.' The words came wheezing from her. 'You must learn to forgive the darkness, but even the conflagration of that waxen taper scorches the lining of my eyes now. I assume the sun still blazes in the illnamed heavens, but I have not confronted it in all these years for here is the realm of endless moonless night.'

'Do you have no visitors?' I asked.

'You will speak when you are spoken to.'

'If I did that I should be almost mute.'

My guardian murmured, 'March.'

But the voice resumed flatly, 'You are the first people I have allowed in this mansion since the great losses.'

'You did not meet a pharmacist by the name of Mr Horatio Green then?' Sidney Grice asked.

'I meet no one and address no soul except to instruct Cutteridge, and my speech is so weak now I must needs use this brass speaking trumpet built into my chair. I passed messages to Mr Green at the gate.'

There was a strong smell in the room like incense, not the frankincense I had smelled in a Roman Catholic Church but more like the masala incenses of India — cedarwood and something sickly.

'It is good of you to allow us in,' I said ironically and she coughed rapidly three times in what may have been a laugh.

'There is no goodness in *me*, young lady, and I am enervated already. Tell me your business.'

'I have come to ask you about a society which we have been told you joined,' Sidney Grice said.

'The Death Club? I did not join it. I conceived, gave birth to and suckled it. It is the bastard child of my unhappy fancies and now I have sent it out into the world.'

My guardian craned forward. 'And may I ask why, Lady Foskett?'

'I have heard about your profession and it does not dumbfound me. You were always an insufferably inquisitive child.'

'I mean no impertinence.'

'It was you who showed my second cousin, Mr Hemingway, his wife's love letters to his father. He shot them and himself as I recall.'

'If I had kept the correspondence from him I should have been an accessory to her deception.'

'You were always an arrant prig, Sidney Grice.'

'I have a love of the truth, Lady Foskett.'

'The truth?' The voice became distorted. 'You may stride around and about this noisome earth until the last fire grows cold upon it and never find such a thing.' She said something inaudible to me and then, 'I formulated the society because it amuses me. I do not read — why be perturbed by the trivial meanderings of men when I can wallow in the depthless mire of my own morbidity? But Cutteridge scours the newspapers on my behalf, clips out the obituaries and delivers them to me on a copper salver. What greater pleasure could I have than to discover obituaries of everyone I knew, all those coruscating perfumed ladies with their gorgeous powerful husbands and their beautiful precocious children. Those strutting, pomaded, shiny-skinned, fine peacocks and their toadying flunkies — what are they now?' Something rattled in her throat. 'Putrefying matter in their marble tombs.' She coughed drily. 'Rotting flesh on crumbling bones in their splendid sarcophagi.' The baroness fought for air. 'But there is a great famine of deaths for me to crow over in this age of steam and drains and telegraphy, and so I must devise some more: people whose complete corporal necrosis will bring me the additional gratification of fiscal advantage.'

'But, Lady Foskett,' Sidney Grice said, 'you must realize that your death is also to *their* advantage.'

Something bumped and the baroness exhaled heavily.

'I cannot die,' she whispered. 'I essayed to quench my thirst for death with a draught of vitriolic oil, but whilst it corroded my voice yet it did not kill me. It flows through my veins now. For two years I took neither food nor water. I willed my vital forces into extinction but whilst this wretched body grew weaker, my aspirations availed me naught and I found I could not die.'

'But surely that is not possible,' I said, and for a while all I could hear was her amplified breathing.

'I feed on my hatred,' she said. 'It is a thin food but pure.'

'But what about your friends?'

'Every man with a pulse, every woman with uncoagulated blood, every infant with a fluttering heart — they are all abominations detestable to me, every one of them my irredeemable enemies now.'

'But I am not your enemy, Lady Foskett,' Sidney Grice said, the shadows dancing on his cheek.

'From henceforth you are.' And for the first time since I had known him, when I looked at my guardian in the candle's flicker, I saw that he was shocked.

He put a hand to his brow and then his scarred ear. 'You know that Mr Edwin Slab died?'

'I rejoiced in my gelidity to hear it.'

'And Horatio Green?' I asked.

'The very fetidness of my soul exults. How and when did he die?'

'Yesterday, of poisoning, in my house.'

'You should take better care of your clients, Sidney' — the whisper was fading now — 'or soon you will have none left.'

'I hope to take care of you, Lady Foskett.'

The air soughed from the speaking tube and as my eyes learned to capture more light, I could just make out the outline of a figure through the black netting, a small woman seated motionless on a high throne. 'Enough . . .' A long sigh and a longer silence. 'Enough . . . enough.'

'I am sorry, sir, miss.' For the second time that day Cutteridge made me start. I had forgotten he was still behind us.

'Of course,' Sidney Grice said. 'Thank you for receiving us, Lady Foskett. We shall not tire you any further.'

'How weary, flat, stale and unprofitable seem to me all the uses of this world.' Her words were cracked like old leaves. 'There is no rest for the damned in this world or the next. I shall always be tired even beyond the end of time.'

Cutteridge blew out the candle and we followed his silhouette out of the room. He closed the door and took us down the creaking stairs.

'You will try to save her ladyship, sir?' His old eyes blinked anxiously as we set foot in the hall.

'I will do everything I can to protect her,' my guardian promised.

'May I shake your hand, sir?'

'It would be a privilege.'

Cutteridge's hand was huge. It wrapped around my guardian's and held on. 'We are dependent upon you, sir.'

'One vital question before we go,' Sidney Grice said. 'Where is the nearest tea shop?'

Cutteridge smiled. 'I see you have not lost your affection for that beverage, sir. Might I suggest Trivet's Tea House, just down the road to the right? They serve a good potted meat sandwich as I recall.'

We stepped out, dazzled by the greyness, and Cutteridge followed to lock the gate behind us. I heard the lock clank as we crossed the road, but when I looked back he had gone.

'That was an odd thing for him to say — asking you to save her,' I said, and Sidney Grice chewed his lower lip.

'There was something very wrong in that room,' he told me.

The crowd was thinning outside the gardens and a few cabs were waiting to pick up fares.

'Only one thing?' I asked and he flipped a peach stone into the gutter with his stick.

'Apart from all the obvious oddities that even you would have noticed,' he said, 'there was something else, something I heard but I cannot think what. One thing I do know is that Lady Foskett must be extricated from that awful society at the first opportunity.'

A woman of about my age wobbled past on a velocipede.

'How indecent,' Sidney Grice said.

'It looks like fun to me,' I said.

'Sooner or later you will come to realize that all fun is unfeminine.'

'I hope it is later then,' I said. 'Anyway, I do not think Lady Foskett wants to be removed from the society.'

Sidney Grice put on his gloves. 'Lady Foskett is a woman of the highest breeding and intelligence,' he replied, 'but when all is said and done, that is all she is — a woman.'

'There he is again.'

The boy in the yellow jacket was hurrying towards us.

'Fought you'd come back this way.' He looked up at me with his big child's world-exhausted eyes. 'Can't keep it.' He reached inside his shirt. 'Not after the kindness what you did me.'

He held out my purse and I took it.

'I will wager it is empty,' Sidney Grice said as the boy raced away.

'Every penny is still here.'

'The dirty blighter,' my guardian said. 'He has stolen my handkerchief.'

'Where there are crowds there are

126

pickpockets,' I reminded him.

We had only just returned when a black carriage stopped outside with curtained windows and a darker shape on the paintwork where a crest must have been removed.

The groom jumped down and lowered the steps for a tall man to disembark. He reminded me of a frog with his bulbous eyes, thin tight lips and slack throat, but his movements were stately, deliberate and precise as he glided erect across the pavement.

Sidney Grice groaned. 'What the deuce is he up to now?'

'Who?'

I did not have to wait long for an answer, for Molly was dusting the hallway and answered his ring almost immediately.

'It's that Honourable Sir Whatsisname again, sir.' She presented his card on a tray but her employer waved it away.

'Send him in.' He climbed reluctantly to his feet, ran his hand through his hair and checked his cravat and eye patch.

'Mr Grice, how good of you to see me at such short notice.'

My guardian grunted and indicated a chair, but both men remained standing.

'What is it this time?' he demanded and

our visitor glanced meaningfully at me. 'You can rely on Miss Middleton's discretion.'

The man's face stretched politely. 'Miss Middleton. My master expressed a wish to meet her, after the newspaper accounts of your last case.'

'It was not my *last* case,' Sidney Grice told him, 'and no such meeting shall take place whilst she is in my care.'

Our caller scrutinized me and turned up his lordly nose. 'Probably just as well to avoid disappointment.'

'Yes,' I said. 'I hate being disappointed.'

His lip quivered with unspoken retorts. 'If you are quite sure . . .'

'You have my word,' my guardian said and the visitor narrowed his eyes.

'My master finds himself in an embarrassing situation.'

'When does he not?'

The man flushed. 'My master had what I might describe as an indiscreet correspondence with a well-known lady of the theatre. When their . . . *friendship* ended the lady exacted a large sum of money upon receipt of which she returned all of my master's letters to her and a photograph which he had signed with expressions of an indelicate nature. The letters were burnt but the photograph seems to have disappeared.

Were it to fall into the wrong hands . . .'

Sidney Grice threw his arms into the air. 'When will he ever learn and start behaving like a grown man?'

Our visitor bridled. 'I really cannot allow you to speak of his . . . my master in such terms.'

Sidney Grice tossed his head. 'I do not have time for all this twaddle. Tell your client to look under the false bottom of his escritoire drawer.'

The man looked flustered. 'Is that the message you wish me to convey?'

'Convey whatever message you choose,' my guardian said. 'Just tell him to be more careful and to stop wasting my time.'

Our visitor tightened his tight lips. 'Very well, Mr Grice. Please ring for me to be seen out.'

'Not your favourite client?' I asked when he had gone.

'I am sick of playing nursemaid to middle-aged children.' Sidney Grice fell back into his chair.

I rang for tea but did not ask him about the Prince of Wales's feathers on the visitor's cravat pin.

15

THE DOCTOR AND THE BERRIES

Bryanston Street looked quite similar to Gower Street with its white stone-faced ground floors and the red-brick uppers, alongside the railings and the basement moats of the long Georgian terraces. After fifty yards or so we turned right down a mews, a narrower street with rows of stables to the left and tall, ramshackle houses to the right. My guardian rapped on the roof of our hansom and we came to a halt. He paid the cabby with a large tip.

'I will give you the same again if you wait.'

The cabby showed no sign of hearing him, but lowered his head and allowed his horse to do the same.

Dr Berry's consulting rooms were on the ground floor and a dowdy middle-aged maid with gappy, crooked teeth showed us straight in. A sombrely dressed woman about ten years older than me sat behind a desk, writing notes. She stood and held out her hand, which Sidney Grice took suspiciously.

'You are the doctor's wife?'

'I have no husband,' she said.

'But you are wearing a ring.'

'It wards off unwelcome advances from male patients.' The lady smiled. 'I shall not toy with you, Mr Grice, as I am all too used to the confusion I cause by my choice of profession. I am Dr Berry.'

'A woman.' My guardian put his hand to his mouth. 'How revolting.'

Dr Berry smiled again. 'If you have come to see me about your revulsion for women I can do nothing for you.'

'It is not an illness.'

'That is debatable.'

Sidney Grice recovered with great effort. 'I have come to see you about a Mr Edwin Slab who, I believe, was a patient' — he was unable to disguise his incredulity — 'of yours.'

'Mr Horatio Green told me to expect you,' Dr Berry said. 'I have heard all about their ridiculous club.'

'You certified the cause of death as a seizure,' my guardian said.

'Provisionally,' she agreed. She had short black hair, clipped severely back, but it could not disguise the gentleness of her nature. 'I was not present at Mr Slab's death and his family opposed my request for a full post-mortem examination. Unfortunately, the coroner held the same misguided opinion of women as you, Mr Grice, and respected their opinions more than mine.'

Sidney Grice bristled. 'My opinions are never misguided.'

'Another misguided opinion,' the doctor countered and I laughed. She had a faint accent that I could not place.

'Do you mind if I ask where you are from?' I enquired.

'Everywhere and nowhere,' she told me. 'I have never stayed anywhere long enough to say that I belong there. My parents were travelling performers.'

'Gypsies,' Sidney Grice said.

'Yet another misguided opinion,' Dr Berry responded and Sidney Grice looked at her. I expected him to be indignant at her presumption but he looked, if anything, mildly amused.

'Gut gesagt,' he said quietly.

'They ran and acted in a small theatre company,' she continued. 'I was educated in whichever country we toured for a season. You pick up a lot of languages quickly when you have to. So when I found that no British university was willing to award a degree to a member of the superior sex, I studied medicine in Paris and surgery in Bern.'

'Two of the ugliest cities in the ugliest countries in Europe,' my guardian pronounced and Dr Berry laughed.

'Casting your prejudices aside for one moment . . .'

'The mind of a man without prejudices is a train with no coal,' he asserted. 'It may be on the right track but it goes nowhere. I think you will find that all my prejudices are based on logical processes.'

'Then perhaps the premise on which you found each conclusion is flawed,' she suggested. 'But, to move on, how can I help you?'

Sidney Grice picked up her pen to examine it.

'How long had Edwin Slab been a patient of yours?' I asked.

'Only a few weeks,' she told me. 'I visited him twice because he had a bout of laryngitis which he was convinced was scarlet fever. I gave him a bottle of laudanum, more to calm him down than anything else, and told him to send for me again in a week if he was no better. Five days later I was called in by his housekeeper and told that he had had *an episode.* By the time I got there he was dead.'

'In bed?'

'No. In his workshop. Mr Slab was something of an amateur taxidermist and he appeared to have suffered a fit and fallen into a tank of formalin. His housekeeper and maid were unable to lift him out without help from the gardener and his boy.'

'Was he a big man?' Sidney Grice asked.

'Quite. But the task was made more difficult by the unusual degree of rigor.'

Sidney Grice put the pen back on a brass tray. 'Go on.'

Dr Berry began to pace the room. 'His housekeeper described to me how Mr Slab suffered from occasional epileptic fits, following a head injury in a carriage accident many years ago. He would go into violent convulsions and froth at the mouth, and it was obvious, when I saw his body, that he had had some kind of seizure. There was a great deal of vomit on the floor; he was cyanotic and his eyes were extruded with dilated pupils, but . . .' Dr Berry stopped by a large rubber plant and peered out of the window.

My guardian clicked his fingers and said, 'You fear the fit may have been induced?'

She spun to face us. 'Two things concern me particularly. The stiffness of his body was extraordinary, especially so soon after death, and I have never seen such a dramatic case of opisthotonus —'

'Which is?' Sidney Grice enquired shortly.

'When a body goes into such violent contractions that it lies arched with only the top of the head and the heels touching the floor,' I said. 'I have seen it in a fatal case of tetanus.'

Dr Berry looked at me. 'And where did you get your medical experience?'

'In India mainly, but also Afghanistan. My father was an army surgeon and he did not trust army nurses to assist him.'

Dr Berry smiled briefly. 'I can sympathize with that.' And her face fell again. 'All of which led me to at least consider the possibility of poisoning with —'

'Of course,' Sidney Grice interjected, 'strychnine.'

Dr Berry raised a crooked finger. 'I have also heard of it occurring with other alkaloids and chemical dyes, but I have never come across it myself.'

My guardian took two halfpennies from his waistcoat pocket. 'And your other concern was?'

She sucked her upper lip. 'When I tapped Mr Slab's chest it did not sound congested.'

'That was thorough of you.' Sidney Grice rattled the coins in his left hand. 'Which would suggest . . . ?' He turned to me.

'That he was dead before he was submerged,' I said.

He tossed the coins and caught them. 'Or that the fluid drained from his lungs as he was hauled out.'

Dr Berry nodded. 'I did point this out to the coroner, but he told me I was letting my imagination run away with me.'

'Perhaps you were overwrought.' My guardian ignored her indignation. 'But I am acquainted with Vernon Harcourt, the Home Secretary, and he owes me nine favours. I shall get the body exhumed.'

'Perhaps you should wait a day before you take that step,' Dr Berry said. 'My concerns were so strong that I took a sample of Mr Slab's vomit and sent it to the pathology department of University College for analysis. The results are due back tomorrow.'

Sidney Grice went down on his haunches to look at her black leather medical bag on the floor by her desk. 'That is an unusual design.' He lifted it and I saw four inch-long legs on the base.

'Yes,' she said. 'I had that made by a man off Charing Cross Road. I have been in houses where raw sewage flows over the floor and my last bag was ruined.'

'Why are there three balls on each foot?' I

136

asked and she laughed.

'Oh yes. They are meant to be berries — just a bit of fun.'

'Fun?' Sidney Grice echoed.

'You are unfamiliar with the word?'

'No. Just the experience,' I said.

'What a resourceful person,' my guardian commented as we left the house, 'and such a good clear analytical mind. But what a pity it is wasted on a woman. And what did you mean by implying that I never have any fun? Why, only the other day I got you to calculate some Gaussian eliminations. That was fun.'

'Highly comical,' I said.

'Yes. Especially when you confused co-primes with prime numbers. I . . . Blast that man!' Our cabby had gone. 'We shall have to walk to Oxford Circus if we are to have any hope of getting a ride.'

'What shall we do tomorrow?' I asked as we made our way back up the mews.

My guardian buttoned his Ulster coat. *'You* are going to do nothing. You have been looking decidedly unattractive in a hearty sort of way recently, so I hope a morning's inactivity might drain the colour from your cheeks. *I'* — he primped up his cravat and ran a hand through his hair — 'shall return in the morning.'

'To see Dr Berry?'

'To see if the laboratory report is back yet.'

'And see Dr Berry.'

Sidney Grice twiddled with his cane. 'Well, I shall need to discuss a few aspects of the case with her, yes.'

And it seemed to me that I was not the only one with colour in their cheeks.

Colour was the first thing I noticed about India before I was overwhelmed. From the deck of the ship I saw the coolies, their black bodies stripped to the waist, clad only in baggy pyjama trousers. But it was the women who really caught my eye. They were dressed in sarees, yards of cloth in one strip wrapped closely around each body and dyed in so many colours — bright saffrons, glowing golds, dazzling crimsons, vivid greens of every hue, some bordered with rich tapestries, some ornamented with silver or glittering with tiny mirrors.

Once we had docked, everything was confusion, a jumble of shouting and jostling all around us, the pleas of beggars and the cries of children, the rattle of rickshaws, the stench of the mob and animal dung and open sewers, the merci-

138

less heat of the midday sun, the heaviness of the air saturating my clothes and hair and dragging me down.

Colour was what first attracted you to me, you said, the way I flushed when I was angry — and there was so much to be angry about in India — the living conditions, the corruption, the arrogance, the bureaucracy and you. You were always so optimistic, so nice. It used to drive me to distraction, but . . . Oh, how I wish I could be angry with you now. I should like to shake you until your buttons flew off, and bury my face in your tunic when you begged for pardon. We always made up but we can never forgive each other anything now.

I carried my gloves. I have always hated wearing gloves but my guardian insisted I brought them. The sun was shining now through the fumes and the rooftops glistened with the remnants of a drizzle, but the people were pallid and their clothes were black and brown and grey as ashes.

16
QUICKLIME AND VELVET

There were several dozen mounds in the field, mostly overgrown and very few with headstones.

The air was still cold and thick with a misty drizzle. My umbrella could not hold it off and the hood of my cape did not stop my hair from clinging damp to my face as I stood and waited for the hearse to arrive.

It came with more speed than was usually considered decent, a low black carriage with one black horse tossing its blinkered head restlessly. The hearse stopped and four undertaker's men climbed out. Close behind came a covered carriage from which emerged a tall, broad woman in full mourning.

'Is this the funeral of Mr Horatio Green?' I asked one of the men as he dusted himself down.

'What there is of it.'

They hauled the coffin out and walked

with it, not on their shoulders but holding it low by the handles. It was a fine oak casket with brass fittings and a nameplate on the lid. The woman followed, her head defiantly high and her face fixed, though her dark-ringed eyes belied her lack of expression. She bore little resemblance to her short, plump brother. The ground was boggy and sucked at my sinking boots with every step.

A tarpaulin lay over a long pile of soil beside the straight-cut hole just inside the gate and the pallbearers rested the coffin briefly upon it as they took cords from their velvet coats and looped them through the handles and, with only a brief pause to adjust their grips, they stepped either side of the grave, swinging the coffin over it and lowering it quickly. The cords were pulled away and the oldest bearer clapped his gloved hands twice. From behind a yew hedge two men appeared with shovels, and without further ado began to toss the soil back in.

A small cry escaped from the woman and she clutched her mouth as if to keep another in.

'What, no words?' I asked, and she looked across the filling hole and answered, 'No words, no vicar and no holy ground for the suicide.'

'May God receive his servant Horatio Green and have mercy on his soul,' I said, and the woman stared down and said bitterly, 'There is no mercy for those who quit this world in an act of mortal sin.' A robin landed on a clod of turf, picking through it. 'He loved birds.' She choked back a sob and walked away. I went after her and she stopped suddenly. 'Who are you and what were you to my brother? Must I bear another scandal at his graveside?'

'My name is March Middleton. I —' I began, but she interrupted me urgently. 'You were there. Did you see him kill himself?' She clutched my cloak. 'Did you?'

'No.'

'Then perhaps that weaselly detective of yours did it or maybe you.' She pulled her shawl tight around her.

'No, I —'

Her black-laced hand shot out and snatched my wrist. 'Why have you come here?' She started to pull me back through the gates and I tried to break away, but she was a strong woman and I did not want to fight her at her brother's funeral.

'I came to pay my respects.'

'Respects? To gloat more likely.' She dragged me to the edge of the grave. 'It's you who belongs in there, not him.' She swung me round. My feet were on the edge of the hole now and starting to slide, and I grabbed her arm to stop myself falling into it.

'Please. I do not know who killed your brother, but I tried to save him.' My right foot slid into the air. 'I tried.'

'Miss Green, come now.' The undertaker touched her hand and she let me go. I teetered and the younger of the gravediggers caught my sleeve and steadied me.

One of the pallbearers led Horatio Green's sister away, but she twisted her head and I had never seen such hatred blaze in a woman's eyes. 'You shall have a quicklime grave for this,' she shouted, 'and I shall come and spit on it.'

I stood and watched her being ushered back into her carriage and the pallbearers clamber back into the hearse and the grooms take up their reins and go back up the drive, more slowly and respectfully than they had arrived, and I wondered how she would react when she found she was excluded from her brother's will.

'You all right, miss?' It was the gravedigger who had saved me.

'Yes.' I fumbled in my purse and gave him two shillings. 'Thank you.'

'Only paid to bury 'em one at a time,' he

told me with a grin.

You would have loved your funeral — the parade-ground precision, the praise of your courage under fire. You saved a comrade by putting yourself between him and the enemy, they said. They gave you a medal and sent it to your mother. How proud you would have been. How proud I must have been, they told me. They were impressed by my stoicism, not knowing how guilt makes heroes of us all.

I would have shared your grave willingly or taken your place if I could, but life is no fairer than death. And so I stood and watched as my heart was lowered to the accompaniment of a rifle salute, and the red soil thumped in reply. The Union Jack fluttered half-mast, a rectangle of cloth dyed in the three crosses that, we were told by a perspiring padre, you and your comrades died to protect.

It all sounded so noble to those who did not see the surgeon's knife or hear the screams of boys not even pretending to be men.

They did not know you died because of me. If only they could have buried that knowledge so ceremoniously.

17
THE MAN WITH NO ARMS

I waited until the hearse and carriage were out of view and lit a cigarette. My hand was steady but my heart still thumped. It was a long walk back to Bloomsbury but I needed it.

A man came running up to me. 'Spare a copper for a war vet'ran, miss.' He had no arms.

I kept walking because I knew I would be mobbed if I did not, and he trotted alongside. 'Where were you injured?'

'Waterloo, miss.'

I surveyed his face. 'You are about forty years too young for that one.'

'Most foreigners don't know that,' he said. 'They've 'eard of Waterloo, though.'

I laughed. 'What makes you think I'm foreign?'

'You don't live round 'ere,' he said. 'So you're foreign.'

'How did you really lose your arms?'

'Printin' press. I was resettin' it when they switched it on. Bam! Down it comes and splat — my arms is all over the front page.'

'Did your employers compensate you?'

'Oh yeah.' He wiggled his head vigorously. 'They was most generous. Twenty quid they gave me — five weeks' wages 'cause I was skilled, you see.'

I brought out a shilling. 'But how will I give it to you?' He had no pockets in his shabby clothes.

'Toss it in the air, miss.' I did and he caught it in his mouth. 'Gawd bless you, miss.' The coin appeared between his brown teeth. 'I'll keep it 'ere for safety.' The shilling disappeared again. 'You shouldn't be walkin' these streets by yourself.'

'I have been down worse.' I walked on and he fell back.

There was a public house on the corner — The Boar's Head — and I needed a drink, but hearing the drunken arguments going on inside, I dared not go in by myself. I thought about asking the beggar — but how could he have protected me? I was just about to walk on when I saw a man shambling towards the entrance. He was dressed in a grubby suit and his shoes were unlaced. His head was bowed and turned away from me, but there was something about him that

I recognized. I hurried over and caught his profile.

'Inspector Pound?'

The man spun round. 'You.' His face was thick with stubble, his collar undone and his trousers splattered with mud. 'Clear off.' He flapped his hand as one might to a persistent stray and stepped backwards.

'But I have been worried about —'

'Take your worries and stuff them.' His voice was hoarse and his eyes bloodshot. 'And keep your trap shut.'

Two men worked their way out, half-supporting and half-pulling each other over in their intoxication. 'Bit of trouble with your strump, mate?' one asked.

'Nothing I can't handle.'

'Give her a bun, did yer?'

The Inspector Pound I knew, the urbane figure of authority, would have rounded on anyone who spoke to me like that. But he laughed coarsely and said, 'Who'd touch that old haddock on a dark night? Not me.'

The two men guffawed and the shorter one was slightly sick down his front.

'How dare —'

'I dare what I dare,' Inspector Pound snapped. 'And keep your trap shut if you don't want a taste of this.' He raised the back of his hand.

I swallowed. 'Very well, Inspector. I will —'

'Inspector?' The taller man burst out and Inspector Pound flinched.

'I used to inspect 'buses,' he said, 'before I found I liked inspecting bottles more.' They all laughed. 'Come inside, mates, and we'll inspect a few together.'

The two men turned unsteadily and with some difficulty, and were just about to go back in when another voice said, ' 'Buses my backside. I knew there was somefink funny about you.' A tall black-stubbled man with a shaven head and gold-capped teeth had come up behind us. He took a long, narrow butcher's knife from a sheath inside his jacket. 'I knew you was a copper's nark the moment I saw you. Get a nose for crushers when you've been done down and nibbed as often as me.'

'What you talking about, Smith?' the inspector asked. 'Come and have a drink with us.'

'I don't drink with bluebottles.' He adjusted his grip on the knife, holding it at hip level.

Inspector Pound spread his hands innocently. 'What, me? Don't make me laugh. I —'

'You will come home with me this minute,'

I said. 'The kids want you and I came to tell you they said you could have your job back at the depot if you turn up sober on Monday.'

Smith sneered. 'Nice try, lady, but I never met a dutch yet who called her old man *inspector.*' With that last word his arm shot forward, the knife flashed, and the blade ripped through Inspector Pound's jacket and shirt, and in one clean movement plunged into his stomach all the way up to the hilt. I heard it cut through him, swishing like a spade in the earth.

We froze, Smith leaning forward clenching the bone handle, the inspector staring into his eyes. A deep stain appeared all at once and Inspector Pound grunted as if he had been punched. He looked down and reached for the knife, but Smith twisted it and pulled it out almost as quickly as it had gone in, and a gush of blood followed it. The inspector clutched at the wound and bent forward. Smith pulled his weapon back, ready to strike again, and I lashed out. I aimed for the eye but Smith was fast. He jerked his head back like a prizefighter and I caught his cheek with the handle of my parasol. He snarled angrily and swung his left arm out, crashing into my neck and sending me sprawling on to the pavement.

The two drunks backed hastily into the pub. Inspector Pound was almost doubled up and I saw his knees buckle as I scrambled up, swinging my handbag wildly and uselessly into Smith's shoulder as he pushed me aside. 'Want some?' he challenged. 'Well, just you wait your turn.'

He raised the knife for a downward blow on the crouching man. Inspector Pound looked at me. His hands were full and overflowing with his life's blood now. 'Run, March,' he gasped. 'Run, my dearest.'

I jabbed Smith in the side with my parasol. 'Drat you.' He wrenched it from my hands. 'Can't wait then?' He threw it into the road and turned to me. The inspector tried to lunge at him but tumbled helplessly to the cobbles. Smith took one step towards me and the knife went back, its blade already wet.

'Leave 'er.' A boot flew up. I saw it clearly — no laces and hardly any sole. But the toe cracked hard into Smith's groin and Smith let out a yelp and grabbed himself, but the knife stayed firmly in his grip. And I saw that the wearer of the boot was the man with no arms, and as Smith spun furiously towards him, the beggar smashed his head hard into Smith's face and Smith blinked and toppled, straight and heavy like a felled tree, cracking the back of his head on the edge of the kerb.

'Run, miss, before 'e comes to.'

'Like hell I will.'

'Go,' Inspector Pound said weakly as I ripped open his shirt. It was a savage cut, gaping wide and pumping steadily. I pulled off my scarf and rammed it into and over the hole, and the inspector groaned and twisted away.

'I am sorry.' I clamped his hands over the scarf.

He gritted his teeth and closed his eyes.

The armless man shouted into the bar. 'We need 'elp 'ere.' But the men inside did not move.

'It's you who'll be needin' 'elp when Smith wakes up with a sore 'ead.'

'You'll all get done if 'e dies — accessories to murder.'

'Where is the nearest hospital?' I asked.

'The London,' the man with no arms told me. 'Ten minutes' walk and you won't never get a cab this way.'

There was a big red-haired man with shaggy sideburns behind the bar.

'Are you sober?' I asked.

'Don't drink, miss,' he said. 'Daren't in my trade or I'd never stop.'

I looked at my watch. 'It is seven minutes

to twelve,' I said. 'I will give you ten pounds if you can get this man alive to the hospital before noon.'

'I'll help,' an old black man called from his corner chair, and suddenly the saloon was full of volunteers.

'Just him.' I pointed to the redhead who was vaulting over the bar and out on to the street. He kneeled quickly by Inspector Pound, put one arm under his neck and another under his legs, and heaved him up, getting to his feet as he lifted the inspector like a bride at the threshold. The inspector moaned.

'Oh good Gawd,' the armless man said. 'I've gone and swallered me tin. Ne'er mind. I'll find it in the morning.'

'Out the way,' the redhead shouted. And he was off.

I have watched men run for their lives from a rogue elephant in musk or a wounded tiger in a botched hunt, but I have never seen a man run so fast as that barman went. I was unencumbered but I could not keep up with him as he sprinted along the street and through a court then down a long straight road. There was a massive redbrick building which I hoped was the hospital, but it was so far away and the streets were getting more crowded. On he pelted, hollering, 'Make way. Dyin' man. Make way.'

There was a market with stalls selling rags, buckets and re-caned chairs, and the man weaved between and around them, swerving like a rugby player going for the winning try. I crashed into a rack of battered saucepans and heard it clatter behind me.

'Frebbin' cow,' the woman in charge of it raged. But I had not time to stop and was too winded to apologize.

I was getting a stitch as we turned left into Turner Street and the man was twenty yards ahead of me by now. I could see his back and Inspector Pound's head and feet bobbing up and down as they reached the main gates.

'Man dyin'. Man dyin',' the red-haired man shouted as he forced his way through a heavy queue on the entrance steps.

I caught up with him in the lobby — an immense marbled hall in the palace of disease — both of us fighting for oxygen. The red-headed man slumped down on the bench, scattering a family that was already settled on it. His efforts had finally proved too much and it was all he could do to point to the clock high over the reception desk.

'One minute to twelve,' I gasped.

'Just in time,' he managed to say and

153

looked down. 'Don't know about him, though.'

Inspector Pound's face was waxen white and when I lifted his arm, it was limp and heavy and his skin was clammy cold. I put my fingertips into his wrist, searching for a pulse.

'Oh dear God.' I moved my fingers around and dug them in deep, hunting for the faintest of beats but, hard as I tried, there was nothing but the dark weeping from his wound.

18
THE BLOOD OF A LION

A nurse came over. The red-headed man struggled to his feet and laid his burden on the bench.

The nurse leaned over and I saw she had thick stains on her apron. She pulled up Inspector Pound's top left eyelid with her thumb and peered into it. The pupil was tiny and fixed on the ceiling.

She let the lid go and looked at his other eye.

'He is dead,' she said flatly. 'I'm sorry. Somebody will come and take him.'

'Dead,' I whispered, though nobody heard me, my name in droplets of blood on my face.

She bustled away and I put an ear to the inspector's nose, but the clatter of feet and the cries of the sick were too loud for me to hope to hear anything. I touched the side of his throat and thought I felt a trembling under my third finger, and saw the blood ooze from his wound in time with the flutter of his heart.

I put my mouth to his ear. 'You are not dead,' I said, 'and you are not going to die. If Mr Grice were here he would absolutely forbid it.' And something tickled my cheek. It may have been a wisp of air or perhaps his eyelashes, which were flickering now.

'Nurse,' I called out, but she was dealing with a baby. 'We need a doctor,' I shouted.

'You and two hundred others before you,' a young woman said. She was holding a filthy cloth to her eye.

'Doctor,' the red-headed man bellowed. He had a fine loud voice and several people glared at him. 'Man dyin' 'ere.'

'And a dozen others in this room alone,' the nurse called. 'Hush yourself and wait your turn.'

'He is a policeman,' I said, but she only saw his pretence of a vagrant.

'And I'm the queen of Siam,' she jeered.

The man with no arms came panting into the room. He took one look, threw back his head and crowed like a cockerel. Three times he did it, ear-splittingly loud. And, as if he had been waiting for the summons, a doctor came into the waiting room, his coat off and his sleeves rolled up.

'What in heaven's name is that appalling racket?'

I ran over and grabbed his arm. 'This man is a police inspector working in disguise. He has been stabbed.'

The doctor crouched. 'He certainly has.' He stood. 'You men take a limb each and carry him through there.'

Four bystanders grabbed hold of his arms and legs and marched across the room.

'Be careful,' I said, and was alarmed to see how loosely his head hung back and that he did not even wince. The wound pulled open again and there was another spout of bleeding.

'Through here.' The doctor indicated a side room and they dropped him heavily on his back on a long table and departed.

'Wait out there,' the doctor told me.

'I have nursing experience. Can I help?'

'We have our own proper nurses. Goodbye.'

I went back to the bench. It was occupied now by five crying girls. The man with no arms was crouched in a slurry of Inspector Pound's blood and trying to reassure them. They had vivid pink rashes on their ears and necks.

The red-headed man was standing nearby.

'I 'ope 'e makes it.'

'You did your best.' I reached into my purse. 'Here is my card. If you call tomorrow I will give you the money.'

He took the card and left. The armless man stood up, nodded at me, 'Good luck, miss,' and turned for the exit. I chased after him.

'What is your name?'

'Charles Sawyer. My friends call me Chas.'

'You may have saved a man's life today, Chas, and you certainly saved mine. Thank you.'

Chas looked abashed. 'I don't like to see a lady knocked abart and you was kind to me.'

'Take my card,' I said. 'And if you come tomorrow I will reward you.'

'I don't expect —'

'And I did not expect to be rescued.'

'Show me the card.' He looked down. '125 Gower Street. I won't forget.'

He walked out and I waited and watched the nurse trudging wearily between patients, telling some to wait and others to go. And I wondered if I had been like that, too exhausted to show compassion. A boy with an injured mongrel was chased away. The five girls were herded out to be put in isolation. The doctor returned. 'I have stopped the bleeding but he is very weak. He needs more blood.'

'A transfusion?'

He wiped his hands on his coat. 'I have done a few and sometimes they work, but other times they hasten the patient's death. We think that there are different kinds of human blood and some do not mix well with others, but we have no means of distinguishing between them.'

'Take my blood,' I said. 'It is my fault he was stabbed.'

We went through to the side room where Inspector Pound lay grey as a corpse, his chest hardly rising. 'I have cleaned the wound with carbolic acid,' the doctor told me. 'There is some evidence it prevents suppuration and I have sutured what I could.'

A nurse was sharpening a needle on a stone. She tested it with her finger as I rolled up my sleeve.

'Sit there at his head.' The doctor wrapped a tourniquet crushingly tight round my arm and plunged the needle in at the inside of my elbow. He had some trouble finding a vein in the inspector's arm — they were empty and flat — but eventually he slid a needle in before releasing the pressure on my arm, and I watched my blood run into a sealed jar as the doctor operated a lever to pump it into the patient.

'Dr Lower was doing transfusions two hundred years ago,' he told me. 'He tried putting the blood of a sheep into a patient who had a violent temper in the hope of making him gentle as a lamb.'

The needle was burning in my arm. 'And did it work?'

'According to witnesses, the patient was so ill during the first course that he refused further treatment.' The doctor adjusted a connection in his tubes. 'Apparently Dr Lower was also planning to inject the blood of a lion into a coward to make him braver, but all his suitable cases' — his weary face twitched — 'were too timid to consent to treatment.'

I laughed. 'Perhaps you could give me the blood of a beautiful woman.'

The doctor assessed me. 'I doubt it would help.' It was a long process, but eventually he stopped. 'You must have given a couple of pints by now.'

'I feel fine. You can take more.'

He pulled the needle out and gave me a wad of cotton wool to hold over the site. 'I have enough patients as it is.'

I watched them lift the inspector on to a trolley and wheel him away. And it may have been wishful thinking but I thought he had some colour in his face.

I stood up and felt quite dizzy. The cold outside air helped a little as I made my way cautiously down the steps but, strangely, a nip of gin from my flask only made me feel worse. It took another two nips to fully revive me.

19
BLOTTING PAPER
AND GOLDFISH

An old man helped me into a cab and I would have been more grateful if he had not taken my brooch in the process. Luckily for me, it was not a favourite and I was too shaken to care. I slouched back in the seat, staring out in front of me, but all I could see was that knife flashing forward and sliding so easily and so deeply into Inspector Pound's stomach, and his look of stunned disbelief.

My guardian came into the hall the moment I got home. He settled me in my chair by the fireplace and went out to pay the driver.

'Let me see your neck . . . You have a nasty bruise but a high collar will hide that.'

'Inspector Pound —'

'Hush, March.' He touched my shoulder. 'Did you really think something like that could happen without my knowing it? Inspector Grant of the Commercial Road

Station was informed by a constable who was questioning an attempted garrotting victim there, and the inspector sent word to me under the illusion that Pound is my friend. I was about to send Molly to collect you when you arrived.'

There was a bottle on a lacquered tray on the round table. 'What on earth were you doing in that area in the first place?'

I struggled to remember. It was so recent but too long ago. 'I attended Horatio Green's funeral.'

He went to the table. 'That was unwise but only what I have come to expect of you. How did you know where and when it was?'

'I stopped one of those girls who are always throwing stones at the house and told her there was a sovereign for whoever could find out which undertaker had the body. Rayner and Sons said that Mr Green's sister was expected to be the only relative in attendance.'

'That shows the best and worst sides of your character.' Sidney Grice took a small penknife off the tray. 'Initiative and extravagance. A shilling would have been more than sufficient. You are inflating the price of bribery, March. On top of which you could have asked me.'

'Would you have told me?'

'No.' He cut the foil on the bottle. 'And, in case you are thinking of traipsing back to the East End, the inspector is not allowed any visitors until he has been moved to a safer area. We shall discuss the incident in the morning when you are recovered.' He put down the knife and took up a corkscrew. 'Now the best thing for anaemia, Dr Berry tells me, is red wine. So . . .' He twisted the corkscrew in. 'I am afraid you will have to consume several glasses of vintage claret over the next few days to restore yourself.'

'Poor me,' I said.

'You must be brave,' he told me with no hint of irony. 'If I ever manage to get this preposterous' — he held the bottle between his knees and hauled — 'cork . . .' There was a pop and the wine splashed over his trousers. 'Out.' He poured a generous glassful and handed it to me.

I could see the surface wobble as I raised the glass to my lips. 'So how did your visit go this morning?' Wine was not my favourite drink but this was not at all bad. I drained it in three gulps.

'Exceptionally well.' My guardian touched his cravat and almost smirked. 'Dr Berry is a truly exceptional woman. We had a fascinating chat about Euclidean algorithms. And her geographical knowledge is astonishing. Do you know that she can give you the map reference for almost two hundred cities, towns and villages in England?' He refilled my glass, though not quite as generously this time.

'It sounds like an uproarious morning.' I could feel the effects already. 'And how many can you recite?'

'Oh, I know them all.' He waved his hand airily. 'Guess what she gave me. No you cannot. It —'

'Oh, do let me try,' I begged. 'A goldfish in a bowl.'

'No, she —'

'A coconut?'

'Now you are being silly.'

'A kiss?'

'Now you are being coarse. You remember I was interested in her pen? No, of course you do not. You never remember anything other than soppy poetry. Well, it turns out that Dorna —'

I could not let that pass. 'Dorna?'

'Dr Berry,' he corrected himself, 'designed the nib of that pen herself. It has a fine, flexible point to allow fluid legible handwriting at a much faster rate, and I am going to see if I can adapt it to fit my pen. We shall call it the Grice-Berry Self-Filling Flexible-Nibbed Patent-Pending Pen.'

165

'It will have to be a very long pen to print all those words on it,' I said and he pursed his lips.

'We have thought of that and agreed that a tasteful copperplate-style G&B embossed on the side will suffice. Just think of it, March. This pen will revolutionize commerce. Think how it would be if every office clerk could effortlessly increase his output by up to twenty per cent a day.'

'But surely the typewriting machine will do that and it produces much more legible results,' I said, and Sidney Grice put his hands together as if in prayer.

'I dare say these novelties have their uses,' he said. 'But try slipping one into your pocket. No, March, the Grice-Berry Pen represents the future of chirography for the next hundred years.'

I swirled the wine in my glass. 'So what did the laboratory tests show?'

My guardian stopped his rhapsody and said, 'Oh, that. The results are not back yet. I shall have to call on Dr Berry again in the next day or two.'

'What a nuisance for you.'

'Yes.'

'Shall I come too?'

'You will not be required.'

'So you will have to be all alone with that

monstrous woman,' I sympathized.

Sidney Grice looked at me. 'I shall manage,' he said stiffly as the mantel clock struck. 'But we have no time to squander in brainless chitterchat. Drink your wine, March. You must keep your strength up. Tomorrow we have an appointment at —'

'Edwin Slab's house.'

My guardian looked askance. 'And you acquired that information how?'

'After you wrote a telegram with your wondrous pen,' I explained, 'you blotted it. As I am sure you know, it is a simple thing to read blotting paper in a mirror.' I was feeling dizzy again.

'How inquisitive you are,' he said, not entirely disapprovingly.

'I need to be,' I said, 'if I am to become a personal detective.'

'Dear child,' Sidney Grice selected a journal from the rack beside him, 'that is one thing you shall never be.' I was too worn out to argue with him. My neck ached from the blow and my arm throbbed from the needle. 'There is an interesting paper in this month's *Anatomical News,*' he continued. 'Not only do women have much smaller brains but they have only a quarter of the number of nerve cells per ounce compared to those of a man. Apparently, large areas of the female brain are filled with fluid — not so much grey matter as grey water. Oh, March, you have carelessly splashed your wine in my face. How on earth did you manage that?'

'I cannot imagine.' I closed my eyes and let the sound of sloshing in my head lull me to sleep.

You could never hold your drink and I am not sure you ever really enjoyed it, but a subaltern who did not drink would have been like a vicar who did not pray. I always had a good head for it. My father said I was hardened to alcohol from infancy because my nanny used to put brandy in my milk to get me off to sleep, then top me up if I awoke in the night.

Once, in a silly dispute, I recklessly challenged you to a drinking competition. It would not have mattered really, but I was your guest in the mess and we quickly gathered a crowd of your comrades round us. Only a man could handle whisky, you said, and we matched each other glass for glass. After ten glasses I felt quite woozy, but you were slurring and spilled your eleventh down yourself. You had to take a double drink in forfeit for that and I could see that you were having trouble getting it down, so I dropped my glass and pretended to pass out, and not a moment too soon. I had hardly slumped in my chair when you toppled sideways out of yours.

I was ill the next morning and my father was furious when he found out the cause.

'How irresponsible,' he fumed, 'leading a young innocent astray.' And he stalked out of the house, cane in hand, straight to the junior officers' quarters to commiserate with you.

20
THE HOUSE OF BEASTS

Edwin Slab had lived in a large white house set nicely back from a well-swept street just off Prince Albert Road, the tidy garden secluded from public gaze by a low wall and a high privet hedge. The clatter of traffic was muffled by the tall grand houses over-looking Regent's Park but still audible as Sidney Grice rattled the knocker.

'I wonder why' — he ran the toe of his boot backwards along the path — 'anyone would use shingle from Llandudno beach when there are so many supplies of gravel closer to home.'

'Does it matter?' I asked and he raised an eyebrow.

'The truth always matters, March. If you mean "is it pertinent?" the answer is almost certainly no.' He eyed two pigeons uneasily as they landed in a lilac tree.

We were greeted by a small elderly lady in a grey dress and a voluminous black wig,

170

masses of curls with long ringlets dangling about her face.

'Have you come to evict me?' Her voice quavered.

'No,' I said. 'We just want to talk to you.'

'Do we?' Sidney Grice tapped a stone unicorn with his cane.

'Well, there's nobody else here, sir,' she told him. 'The owner, Mr Slab, has passed away and the rest of his staff have upped and gone.' She made a dipping arc with her arm as if introducing them. 'Maissie and Daisy and Polly and Mrs Prendergast — all skidooddled. But I'm eighty-six, you know, and who would take me on?'

'Not I,' Sidney Grice said. 'Not even in your heyday — if you ever had one.'

The woman swallowed a wounded gulp.

'My name is March Middleton,' I said, and she perked up.

'*The* March Middleton?' Her voice rose excitedly. 'I've read all about you in the papers. You must be the one who works with that horrible Sidney Grice, the man what kills everyone.'

The man what killed everyone scowled, but I laughed and said, 'Not quite everyone. This is Mr Grice in person, and who are you?'

'Miss Flower,' she said. 'I'm eighty-six,

you know, and my mother called me Rosie.'

'Then I shall too,' I said. 'Can we come in, Rosie?'

'Of course we can.' Sidney Grice pushed past her into the house. 'What is your position here, old woman?'

'Housekeeper,' she said, 'or at least I used to be until I got too old. Mr Slab only kept me on out of charity.' She dabbed the corners of her eyes with a black-bordered handkerchief which she had tucked into her sleeve. 'Full of kindness, Mr Slab was. He didn't deserve to die like that.'

'To judge him by his taste in furnishings, I am not so sure,' my guardian said. The floor of the entrance hall was scattered with zebra skins and the pine-panelled walls were hung with them. 'Where did your employer die?' He fingered her hairpiece.

'In his workroom,' Miss Flower said, 'if you would like to follow me.'

'I should not like it in the least. Hold still, woman.' He picked a piece of fluff out of her wig and popped it into an envelope. 'I am most particular about whom I follow, why, when and where, and I shall not have witnesses dictating the sequence in which I collate evidence. At best your suggestion is impertinent. At worst it might be construed as suspicious.'

Rosie Flower blinked. 'Suspicious, sir?'

'But since I am unfamiliar with the topography of this building . . .' He took off his gloves and dropped them into his hat. 'Show me his study.'

'Study, sir?' She placed his hat on the hall table and my parasol in a stand made of an animal's leg.

'It would seem that Mr Slab, not content with filling up beasts, employed the services of a parrot.'

'Parrot, sir?'

'Study,' he snapped. 'There is not a man in England worth over four thousand pounds who does not possess one. Take me to it . . . *now.*'

Rosie indicated an open door on the left and Sidney Grice brushed past her again. 'Come along.' And Miss Flower tottered after him with me at the back, scrutinizing the decor.

A zebra's head hung over the interior porch, mouth agape as if remembering the nasty shock it must have endured, and the black-and-white striped curtains were tied back with tasselled tails.

'He called this the Hyena Room,' Rosie Flower announced as we entered.

'I cannot think why,' my guardian murmured. Stuffed hyenas posed self-consciously all around the room, their fur patchily spotted, their black lips pulled back to reveal gapped spikes of orange teeth and dark tongues, their faces a curious cross between bears and wild dogs, with big oval ears and ugly, cold yellow eyes.

'Because —' Rosie Flower began.

'Was this his chair?' Sidney Grice pointed to a hairy armchair with a hyena crouching as a resentful footstool.

'The very one he sat in every evening,' Miss Flower said.

He went down on one knee and patted the seat cushion. 'Left-handed.' He dabbed the tip of his middle finger on the tip of his tongue. 'And a lover of chocolate éclairs.' He lifted the cushion. 'You were not lying about him being kind.'

Rosie Flower looked bewildered. 'But how can you tell?'

'The undersurface of this cushion has not been cleaned since before eighteen seventy-seven. There are five distinct rings of *Erysiphales Espanola* — Spanish mildew also known as oak mould, not because it grows on oak trees, but because it does so in an incremental annual annular fashion.'

'I don't understand, sir.' She sucked her lips in.

'I am merely pointing out that no one

other than a soft-hearted dolt would have employed the services of a maid who was so slovenly, nor a housekeeper who was so decrepit as to allow such laxity.'

Rosie's eyes welled up. 'Mr Slab was always very appreciative of our labours.'

Sidney Grice snorted. 'Hence my choice of the word *dolt*. Why are there buckets of sand in every corner?'

'Mr Slab was terrified of being caught in a fire, sir. He had ropes fixed inside all the upstairs windows to climb down but I would die if I tried using one of those.'

I trod on an outstretched paw and jumped. 'Did he kill all these himself?'

'Oh no,' Miss Flower said. 'He did love killing things, but he never travelled further abroad than Winchester. All of these came from the zoo. The man who brought them was most anxious to reassure me that they had all died of old age.'

'But this one is a cub.' The pole of a table lamp projected from its head.

'That one died of young age,' she said.

'If only you had followed its example,' Sidney Grice told her. 'Were you with your lackadaisical employer when he died?'

'No.' Miss Flower polished the tip of a hyena's nose with her sleeve.

'Did you discover him?' I asked.

175

'Yes.' She ruffled its spiky mane affection-
ately.

Sidney Grice walked round an onyx table
supported on the heads of four sitting
hyenas. 'Tell us.' He snapped his fingers.

'Well, I was having my supper downstairs
with Maissie and Daisy and Mrs Prendergast when —'

'Where was Polly?' my guardian interrupted.

'It was her afternoon off, sir.' Rosie twisted
her handkerchief. 'I expect she was spoon-
ing in a pleasure garden with her young
man.'

'And his name is?'

'Richard Collins.'

'Then what happened?'

She reddened. 'I'm trying to tell you, sir.'

'Get on with it.' He brought a short pair
of tweezers out of his satchel.

Rosie Flower's right hand twizzled in
agitation. 'I'm eighty-six,' she remembered.
'Or seven.'

I took her arm. 'Please tell us what happened to Mr Slab the night he died.'

'Well, I was having my supper downstairs
with Maissie and Daisy and Mrs
Prendergast,' she began as Sidney Grice
plucked a tuft of hairs from a snarling
hyena's head, 'when Mr Slab rang the bell.'

'How do you know it was Mr Slab?' My guardian dropped his sample into a white envelope.

Rosie Flower twiddled with a ringlet. 'The bell came from his workroom and so —'

'And so you made the illogical but possibly true assumption that it was your employer who rang it.' He scribbled on the envelope and sealed it with a metal clip.

'But there was nobody else in the house, sir.'

'The fact that you did not observe anybody else in the house does not mean there *was* nobody else.' Sidney Grice poked a straight length of wire in the specimen's ear. 'Proceed with your account but do try to gather your senile mind.'

'Just ignore him,' I said.

He grunted and pulled out the wire to scrutinize the end.

'I went to see what he wanted.' She tickled behind a hyena's ear.

'Why you?' he asked as she patted its head.

'Because Maissie was scullery maid, Daisy was having her cow-heel jelly and Mrs Prendergast was Cook.'

'Continue.' Sidney Grice sat behind the desk in a brown leather captain's chair and pulled open the top drawer of the desk. He brought out a stack of letters and undid the string tied round them.

'You shouldn't be looking at those, sir.'

'Which is exactly why I am.' He unfolded the top letter. 'What happened when you answered the call?'

Miss Flower wrapped a string of fur round her finger and said, 'Poor Mr Slab was lying in his tank.'

'What tank?'

'His pickling tank. I can show —' She started towards the hall.

'Stay exactly where you are.' Sidney Grice paused from measuring the hyena's teeth. 'I shall not have you deliberately or inanely misleading me with your false impressions. Was the tank full?'

'Yes, sir. It was full of Mr Slab and over-flowing with pickling water.'

'Was he face-down?' I asked.

'Sort of.' She unwrapped her finger. 'He was all bent backwards in a funny way — except it wasn't funny — and the poor man had been sick everywhere.'

'He cannot have been sick on the ceiling,' my guardian pointed out. 'Be more specific, woman.'

'Everywhere,' she said. 'All over the floor. There was a lovely donkey-skin rug soaked all through. We had to throw it away.'

Sidney Grice snatched at the words. 'You

admit you destroyed evidence?'

'I was just clearing up, sir, me and —'

'Where else did he vomit?'

'All over his cutting-up table and Veronica too.'

'Who is Veronica?'

'A mangrove.' Miss Flower tapped on the snout of a hyena. 'A sort of otter what kills snakes.'

'I think you mean a mongoose,' I suggested.

'Do not attempt to put words in the witness's mouth,' my guardian snapped.

'Took me all morning to clean her up and she's still damp. And he made a terrible mess of Sidney.' She pointed to an especially mangy wolf near a magazine rack. 'We brought him up here to get dry.'

I laughed. 'Is that really its name?'

'It is now.' Rosie Flower winked.

'What else did you remove from the scene?' Sidney Grice snapped. 'A gun or a knife perhaps? Do not answer that. Proceed with your rambling.'

Rosie Flower pulled down her lips and tensed them for a moment. 'I went over to the tank and he didn't look at all right, sir. Apart from being dead and curved up like a humpback bridge, his eyes were near popped out of his eyeholes like tennis balls, they were, but the worst of it was he had this horrible grin, like a cheddar cat it was, and he had ground his teeth so hard that they were all smashed up.' She shook out her handkerchief. 'Oh, miss, it was most distressing.' Rosie Flower dabbed her eyes.

'Continue,' my guardian said and she raised her chin.

'Pardon my saying so, but you are not a nice man, Mr Grice,' she said as he strolled round her. 'Then I ran to the top of the stairs and shouted down to Maissie, *Go fetch Dr Berry.* She has young legs. *And be sharp about it, you idle good-for-not-very-much.* But he was dead by then. I'm sure of it. Oh, the poor man. He was . . .' Rosie Flower's mind strayed far away. 'He was . . .' she repeated distractedly.

My guardian clicked his fingers. 'Did he have any callers that day?' And she jolted back to us and said slowly, 'Not a rich man nor a poor man.'

'Or the day before?'

'Not a saint nor a sinner, nor the day before that, nor any other day this side or the other side of any day you trouble yourself with, sir.'

'Why not?' I asked.

'Why, he had no time for callers with all his work, taking innards out and stuffing

stuffing in and dealing with all his visitors.'

He regarded her through a glass paperweight. 'You led us to believe that he had no visitors.'

'No *callers.*' She pushed the wig up her forehead. 'Callers come to the front. Visitors go round the back and there was no end of those — people with pets what they wanted done. We had a horse last month, but they were too slow bringing it and the gases exploded it. All its insides were outside.'

'Did he have any visitors on the day he died?' I asked.

'I expect.' She pulled the wig down again. 'But we never really knew who was there or not.'

Sidney Grice folded the letters and tied them in a bundle again. 'Where is the workshop?'

'Down the end of the hall to the left, sir.'

He waved the letters at her. 'Show me.' And let them fall on to the desk top.

21
THE REGIMENT OF COSSACKS

Off we set back into the hall and down a long colonnaded vestibule, our footsteps clicking on the green marble floor. On either side the walls were plastered and painted with garish jungle scenes. Improbable tigers peeped from behind palm trees and unconvincing lions poked their heads through bamboo screens, and all along the arched ceiling peculiar serpents stretched and coiled in iridescent greens with impossibly daggered fangs. A stuffed black bear stood sullenly in an alcove and a brown one in another. Their paws were probably meant to be slashing, but they looked more like they were waving mournfully to each other.

We got to the end and Rosie Flower unlocked the door. 'Here we are.' It opened into an enormous conservatory. I had not seen anything so big since my father took me to Chatsworth House, and for an instant it was like stepping into an indoor zoo.

There was not a beast I could think of that was not present in that room. Mice played around cats who dabbed at mastiffs and Great Danes. These in turn looked up at ponies and carthorses, an elephant and two giraffes. Panthers, leopards and wolves stood in a peaceful circle, watched happily by a dozen owls perched on the leafless branches of a gnarled olive tree.

Unlike a zoo, however, there was not a cage in sight and every creature there was silently frozen, while our noses were assaulted not by animal odours but by the sting of formalin and the sickly sweet pungency of mothballs.

We made our way through the dead menagerie into a windowless white-distempered room that was more reminiscent of a mortuary. To one side stretched a huge operating table with a rack of gas lamps hanging low over it. Rosie turned the lights up. Surgical saws glinted on hooks along the wall and there was a row of knives arranged in order of size, from scalpels to butchers' skinning knives and cleavers. Four covered bins stood below on the white tiled floor. A stepladder was propped against the wall. To the right was a glass tank about six foot high and five foot square, I estimated. It was three-quarters full of a murky liquid and reeked of formaldehyde.

I tried the handle of the back exit. It was locked. 'Where does this go?' I brushed against a sack and got white powder on my dress.

Rosie blew her nose. 'It opens on to Hatter Street. His visitors came and went this way.'

'And you never saw them?'

'Not unless Mr Slab called me in, which wasn't often enough to be called often.'

'Where is the key?' Sidney Grice took a large femur from a wooden box on a shelf.

'On the wall there, sir.'

He took it off the hook and opened the door. On its outer side was a brass plaque. EDWIN SLAB, TAXIDERMIST TO THE GENTRY. PLEASE RING. The street outside was deserted and it was raining heavily. He stepped out and tested the bell. 'It has been disconnected.'

'Children used to ring it and run away, sir. Customers knew to knock five times.'

He shut the door and locked it. 'This room stinks of bleach.'

'We had to clean up, sir.'

'And destroy evidence.' He pushed his wet hair back. 'That could go very badly against you in court.'

Miss Flower's lower lip quivered. 'Court, sir?'

He picked something off a shelf. 'This syringe is broken and by the small cuts on your right thumb and forefinger you may come under suspicion of having caused the damage.'

Miss Flower bit her lip. 'I picked it up, sir . . . from the floor over there.'

'Your answer to the next question may have terrible consequences for you.' Sidney Grice put his face very close to hers and peered into her old eyes through his pince-nez. 'Did you bend the needle accidentally or on purpose?'

'Neither, sir. It was already —'

'Who washed the floor?' he asked angrily as I opened a cupboard to find it stacked with pelts steeped in camphor.

'Why I did, sir, with Polly.'

He replaced the syringe. 'Then perhaps you would like to describe every footprint upon it, the size and shape of the boots that made them, any distinctive defects of the soles or heels, the movements conveyed by their patterns but then' — Sidney Grice banged his cane on the table — 'perhaps you cannot. No more than you can tell me where every fibre was, its length, thickness and colour, whether it lay on the dust or partly or completely under it. Of course you cannot because you are a senile and witless short-sighted old —'

I slammed the cupboard door. 'That is enough.'

My guardian jerked his head back as if avoiding a blow. 'Kindly do not interrupt my interrogation of a suspect.'

Rosie Flower quailed. 'Suspect, sir?'

'She is a frail old lady,' I said. 'And please do not trouble to tell me about the frail old lady who single-handedly wiped out a regiment of Cossacks with a cheese wire.'

He looked puzzled. 'I am unfamiliar with that case.' He put his head into an open wall safe and Rosie Flower stepped back uneasily.

'That is all for now, thank you,' I told her as my guardian's head reappeared.

'I have not finished questioning her yet,' he bridled.

'Yes, you have,' I said, and to my surprise he acquiesced, shutting the safe as if it were delicate, then opening it again and wiping his hands on a white cloth from his satchel. 'Well, congratulations, Miss Flower. You have carried out the most professional obliteration of clues that I have ever been honoured to witness. And I speak as a man who has worked with — or in spite of —

the police forces of eight different nations. What a pity for your employer that you were not always so assiduous in your duties.' Rosie Flower opened her mouth in protest but thought better of it. 'There is nothing to be gleaned here.'

We made our way back through the conservatory, skirting a splendid crocodile that I had not noticed before, with a kid goat lying placidly between its jaws.

Miss Flower straightened her wig. 'Shall I see you out, sir?'

He shooed her away. 'We are not leaving yet.' He went back into the study. 'And do not attempt to flee.'

'Where would I go, sir?'

'Are you asking for my advice on how to escape justice?'

'No, sir. I should be glad to see some justice one day.'

He turned his back on us.

'Do not let him upset you,' I told her. 'It is just his way.'

'If he were my charge I should tell him to mend it.'

'What will happen to you now?' I asked and she trembled.

'I'm sure I don't know, miss. I shall stay here until they throw me out. In the meantime I have food and shelter. After that, what is there for my sort? I'm eighty-six, you know, and I have no savings to speak of — just a few shillings I was putting aside for some pretty pink ribbons for my hair — and I shan't go in the workhouse, miss. I shan't.' She stamped her foot and nearly toppled over.

'Have you no family?'

'Brothers and sisters all dead.' She steadied herself on the edge of a zebra-skin stool. 'They never had nice employers like Mr Slab.'

'Are there no charities that can help?'

'Oh, miss,' she exclaimed, 'there's precious little charity in this fine city and what there is goes to fallen women, and the trouble is I never fell.' She smiled shyly. 'Wish I had now.'

I laughed. 'It is probably a little late for that now.'

Rosie Flower put her hand on my arm. 'Never too late to fall, miss.'

I remembered Harriet Fitzpatrick telling me about a new charity for old servants. 'I shall make some enquiries,' I promised as I turned away.

22
THE HYENA IN THE ROOM

There was a stack of paperwork on the captain's chair when I returned. My guardian had pulled all the drawers out of the desk and was on his knees, peering inside its empty shell.

'What are you looking for?'

Mr G emerged, looking a little grubby. 'A scientist records all the information he observes and a good scientist observes everything.' He turned the drawers upside down and banged on them. 'You would be astonished how many people think it is safe to hide things by affixing them under drawers. I have sent two women to prison simply by inspecting their bureaux. But it is difficult to persuade the average policeman to search anything, let alone underneath it.' He slid the drawers back into place. 'Desks are usually a cornucopia of information. They have diaries noting important rendezvous, letters revealing romantic liaisons;

incriminating documents, hidden weapons, locks of hair. But this is the most unrewarding piece of furniture I have come across since I searched your bedside cabinet last week.'

I clenched my jaw. 'You searched my bedside cabinet?'

'It would appear that Miss Flower's psittacine tendencies are contagious,' he said and I was just working out that psittacine referred to parrots when he asked, 'What is the first thing you notice about this room?'

'The hyenas,' I replied and waited for a sarcastic response.

'Very good,' he said. 'Grice's third rule of detection is not to ignore the obvious. What else do you notice?'

I thought about it. 'There is only one armchair.'

'Precisely,' he agreed. 'So presumably that scuttle-brained housekeeper was telling the truth about her master never entertaining callers, at least not in this room. Take a look around and see if the other rooms are more sociably equipped, and do try not to destroy any clues.'

'Everything is a clue,' I reminded him.

'Remember that and you might be slightly less of a nuisance.' He crawled round the desk. 'This is only the second time I have come across this type of varnish used on walnut veneer.' He lay on his back with his arms stiff at his sides. 'What is the easiest way to give somebody poison?'

'Put it in their food or drink . . . providing the flavour is masked.'

He crossed his ankles. 'Would liqueur-filled chocolates do it?'

'I imagine so.'

Sidney Grice pointed lazily and I followed his hand. In plain view on the mantelpiece was a wooden box. 'Open it, but do not touch the contents.'

There were five chocolates in the box with a space just the right size for a sixth.

'So you think —'

My guardian put a finger to his lips.

'Attempt neither to anticipate nor to interpret the complexities of my intellect.' He closed his eyes and began to hum loudly and as tunelessly as ever.

I left him to it and crossed the hall into a dining room, decorated with fish: brown trout over the fireplace; sticklebacks suspended in an aquarium amongst wilted reeds; and a giant tunny fish in a case on a low stand. A rectangular table surrounded by twelve chairs dominated the room. All but the carver at the head were covered in dust sheets.

Further down I found a sitting room. Birds were the theme here — sparrows, owls, hawks and seagulls, two eagles with wings outstretched, an unhappy-looking robin on a twig and a kingfisher frozen in mid-swoop. In this room too there was only one armchair.

From somewhere above me I heard a dull thump and the sound of feet scrabbling. It did not seem likely that Miss Flower would be scurrying about so energetically. I went quickly to the study.

'This room has been searched by someone else and recently.' Sidney Grice had turned a small rug upside down and was dabbing the undersurface with a strip of gummed paper.

'There is somebody upstairs,' I said. 'I heard feet running.'

'Is there any point in telling you to stay here?' My guardian snatched up his cane.

'No,' I said, and we hurried into the hall and up the wide staircase. It turned back on itself on to a well-lit square corridor.

'It was over the sitting room' — I pointed — 'which should be that way.'

The door was ajar but I could hear nothing now. Sidney Grice twisted the handle of his cane until it sprung out to twice its original length, motioned me to stand to one side and prodded the door. It swung open easily. The room we found ourselves in was bright and cheerfully decorated. It had floral wallpaper and a pink Persian carpet. There was a single bed with a red counterpane and a lacquered dressing table with a set of brushes and a cheval mirror on it. The wardrobe was open with one plain dress hanging in it.

'Mr Slab certainly treated his servants well,' my guardian observed.

'There is the rope she spoke of.' There was a thick four-ply cable spliced into a loop and attached to a hook under the sill. The other end hung through the window.

'It is taut.' My guardian ran towards it and I hurried to join him, and the first thing I saw was Rosie's wig in the upper branches of the lilac tree. I leaned out further and straight below me was the back of a bald head and a grey dress billowing in the breeze.

'We must get her down,' I said. 'I hope she is not tangled in those branches.'

'She will pass through,' he assured me. Sidney Grice gripped the rope in both hands and hauled to create a little slack, and I unlooped the rope from the hook. He put a foot on the wall, then leaned back and paid out the rope. 'I have her.' His face was purple with the strain. 'Go to her, March — quick as you can.'

I raced from the room, down the stairs and out into the front garden, almost crashing into the unicorn in my haste. Miss Flower was about four feet from the ground, facing the house and creaking downwards. I ran under the tree and reached up, grasping her under the arms as she descended.

'I have her,' I called up and the rope snaked down, crashing through the branches, her whole weight suddenly in my hands. She was heavier than I expected and I staggered back, almost toppling over with her on top of me, but the trunk steadied me as I laid her supine on the gravel.

Rosie Flower's face was swollen black, her eyes wide and bloodshot, and her chewed tongue stuck out through a bloody froth. I pulled at the knot but it was embedded into the crêpe skin of her bruised neck. Sidney Grice appeared breathlessly. He brought out a clasp knife and sawed, but the rope was tough and it was several minutes before he was able to stop and rip the last few strands apart.

Her body was very hot but lifeless.

'I must have heard her feet drumming on the wall,' I said. 'I did not realize . . .' I stopped. 'She talked about falling. I thought she meant . . .'

My guardian touched my shoulder. 'If there *is* a beneficent God, she is happy; if there is not, she is at peace.' He proffered me a big white handkerchief with DB embroidered in one corner. I did not need it, but I accepted it because I knew he was trying to comfort me.

I took some twigs from her sleeve and Sidney Grice lifted the old housekeeper as one might a child, his left arm under her shoulders and his right below her knees, and carried her back to her room. We laid her on her bed and I closed her eyes and crossed her arms, while he fished out her wig with his cane. I raised her head to put it on, but could only create a travesty of the woman we had met little more than an hour ago. I prayed quietly but, though he stood in respect, my guardian's lips did not move.

'I will arrange for an undertaker,' he said, white-faced, and later, in a steadily swaying hansom, he asked, 'Where did you read about the woman who killed a regiment?'

'I was probably confused.'

He sucked his lower lip. 'Yes, you usually are.' He coughed and put a hasty hand to his eye. 'Perhaps Miss Flower was right and I do kill people.'

'It was not you,' I said. 'This Christian world of ours killed Rosie Flower.'

23
KALI AND THE TOOTHPICK

We went home. Sidney Grice adjourned to his study and I to my room.

I read your letter, the one you wrote when you were sent to the hills. Several British and Indian travellers had gone missing in the district and it was rumoured that the Thuggee cult had been revived in the area. The Thuggees, you told me, were bandits driven by their fanatical devotion to Kali, the goddess of darkness and death. It was their practice to befriend groups of travellers and, having gained their confidence, strangle them with knotted handkerchiefs. The bodies were then mutilated and disposed of in wells.

You were worried that you might not get the chance to confront them. I was worried that you would. I was scared, of course, that you might get killed, but my greatest fear was that you might kill somebody. I could not imagine you doing that. Those big gentle hands that cradled my face were not those of a killer.

As always, we dined by ourselves — cold potatoes and a salad drenched in vinegar. My guardian was occupied with some old case notes, so I turned to Tennyson's 'In Memoriam'. Sometimes it comforted me, but not tonight — the doubts and hopelessness of the verses pressed too heavily upon my heart.

'Ha,' Sidney Grice called out triumphantly. 'Although there are nine known cases of death by nitrous oxide poisoning in this green unpleasant land of ours, four were at the hands of incompetent dentists, another four were accidental overdoses at parties and one was during a demonstration on stage in Piccadilly. Silas Braithwaite could be the first case of murder or suicide by laughing gas ever to be documented. A bit of a feather in my cap, what?'

'Tis better to have loved and lost than never to have loved at all. I closed my book. 'I am so happy for you,' I said.

'Thank you, March.' He clapped his knees.

'And how many cases of elderly housekeepers hanging themselves have you come across?' I asked, and my guardian blew some air between his lips.

'Oh, they are two a penny.' He popped out his eye. 'It would have to be a very quiet week for that to make even the local press.'

There were slug holes in my lettuce.

'So' — he put his eye into its velvet pouch — 'what are we to make of Mr Slab's unpleasant demise?'

'He was probably poisoned with strychnine and possibly drowned in formalin,' I said.

'I am pleased to note that you have qualified your conjectures.' He whipped a folded black patch out of his jacket. 'So how was he poisoned?'

'The chocolates.' I wiped something grey off the surface of a leaf with the corner of my napkin and added hastily, 'Perhaps.'

'Probably not.' He deftly tied the patch behind his head. 'I kept one of them for analysis and gave the rest to Molly. She sucked them up like a McGaffey Whirlwind, well over an hour ago and — to judge by the shrill attempts at civilized speech drifting up the dumbwaiter shaft — she is still alive and as well as she will ever be.'

I swallowed, though I had nothing in my mouth. 'You used Molly as a guinea pig?' And he waved a hand.

'Molly has unwittingly tested five suspect

substances without ill effect since she came here, though she did become horrifyingly skittish after sampling an extract of *Cannabis indica* leaves once.'

I knew better than to argue about the morality of his deed. 'So how do you think he was poisoned? With the syringe?'

'That is the most likely.' He straightened his patch. 'You may remember, if you were paying attention, that I questioned the late Miss Flower about the needle and she assured me that she had not bent it.'

'It could have been bent by being dropped.' I cut a black bit out of a potato.

'We have not established that it *was* dropped.' My guardian drummed his forehead with his fingertips. 'But, even if it was, the needle was bent to the left, back on itself and into a sigmoid shape, which would suggest that there was a considerable struggle whilst it was being inserted and, since none of Mr Slab's specimens were capable of active resistance, he would seem to be the most likely recipient of that needle.'

I cut open another piece of potato but that was even worse. 'But if he was injected with strychnine he would have died within a minute or two anyway. So why put him in the tank?'

He refilled his tumbler from his carafe of

200

water. 'To make sure that we knew he was murdered. A fit man would have some difficulty scaling a six-foot high glass wall and the stepladder was at least ten feet away. It is inconceivable that a man in the agonizing muscular contractions that strychnine produces could have done so. Unless we are willing to entertain the idea that he climbed into the tank unaided — and do not forget that Mr Slab was eighty-one years old — then injected himself with the poison.'

'It does not seem likely.' I pushed the potatoes aside.

'Why do you suppose that Mr Slab gave his servant such luxurious accommodation?'

The skin on my tomato was wrinkled and splitting.

'I do not think there was anything untoward going on,' I said and Sidney Grice puffed.

'Neither do I. I suspect it was, as Miss Flower told us, because he was a kind man and kind men are often easy victims.'

'He was not kind to animals.'

'The most gentle man with whom I am acquainted goes to Spain every summer to watch men in gaudy costumes goading bulls to death.' He gestured sharply. 'Dash it all, March. Why does nothing seem to fit together? What am I missing?'

'A good cook,' I said. 'Other than that I do not know. Why were you so hard on Rosie Flower?'

'To find out if she was telling the truth about only trying to clean up when she destroyed the evidence. Guilty people are resentful when confronted with their wrongdoing. They may become truculent and they almost always try to stare you out or fix upon the floor. Miss Flower was upset and confused but said nothing to incriminate herself.'

I turned the plate round but my dinner looked no more attractive from a different angle.

'I have had a message from Dr Berry,' Sidney Grice told me as I forced myself to eat a slice of shrivelled cucumber. 'She will have the results first thing tomorrow.' He speared a radish with a flourish of his fork. 'So you will have to entertain yourself for the day.'

'It will take all day?' I queried as he chewed a stick of limp celery.

'Well,' he said, 'I have promised to take her for lunch so that we can discuss the case at length, and then I intend to consult Mr White Senior of White, Adams and White, in an effort to find a clause that will allow Baroness Foskett to dismantle her society.'

'But Baroness Foskett does not want it dissolved.'

'Baron Foskett saved my life' — my guardian stabbed his tomato so hard that it squirted over his napkin — 'and I have a sacred duty to save his widow's.'

'What happened?' I asked and he wiped his mouth.

'My tomato burst.'

'No, I meant —'

'Besides,' he spoke over me, 'I am half-convinced that Baroness Foskett is a very frightened woman indeed.'

'Why not visit her again?'

He took a drink of water. 'I wrote to her this morning and had a reply by return. She has granted me an audience the day after tomorrow, but only on condition that you come too.'

I nibbled a stalk of watercress. 'She probably wants to gossip about the latest fashions from Paris.'

Sidney Grice looked pensive. 'I think that very unlikely.'

'Silly me.' I slapped the back of my hand.

'Indeed,' he said.

I did not trouble to tell him that he had smeared tomato juice over his cheek.

'Speaking of visits, is it not about time we

called upon the other lady member of the club?'

'Ah yes.' He looked towards the ceiling. 'The reputedly merciless and disconcertingly young Miss Primrose McKay.' My guardian rattled his fingernails on his carafe. 'You may be interested to learn that I had news of Pound while you were upstairs.'

'Well, of course I am.'

Was it my imagination or was he hesitating and avoiding my eye?

'It appears' — he smoothed a crease in the tablecloth — 'that the inspector has departed.' I dropped my knife. The room went out of focus and his voice became muffled, but I could just make out the words. '. . . from the London Hospital and been transferred to the University College Hospital.' I steadied myself on the arms of my chair as he continued. 'And, since it seems ordained by a higher but tedious power, that we talk of nothing but visits this evening, I believe that the Liston Ward is open to public invasion every evening and some mornings.'

'Thank you,' I whispered.

'You are welcome.'

'I was talking to God,' I told him as I retrieved my knife.

'Let me know when he replies.' He turned

a chunk of cucumber over.
  'He already has,' I said.

24
THE BIRTHDAY SLAUGHTER

The horse was hobbling, stumbling in every dip in the road and scarcely able to lift its feet over the bumps.

'Is Miss McKay very wealthy?' I asked as my guardian gave up his attempts to pour tea from his flask.

'Eight years ago' — he banged the cork home with the heel of his hand — 'Primrose McKay was the sole heiress to a considerable fortune. Her late father's coffers were bloated to the point of pathological obesity with every tube of swine flesh, gristle and sawdust that his factory produced.'

'You are making my mouth water,' I said and he tisked.

'That was not my intention.'

Our horse tripped but just managed to recover its stride, almost throwing us over the flap.

Sidney Grice knocked on the roof. 'Have a care, man.'

'Your horse needs rest,' I called and the hatch shot open.

'Needs a good thrashin', she do.' He cracked his whip. 'Lazy good-for-nuffink bag o' bones.'

'Perhaps you should try feeding her,' I retorted, but the hatch slammed.

'Do you believe that story about her killing a sow on her tenth birthday?' I hung on to a strap as we rounded a corner.

'When I was investigating the disappearance of Canasta — Lord Merrow's prize hog — in '76 I interviewed a slaughter man who mentioned that he held the sow still for little Miss McKay.'

'What an odious creature she must be.'

He caught his satchel as it slid off the seat. 'Hypocrites are always repelled by the lack of hypocrisy in others. You have no objection to pigs being killed on your behalf.'

'Yes, but to enjoy doing it and at such a young age . . .' I stopped, appalled by the thought.

My guardian put his flask away. 'Not an endearing trait, I grant you, but it does not make her a murderess.'

'It has to make her a more likely suspect.'

He snorted. 'There are few things less likely than a likely suspect.' And while I pondered over that we paused for a funeral cortège to pass by.

By the time we reached Fitzroy Square the horse was struggling so badly that the driver had to pull over to let us off. There was a cold wet stillness in the air.

'You'll be cat meat before this day is out if you don't git goin'.' The driver lashed his mare pointlessly as she crumpled to her knees.

'There is a foul pit in hell for people like you.' I shook with anger and he laughed mockingly.

'Live there already, darlin'. Only it's called Peckham.'

'If I ever see you on Gower Street again I will have your licence.' Sidney Grice flung him his fare.

'Never 'ad one anyways,' the driver shouted after us. 'So don't fink . . .' but his voice was drowned out by the raucous cries of the newspaper vendor, 'Brave British boys face Russian fret to India.'

My guardian shuddered. 'I knew I should have killed the tzar when I had the chance.'

I looked askance at him but he did not seem to be joking. 'Do you think there will be another war in Afghanistan?'

'Undoubtedly,' he said. 'And when we have won it we should march on to Moscow.'

Miss Primrose McKay lived in a grand house just off the square, the third in a smart Georgian terrace, clad in white stone with a burgundy front door.

'Make an observation,' Sidney Grice said and I looked about me.

'The pavement is uneven.'

'Good. And what conclusion do you draw from that?'

I pulled my cloak tighter around me. 'It needs repairing.'

He clicked his tongue. 'What about the pattern of the unevenness?'

'I cannot see any.' My cloak was heavy with damp.

My guardian sighed. 'Everything has a pattern even if it is random. In this case it is not. The slabs are tilted or even cracked close to the coal holes where sacks of fuel have been dropped carelessly over a period of many years. The pavement outside this dwelling is unscathed which shows . . .'

My mind raced. 'Either they do not have coal delivered — which seems unlikely for a house of such grandeur — or the servants ensure that the coal merchant takes care.'

'And how will we ascertain the more likely conclusion?'

'By testing their efficiency.' I twisted the bell and scarcely let go before I heard two

209

bolts slide back.

'Case proven,' I said and my guardian put his cane on his shoulder.

'If one ignores the multiple other interpretations which spring immediately to mind.'

We were confronted by a footman in green and gold livery — tall and heavily built with a pox-scarred face.

'Thurston Gates.' Sidney Grice raised his cane as if prepared to use it.

'Mr Grice.' The footman eyed us icily. 'I was told to expect you.'

My guardian lowered his cane. 'What a pity for you that you did not expect me when I exposed your protection racket.'

Thurston sneered lopsidedly. 'It was an insurance scheme. Nothing was proved against me.'

'Only because the shopkeepers were so terrified of your brothers.' Sidney Grice dragged the sole of his boot over the scraper. 'Still, we must not reminisce all day.'

The footman grunted and stood back to admit us.

25
DEAD DOGS AND DANCING MANDARINS

We were taken to the music room, high-ceilinged with full-length windows and ivory silk curtains pulled back. Through the voile I made out a knot garden, the low box hedges laid out in a series of concentric circles within squares.

Chairs were set out on the parquet floor as if for a soirée, facing a raised platform scattered with empty music stands and dominated by an inlaid rosewood piano at which Miss Primrose McKay was seated side-on to us, stabbing out a one-fingered scale. There was something mannered about her posture, her left elbow on the lowered top lid and her forehead resting on her fingertips in a studied pose of pain. Her dusty pink floral dress was arranged in flowing folds as if by a portrait painter. Her yellow tresses hung freely down her back. She did not stand or even raise her head as Thurston announced us.

'Mr Grice,' she said as if I had not been mentioned and was cleverly camouflaged. 'I was beginning to think that you were not coming.'

'We are only five minutes late,' I pointed out as we walked down the aisle towards her.

She struck three middle C's. 'Try holding your breath and tell me five minutes is not a long time.'

'Wait until you are told that you have five minutes to live and then tell me that it is,' I riposted and her right eye met mine in open hostility.

There was an etched glass saucer of champagne on an oval loo table at her side and a folded fan beside it.

'Very few women are blessed with brains *and* beauty.' Her voice was jagged and brittle. 'It would appear that you have neither.'

'There is more to beauty than looks,' I said and she emitted an amused bark.

'Whoever told you that?'

My father did, and Edward, but I was not going to expose them to her ridicule.

'I know ugliness when I see it,' I said as we stopped a few feet away from her.

'You only need a mirror.' She looked me up and down. 'Did you make that dress yourself?'

'You —' I began, but Sidney Grice touched my wrist.

'I am sorry about your dog,' he said, and she struck a clashing chord.

'How did you know about that?'

'Its image is in your locket. Nobody wears the picture of a living pet and the clipping of hair has not had time to fade, hence its loss was recent. Plus few people mourn an animal for more than five months.'

Primrose McKay inclined her head a fraction. 'You are very observant.'

'It is my job,' he said, and she responded scornfully, 'Ah yes, I almost forgot — you *work* — how inexpressibly vulgar.' She sipped her champagne.

'I suppose you think a life of self-indulgent idleness is ennobling?' I said, and my guardian put a finger to steady his eye.

'I am not completely idle.' She tossed her head but in an oddly careful way. 'I have invested in a number of racehorses and a stud farm in somewhere called Suffolk.'

At least that was one interest we had in common, though I could only afford to follow the sport with small wagers. 'And have you had any winners?'

'Not yet.' She pursed her pale pink lips. 'But they shall win because I wish them to.

213

Besides' — she blew me a kiss — 'the noble do not need ennobling.' She played a trill.

'I shall refrain from commenting upon your father's beginnings as a swineherd,' my guardian said, and she slammed the palm of her hand on to the keys. 'What happened to the other figurine?'

'What?' she snapped and he made a flourish towards the yellow, green and white statue of a Chinaman in robes, standing on a black-and-gold oriental table in front of a mirror on the wall.

'Sui dynasty from Henan,' he pronounced. 'I have only seen a dozen dancing mandarins before and never one in such a pristine state, but no lord would dance without his lady and I cannot believe you could not afford the pair.'

'Oh, that old thing.' Miss McKay did not trouble to follow his hand. 'I would not know. Papa collected curios on his travels. I believe we had the lady until a stupid maid smashed it. I had her beaten, of course.'

'You had your maid beaten?' I half thought I must have misheard.

'You could hardly expect me to do it myself.' She rose from the stool in one smooth effortless movement. 'Besides which Thurston is so enthusiastic about his work and knows how not to inflict visible damage.'

Primrose McKay was tall and slender, pale and finely featured, and her hair was combed over the left side of her face, hanging almost to her breast. As if I did not dislike her enough already, I hated her for that hair. Mine is brown and frizzes at the ends. Hers glinted in the light like threads of gold.

My guardian took one step towards her before he spoke. 'The Last Death Club.' He watched her closely.

'What of it?' She picked up the fan.

'Why did you become a member?'

She gazed coolly back at him. 'Why should I not have some fun?'

'Because such *fun* can gain you nothing but money — which as sole heiress to the McKay fortune you surely cannot need — and may very well cost you your life.'

Miss McKay flipped her fan open to reveal a jade-coloured carp swimming beneath pink blossoms. 'I am sorry to contradict you, Mr Grice, but it gives me an interest in life which has been lacking since my dear papa was taken from me.' She peered down at him over her fan. 'Besides, it is unlikely to result in my demise since I am under your protection.'

He separated his hands by a few inches. 'I am not employed to be your bodyguard,

215

Miss McKay.'

She brushed a fly off her forehead with the fan, and the waft of air lifted her hair. At first I thought it was a shadow, but then I realized that she had a birthmark, a dark stain around her left eye spreading over her cheek to her ear and on to her upper lip, which was swollen to her nostril.

'I am aware of that.' Her voice hardened. 'But the fact that you would be certain to capture whoever killed me is surely deterrent enough for any sane man.'

Her hair sank back but was still parted.

'Assuming that the killer is sane and a man,' I pointed out, unable to take my eyes off her blemish. It was as if an expensive porcelain doll had been dropped into mud. 'But surely you know that you have made your death profitable to every other member of the club.'

Miss McKay blinked slowly. 'My death will always be profitable to someone, Miss Middleton. My detestable younger sister stood first in line until I had her committed. A cousin in Canada was next before a wounded grizzly bear tore him asunder.' She swatted the fly off her sleeve and it arced into her glass. 'Beyond that' — she turned languidly to watch its death struggles — 'the surviving McKays may strip my fortune like piranhas with a dead horse.'

'You are very young to be a member of such a club,' Sidney Grice observed. 'What reason could the other members have for expecting to outlive you?'

Miss McKay stretched tiredly. 'The walls of my heart are like tissue paper.' She pushed the fly under with the tip of her finger. 'And they are liable to burst at the slightest exertion. The finest physicians in London have signed certificates to that effect.'

'Then it should be a simple matter to finish you off.' Sidney Grice strolled over to a cello propped on its spike against a beechwood rack.

'You might imagine so.' Miss McKay gave him a sugary smile. 'But I have evolved a clever plan.'

'Clever plans are rarely clever.' Sidney Grice plucked the A string. 'If an idea has occurred to you, it will have occurred to a million other minds. If you had an original thought in your head you would not be wasting your life away, lolling like a solitary basking seal.'

Miss McKay's mouth tightened and the right side of her upper lip blanched. 'I have a good mind to tell Thurston to thrash you for your impudence.'

'Your footman tried to hurt me once before.' He turned the tuning peg and retried the string. 'And you would be inconvenienced were I forced to disable him again.'

Miss McKay stared at my guardian. He had the string tuned to a B flat now.

'May I ask what your plan is?' I enquired as she picked up the saucer.

'It is clever because it is simple.' She looked at the ceiling. 'I shall wait until every other member but one of the club is dead and he has been arrested. At this rate I shall not have to tarry long.'

'There were other members who probably thought they could sit it out,' I told her, 'but they have paid dearly for their mistake.'

She turned her face away. 'They were all sheep.' Her neck was long and white, but I saw another dark stain appear from just above her collar. 'They sat and awaited their fates like tethered ewes, whereas I have made a pact with the wolf.'

'Do you imagine Thurston will keep you safe?' Sidney Grice twanged a C sharp and seemed quite satisfied with the result. 'He would sell you tomorrow if he thought he would be a farthing better off.' He selected a bow and twisted the key to straighten the ribbon.

'That is where you are wrong, Mr Grice,' Primrose purred. 'You see, I give Thurston rather more than mere money.' Her body undulated and my guardian looked nauseous.

'What pleasure can you get out of the club?' I asked and the surface of the champagne trembled in her left hand.

'It is difficult for you who have nothing in the way of looks, style or money to know what life is like for one who was born to everything. Beauty, wealth, taste and intelligence are such a burden, such a bore.'

'How do you bear it?' I asked and she replied with no apparent irony, 'It is a duty, but even I must relax and death amuses me.' She dipped her finger and thumb into her drink and took out the fly.

'Let us hope you die laughing,' I said and she blew my words away as if they were cigarette smoke.

'Harbour no fears on that account, Miss Middleton, for I have no intention of dying.'

'Everybody dies,' I said.

'Yes, but I am not *everybody.*' She popped the fly into her mouth, chewed twice and swallowed. 'I do not want to die and I never do anything that I do not want.'

Sidney Grice replaced the bow and said without raising his voice, 'You may see us out now, Thurston.'

The footman joined us at once and led us out with an insolent swagger. 'Put you in your place,' he remarked to my guardian as he opened the door.

'At least I know mine,' Sidney Grice retorted and Thurston turned puce.

'How are the mighty fallen,' I said as I got to the front step. 'From criminal mastermind to grovelling lackey.'

Thurston Gates jabbed his finger under my nose, livid with fury. 'It is you who will grovel one day, girl.'

'But not to you,' I said as the door slammed.

'There was a time that Thurston would have broken your neck for speaking to him like that,' my guardian told me, 'but he has to keep a lower profile these days. I imagine Miss McKay rewards him handsomely.' He waved to a cab, but it was already pulling over for two men in the Campbell tartan kilts. 'Few will gainsay her with Thurston Gates at her side.'

'What a horrible woman she is,' I said as a line of occupied hansoms passed by.

'For once I quite agree with your assessment.' Sidney Grice waved his cane at a vacant cab but the driver ignored him. 'But I wish there were more like her.'

Another cab went by as if we were invisible. 'A quarter of the problems of this world are caused by rich women pretending to be useful and getting in everybody's way. Oh, dash it, there goes another.'

I put my first and second fingers between my lips and blew a good piercing whistle. My guardian stared. 'The word *washerwoman* springs to mind,' he said.

'It did the trick, though,' I told him as the driver tipped his battered bowler and wheeled sharply back to us.

26
MELTON MOWBRAY
AND LUCINDA

The corridors were crowded as I made my way to the Liston Ward of University College Hospital. I had heard of Robert Liston from my father, who had seen him at work. He was a surgeon who boasted of being able to amputate a leg in less than thirty seconds. He was a great showman but his speed was not just theatricality. The quicker the operation in those days before anaesthesia, the less likely the patient was to die of shock. It was a pity, though, that he held hygiene in contempt, for a great many of his patients died later of infection.

There were about thirty beds on either side of the long ward and most of them were surrounded by visitors. Some patients lay glumly alone and some slept, oblivious to their weeping families.

Inspector Pound was in the end bed on the left-hand side under a window. There was a woman sitting at the head of the bed and a man standing with his back to me.

'Miss Middleton.' The inspector was grey. 'May I introduce my sister, Lucinda?'

My first impression was one of sourness. I went to her and we shook hands. 'Your brother speaks very fondly of you,' I said and she stretched the corners of her mouth briefly, a tiny, pointy-chinned woman with pink cheeks and hair pulled severely back.

'But he has not mentioned you,' she said warily.

'That is because there is nothing to tell,' I assured her and turned to Inspector Pound. 'I have brought you a little whisky for your pain.'

'You should not have troubled,' he said tiredly.

'Oh, it was no trouble,' I assured him. 'I found it in my handbag.'

He snorted in amusement and his sister drew in her thin lips. 'The devil's brew,' she said and I decided that my first impression was correct.

'Did Christ not make alcohol for his first miracle at Canaan and bless it at the last supper?'

'I must be off,' the man said, and I looked across to see that it was Inspector Quigley.

'Good morning, Inspector,' I said. 'And what is your conclusion — attempted suicide or accidental stabbing?'

Inspector Quigley reddened. 'You are getting quite a reputation in the force, Miss Middleton.'

'A good one, I hope.'

'Hope springs eternal.' He picked his hat off the bed. 'Good day, Pound, Miss Pound, Miss Middleton.'

'I suppose it was nice of him to visit you,' I said as he passed into the corridor, and Inspector Pound frowned weakly.

'Much as I admire his detection record, there is not much nice about my colleague.' He put a hand over his stomach and winced. 'He came to make sure I would be out of his way for the next few weeks, and I think he is going away satisfied.'

A child's wails cut through the general chatter.

'I must go, George,' Lucinda said and looked at me sideways.

The sheet was being lifted over a young man's head across the ward.

'I am sure I shall be quite safe with Miss Middleton. You will come again tomorrow?'

'If I can. There is so much to do in the house.' She bent and pecked his forehead. 'Goodbye, Miss Middleton.'

We shook hands.

'You mustn't mind Lucinda,' Inspector

Pound said when she was out of earshot. 'My sister had to be a housekeeper for our uncle and a mother to me when she was fourteen. He was a demanding man and I was not the easiest of boys.'

I sat on the vacated chair and leaned towards him. It was difficult to hear above the babble of conversations. 'I do not suppose she will be very fond of the woman who nearly got her brother killed.'

'I haven't told her that bit.'

'I am sorry,' I said. 'It was stupid of me not to realize that you were doing your job.'

Inspector Pound put his finger to his lips. 'You fought to protect me when you could and should have run away. You staunched my bleeding. You got me to hospital and gave me your blood.' He winced. 'I think that more than makes up for it.'

'Does it hurt very much?'

'Not in the least.'

'You have more colour in your cheeks.'

'The doctor has prescribed two pints of stout a day to put iron back in my blood. I would prefer a pint of bitter from the Bull, but it seems to be doing the trick and this will help.' He slipped the bottle of Scotch under his blanket.

A nurse came by with a bowl of broth and I took it from her. 'I will give it to him.'

'Please don't,' he said. 'They moved me here because they thought I would be safer away from the East End, but to go by the food I am not so sure.' And I looked at the greasy globular mess.

'Oh, I see what you mean — but you must eat something.'

'You try it.' He shifted uncomfortably. 'What wouldn't I give for a Melton Mowbray!'

'There is a pie shop down Judd Street. I will bring you something tomorrow — if you do not mind me visiting again.'

'I will be still here — I hope.'

The rain rattled on the windowpane.

'I shall take that as a formal invitation.'

A nurse rang a handbell, shaking it so violently that an old man sitting dozing nearly fell off his pillow.

'Sounds like visiting time is over,' I said.

The ward was emptying swiftly as I stood. Nobody wanted to risk the wrath of Matron. The inspector raised his hand and cleared his throat. 'May I ask you a favour, Miss Middleton?' He spoke haltingly. 'If my men ever found out that you came to my aid in a fight or that I have a woman's blood in my veins . . .'

'It will be our secret,' I said, and for the first time I wished I was Lucinda and could kiss his forehead. 'Goodbye, Inspector.' I touched the back of his hand.

I glanced back as I reached the exit. His eyes were screwed up and his face was drawn.

'Is there anything more to be done for him?' I asked the matron, who was marching in.

'Everything *is* being done,' she told me.

'I just wondered about the food.'

'The Queen of England does not dine better than the patients here.'

'No wonder she is so skinny.'

Her jaw tensed. 'Goodbye.'

I had lived long enough with Sidney Grice to know when there was no point in arguing.

'I have received a correspondence from Mr White Senior of White, Adams and White,' my guardian told me over a parsnip soup, 'and he has confirmed that the terms of the Last Death Club are contractually binding. The only way to quit the society is to quit this life.'

'So your friend the baroness will have to take her chances.' I shook more pepper into my soup but it was not improved.

Sidney Grice lowered his spoon into his bowl. 'Lady Foskett is not my friend,' he informed me coolly. 'Her husband saved me and she did me a great kindness once, but I am trying to forgive them.'

He turned back to his soup and the conversation was at an end.

Edward loved his writing box and we had great fun watching him trying to find the hidden drawer. Eventually he too gave up. My father showed him and left. Edward and I were allowed a little time alone together now that we were engaged.

'The very first person I shall write to is you,' Edward promised.

'I shall not hold my breath,' I said. 'It took you three weeks to reply to your brother's last communication.'

'Well, this time you can.' Edward pulled out a chair and sat at the table.

'What?'

'Hold your breath,' he said.

I took a deep gulp and stood peering over his shoulder as he dipped the nib of his pen.

'My Darling March,' he wrote. 'Thank you so much for my wonderful present. I shall treasure it always but not one jot as much . . .' he re-dipped his pen, 'as I shall treasure you for the rest of my life.' He glanced back and up at me pinching my nose and going red with the effort, as he finished with deliberate slowness. 'With all my heart, your ever-loving . . .' he paused as I went purple, 'Edward.'

I let out the air and took a deep a breath. 'Beast.' He blotted the paper. 'And you haven't put any kisses on it.'

'I did not think you had enough breath left for those.' Edward smiled and stood up. 'And I have not enough ink to give you all the kisses that I want to. Besides which . . .' He took me in his arms. 'I wanted to give them to you myself.'

No one can describe love or happiness, but at that moment I had so much of both that I thought I would burst.

27
POISON AND PREDATORS

Kew was much quieter than it had been for the royal visit and, without the crowds, there were no stalls or beggars — only a crossing boy sweeping the road with a tied bunch of twigs, some fine ladies flaunting their peacock-feathered bonnets in their carriages, and a salt carter clacking his rattle for the kitchen maids to run out of the big houses and purchase a block.

'Why do we alight so far from the house?' I asked as we walked along the side of the gardens.

'It is a question of honour.' Sidney Grice tugged his hat a little lower. 'We cannot turn up at the front in a two-wheeler. It would be an insult to the noble blood of our hostess.'

I stumbled on a loose slab. 'Can I ask what happened to Rupert?'

'You can and you have.' He puffed out his cheeks. 'Rupert was a lion fed to the Christians. He forgot all my refutations and allowed the desperation of hope to drown his logical abilities in the swamp of blind faith.'

'Are you an atheist?' I asked and Sidney Grice paused in his stride.

'When I have the time I shall investigate the matter. If there is a God, be sure of it, I shall track him down. And when I do, he has a great many things to account for. Rupert was a missionary in the tropics, but the natives decided they would rather eat a white man than listen to his sermons. They cooked him live for two days over hot coals, I was told. Apparently they believe that the louder and longer their victim screams, the more evil spirits he frightens away.'

He cupped his nose and mouth in his left hand.

'All the more reason to bring them the word of God,' I said. 'At least he died doing that.'

'I am sure it would have been a great consolation to him.' He closed his eyes briefly. 'A good master looks after his servants. One cannot help but wonder if God is a gentleman.'

'Perhaps he is a she,' I suggested.

We turned the corner.

'What a terrifying thought.' He rang the bell and Cutteridge appeared almost at once from the ruins of the right-hand gatehouse. 'Though it might explain the illogicality of creation.'

'Do you think God could be a woman, Cutteridge?' I asked when he had admitted us.

'I do not imagine that a woman could be so cruel, miss,' he said.

'Also, there are no fashion tips or knitting patterns in the Bible,' my guardian said and I laughed.

'Why, that was almost witty,' I said and he looked mildly indignant.

'It was a serious theological point.'

As we made our way through the under-growth, Sidney Grice stopped to listen. 'The dogs sound restless.'

'Mastiffs do not like being kennelled, sir. I let them out at night to patrol the grounds.'

A clamour of snarls and yaps cut through the air.

'Are they as aggressive as they sound?' I asked as we rounded a huge flowerless rho-dodendron.

'A would-be burglar and his boy scaled the wall to the north of the property once,' Cutteridge told me with a small shudder. 'We heard their cries from inside the house. There was a full complement of staff in those days. Three gardeners and two footmen tried to beat them away with poles, but her ladyship was the only one who could command them. By the time she had been roused and called them off, it was difficult to imagine that what was left had been human.'

'But how do you control them now?' I stepped sideways to avoid a patch of thistles and almost trod on the remains of a viper curled in the soil and riddled with maggots. The head was missing. Whatever had taken that — a fox perhaps — would surely be dead by now.

Cutteridge tilted his head in the direction of the barks. 'I don't, miss. I open the cage with a wire from the scullery and I throw horsemeat into it to lure them back. You can see the enclosure from the window. Once I miscounted and one of them got into the house and tried to mount the stairs. I was compelled to run it through with the fourth baron's double-handed sword. Mind your face, miss.' He held back a bramble for me. 'Her ladyship was most annoyed and docked the cost from my wages.'

'How many dogs are there now?' Sidney Grice asked as we came to the gravelled clearing.

'Fifteen, sir.'

We turned another right and all at once it

came upon us — Mordent House, tall, bleak and forbidding, its emptiness taking us in as we climbed the algae-green marble steps, its rancid air suffocating me as we entered the decayed hall, its corruption crushing me as we mounted the quivering stairs.

'Did you observe that the lacewing has gone?' my guardian asked me in hushed tones as if still mourning its passing.

'It has probably been eaten.' I hastily stepped up as a board cracked under my weight.

'What a fine portrayal.' Sidney Grice pointed to a darkly varnished painting on a far wall — Actaeon, having been turned into a stag, being torn apart by the goddess Diana's dogs. 'If you look carefully you can still make out gouts of his flesh dripping in the first hound's mouth.'

'And you thought a female god would be kind,' I said, but Cutteridge made no sign of having heard me. He seemed to age with every step we ascended and his hand was shaking as he tapped on the oak panel.

'Wait here, please.' He entered the darkness, and a match flared and died while the candle flame grew into a glimmering halo, giving just enough glow to show us the outline of our chairs and the gauze box before us.

'Sidney,' the speaking tube hissed the moment we were seated, 'is there no escaping you?'

'Many have tried,' my guardian said.

'And many have succeeded,' the baroness responded and his face fell. 'Perhaps too many to enumerate, but permit me to essay. Thomasina Norton, *exempli gratia.* I am accurately informed that she slew two men whilst entrusted by her progenitors to your incommensurate care. I hope your present ward has no murderous intents.'

'Not yet,' I said and she rasped, 'You have spirit, child, but do not fear. He will soon destroy that as he lays waste all things that are lured into the lair of his existence.'

'Mr Grice has given me his protection,' I said.

'Just as he did with Horatio Green and Edwin Slab? A flimsy shield indeed behind which to shelter.'

'I offered them no protection, Baroness.'

The speaking tube clattered.

'I am bored with you already — stifled and stultified almost to a state of mental paralysis. Why have you come?'

'I am concerned for your safety, Lady Foskett. It does not appear that you can extricate yourself from that death society —'

'I have already made my position clear,' the voice broke in, husky and metallic, 'and you cannot possibly have misconstrued it. The Last Death Club is my whoreson progeny and I mean to sustain it to its sour conclusion. I shall not permit any member to withdraw from their compact with me, nor shall I tolerate any interference with its constitution from you or any other man of woman born.'

I saw Sidney Grice's fingers twitch on his knees. 'At least will you take some steps to protect yourself?'

There was a dry throaty rustling. 'Who can harm me when I cannot harm myself? Do you think Cutteridge will let an assassin into the house?'

'He is only one man,' I said.

'I have a title, child. Kindly use it.'

'And so have I,' I said. 'It is *Miss*. I may be a child to you, Lady Foskett, but you are elderly and I do not address you as *old woman*.'

The baroness wheezed furiously. 'You are an impudent hussy.' She coughed four times. 'But you are right. I am not dependent only on Cutteridge for my security, *Miss* Middleton. I have my dogs of war and when they are unleashed there is not a man on the slime of this earth who can hope to overcome them.'

'Even so, your home is not impregnable, Lady Foskett,' my guardian told her. 'Two members of your society have been poisoned already. Will you at least have your food tasted?'

'I could employ the services of small children.'

'An excellent idea,' my guardian said.

'Ah, what unbridled joy I could obtain in observing their terror, perhaps even watching them writhe and die.'

'I was thinking more of using their sensitive taste buds to detect any toxins.'

There was a thump of boot on wood. 'Stick to the terms of your employment, *Mr* Grice. When, as I so fervently desire, my rancid soul absconds to join the ragged battalions of the damned you will be at liberty to investigate its departure with all your limited powers. But, for so long as the sulphurous fumes of this tortured world continue to flood my alveoli, leave me in my squalid solitude.'

Sidney Grice shrank where he sat. 'Lady Foskett . . .' he began, but did not seem to know how to continue.

'See them out, Cutteridge,' the voice exhaled and I felt a hand on my shoulder. 'Out . . . out . . .' The voice faded.

My eyes were getting accustomed to the light now and I could just make out her figure, tiny and erect in the high-backed chair, a long dress flowing over the platform, a veil over a shadowed face.

'If you please, sir, miss.'

We stood up and in the fluttering candle-light our projected darknesses stretched and bent, separated, twined and swayed, spectres of Sidney Grice and me locked in a *danse macabre* before we were torn apart again.

'Goodbye, Baroness Foskett,' I said, but only an exhalation responded.

The stairs creaked more than ever and twisted under our feet as we made our way down.

The sky was overcast and the path slippery and waterlogged by a shower. 'The wind is getting cold,' I observed as Cutteridge unlocked the gate.

The dogs were clamouring and Cutteridge surveyed the sky. 'There is a storm gathering, if I am not mistaken, miss.'

A crow shrieked.

'Predators.' My guardian buttoned up his coat. 'They are everywhere.'

28
TWO NURSES AND THE MARQUESS OF SALISBURY

Two nurses were stripping the bed next to Inspector Pound's when I arrived.

'Nice old chap,' he said. 'Came in with a cut finger and ended up with his arm off. He never recovered.'

'And how are you feeling?'

'Never felt better.'

He did not look it. His face was white again and beaded with sweat, there were dark hollows beneath his eyes and a slight tremor in his hand as he held it out to me.

'I have brought you a pork pie. It is still warm.' I opened my brown paper bag to show him, and he twisted his head but could not lift it to look. 'And two bottles of bitter from the Bull, poured less than twenty minutes ago. Would you like some pie now? I have a knife.'

'Thank you. Perhaps later. I feel a bit green to tell the truth — and hot.'

I pulled the blanket down and saw that

his sheet was stained brown with old blood and that his gown was damp and clinging to his shoulders.

'This patient's bedding needs changing,' I told the nurse and she snapped round.

'Did it this morning.'

'She did,' he confirmed. 'I expect the wound is weeping a bit. A couple of stitches pulled out but the surgeon is coming tomorrow.'

'Let me see.'

Inspector Pound clutched his blanket. 'Hold on, Miss Middleton.'

'I have worked as a nurse in three different countries,' I said and took hold of the sheet.

Inspector Pound let go and closed his eyes, as if not seeing me looking at him made it more respectable. Perhaps it did for him. I loosened his bandage and saw the wound was seeping pus. I pressed lightly on his stomach and he yelped involuntarily. His skin was hot and rigid with muscle contractions.

The nurses were going.

'Get me some carbolic acid,' I said and they looked nonplussed. *'Now.'*

'You can't order us about.' They put their hands on their hips.

'I will give you two minutes,' I said and

they both hurried away.

The inspector managed a smile. 'I could do with a few of you in the force.'

'Women?'

He shivered and I covered him again.

'I didn't mean that,' he said. 'It's hard to think of you as a woman sometimes.'

He meant it as a compliment, but I knew how he would have reacted if I had told him he was not like a man.

'Do you believe in germs?' I asked as he gingerly put a hand to his side.

'I am not sure. I know Florence Nightingale says they are nonsense.'

'Florence Nightingale is a wonderful woman,' I said, 'but she believes that fresh air cures everything. If that were the case why would agricultural workers be decimated by disease?'

'By the poisonous miasma produced by the smells of cow dung.' His voice was fading as the nurses returned with a blue bottle, a bowl and a stack of cotton squares.

'Hold his arms,' I said. 'I am sorry but this will smart.' I pulled out the cork and the fumes stung my eyes as I poured it on to his stomach. The inspector arched up and cried out.

'Ruddy hell!'

'Kindly moderate your language,' the

younger nurse scolded.

'Cripes!' he yelled, writhing as I wiped the muck from the wound.

'I am sorry,' I repeated and tossed a foul-smelling swab into the bowl.

He cried out again and mercifully fainted.

Matron marched over. 'What do you think you are doing?'

'What you should have done,' I said, scooping out what infected matter I could and throwing the wad away.

'You will leave this instant.'

I trickled some of the carbolic over the wound. 'He needs a clean bandage,' I told the older nurse, 'and please wash your hands first.'

I wiped my hands as best I could on the remaining squares. 'You can watch this man die or you can try to kill the cause of his infection.'

She wagged a fat finger at me. 'You are an insolent little madam.'

'I am also the Marquess of Salisbury's goddaughter,' I told her. 'The choice is yours.' And I left.

My father and I had seen the marquess go by in a landau on his way to the India Office once so I was only exaggerating a bit.

'Do not be such a baby,' I said as you

clung on to your trousers.

'If I were a baby I should not mind, but I am a man and it is not decent.'

'Very well then,' I said. 'Bleed to death.'

You tried to tell me it was only a scratch, but your trouser leg was saturated and when I eventually managed to coax you and clean the wound I could see your femoral artery exposed, as if by careful dissection rather than the careless slash of a comrade's sabre in a mock duel. I saw your life pulse through it. One sixteenth of an inch more and you would have been dead. They say it takes less than half a minute. My father arrived with his suture needle and you fainted clean away, though we told you afterwards that you had not.

You had a bit of a limp after that but I suspect you played it up, hoping the men and other girls might think you had been injured in action, besides which everyone knew that Lord Byron had a club foot so it was dreadfully romantic. You did not need to fake it for me. There never was a more romantic man. I still have that rose crushed and dried in my journal to prove it. Who else would risk their life because I loved a flower?

'I have just been to see Inspector Pound,' I

told my guardian on my return.

'I know.' He was fiddling with the levers on a metal box, another of his inventions.

'How?'

'You reek of carbolic acid. It almost masks the smell of tobacco and gin and parma violets. So, since you are clearly anxious to tell me, how is he faring?'

'Not very well,' I said. 'His wound is suppurating and he has a fever.'

He rifled through a tangle of wires and bolts and tools on his desktop and extracted a small screwdriver. 'He is a strong man.'

'Will you not visit him?'

He tightened two screws on the side of his machine and turned it upside down. 'For what reason? He is not involved in any of the cases I am investigating.'

'To see how he is.'

'You have just told me how he is.' He took a bolt out and put it to one side. 'I must find someone who will make a better coiled spring.' He hinged a panel sideways to open a square hole.

'To show your concern,' I suggested.

'How can I show that which does not exist?' He picked up a pair of pliers.

'Do you really not care?'

'He is a good policeman in a world of incompetence and corruption and I should miss that, but my weeping at his bedside will not heal him any the quicker. Give him my regards if you wish.' He poked the pliers through the hole and grasped something. 'Now' — there was a loud click — 'if Cook uses this as instructed we should never have another lump in our creamed potatoes again.'

'Anyway,' I said, 'how was your visit to Dr Berry?'

'Most pleasant.' He twisted the pliers a fraction clockwise. 'She had a pretty blue dress on and —'

'I meant the tests,' I said and he looked up again.

'Oh, those? Yes, they were all positive. Edwin Slab was definitely poisoned with strychnine. She had a frilly collar and matching cuffs too. Something like that would flatter even you, March, if you were not so studiously occupied with looking dowdy.'

'There is nothing studious about my dowdiness,' I retorted, uncertain what I meant but feeling it was probably sufficiently withering to merit flouncing out of the room.

29
WEALS, FLARES AND THE FIGURE OF DEATH

'The trouble is,' Sidney Grice said over breakfast the next morning, 'I have not been focused. There are too many strands in the web of these murders and I have allowed them to lead me in different directions when I should be tracing them all back to the centre.'

'I am not sure I know what that means,' I said.

'Neither am I.' He nonchalantly crumbled his charred toast into his prune juice and over the tablecloth. 'It seems reasonable to assume, though not to take for granted, that the deaths of Messrs Green, Slab and Braithwaite were connected. Horatio Green and Edwin Slab were both members of that ludicrous society, which makes them self-selected targets, but why Braithwaite? His only connection that we know of was that he was Horatio Green's dentist. I rifled through his meagre patients' records and scantily filled appointment book and none of the other members have ever consulted him. So why would he be a victim?'

'Perhaps he knew something that would incriminate the murderer,' I suggested.

'That would seem the most likely explanation.' He felt the teapot and pushed it away. 'Though the fact he said nothing to us indicates that he might not have even realized the significance of his information and, if my profession has taught me anything — which it has — the most likely explanation is often the wrong one. Perhaps the delightful Quigley was right — and what an unappealing idea that is — and Braithwaite killed himself accidentally.'

'But what about the marks on his wrists?' I reminded him. 'Could he not have been tied to his chair and only released when he was unconscious or dead?'

'The marks on his wrists were at least a few days old,' he declared. 'Long ago I observed that rope marks cause a triple-layered inflammatory response — a red impression, bordered by a paler, less well-delineated flare, bordered by a weal mark. It takes some time for these marks to fade depending on the severity of the trauma. The flare and weal had disappeared, but the inner lurid colouration was still evident even

247

to your poorly trained eye. Hence the marks were not made immediately ante-mortem.'

'So how do you explain them?'

He refilled his cup. 'I was not aware that I was obliged to do so.'

'Do you think that when Jenny referred to Mr Braithwaite wanting her to play games he —'

'Quite possibly.' He opened his egg with a teaspoon but I did not bother with mine. It was crypt cold and my toast was soggy but just about edible.

Molly came in with a copy of the Man-chester *Guardian* and her employer dabbed the cover with his middle finger. 'This has not been pressed,' he told her. 'Go and do it immediately.'

'I started to press it,' Molly said, 'but there's a lovely funny picture of you on page four, sir. So I thought you would want to see it straightways. I know how much you love a good hoot.'

Sidney Grice looked at her as if she were a changeling, rustled through the pages, tut-tutting at the ink stain which had miracu-lously migrated on to his shirt front.

'It's ever so good ain't it, sir?'

'One shilling off your wages,' her employer said absently. His face clouded and he put a finger to his eye. He rammed the paper back at her. 'Take it away and burn it . . . *now*.'

'Can I see?'

'No, you may not,' he said, but I had already whisked it out of her hand. It was a cleverly executed cartoon and there was no mistaking Sidney Grice with his eye patch on and the cruel exaggeration of his shortened left leg, but even worse were the corpses strewn about his feet, every one of them named — Sarah and William Ashby, Judith Stravinskij, Sir Randolph Cosmo Napier, Alice Hawkins, Horatio Green, Edwin Slab, Silas Braithwaite, Rosie Flower. And Sidney Grice stood over them, holding a scythe and dressed in the hooded robes of Death.

'What in the name of everything unholy has Rosie Flower got to do with me?' Sidney Grice demanded. 'And how the devil did they find out about her?'

'Ten shillings off your wages for strong language,' Molly whispered as she skipped heavily out of the room, and my guardian threw his napkin after her.

'Sarah Ashby was dead before I had even heard her name,' he fumed, 'and William Ashby, who is portrayed as an innocent dupe, was a murderer tried and found guilty by twelve men good and true in an almost fair trial.'

'But he was your client.'

'Then more fool him.' He swept out his hand, sending his egg flying into the coal box. 'He wanted the truth and he got it.' He wiped his fingers on the tablecloth. 'And nobody can blame me because Napier and Hawkins got in the way.'

I put my toast down. 'Got in the way? I can hardly believe you have said that. Alice Hawkins was —'

'A corpse,' he interjected, 'before I even took on the case, and Quarrel — not I — killed them all.' He knocked his teacup but caught it as it spun off the saucer. 'None of the others was ever a client of mine except for that that damned fool Green, and I am in the process of bringing his murderer to book as I speak.'

'I hope so,' I said. 'But who was Judith Stravinskij?'

'I throttled her,' my guardian conceded, 'but it was all an innocent misunderstanding on her part.' He looked at the ceiling for a moment. 'Besides which, it is the unnamed figure that really injures me.'

I looked again and in the bottom right-hand corner was a faceless dead man that I had not noticed before. This body was simply labelled *next client*.

'Will you sue?' I knew of Sidney Grice's

predilection for bringing civil actions against his detractors, but he shook his head. 'The editor of the Manchester *Guardian* knows things about me that I would rather he kept to himself, and I have information about him that would destroy his marriage, finish his career and quite possibly put him in prison. We would be like two drowning men, clutching at each other and dragging each other under.'

I remembered Eleanor Quarrel and Father Brewster, and imagined how it must have been for them as the stormy seas closed over their heads. She murdered members of her own family in cold blood, and so many others. Did she repent in her terror or did she only fear for herself? Could her own death make atonement for what she did? I prayed so every night.

'Shall I burn it?'

'No,' he said. 'I shall save this scurrilous rag and the next time I meet Mr Charles Prestwich Scott and his amusing sketch artist, I shall take great pleasure in making them eat their words — preferably literally.' He turned back to the carbonized slurry in his bowl and I tried to shake off my thoughts.

How could she have laid Sarah Ashby on the ground, stabbed and hacked at her and

251

calmly sliced that angelic face through the soft skin and warm muscle down to the teeth and bone?

Sidney Grice let his napkin fall on the floor. 'Come, March.' He scraped back his chair. 'Today we shall visit the displeasingly named Mr Piggety.'

30
PIGGETY'S CATS IN BIG WHITE LETTERS

There had been a fire in Euston Square and the Metropolitan Brigade was still fighting it with water wagons connected to a rattling steam pump, leaving hardly any room for traffic to pass by.

'The subterranean railways were supposed to alleviate our transport problems,' my guardian said, 'but I suspect they have merely added to them by enabling the vulgar herds to invade our capital at will.'

'This is nothing to the chaos I encountered in India.'

He looked away. Firemen were breaking open a window with their axes and the smoke rolled blackly out, stinging the eyes of the onlookers and startling a team of dappled horses harnessed to a stonemason's wagon which skewed across the road, slowing our progress even more.

'There is another approach we could take to these investigations,' Sidney Grice said. I liked the *we*, though I suspected he meant himself rather than me. 'We could just wait until all but one of the club members is dead and arrest the sole survivor. At the rate they are dying it should not take very long.'

'You cannot mean that,' I said as we edged round the obstructions. 'Surely it is your job to protect these people.'

My guardian undid the clips on his satchel and brought out his patent heat-retentive flask.

'On the contrary.' He poured some tea into his new specially designed tin cup, tall with a slight internal lip to discourage spillages. 'If you recall the terms of my engagement, I am employed to investigate the deaths of the members, not to nanny them and, if they do not die, I cannot do my job.'

'But surely your instincts are to save them?'

He recorked his bottle. 'The beasts in the field have instincts. I have intellect and I do not need to exercise it overly much to know that any other deaths will reflect badly on me, and my professional standing has already been battered like the wreck of the Deutschland. Besides, it is an inelegant solution.'

'It helps that we only have five suspects,' I said as he put his flask away.

'Not necessarily.' He steadied his cup as we swung round a fireman carrying a night-gowned old man like a child out of the house. 'Someone who is not even in the society may hold a grudge against the victims. Besides which' — he put his hand over the cup — 'numbers are immaterial. There were one hundred and three suspects when Granny Griggs was sawn in two at four post-meridiem, but I apprehended the culprit before the clock had struck the quarter. Conversely, it took me four years to prove the guilt of Lorraine Merrylegs when she was the only person present at three different murders. If she had remembered to brush behind her teeth, she could still be about her work now.'

'I have never heard of her,' I said, 'and I read all the shilling shockers.'

'The Lord Chancellor begged me to keep the matter quiet for reasons which I am un-able to divulge until this century has reached its inglorious conclusion.' He drank a little tea. 'Anyway, you are forgetting there is a sixth suspect.'

I thought about it. 'Who?'

'Myself,' my guardian said. 'I also stand to gain a tidy sum of money pursuant to the deaths of all the members.'

I laughed. 'You cannot seriously suspect

yourself.'

'One must always consider all the possibilities,' he said. 'However, I have sufficient intimate knowledge of my actions to enable me to discount myself as the guilty party with a reasonable degree of confidence. You, however, may keep me on your list.'

'I shall bear that in mind,' I told him as we jolted over a pothole that nearly caused him to choke on his tea.

We turned off Euston Road but our rate of progress did not improve. Two men were loading furniture into the back of a van and our cabby had to threaten them with his whip before they would move it to one side. The streets became narrower and shorter and the houses smaller and shabbier the further we went east, and there were fewer carriages and more pedestrians, until ours was the only hansom in view, pushing its way through the bustling crowds.

'What a fine history this place has.' My guardian raised his voice above the general din. 'Over there is The Prospect of Whitby, formerly and more aptly known as The Devil's Tavern. The great Hanging Judge Jefferies frequented it, and his house stands nearby with a noose in the window to commemorate his glorious career. Why, in two particularly productive days of September 1685, he condemned one hundred and forty-nine people to death.'

'What a jolly card he must have been.'

The streets were slightly wider now but more oppressive with their high sides — the towering windowless walls of warehouses, their red bricks blackened by the sooty London air and joined across the road by a mesh of wooden walkways at every level. The alley opened out into a seething mass of porters and lightermen, heading their way to and from the docks, many burdened so heavily that they were bent double under their loads of sacks and crates.

'They used to call this Execution Dock.' He strained to make himself heard. 'It was a favourite site for dispatching pirates and mutineers. They really knew how to hang a man in those days. If the executioner did not pull his legs to finish him off a man could jiggle on a short rope for the best part of an hour — the *Marshal's Dance* as they called it. My father came to watch the last hanging here and told me it was quite wonderful.'

'Like father like son,' I said and he beamed.

The hansom came to a halt. 'That's as far as what I go,' the cabby shouted and my guardian passed up his payment.

'Keep the change and there's a guinea for you if you wait.'

'One hour,' the cabby said and wrenched the reins to urge his horse out of the way.

'Keep your eyes skinned,' Sidney Grice told me. 'We are looking for Piggety's. No need. There it is.'

I followed his hand to see a tarred wooden building, two storeys high, built against the side of a sugar warehouse with a hexagonal tower on top and a row of skylights in the roof, a sign on the side bearing the legend *Piggety's Cats* in white letters three feet high.

We pushed our way through a group of dockers who were bent over a game of Find the Lady. A fat man with a wooden leg was sitting on the cobbles, putting a stone on a tray, then covering it with one of three mugs and shuffling them about while the audience placed bets on which mug he had used. We watched for a while and he was very fast. I could never guess the correct mug.

'Left,' Sidney Grice said and it was. 'Centre.' He was correct again.

The fat man looked up. 'You 'aving a punt, guv?'

'I never gamble,' my guardian told him,

'even on certainties like this. Left again.'

I was aware of a man in a green jacket standing behind us, and turned to see him grasping a wicked-looking cudgel bristling with spikes.

'Time to go before I smash your pretty face.'

Sidney Grice seemed to be engrossed in the game. 'Centre,' he said.

'Thank you,' I said. 'I am not often accused of being pretty.'

'I was talkin' to your old man.' The man in the green jacket moved in close and raised the cudgel. I felt it prick my chin. Instinctively I raised my parasol and accidentally caught him in his right nostril. It was quite a hard jab and he was so taken off-guard that he dropped his weapon and clutched at his nose.

'Centre.' My guardian spun round and I looped my arm through his.

'Take me away from these ruffians, Mr G,' I said as the man scrambled for his club.

Sidney Grice kicked it skittering away. 'Certainly, Miss Middleton,' he said and glanced over his shoulder. The man had retrieved his weapon but made no attempt to follow us.

'Why did you call me Mr G?' he asked as we came up to the shed.

'I was not sure if you wanted them to know who you are,' I said. 'Anyway, I think I quite like it.'

A cesspit was overflowing down the slope towards the water's edge.

'So do I.' He lifted the knocker. 'It manages to be informal and formal simultaneously.' He rapped on the door, which flew open almost immediately, and the stench struck us so forcibly that we both staggered backwards.

31

THE CURIOUS INCIDENT OF THE CATS IN THE DAYTIME

'Oh, you'll soon get used to that.' The man who answered our call was so short and onion-shaped that, had he been wearing a peaked cap, I would have been tempted to ask where Tweedledee was.

'I think not.' Sidney Grice put a hand over his mouth and nose.

Our greeter put his hands damply together. 'Think of it as the smell of money.' The front of his head was flattened, sloping downwards, giving him a curiously low brow.

'I shall not be putting it in *my* purse,' I assured him.

'Sidney Grice.' My guardian held out his card. 'And this is Miss Middleton. You must excuse her peculiarities.'

'Prometheus Perseus Piggety.' He took the card and turned it over, as if expecting to find a personal message. 'I can forgive a beautiful lady anything,' he said, quite gallantly, until he added, 'but this one will have to mind her p's and q's.'

'I will tell her that,' I said, 'but I doubt that she ever will.'

Piggety screwed up his eyes and pushed his face quite close to my guardian's. 'How very like your cartoon you are.' And Sidney Grice whipped his card away.

'Were your parents fond of Greek myths, Mr Piggety?' I put in hastily.

All the time we were speaking Mr Piggety was shuffling backwards, like a flunkey in the presence of his monarch, to admit us to his premises.

'I hated them,' he said, 'and they hated me. So they changed my name from Samuel when I was fourteen.'

'How could anyone hate you?' I sprayed some perfume on to my handkerchief.

'Many people have asked me that question and I have yet to provide an answer . . .' He licked his lips. 'For there is not a more loveable man in this land than me.' He locked the door. 'The only one ever cut' — he held up a long, steel key with rows of teeth set at various angles around the cylindrical shank — 'and one that cannot be copied. Security is my watchword, my guiding light, my beacon, my —'

'A Williams-Hazard deadlock,' Sidney

Grice interrupted.

'You know your locks, sir.'

'Mr Hazard paid me three hundred guineas to attempt to pick his prototype.'

'And did you manage?' I asked.

'He paid me another two hundred guineas to keep that information confidential.'

We were standing on a concrete platform with waist-high railings, looking down to a large, well-lit room with four long, parallel rows of cages stacked three high and resting on trestles.

'This used to be a factory for canning soup,' Prometheus Piggety told us, 'until people realized what a useless idea that was.'

'But surely it preserves the food,' I said and Prometheus Piggety snickered. He was neatly if slightly shoddily dressed in a shiny-elbowed, bottle-green coat and good-quality black twill trousers which needed pressing, but his shirt collar was stained a vivid red with a blue tint.

'Yes, dear girl, but how do you get it out again?'

'I am sure I could design an opening device,' my guardian said, half to himself, and Mr Piggety snickered again.

'I should not trouble yourself, sir. It is just a passing frivolity like paraffin. What is the point in that when we have an endless supply of sperm whales already?'

I was about to point out that paraffin was cheaper, cleaner and kinder, but Sidney Grice said, 'You have an interesting business here.'

'Come and see for yourself.' Mr Piggety led the way down a flight of open metal steps into the great hall and stopped at the first cage we came to. It contained five white kittens.

'Aren't they gorgeous?' Mr Piggety opened a cage, lifted one out and handed it gently to me, a tiny thing with big green eyes and soft pink paws. I stroked its head and it nuzzled my hand. I put my finger under its throat and felt nothing.

'How very odd,' I said. 'It seems so happy and yet it does not purr.'

'There is something very curious about the noise these cats are making,' Sidney Grice said.

'I cannot hear anything.' I tickled behind its ears.

'That is what is so curious.' My guardian rattled his cane along the bars of a row of cages and the occupants jumped back and, though some opened their mouths and bared their teeth, not one of them hissed or meowed at him.

Mr Piggety made a high whinnying sound.

'Well spotted, sir. Do you know I have shown countless gentlemen around this establishment and not more than two of them observed that fact until their attention was drawn to it?'

The kitten dabbed a button on my coat.

'Why do they not make any noise?' I asked and Mr Piggety whinnied again, but in a lower register.

'These cats all came from a remote valley in an area of Spain called' — the whinny rose — '*Cat*alonia. Rather good, don't you agree?'

'Not remotely.' Sidney Grice genuflected to peer under a cage.

'I bought a job lot of cats' — more shrill hilarity forewarned of another pun — '*fur* three pounds, but I realized at once these were absolutely *purr*-fect for my purposes: snowy white, wonderfully soft fur and every one of them dumb. What more could you want?'

'Money,' my guardian said and Mr Piggety heehawed.

'You and I could be brothers,' he said and Sidney Grice recoiled. 'For the love of lucre is exactly why I purchased this magnificent edifice.'

'How many cats do you have here?' I asked.

'Four thousand, four hundred and twenty-two,' Mr Piggety replied, taking the kitten from me and putting it back in its cage where it mewed silently. 'I shall start marketing them before the end of next year.'

'But why have you not sold any yet?'

'Two reasons,' Mr Piggety said. 'First, we have to sell by the hundred to make the business viable.'

'But surely people buy cats individually.' I brushed some fine hairs from my collar and Mr Piggety snickered.

'What on earth could you do with one cat?'

I was about to tell him when my guardian said, 'What is the second reason?'

'Why, to let them grow, of course.'

'I would have thought most people want kittens,' I said and Mr Piggety neighed.

'Goodness, miss, but you have a lot to learn. Let me show you.'

We passed between two rows of cages, the occupants pressing their little pink noses out or playfully poking their paws between the bars.

'Every cage has its own bowl of fresh water and a twice-daily supply of minced horsemeat,' Mr Piggety pointed out.

'They seem very well cared for,' I said.

'Indeed they are, miss. Indeed they are,'

266

Mr Piggety agreed. 'We have a system of steam pipes to warm the room in winter and all those skylights can be opened to cool it in the summer. It is important to maintain exactly the right temperature.'

'Sixty-two degrees,' Sidney Grice said, pointing to the far wall and a thermometer so small that I could only just see its outline.

Piggety rubbed his hands together. 'Too cold and they become ill, too hot and they moult and that would be a complete disaster. The steam is piped from my offal-boiling factory on Offal Lane just behind this factory, so I have a constant supply without the need to buy coal or employ a layabout to stoke up a boiler when he feels like bestirring himself.'

'What has happened to your shirt?' I asked. The stain seemed to be spreading and Mr Piggety looked abashed.

'I suffer from *Chromhidrosis*,' he told me, 'an embarrassing condition which stains the sufferer's sweat green, yellow, black or — in my case — bluish-red.' He spoke so sheepishly that I was about to apologize when Sidney Grice gave up examining the hinge of a cage and asked abruptly, 'How many businesses do you own?'

Mr Piggety narrowed his eyes. 'You are not from the ministry of taxation?'

267

'Do I look like a civil servant?' Sidney Grice bristled as we came to a door at the far end.

'There is not much civil about you,' Mr Piggety observed. 'But since you ask, I have three other businesses, the production and marketing of clockwork animals — mice and dogs mainly — a second-hand sock warehouse, and another factory for the manufacture of false hands — very much in demand in Hungary for some reason. Perhaps they are very . . .' he smirked '. . . *Hungary.*' He paused for effect. '*Hand* they eat hands.'

I cringed and my guardian threw him an atrophying look, as Mr Piggety opened up and stood back for us to go through into a smaller rectangular room. Here there were hooks hanging from two parallel belts of chains either side of us, running the length of the room towards two big enamelled circular vats.

'When this is fully functional,' Mr Piggety said, 'four men should be able to put two hundred and forty cats through here in an hour. These,' he picked up a heavy wooden cosh, 'are what we will pretend to kill them with.'

'One moment,' I interrupted his happy flow. 'Why would you want to *pretend* to kill them?'

Mr Piggety shrieked with merriment. 'No, miss. We won't pretend to kill them — we'll pretend to kill them with the clubs.'

'Let me see,' my guardian said and marched over to a vat to peer in and back to us, pausing to examine an array of wheels and levers halfway down. 'So your intention is to tie the cats to the hooks.'

'Using only these silken cords so as not to damage them in any way,' Mr Piggety affirmed.

'I still —' I began but Sidney Grice carried on over me.

'Presumably you will fill the vats with hot water.'

Mr Piggety clapped his hands. 'There you have it, sir. The cats will be transported from here to the tubs in a continuous line to be automatically lowered into the vats.'

'For how long?' Sidney Grice enquired.

'From experiments I have conducted so far, about one minute,' Mr Piggety said. 'As a good rule of thumb, we will just wait until the water stops frothing.'

'So you are going to put live cats into scalding water?' I hoped I had misunderstood him.

'Quite so, miss,' Mr Piggety said proudly. 'The clubs are only there to allay the suspicions of goody-goody milksoppers like the RSPCA should they decide to pay us a visit. I had the room soundproofed for the same reason, though I would not have troubled had I known I would come across such conveniently mute creatures. There are ridiculous laws now based on fanciful ideas that animals are capable of suffering the same as we are. Why, these cats cannot even squeal, and it is a well-known medical fact that a dumb man does not really feel pain.'

'But why not at least stun them first?' I asked.

'Oh, you ladies.' Mr Piggety winked at me and then at my guardian. 'So soft-hearted. Three reasons not to club them, miss. First, it takes time, second, there is a risk of damaging their pelts and, third, the skin is looser on a live cat and the writhing makes it more so. Also, it tenderizes the meat, which we intend to make into a very superior food for the discerning dog owner.'

'Discerning dog owners do not eat the flesh of cats,' Sidney Grice pointed out.

'Perhaps you would like to see the skinning room next.'

I felt queasy. 'What a repellent man you are,' I said, and Mr Piggety flared.

'I wonder if you will be so childishly sentimental when Mr Grice gives you a lovely soft white fur coat for Christmas.'

'You are —'

My guardian stepped between us. '— a member of the Death Club.'

'What is left of it,' Mr Piggety agreed merrily.

'You realize, I assume, that — since some of your members have been murdered already — you must be a suspect yourself?' my guardian enquired, and Prometheus Piggety sniggered sneezily.

'Suspect away,' he said, 'but you would be better employed suspecting the real killer.'

'It causes me no sorrow to tell you that you are going to die, Piggety,' Sidney Grice said, 'horribly and soon. If you are not the murderer you will be murdered, and if you are the murderer I shall experience great *Schadenfreude* in seeing you hanged.'

'I hear you have a fondness for executing innocent clients,' Mr Piggety sneered.

Sidney Grice's grip tightened on his cane.

'Why, you —' he began, but I jumped in with, 'Are you not concerned that the other members are being murdered?'

'Concerned?' Prometheus Piggety took off his gold-rimmed spectacles and hurred on them. 'Delighted, more like. Why, every death brings me closer to a considerable fortune.'

271

Sidney Grice brought his anger under control and said, 'It does not take a giant stride of the imagination to know that the person most likely to benefit is the murderer himself.'

'Nor does it take a giant stride to know that when there are two of us left, I shall turn the other member in to the very first peeler I bump into. I do hope it's the vicar. I should love to see a vicar swing.'

'But what if you are not his last intended victim?' I asked, and Mr Piggety sniggered yet again.

'Dear girl.' He polished his spectacles with a square of chamois leather and held them up. 'Though I can tell you have taken a shine to me already, you need have no fears on my behalf. I have already taken out an insurance policy which will guarantee Mr Grice will have to do everything in his power to keep me alive. I have placed a notice in tomorrow's *Times,* announcing that I am under his protection.'

Sidney Grice wiped his cheek with the back of his hand. 'Then I shall place a larger notice making it quite clear that you are not.'

Mr Piggety wiggled his fingers as if warming up to play the pianoforte. 'It is of no matter. I had my palm read by an old smelly gypsy woman when I was fifteen and she forecast a number of things correctly, such as that I should grow up irresistible to members of the gentler sex — and please do not trouble to deny it, miss — but also that I should die in my bath before my eightieth birthday, so I am not expecting a visit from the grim reaper for many a year yet.' He hooked his spectacles behind his ears.

'You cannot really think anyone can tell the future by the creases in your palm. If that —' I began, but Prometheus Piggety said over me, 'According to Professor Stone, who has a chair in mathematics at Cambridge, palmists and fortune-tellers are more often correct in their forecasts than economists or weather forecasters.'

'That is like asking who is the most blind man in the country of the blind,' Sidney Grice commented, and Prometheus Piggety giggled.

'I have heard that you are half-blind yourself, Mr Grice.'

My guardian blanched and put a quick finger to his eye. 'I wonder if your gypsy told you what a gullible, conceited, shrivel-brained small man you would become, or if she forecast how odious and malodorous you would be, or perhaps she did not

trouble since you possessed all those qualities already.'

'Small?' Mr Piggety clutched the edge of a
table to steady himself. 'How dare you, sir?
You come barging in with your . . . dun-
headed bat-faced —'

'No wonder your parents did not like you,'
I told him. 'I am only astounded that you
had parents in the first place.'

Mr Piggety drew himself to his full height,
but even then he was a good three inches
shorter than me.

'I will thank you to quit my premises.'

'There is no need to thank us,' I said and
spun on my heel, trying to pretend I had
not caught it in a grating. 'It will be our
pleasure.'

'I shall have you closed down by the end
of the week,' Sidney Grice told him, but Mr
Piggety jeered.

'I think not, sir. Several senior members
of the Cabinet have invested heavily into
this project,' he called after us as we climbed
the stairs.

'To think we are governed by such people,'
Sidney Grice bemoaned when we rejoined
the swell of dock workers. 'If the British
Empire should last a thousand years, men
will say this was their most squalid hour.'

'Wotcha, Mr Grice.'

I turned and saw an urchin sitting on an algae-coated mooring post. My guardian did not turn his head towards him but replied through frozen lips, 'If ever you acknowledge me again, you and all your verminous gang can report to Wandsworth for a flogging.' And he spun the boy a shilling as we walked past.

'Dr Berry told me something interesting yesterday,' Mr G said as we went in to his study. 'The previous afternoon she was in Tavistock Square on her way to see a patient when she glanced up and saw a woman looking out of a window.' He thumbed through his mail. 'Guess where.' He sliced open an envelope using a wicked little stiletto, the very one — he once told me — that Jimmy Makepeace had used to cut the throat of his father.

'Silas Braithwaite's waiting room,' I exclaimed. He nodded and I thought about it. 'It could have been a cleaning lady sent by a letting agent or a relative looking —'

'Dr Berry could not be sure,' he threw the letter over his shoulder straight into his wastepaper bin, 'but she thought there was a dark stain on the left side of the woman's face.'

'Primrose McKay.'

'Hardly a titan stride of the imagination to imagine so.' He threw another two letters away unopened. 'And she felt that the postulated Miss McKay was watching her, but then you know my views on feelings — they belong in a compendium of fantasies and myths.'

'But why would Primrose go there?'

He tore a letter in half and put one part under his desk lamp. 'You are the one who is besotted with speculation.'

'To check there was no sign of her there — her name in his files, a letter from her or an entry in his diary.'

'Goodness, you *are* feeling creative today.' He sneezed.

'Shall we call and ask Miss McKay about it?'

'You go if you want to.' He blew his nose. 'I do not share your enthusiasm for wasting my days. How many times must I tell them?' He waved a thick document under my nose. 'I do not want to be president of —' But the last word was lost in another sneeze.

32
CHOREA AND THE WHALE

The cries were reverberating down the corridor as I made my way along it. It sounded like two people, an adult and a child, but it was difficult to tell and none of the visitors was paying any attention. Pain was all too common in the treatments that were supposed to alleviate it.

There was no sign of the matron as I went into the Liston Ward and to Inspector Pound's bed. His eyes were closed and his breathing shallow, and his skin had a waxy glaze to it. I felt his pulse, weak and rapid, and pulled the blanket down. The sheet looked clean at any rate. I lifted it away.

'Don't tell Matron or we'll lose our jobs and never get another,' the older nurse pleaded as the two of them approached, 'but we've been cleaning him up with the carbolic like you said.'

'I can see you have changed his bedding.'

'The wound looks a lot better too,' the

younger one said.

'Then I shall not disturb it.' I replaced the sheet and blanket. 'Has he been unconscious long?'

'All day,' said the younger one. 'He had a bit of that pie but he could hardly keep it down.'

His moustaches were damp and ragged.

'Who is his surgeon?'

'Mr Sweeney,' the older nurse said. 'He's Irish but he's very good. I once saw him cut out a live baby unharmed and the mother lived.'

An old man was shouting — something about Lord Raglan. He repeated the name five times, each time more faintly, the last time breaking up. I saw him struggle to sit up but a nurse pushed him back into his pillow.

'Is he here today?'

'He does a ward round in about half an hour usually, if he hasn't been held up in surgery, but they won't let you stay while he's here.'

I took a card from my handbag — it had a print of a robin on it — and propped it up on the side table.

'How can I recognize him?'

The younger nurse giggled. 'You can't miss him. He nearly fills the corridor and he's got mutton chops like privet hedges.'

'That's no way to speak of a doctor,' the older nurse scolded. 'You won't mention us, will you, miss?'

'No. And thank you for what you are doing.'

I stood a while after they had gone and tidied his hair, and bent over to kiss his brow, but before I could reach him one eye opened a crack.

'Don't fuss, Lucinda,' he mumbled and the eye drifted shut again.

They were covering the old man's face as I left. I went to the chapel and sat at the back, and prayed for the man I never knew and the man I hoped to know again. A couple came in, smiling.

'Thank God,' the husband said. They put some money in the box and left, and I put my face into the cup of my fingers.

'Give me something to thank you for,' I whispered into my hands. People make deals when they want something from God. They promise to be good or give alms or go to church every day, but what could I bargain with that was worth Inspector Pound's life?

I opened a Bible and leafed through to the account of the centurion asking Jesus for help. *Say but the word and my servant shall be healed.* I used to find the words inspirational but now they seemed empty. I looked for something else, opening the book at random, but nothing brought me any comfort. Time passed and I went back up the stairs.

The nurse had not exaggerated. Nobody could have missed Mr Sweeney as he progressed along the corridor. He was a man of truly enormous bulk, swaying side to side, his face almost hidden behind a shrubbery of whiskers, and followed by a gaggle of students and junior staff.

'Might I have a word, Mr Sweeney?'

He lumbered on. 'I never discuss patients with relatives.' His voice boomed like an operatic bass.

'I know how busy you must be. My father was a surgeon.'

He paused in his stride but did not stop rocking. 'What was his name?'

'Colonel Geoffrey Middleton.'

'Never heard of him.'

'He spent most of his time in private practice and the army. He was the first to describe Middleton's Chorea.'

'Was he, by Jupiter?'

'I am Inspector Pound's . . .' my brain raced, '. . . fiancée.' *Friend* sounded slightly indecent and he may have met the inspector's sister already. 'I wonder if you would consider giving him some more blood.'

He guffawed and said over his shoulder. 'And how do you suggest I do that — pour him a glass of it?'

The acolytes tittered.

'By transfusion,' I said and the swaying stopped. 'I assisted my father for many years so I know something about it.'

'Then you will also know that three-quarters of patients being given blood go into acute circulatory shock and die during the procedure. Good day, Miss Middleton.'

'I gave him blood at the London Hospital with no ill effect on either of us.'

Mr Sweeney raised one eyebrow. 'Did you, by Jove?'

'Yes, and I was not aware that University College lags so far behind that it is unable to carry out the same procedure.'

The students gasped in a way that would have done credit to the final act of a melodrama, if only they had remembered to throw up their hands. The great bulk of Mr Sweeney tilted alarmingly and examined me. 'You are a highly presumptuous young lady.'

'I am often told that,' I informed him. 'But perhaps in this case I was right to presume things. I presumed that you were one of the

281

finest surgeons in London. You may not have heard of my father but he often spoke highly of your contributions to *The Lancet*. Perhaps it was *his* presumptions which were wrong.'

I could almost swear two juniors threw up their hands, but I was too busy trying to fix his watery brown eyes to show him I was not afraid.

'Do I look like a fish?' He raised the other eyebrow.

I wanted to say *more like a whale* but I settled for 'Not very.'

The students tried to stifle their amusement. He turned to them and they succeeded.

'You think you can throw me the bait of vanity and reel me in?'

I knew I was in danger of going too far. 'I hoped to appeal to your professional pride.'

He growled softly and said, 'How much blood did you donate?'

'Only about half a pint,' I said. 'So I have plenty to spare.'

Mr Sweeney huffed. 'I am much too busy for all of this nonsense,' he told me as he started to lumber on. 'Come back in an hour.'

He was quick and efficient and I was quite relieved that he only took another pint. I would have given more but I was feeling quite woozy.

'Keep the wound clean with carbolic acid,' he told Matron as he slid the needles out.

And as he was leaving he tilted towards me again. 'There is no such thing as Middleton's Chorea and I have never contributed to that vulgar publication *The Lancet.*'

'I had to say something,' I responded and he grunted.

'Let us hope your prevarications have saved a life.'

Inspector Pound shivered.

Outside the rain had lifted and the sun was forcing its way feebly through that grey-beige that Londoners called a sky.

33
THE DEAD EITHER SIDE

Elm Road was full of life. The baked potato man vied with the cries of the crumpet seller, a boy pulled a block of ice on a handcart and the milkman rolled a churn on its lower rim towards the steps of a cellar.

We turned left down Plane Road and almost immediately the bustle ceased. There were no tradesmen here, only the pig man collecting swill from an imposing house on the corner. I patted his horse and it tried to push its nose into my handbag.

The road had been dug up and some planks laid over two parallel trenches, but the earth was piled so high around the works that it was impossible to cross without our boots becoming caked and the hem of my dress being saturated with wet mud. The workmen were taking a break, leaning on their shovels in their thick coats, except for one in shirtsleeves.

'He must be cold,' I commented, but Sidney Grice was peering into the trench.

'What with all these subterranean railways, passages, cellars, pipes and wires there will soon be more of London below the ground than above.' Mr G scraped some of the sticky clay off his soles against the kerb.

I walked on a few paces. 'Here we are.'

The church grew comfortably from its plot, grey stones, which might have been placed on top of each other three centuries or more ago, rising heavenwards as we walked down the path, the dead either side of us in a small ancient graveyard with the headstones laid flat upon the earth, most of them made illegible by frost and lichen, some half-buried under moss and grass.

'Somebody wept each time these graves were filled,' I said. 'Now nobody even knows who they contain.'

My guardian putted a twig to one side. 'Very few people are worth remembering.'

'They loved and were loved,' I said.

He paused to inspect a footprint on the verge. 'There is nothing clever about that. A flea-bitten cur is capable — and probably more deserving — of affection than the average man.'

We reached the porch and a great oak door strapped to the granite pillars by heavy black hinges studded with square pyramidal iron nails. 'Locked.' Sidney Grice turned the barley-twisted ring handle clockwise. 'It is sobering to reflect that there have only been six periods in the island's blood-soaked history when it has been felt necessary to keep our churches barred and we are living in one of them.' He rapped three times smartly with the handle of his cane and we waited.

'I wonder who will remember me,' I said.

'Nobody at all,' my guardian said, 'unless you put those journals of yours to some use and publish an account of your time with me.'

I was about to tell him that I hoped to mean more than that to somebody some day when a small panel in the woodwork swung inwards and a man's face appeared behind an inset fretwork box.

'Mr Grice?' The voice was high.

'Reverend Jackaman?'

'If you are Mr Grice, prove it by taking your eye out.'

'Step off that kneeler first.'

The face blinked. 'How do you know I am standing on a kneeler?'

'Because I am Sidney Grice.'

The face pondered for a while. 'Very well then. I *am* the Reverend Jackaman and now

I should like you to leave.'

'I am Miss Middleton,' I told him and he looked shocked.

'You may be hardly more than a child,' the reverend said, 'but you must know that a lady never introduces herself to a gentleman.'

'If I should meet one I shall remember that,' I told him, 'but you ought to know that it is neither polite nor Christian to lock out a lady when she seeks access to the house of God.'

'My apologies for that,' he said. 'Now kindly go away.'

My guardian leaned towards the hole and it shut. 'What are you frightened of, Reverend Jackaman?' he called through the panel.

'You,' a muffled voice replied. 'I read the papers. Every soul whom you have questioned regarding that accursed death club has met an horrible end.'

'*A* horrible end,' Sidney Grice corrected him and the panel swung open again.

'Henry Alford would not have agreed with you.'

'Henry Alford would never have agreed with anyone,' my guardian retorted. 'He was the epitome of charm, but one of the most disagreeable men I have ever met when discussing linguistic exactitudes.'

'Who was Henry Alford?' I asked.

'Oh, what a meagre education the young receive and what a mean proportion of that they imbibe,' the Reverend Jackaman bemoaned. 'They are too busy dancing in the afternoons and listening to glee singers.'

'And filling their heads with Byronian trash,' my guardian concurred. 'Henry Alford was, amongst other things, a Fellow of Trinity College, a scholar and a textual critic.'

'And why are we talking about him?'

'I suppose you would rather be discussing ribbons and buttons,' Jackaman snapped. 'I see these girls in my church, Mr Grice. They whisper and giggle during my sermons. They pass each other notes. All they have come for is to flaunt their flounces.'

'It makes one despair for the empire,' Sidney Grice tisked. 'But we digress.'

'Surely not,' I murmured.

'You can at least talk to me, Reverend.'

'Can but will not,' Jackaman rejoined. 'Whilst others put their trust in Grice, I put mine in God. I seek his sanctuary in my own church.' The panel closed.

'You may be meeting your creator sooner than you think if you do not let us help you,' Mr G called.

'What's all this then?' We spun round to

be confronted by a young man in a dazzling checked suit and bright yellow cravat, waving at us from the roadside. He came hurrying across, neatly leaping over an old man who was lying on the pavement. 'Fretnin' a man of the cloth, Mr Grice? Whatever next? Slaughterin' babes in their mothers' arms?'

'The Lord is my Shepherd,' the vicar was reciting loudly. 'I shall not want . . .'

'Blast,' my guardian grumbled. 'It is that blighter from the *Evening Standard*. Ignore him, March.' But I could not take my eyes off him.

The man sauntered up the path. He had a large white carnation in his buttonhole and wore white spats over black patent-leather shoes. 'And who is this lovely lady? No, don't tell me. I want to be able to write *Sidney Grice Seen With Mysterious Dark Female Companion.*'

I laughed and said, 'I am March Middleton, Mr Grice's ward.'

My guardian groaned and the young man tipped his natty bowler hat jauntily back with his silver-handled cane, to reveal dark Macassar-oiled hair.

'Yea, though I walk through the shadow of the valley of death,' came from inside the church.

'Wotta disappointin'ly innocent explanation,' the newcomer said. 'Waterloo Trumpington at your service, miss.' He took my hand and clicked his heels together like a Prussian officer at court.

I laughed again. 'Is that your real name?' And Waterloo Trumpington grinned. He had nice white teeth and his face was smooth and boyish.

'Is anyone's?'

'Mine is.'

'Stop jabbering.' Sidney Grice stood listening at the door. 'And listen.' But all I could hear was traffic from Elm Road and the voice of the vicar inside St Jerome's.

'Follow me all the days of my life.'

Sidney Grice tensed. 'Reverend Jackaman,' he called out urgently. 'Listen to me. Your life is in imminent danger.' He rattled and wrenched at the handle. 'For heaven's sake, open up, man.'

'And I shall dwell in the house of the Lord. What? . . . Who are you? How did you get in here? . . . What? . . . No!'

The last word came as a prolonged piteous cry abruptly cut short. There was the sound of a scuffle and then silence.

34
HALF-MELTED CANDLES AND ANGELS TO SMITE

Waterloo Trumpington's visage changed in an instant. A moment ago he had been nothing more than a careless cockney dandy, but now the grin was replaced by a tight-lipped determination and the dancing eyes were fixed on the figure of my guardian.

Sidney Grice had his ear to the door and signalled us to stay quiet. There was a bump and a low moan, and then a thump like somebody banging a table.

'No,' Reverend Jackaman cried out. 'For the love of Christ our saviour.'

I heard metal strike metal and a scream and then a series of six duller blows, steady and separate, each one accompanied by another shriek.

Sidney Grice stood back and looked at the window.

'Smash it,' Waterloo Trumpington suggested. His voice was calm and strangely detached.

'With what?' my guardian demanded. 'Anyway, it is too high and barred.'

I banged on the woodwork with the side of my fist and yelled, 'Open this door.' But the only reply was a metallic clash and another cry.

'Mighty Lord, send your angel to smite —' But the words were lost in an agonized sob.

The church was joined between two tall houses.

'That' — Sidney Grice pointed to the house on the left — 'is the rectory. Go, Miss Middleton, and ask if there is a side entrance into the church. Hurry.'

The hammering and shrieking began again, each cry more piteous than the last.

There was a wall between the church grounds and rectory garden, with a gateway set into it. I ran across the graveyard, trying to avoid stepping on the tombstones, but the wooden gate was locked so I zigzagged back. Sidney Grice was rooting through his satchel while Waterloo Trumpington leaned languidly back on his stick, observing him. My guardian brought out a twisted piece of metal and rammed it into the keyhole.

'Breakin' into an 'ouse of God?' Waterloo Trumpington mocked. 'It gets better by the minute.'

'Do something,' I shouted.

'I am.' The reporter grinned. 'I am doing my job and leaving your guardian to his.'

'I have no time for this.' I ran back down the path, calling over my shoulder. 'The *Evening Standard* will be very interested in my account of how you stood back and let a man of God die.'

I did not wait for a response but dashed down the footpath, cursing the impediment of my dress as I whipped through a low gate and to the front of the rectory. Panting heavily, I wrenched the bell. It tinkled merrily in the background and I wrenched it again. Ten times I rang, but there was no reply.

I looked in through the window, cupping my eyes with my hands to the glass, but only saw a dull, unoccupied drawing room with an upright piano with half-melted candles in brass candelabras. I tried the bell again, yanking at the handle until I thought it would come off in my hand, and shouted out, 'Hello. Is anybody there?' And then I heard it, clear and loud from the church of St Jerome.

'Help . . . Somebody help me . . . No! Sacrilege. Please God, no!' And that *no* became a wail soaring to the heavens, nothing but terror and pain and then nothing at all.

I ran back. Sidney Grice was wrenching on his lever in the keyhole.

'Now!' he yelled and Waterloo Trumpington ran at an oak panel, flying into it with both boots and landing with great agility on his feet as the door crashed in. He checked his buttonhole and looked over my guardian's shoulder, and the blood drained from his face. His fingers went to his cheek and he half-stepped, half-stumbled backwards.

'Shit me,' he said softly.

'Stay out, March,' Sidney Grice called, not taking his eyes off whatever confronted him. 'And this time I mean it.'

All the more reason to come in, I thought, but, for the first time since I had come to London and ever since that moment, I wished I had obeyed him.

'Sacrilege,' I whispered in an echo of something I had heard a long time ago when I had thought I knew what the word meant.

35
BLOOD AND WATER

St Jerome's looked normal for a moment —
a small austere Norman structure with four
rows of benches parted by a central apse
and two side aisles, a tapestry-covered
footstool lying on its side, and a marble altar
with a silver candlestick on each corner, the
body of the church being lit by a clumsy
stained-glass window at each end. But
Sidney Grice was not admiring the architec-
ture. His attention was fixed on a heavy oak
screen in front of the organ and what was
attached to it.

I gasped and steadied myself on the end
of a pew. The thing I saw was a grotesquery,
a travesty of a man and his redeemer. The
Reverend Jackaman had been stripped to
his blood-soaked calico drawers and skew-
ered to the screen in a depraved mockery of
the Crucifixion. A nail had been hammered
through each of his wrists and a longer one
through his overlapped feet. His head hung

on to his chest, his scalp pierced by dozens of hat pins, some sticking out through the skin of his forehead, and a wooden spar jutted from where it had been thrust deep into his side and up under his ribcage.

'Forthwith there came out blood and water,' I said and crossed myself, but my guardian showed no sign of having heard me. He stood quite still, the red light of the angels cast across his face as he gazed at this thing, the priest who had become obscenity and suffering.

'Oh, my good Gawd.' Waterloo Trumpington came to stand beside me and I glanced at him. But instead of the disgust I had expected to see, his eyes flashed with excitement and he narrowed them knowingly, with a peculiar look creeping over his lips.

36
COURCY'S CRAVAT AND SUCKING LICE

For a long time Sidney Grice surveyed the monstrosity before us. He put on his pince-nez, leaned forward and took them off again. He whistled seven quick notes softly through closed teeth and crouched. He stood and walked to and fro, not taking his eyes off the body until he turned, paced three steps back and whipped round, as if he were a child playing *statues* and expecting the vicar to have moved. But the Reverend Enoch Jackaman was never again to move on this earth of his own volition.

'May God receive and have mercy on your soul,' I said, and my guardian looked puzzled.

'Mine?' He spoke as if half asleep.

'Reverend Jackaman's.'

He raised an eyebrow and put his pince-nez back on to view the reverend more closely.

'So that is how you did it,' he murmured.

'Surely it is obvious how he was killed,' I said, but my guardian clicked his tongue.

'The truth is rarely obvious and the whole truth never so. Look in your books,' he gestured to a stack of Bibles, 'and tell me how clear it is.'

'There are more answers in the Bible than you seem to think.' I slid on a dark puddle. 'Should you not be chasing the murderer?'

Sidney Grice seemed mildly hurt. 'That is exactly what I am doing.' He walked round the screen. 'Courcy's cravat,' he said as he emerged.

'But you should be finding out how he escaped.'

Sidney Grice pulled his lower eyelid down a fraction to let his eye drop. 'My dear child —'

'Do *not* call me a child.'

He tightened his mouth. 'Then do not behave like one. You think you can blunder into my life for a few months and tell me how to go about my business?'

I tried to calm myself. 'I am sorry. It is just —' But my guardian shushed me gently.

'I *know* how the murderers escaped. They went through that exit by the side chapel, across the rectory garden and through the back gate into Mulberry Street where they will have been instantly swallowed up in the crowds that attend the Thursday toy market. If they can be tracked, your new friend will be hot on their heels as we speak. Waterloo Trumpington clings to me like a sucking louse sometimes, but once he is on the trail of something he is a veritable pig in a patch. He will turn the whole field over until he finds his turnip.'

'Why more than one murderer?' I asked.

'Because one person could not hold a conscious and struggling vicar still and transfix him at the same time.' Sidney Grice pinched the scar on his ear. 'You need both hands just to hold a nail and hammer it.'

'And you are happy for Waterloo Trumpington to catch them?'

Sidney Grice blew his nose. 'I would be delighted if Trumped-up Trumpington came across the murderers because I have no doubt who would come off the worse for the encounter. Do you seriously imagine that the people who did this could be bested by that jumped-up, slandering, penny-print guttersnipe?' He held out a screwed-up ball of paper and shook off a gelatinous clot. 'I found this crammed into his mouth.'

'What does it say?'

He straightened it out until I could just make out the words: *Eloi El* — a bloodstain — *hani*.

'*Eloi Eloi Lama Sabachthani,*' I said. 'My God, my God, why have you forsaken me?'

'A valid question under the circumstances,' my guardian commented.

I looked around the empty church, the clumsy pillars and the cold statues, and tried to clear the jumble from my mind. A life-sized crucifix lay smashed, wood and plaster in one corner. 'What did you mean by *Courcy's cravat*?'

'Jean-Claude Courcy was a war veteran with a grudge against the Grande Armée. He was paralysed from the waist down by a bullet in the spine, but he had been caught stealing from the mess bar just before battle and forfeited his pension. He killed four officers from his wheelchair whilst going round the streets in uniform. If an officer stopped to give him alms, he would speak very huskily so that the victim had to bend his head towards him to hear. Courcy had a noose on a stick, which he would whip over the victim's head, then pull the rope to tighten round the neck. A strangled man can lose consciousness in under a minute. Sometimes Courcy would toy with them by loosening the noose enough for them to come round before he tightened it again. A captain who he had left for dead recovered and told that story. The last intended victim

300

escaped because he had a very large nose and ears, and Courcy had not opened the noose wide enough to go cleanly over.'

I was feeling very hot and sick, but I forced myself to step forward and look more closely.

'I can see the rope mark round his neck.'

'And under the angle of his left jaw?'

'A circular impression.'

He bobbed down to turn a leaf over. 'Made by the end of the stick.' He jumped up. 'That was the first choking sound we heard. The noose was tightened just enough to incapacitate Jackaman. He could then be led like a stray dog to the screen; the pole was passed through a hole in the screen and wedged the other side. At that stage it could be loosened. The killer wanted him to be fully aware of what was happening to him.'

I closed my eyes in a futile attempt to erase the image before us. 'How can anyone hate people so much?'

Sidney Grice crouched to scrutinize a puddle of blood blotting out most of the Latin inscription on a memorial floor-slab. He took a pipette from his satchel and carefully sucked a scruple of darkness into the bulb. He put a finger over the top, took a test tube in his left hand and deftly removed the cork with his little finger, let the fluid

301

flow into the tube and recorked it.

'They may not have hated Jackaman at all.' He put the test tube and pipette away. 'It may be just me.'

This was intolerable. 'Why does everything have to revolve around you?'

He went down on his knees and crawled with his nose almost on the floor in a wide circle round the blood. 'Ah.' He brought out an envelope and scooped a bit of dirt into it.

'Because,' he said simply, 'it always does.'

I could not bear any more — the disgusting suffering of the man who was dead; the disgusting arrogance of the man who regarded everything that happened as an intellectual jigsaw puzzle made only for him to play with. I went outside where at least the dead were at peace.

Angelica, your youngest sister, the darling of your family, had died of scarlet fever at home in Shropshire, and you were very low and very drunk or you would not have told me about the war. You said that in the Afghan Campaign, when the tribesmen of the Northwest Frontier captured a Christian soldier, they would castrate him and then they would tie him to the ground and prop his mouth open with a stick and the women would crouch over him and drown him in their urine.

I am not sure you believed the stories and I certainly did not. I could not imagine anyone being so disgustingly cruel — until now.

I sat on a stone bench with my back to the wall of St Jerome's and looked at a gravestone to my side. A whole family lay there, the parents and five children all dead within a three-year span ending in 1785. For almost a century they had lain undisturbed, awaiting the resurrection of their bodies. I could not imagine a soul and yet I knew we all had one. I wanted a cigarette but it seemed disrespectful. I closed my eyes and prayed until I heard hurried footfalls approaching and Waterloo Trumpington came breathlessly back. 'No sign of 'im.'

'Look in the church,' I said. 'There are plenty of signs of him there.' And then I could not stop myself. Everything came welling out of me in uncontrollable sobs. 'I am sorry.' I took his handkerchief and caught myself. I knew how tears embarrassed men, but Waterloo Trumpington showed only concern.

'What you need,' he touched my arm, 'is a good strong drink . . . What's so funny?'

'I was just thinking' — I wiped my eyes — 'how nice it is to be with a man who does not add *of tea.*'

37
GREAT NAVAL BATTLES
IN THE SNUG

The Black Boy was just round the corner, crowded, smoky and noisy, with a huddle of costermongers bantering round the bar.

'Come in the snug,' Waterloo Trumpington said. 'You won't get ogled there . . . unless, of course, you like being ogled.'

I would not have minded in the least but I said, 'We will go in the snug.' And we passed through to a side room, pine-lined, with three tables made of upturned beer barrels and a fireplace with cold clinker settled in the grate. 'I am sorry I cried.'

Waterloo Trumpington pursed his lips. 'Know why men don't cry? They're frigh'ened to. Women are braver than men.'

'We don't fight in wars.'

He batted the thought away. 'You've got more sense.'

'You have a very good opinion of my sex.'

'I like women. My mother was one.' He clapped his hands together. 'What'll it be?

Port? Sherry?'

'A brandy would be nice.'

'That's the spirit.' He went to the bar where it jutted into the room. 'Couple of big Boney's, sweetheart, and one for yourself.' Then he rejoined me with two very large brandies.

'I hope the alcohol kills the germs.' The rim was smeared greasily.

'The drinks 'ere will kill anyfink,' Waterloo Trumpington told me cheerily. 'Good 'ealth.'

We clinked glasses and I took a swig, holding it in my mouth before letting it course down my throat. I blinked. 'I believe you are right, Mr Trumpington.'

'My friends call me Traf,' he said, 'and I 'ope you will do the same.'

'Is that really your name?'

'Waterloo Trafalgar Agincourt Trumpington reporting for duty, ma'am.' He saluted. 'My old man was very patriotic.'

'Traf is certainly less of a mouthful.' I laughed. 'And please call me March.'

'March it is then. Mind if I smoke?'

'Not if you give me one.'

He grinned approvingly. 'You're quite the twist, March.' And, seeing my bemusement, explained. 'Twist and Twirl — girl — rhyming slang.'

'Like *Adam and Eve — believe,*' I said and he chuckled.

'Why, we'll make a cockney of you yet, March. 'Ow long have you known Mr Grice for then?'

'Only a few months,' I said. 'Though it seems a lot longer.'

'I'll bet it does, living with that old devil.'

'You do not like each other, do you?'

Traf leaned back in his chair. 'Our Sidney dislikes the world and the world returns the compliment.'

'I do not think he dislikes everyone. We met a woman doctor recently and I think he holds her in some regard.'

He swigged his brandy. 'A woman doctor?' he asked incredulously.

I nodded. 'Dr Berry.'

'Oh yeah. I've 'eard of that old 'arpy.'

'Dr Berry is neither old nor a harpy. She is still quite young and pretty and I think what she has achieved is quite wonderful. But he does seem to dislike most people. Do you have any idea why?'

'You'll have to ask 'im that one. I 'ave 'eard it said as 'e was disappointed in love.' Waterloo Trumpington snorted. 'Can't imagine 'im being disappointed in anyfink but 'atred myself.'

'But why you especially?'

'Opposite sides of the same coin, me and Sid. We rake around scandals and we uncover things people don't want uncovered. Only 'e's so hoity-toity he can't stand to be reminded of that.' We smoked for a while. 'Having a spot of bother with 'is latest assignment, ain't 'e?'

'Is he?' I finished my brandy.

'Same again?' Waterloo Trumpington picked up both glasses without waiting for a reply.

'I do not mind you trying to get me drunk,' I told him when he returned. 'In fact I do not mind if you succeed. But you will not get me to talk about him.'

Waterloo Trumpington surveyed me in amusement. 'Scratch me, you're a cucumber.'

'How did you come to be here?' I asked.

'Vicar in a deaf club where the members is dyin' like rats in a ring.' His chair creaked as he leaned towards me. 'It 'ad to be worf an interview. Wasn't expectin' nuffin' like that, though.' And from his expression it was clear he was not disappointed.

I sucked the last of my cigarette, downed my brandy in one and stood up. 'Thank you for the drinks. I had better get back to work.'

Traf raised his glass. 'I know when I'm beaten.'

'I cannot imagine anyone getting the better of you.' I stubbed out my cigarette underfoot and left him to it.

The costermongers had gone, leaving only a handful of old men staring into their futures through empty beer mugs. It was drizzling outside now and Sidney Grice was standing in the graveyard. His nose twitched. 'You have been to a public house.'

'The Black Boy.'

'I do not care what colour, sex or age it was. You went unaccompanied into a drinking establishment?'

'No. Traf . . . Mr Trumpington took me.'

My guardian shot a hand to his eye. 'What did you tell him?'

'Nothing.'

'What did he ask you?'

'How long I had known you. I said a few weeks. Then he tried to get me to talk about these cases, but I told him I would not discuss anything with him.'

'Good. What else did you tell him?'

'Nothing.'

'You are sure?'

'Completely.'

Sidney Grice grunted. 'It is almost impossible to say nothing to the predators of Fleet Street. They could suck the juice from a diamond. However, we shall see what calumnies he begets from your socializing soon enough. I must find somebody to summon the police.'

'At least Inspector Quigley cannot say it is suicide or an accident this time,' I said.

'I would not be too confident of that,' my guardian disagreed, 'but Quigley will not come. He would not want to get embroiled in a case like this at the best of times. No, March, he will send a subordinate or, better still from his point of view, a rival.'

A large middle-aged woman came along with arms full of flowers.

'I am sorry, madam,' I said. 'But the church is closed.'

'Nonsense. I can see it is open from here.' She pushed me aside but Sidney Grice stood his ground.

'One moment, please.' He delved into his satchel like a lady rooting though her handbag. 'Here we are.' He pointed a small, beautifully carved ivory-handled revolver straight at her and said pleasantly. 'If you do not turn round and go away within nine seconds, I will put a bullet into your vestigial brain.'

'How dare —' She clutched her flowers as though expecting to be robbed of them.

'Seven seconds.'

'Well, really.' The woman retreated to the

pavement and called back. 'I shall summon the police.'

'Please do.' He pulled back the hammer. 'And tell them to hurry.'

'That was a little extreme,' I commented as she bustled through the gate.

'I disagree.' He lowered the hammer and put his revolver away. 'It was *very* extreme. But she had the glazed eye of a slow-worm and it would have taken half an hour to achieve the same outcome by conventional means.'

We waited until the police came — four constables, a uniformed sergeant and a plainclothed detective, none of whom I had seen before.

'Miss Middleton saw less than I did,' my guardian said. 'I will not have her questioned.'

The detective was ruffled. 'I shall question whosoever I please.' His voice came from somewhere in the back of his throat. 'Stay there,' he said to me.

I sat on the low wall with my feet at the side of a gravestone. It said *John* or *Joan* and *Be,* which I assumed was the start of *beloved,* and the words of Genesis came into my head: *In the sweat of thy face shalt thou eat bread, till thou return unto the ground; for out of it wast thou taken: for dust thou art, and unto dust shalt thou return.* Was that all there was to it? Could God not protect his own servant who had pleaded with him? I thought even the hairs on our heads were numbered.

I heard some clattering and looked up to see my guardian coming out of the church.

'They are taking him down.' He took my arm. 'Come, March. This is no place for you.'

'It is no place for anyone outside of hell.'

We made our way to the path and turned our backs on the dead.

'You are shaking,' my guardian said. 'What you need is a really strong drink,' he patted my hand, 'of tea . . . What is so amusing?'

'Nothing,' I said. 'Nothing at all.'

There was a pretty tea shop at the front of Bailey's Antiquarian Bookstore and they were about to close, but the manageress cheerfully admitted us and seated us beneath a giant aspidistra plant. Sidney Grice swept his arm back to push away a leaf which was tickling his head.

'Did you find out anything else?' I asked as he shifted his chair away from it and me.

'Two things.' The leaf was caressing his cheek now. 'One tangible, the other intangible.' He delved into his satchel for a brown paper bag and whipped out a greasy cloth cap, holding it up for my inspection.

'The tangible clue,' I guessed.

'Quite so.' He placed it on the table. 'I espied it in the garden, caught in the overhanging branch of a fruitless Plymouth pear tree.'

'Perhaps it was swept off the murderer's head as he escaped,' I suggested.

'It is unlikely to have belonged to the vicar,' he concurred, 'and anyone who was not in an extreme hurry would have paused to retrieve it. The branch was only four feet-three inches from the ground, but then . . .' He looked at me quizzically.

'People bend as they run.'

'Precisely.' He slapped the leaf irritably.

A waitress appeared with our tea in a white china pot with matching cups. 'Shall I hang that up for you, sir?' She viewed the hat with distaste.

'Leave it alone,' he snapped. 'It is not my hat.'

She hurried away and I picked it up. 'The wearer had black hair not pomaded,' I observed, picking out a strand from the lining.

'Or red hair.' Mr G pointed to a few on the underside of the peak.

'One of the men working on the road had

red hair and he was not wearing a hat,' I commented.

'And how do you think he got round the back and into the church in the time available?' He rammed the leaf away but it sprang back. 'Plus there would have been mud everywhere from his boots and clothes.'

'I did not say he did,' I defended myself. 'I merely observed —'

'Leave the observations to me.' Mr G leaned back and snapped the leaf off.

'Are you going to show me your intangible clue?' I joked weakly and he huffed.

'I went out through the back gate to the toy fair and, except for Trumpington darting about like a confused whippet, not a soul had noticed anything at all.'

'That is disappointing.' I poured, thinking that I would rather have had another brandy — anything to dull the sights and sounds that crowded through my brain.

'On the contrary.' Sidney Grice stirred his milkless, sugarless tea vigorously clockwise. 'It is one of the most important clues I have discovered so far.'

'I do not understand.'

A look of alarm came over Sidney Grice's face and his hand shot in the air. 'Waitress. I ordered tea, not last week's pencil shavings.'

I went to see Inspector Pound. He was still unconscious but his breathing was stronger and steadier. The younger nurse came and wiped his face with a damp flannel.

'He came round a bit this morning,' she told me, 'and said something about the robin on the card and his uncle, but it didn't make much sense.'

'It was just a silly joke. His uncle was a mounted Bow Street Runner,' I told her, 'and they wore red waistcoats.' I touched Inspector Pound's brow. 'His temperature has gone down,' I observed. 'Thank you for tending to him.'

The nurse bowed her head. 'He's a good sort, the inspector,' she told me. 'He arrested my brother once and didn't even beat him up.'

38
SLAPPED FACES AND TORN REMAINS

We did not have to wait for the morning. The evening papers were full of the news.

HORRIBLE MURDER OF THE REVEREND ENOCH JACKAMAN, LATE VICAR OF ST JEROME'S CHURCH

But worse was to follow.

THE CURSE OF GRICE STRIKES AGAIN

And:

SIDNEY GRICE, PRIVATE DETECTIVE, WITNESSES TERRIBLE MURDER OF HIS OWN CLIENT

'Personal, personal, personal,' Sidney Grice chanted. 'I am a *personal* detective. There is nothing remotely private about my work at the moment.'

We read them over tea in the study.

'Your new friend devotes a whole column to you, March,' my guardian said quietly and handed me a copy of the *Evening Standard.*

THE TRUTH ABOUT SIDNEY GRICE FROM HIS COMPANION

On the afternoon of the murder while the body of the Reverend Jackaman still hung crucified, dark-haired and dark-eyed Miss March Middletone took our young reporter to one of the many public houses she frequents where she smoked tobacco and consumed great quantities of strong liquor. Only when she was in what we can only refer to as a condition which no lady should be did she consent to give him an interview. Miss Middletone would not comment upon her relationship with Mr Grice at whose address she resides.

'That is disgusting,' I said. 'I shall sue.'

Sidney Grice looked severe. 'What has he said that was untrue?'

'Nothing, but he has implied . . .'

'He will argue that it is only your depraved mind that imagines anything untoward in his article.'

I read on. 'Nor did she deny that his attentions were not always of a nature one

317

might expect from a man purporting to be her guardian.'

'I did not deny it because I was not asked,' I said, 'and what is this about *purporting*? You *are* my guardian.'

'Not in law,' Sidney Grice said softly. 'There has never been a court order assigning you to my care.'

'If ever I see that man again I shall slap his face.'

'Oh, you will see him again,' my guardian assured me, 'and he would love you to assault him, the more publicly the better.'

'And he has misspelled my name.' I folded the paper. 'I shall not read this filth.'

'Read it later,' he advised. 'You cannot defend yourself from attacks if you do not know what they are.'

I dropped the paper by my chair. 'What kind of a man writes these things?'

'The kind of man with whom you go drinking.'

This seemed a good time to divert the topic.

'How did you know that Reverend Jackaman was standing on a kneeler?' I asked.

'If you were paying attention, you will recall me telling you that I met Jackaman's brother once on the crossing to Calais. He was an exporter of cat-o'-five-tails.'

318

'Do you not mean nine tails?'

'No. These were considered kinder for flogging children.'

'How soft-hearted he must have been.'

He carefully ripped a strip from his paper and put it on the table face down. 'At present I am more concerned with his stature. He was five foot and three inches before his back was bent and he told me that he was the tallest member of his family, so Jackaman must have stood on something to peer out of the opening.'

'Why not a chair?'

'Because, unlike the rest of mankind, I use my senses. I heard wooden furniture being dragged. It was not as heavy as a pew and a chair would be too tall to stand on and too low for kneeling. It was obvious. A simpleton could have reached the same conclusion.'

'But I did not.'

My guardian allowed himself an ephemeral smile. 'Precisely.' He picked up the *West London Recorder*.

'You seem very relaxed about all this,' I commented.

'I am rarely what I seem.' Sidney Grice folded his arms and leaned back in his chair. 'Besides,' he continued, 'for the first time in my life, I am too angry to be angry. I have come to expect slanders as a professional risk, along with death threats, assaults and damage to my property. But this man has made vile innuendos about a girl — a young woman — in my care and that is insufferable. If I know one thing for certain, Waterloo Trafalgar Trumpington shall rue the day he put his name to such foul falsehoods.' He crunched the *Recorder* and his voice rose. 'How many times do I have to tell them? I am *not* protecting these people.' And the paper bunched up in his grasp. In a seemingly involuntary movement he ripped it apart. 'Perhaps,' he surveyed the torn remains, 'I am not too angry to be angry after all.'

I leafed through the *Hampstead Times* and did not have to go much further than an account of a mugging on the heath of an ebony dealer before I saw:

THE AFFAIRS OF SIDNEY GRICE
Our reporter has been privy to intimate details of a relationship between private detective, Mr Sidney Grice, and Dorna Berry, a married woman posing as a doctor in . . .

I closed my eyes.
'What is it?'

I handed the paper over and my guardian flushed. 'In a jealous rage, Mr Grice's present female companion revealed that he has developed strong feelings for Mrs Berry, which we have now reason to suspect are not,' his voice rose, 'reciprocated.' He flung the paper down, strewing its pages across the tea tray. 'Apparently I think she is wonderful but refuse to speak of her to you.'

'More lies,' I said, but there was nothing phlegmatic about Sidney Grice's reaction to the papers now.

'What *exactly* did you say to that scoriaceous, grubbing, truth-warping, word-twisting skunk?'

'I only said that I think you like her.'

'*Like?*' He mouthed the word as if it were unclean. '*Like?* You told him I *like* her?'

'Yes.'

'You told that scabrous, excremental —'

'I told him you like her and that was all I said.'

'*All?*' He scrabbled through the pages. 'According to this, I think she is wonderful and beautiful. Explain away that, *Miss Middletone.*'

'I said that *I* thought she has done wonderful things and that she was pretty.'

'Hellfire and blast, March. Why did you not just come out and tell him I was having an illicit relationship with Dr Berry? You have taken that woman's good name and rammed it into the dung heap.'

'You did not mind so much when *my* honour was being impugned.'

He caught his falling eye and clenched his fist around it. 'If your name was sullied it was you who soiled it. I ordered you —'

'Nobody *orders* me to do anything.'

'And more is the pity for that. I told you not to talk to that puffed-up poseur and what did you do? You ran off with him to some sleazy den and confided in him what you salaciously imagined to be my private feelings.'

'I only —'

Sidney Grice stood up. I had never seen him so enraged. 'No, March. You deliberately went behind my back with a man who is my sworn enemy and you smeared excrement over the name of an innocent woman who has done nothing but defend your appalling manners every time I complain about them.'

'So it is all right for you to denigrate me?'

'I wanted advice on how to deal with your waywardness and she suggested tolerance. Well, we see now how her kindness has been repaid. You have turned her life into a freak show for the pavement-scrapings of humanity to gawp at.' His face twisted in pain. 'What you have done to that woman is unforgiveable.' He clutched at his socket and I went to him.

'Is it very painful?'

'Not in the least,' he said. 'It is only ingratitude that hurts me.'

He could have slapped my face and wounded me less. 'I have always been grateful to you for taking me in.'

'And this is how you show it?' He put his handkerchief to the socket and the cotton came away stained straw and red.

'Shall I look at it?'

He twisted his head away. 'I do not want you to look at it and I do not want to look at you.'

I stepped back.

'Then I shall get out of your sight,' I said as Sidney Grice bent and reeled to his desk.

'Damn it,' he said as I left the room and ran upstairs to my memories.

They were fumigating your quarters — a monthly futile battle against the cockroaches, millipedes, columns of ants and innumerable other creatures that crawled into, under, out of and over every surface of every room. Our homes were all raised on wooden piles which helped a little and no one but a griffin — as newcomers were called — put down rugs for horrible things to breed beneath. I learned very early on to shake out my slippers before I put my feet into them. Even then I had a nasty sting from a tenacious scorpion on my great toe once and it was weeks before I could lace up my right boot properly again. But I was lucky, my father told me. The wife of one of the captains had got into a hipbath only for a snake to slither in after her.

You brought a few things to our bungalow for safekeeping. The last time the fumigators had been in your room a penknife had gone missing. The workmen insisted you must have lost it, but you were certain you had left it on your bedside table and you were not usually careless with your things.

Your writing box was slightly scratched and, while you were off on a pig-sticking expedition, I decided to polish it. The wax was fluid in the heat and some of it trickled between the folded doors. I was worried that it would run over your correspondence and spoil it so I opened the lid.

I have always been inquisitive but not a sneaky person. I would never have searched your pockets or steamed open a letter. But it fell out on to the floor and, when I bent to pick it up, I could not help but notice the words.

With regard to your proposed engagement your mother and I can only express our grievous dismay that you should choose to entangle yourself with a girl whom we have never met and of whose background we know so little. You cannot have forgotten Hester Sandler who waits so patiently and loyally for your return and with whom you have a long-established understanding. For your sake she has spurned all prospective suitors and it is only right that . . .

I did not see what Edward's father thought was right, but it was not difficult to guess. I put the letter back in the box and went to join my father at the hospital.

'Everything all right?' he asked but I did not reply.

39
PERSIAN SLIPPERS
AND MAUDY GLASS

I went back to Parbold. The Grange had still not been let so Mr Warwick, the land agent, gave me the keys and I walked up the hill while George Carpenter, the old gamekeeper, drove my luggage with Onion, his ancient donkey, wheezing behind me. It was two miles and a steep climb, but we made it just in time to see the sun sink behind Ashurst Beacon with the Douglas Valley glowing in its embers.

For two days I wandered around the house and grounds, unable to settle. I sat in my father's library, staring at his musty books, but could not bring myself even to open them.

Maudy Glass came to stay. As children we had run down the Fairy Glen together or across the pastures to catch sticklebacks in Jackson's pit, but Maudy was married now and heavy with her second child.

'Do you think you will ever have children?'

she asked.

'I thought so once,' I said. 'Shall we prepare dinner?'

We cooked together on the ancient range — thick lamb steaks and boiled potatoes with mint from the tangle of my father's old herb garden — and I found a bottle of wine in the cellar. But I remembered Sidney Grice's insistence that animal flesh was no different from human and his account of the cannibals eating Rupert, and I could not put it in my mouth.

We cleared and washed and dried and settled in our armchairs.

Once, when we were sitting by that fireplace, I asked my father if he resented me for killing his wife and he told me that he had 'for fully two minutes until I saw you — a scrunched-up magenta monster struggling to get out of your swaddling — and then what could I do but love you?' He poked a log and the sparks flew into the night. 'And I have never stopped.'

'Not even when I accidentally set fire to my bedroom?'

'Not even then.' He patted my hand. 'Besides, you did not kill your mother. A filthy slaughterer posing as a surgeon did that. I will not call it butchery. Butchery is a skill and he had none. If it had not been for you kicking and caterwauling in my arms I believe I would have beaten him to death.'

'It must be terrifically exciting working with the famous Sidney Grice,' Maudy said, and I rubbed my eyes wearily but she chattered on. 'Remember when we were children? We used to go to the attic and play spies.'

'We made cloaks from old curtains,' I recalled, 'and low-brimmed hats from lamp-shades. We must have looked ridiculous.'

Maudy laughed and the shadows lit up for a moment. 'And we used to leave each other secret messages in that hole in the old oak tree. It blew down in the gales last year — but why am I telling you that? You have only been away a few months, but it feels like half a lifetime. I don't suppose I shall ever get away from Lancashire.'

'I thought you were happy here.'

Her face fell. 'Jethro is a good man . . .' Her voice tailed but then she picked it up again. 'You must have had some very excit-ing adventures.'

'Oh, Maudy, if you only knew . . . the things I have seen.'

'You are so lucky.'

'Such things,' I whispered.

Maudy Glass was sleepy now but she sat up in expectation of a thrilling yarn. I could not talk about watching Horatio Green die in the study or finding Silas Braithwaite dead, or lowering Rosie Flowers by the rope round her neck, or seeing Reverend Jackaman crucified, and so I told her about the Ashby case and how Eleanor Quarrel, so alive and so beautiful, had died — drowned when her ship went down and all because of me. I thought that talking might help to heal the wounds but it only burst them open.

'But you acted from the best of motives,' Maudy told me as I sipped my gin by the open fire. Maudy was not taking alcohol even though the doctor had told her she must. She said it made her feel sick, but I managed to persuade her to have a large sherry.

'The road to hell is paved with good intentions,' I said, or think I said, but Maudy was dozing by then, comfortable in the chair that my father had always occupied.

'You would have liked Edward,' I said softly, 'and he would have liked you, Maudy. You would have made each other laugh. I have never told you about him. How could I?'

She began to snore — quite loudly like Bobby, the old retriever we once had.

'I lied to him, Maudy.' I poured myself another drink, almost to the brim. 'I lied without compunction. But I sent him to hell when I thought he had deceived me.'

I raised my glass but the world looked no better through it.

'I lied to everybody. It was my idea and my father went along with it. The army was reluctant to accept the presence of a girl as it was. They would never have accepted what was little more than a child.' I finished my drink and put the glass down a little more heavily than I intended, and Maudy stirred but did not wake. 'So when I met Edward I was sixteen and when we became engaged to be married I was seventeen, though he thought I was twenty and the lie became toxic. I never knew when it would strike my heart or if there would be an antidote. Only he could have told me that.'

'How could you what?' Maudy asked and opened her eyes.

I still lie about it now. It is the only way I can be taken half-seriously — and most of the time I believe it. Sometimes I feel I am an old, old woman — the things I have known — but in my heart all I want is to dance, to waltz with you under those huge Delhi moons, to hold you close and count the countless stars and to be so happy that it hurts.

I damped down the fire and put up the guard and we went to bed, but I could not sleep, so I went down the wooden stairs into the cellars and through the dripping arches, past the wine racks to where Sarah Ashby stood waiting for me. She smiled happily and stepped forwards to greet me, but there was a shadow behind her, Eleanor Quarrel with a knife in her hand, its wicked blade shining, the burnished steel tapered to a lethally fine point, and the edge wavy and razor-thin. I tried to cry out but the hand going over Sarah's mouth somehow gagged me and I saw the blade sweep over and up, plunging into Sarah's chest, and the gush of black blood from her burst heart, and I too doubled up as Eleanor Quarrel rushed towards me, hissing, clawing at my hair and gouging at my eyes.

I jolted out of bed and went to the window to look out at the moon over Hunger Hill. My father had owned this land, and his fathers for over three hundred years, and what had I done with it? My heart was still pounding so I had another gin, and I must have fallen asleep in my chair because the front bell was clattering and I went out to find young Sam Vetch breathlessly presenting me with a telegram.

MARCH RETURN AT ONCE STOP I NEED YOU
STOP SIDNEY GRICE

I found a piece of paper and printed in pencil *Will arrive tomorrow stop March.* This left hardly any time even to think about what I had to do, so I crossed out *tomorrow* and wrote *today.*

And so, four days after I had set off for Lancashire, the process was reversed — George Carpenter and Onion, keys to Mr Warwick, then the train, changing at Wigan and disembarking at Euston. London was still quite new to me then — the biggest and wealthiest city on earth, capital of the greatest empire the world had ever known, the noise and bustle crashing around me as I walked towards Gower Street.

I saw a girl, probably no more than ten years old, the skin of her naked limbs tight around her bones, with a sunken-faced baby tied in front of her in a sack. She was crouching in the gutter picking at a rotting fish head, chewing the morsels and feeding the pap to her sibling. I went over to offer her a few coins but she saw me approach and scuttled away, snatching a ride on the back of a coal wagon before the carter saw her and stung her off with his whip.

It was quieter in Gower Street. Two men were carrying a rough pine coffin out of University College Hospital and across the wood-blocked road into the Anatomy Building — another person that no one cared to bury and would get more medical attention dead than he or she would have had while alive. I crossed myself and walked on.

Molly let me in.

'Oh thank Gawd.' She was still snuffly with her head cold and had boot blacking on her hands. 'I've been so worried about him, miss, stuck up in his room, most likely indulging in his secret vice.'

'What *is* his secret vice?'

Molly scratched her neck. 'Why, miss, it is so secret I doubt as even Mr Grice knows and he knows everything.'

'Is he still up there?'

Molly looked at the ceiling as if checking. 'Still is the word,' she said. 'I haven't heard so much as a scamper from him for ever so long and, oh, miss, he hasn't eaten for days. He must be ravished.'

'He certainly must have been desperate to have sent me that telegram,' I said.

'Well —' she began.

'What telegram?' Sidney Grice appeared at the top of the stairs.

He had his paisley dressing gown on and Persian slippers, and a tasselled red velvet fez.

'I came back,' I called up.

'Why?' He adjusted his black patch. 'Where have you been?'

I looked at him and then at Molly who was screwing her apron into a black ball in front of her.

'Nowhere special,' I said, and my guardian humphed and drifted away. I heard his bedroom door close and the four bolts slotting into place.

Molly's face was a fashionable Perkin's mauve.

'You,' I said and she blinked.

'And Cook.' She smudged her hat with four fingerprints. 'She helped with the spelling and grammaticals.'

'I did not know you could be so duplicitous,' I said and she grinned. There was blacking on her nose now.

'Why, thank you, miss.' She attempted a curtsy and scurried away.

40
FRENCH BLOOD AND COMMODORE BRACELET

I did not see Sidney Grice — though I thought I heard him cry out once — until he joined me for dinner. He had his patch on and a smoking jacket, which struck me as a peculiar choice for a man who abhorred tobacco.

'Molly was worried about you,' I told him, 'locking yourself away.'

'It is the only way I can get any peace.'

'But you did not eat.'

'It has long been a habit of mine to fast intermittently. It cleanses the liver and hence the mind.'

'But you are eating tonight?'

My guardian rubbed his hands together. 'Indeed I am. I told Cook, when you wandered off, that you were bored with our usual fare and she was as taken aback as I was. Nevertheless, she has manufactured a special treat in honour of your return.'

'How exciting,' I said uncertainly and

added, 'I did not think you knew I had gone.'

He slipped his napkin out of its ring, an ornately carved cross-section of femur from the first man he had brought to the gallows. 'Did you seriously think that I do not know who is or is not in my own home, or that the servants could connive to send a telegram without my knowledge?'

'Not really,' I said. 'Have there been any developments whilst I was away?'

'Very few.' He unfolded his napkin. 'But I have not been entirely idle. After you left I paid three visits, first, to Horatio Green's shop where I made sixty-two observations, three of which may be significant. The shelves were quite high, presumably to stop bottles being accidentally knocked off them; second, the poison book lists strychnine as having been sold the day before he so inconsiderately died, though the name of the person he sold it to is clearly fictitious.'

'How can you be sure of that?'

Mr G shook the napkin vigorously. 'People creating names tend to be a little too creative for their own good. They often give themselves knighthoods or even peerages. This person was a little less ambitious and settled for a commission in the Royal Navy. There are no acting or retired Commodore

Bracelets on the naval list.'

'And third?' I inquired.

'Mr Green did not stock prussic acid, making it unlikely that he accidentally gave it to himself. Other than that, it has been very quiet.' He laid the napkin on his lap. 'Perhaps it is you and not I who attracts disaster.'

'Quite possibly.' *I certainly brought it on you, my darling Edward.* 'Where did you go for your second visit?'

'To St Jerome's Rectory.' He corrected the alignment of his cutlery. 'And there I interviewed Reverend Jackaman's old housekeeper — a delightful lady who makes a splendid cup of tea. She told me the rectory was evacuated an hour before we arrived because of a gas leak from the road works.'

Molly came puffing up the stairs, her face still smudged, opened the dumb waiter and brought out two covered plates.

'Can I stay and watch?' She plonked mine in front of me.

'I do not see why not.'

'No,' her employer said and she shuffled away. I saw my face squashed wide in the silver dome. 'Feeling nervous?'

'Yes.' We whipped off the covers and I surveyed the offering. 'It looks very like another vegetable stew to me.'

337

Sidney Grice was actually smiling. 'What is it on?'

I forked some of the washed-out, grey-green porridge to one side. 'Rice pudding.'

He waited. 'Do you still not know what it is?'

'Vegetable stew on rice pudding.'

'Curry.' He rubbed his hands together. 'We thought it would remind you of your days in India.'

I need no reminding of those. I carry India like your unborn child.

'Curry has spices.'

'Exactly.' He dug into the mound on his plate. 'So Cook put pepper and nutmeg in it.' He chewed a forkful appreciatively. 'And I detect a very generous pinch of mustard powder. Tuck in.'

I speared a flaccid carrot peeling. 'It was a kind thought.'

Sidney Grice swallowed. 'Dr Berry said you needed a more varied diet.'

'She is right about that. Have you seen her since . . . ?'

He waved some sludge around on his fork. 'She is taking advice about their aspersions on her professional qualifications,' he said. 'But she has suffered worse libels than that.

338

She tried to tell me I was harsh with you.'

'I cannot imagine why she would think that.' But, as always, my irony was wasted.

'Exactly what I said.' The sludge splotched back on to his plate. 'You have not asked about my third visit, but I shall not allow that to deter me from describing it to you.' He replenished his fork. 'On the morning you fled this house, I made a call on the last member of that abominable society, the splendidly styled Mr Warrington Tusker Gallop.'

'And did you discover anything?'

'I always discover something.' A sticky brown liquid was dripping between the tines. 'Mr Gallop is allegedly away in France' — his mouth curdled at the last word — 'buying supplies for his snuff shop. According to his housekeeper, he has been absent from our shores since the day before Mr Green died. Do you find that suspicious?' He took another mouthful.

'Not necessarily.' I sniffed my food and wished I had not. 'Though he may have been killed, or he could be in hiding and committing the murders, using the trip to provide him with an alibi.'

He swallowed. 'You know, March, your excursion seems to have done you some good. You have constructed an entire sentence of rational thought.'

'You are the only man I know who can turn a compliment into an insult.'

He looked quite pleased at that remark, but only wiped his mouth and said, 'I am always wary of anyone or anything connected to the land of revolution, infantile paintings, bad cooking and slipshod tailoring, and so, for the time being, I am more inclined to classify Gallop as a suspect than a victim.'

I laughed. 'Because you do not like the French?'

'Because nothing good has come from there since Charles Le Grice in 1066.'

'So you have French blood in your veins.'

Mr G winced. 'Norman blood before it was contaminated by breeding with the French.' He ate some more and smacked his lips. 'I am not partial to this modern fad for giving food flavour, but I shall certainly get Cook to make this again.'

I tasted a sample and wished I had eaten my steak when I had the chance.

41
PIKESTAFFS AND TELEGRAMS

Sidney Grice was at the table before me the next morning, engrossed in volume one of Clarke's *Physiognomy of the Criminal and Imbecilic Classes* and huffing to himself.

'Tosh.' He ripped out a page, screwed it up and threw it down. 'Balderdash.' Another page followed. 'These people think you can detect a murderer by the shape of his ears and the length of his nose. Why, Richard Batty had the face of Apollo but he still took a pikestaff to the bridesmaids at his own wedding.' He ripped out two pages at once, quickly rechecked something and threw them away. 'If these sham scientists were correct, then all I should need is a serviceable tape measure and I could round up every ne'er-do-well in London before he or she had even dreamed of transgressing. Molly is on her mettle today — only twenty-eight seconds to answer the summons.'

'How can you be so precise about the

time?' I had not heard the bell ring and he had not taken out his watch.

'Because I have a built-in clock.'

'Does it tick?'

'Yes.' He ignored my facetiousness. 'And I am discouraged to learn you have not heard it. It is built into the cabinet behind you.'

'Oh,' I said. 'I had forgotten about that.'

'There is no point in observing things if you do not remember them.'

Molly came in, her hands and sleeves grey. 'Telegram, sir.' She held out the tray.

'Lower the tray,' her employer told her. 'Raise it.' He scrutinized the undersurface through his pince-nez. 'Why is it covered in scratches?'

'Well, I have to put the ashes on something,' she said.

'What is wrong with the dustpan?'

'Nothing much, sir,' Molly said, ' 'cept that it was downstairs and I was up.'

Sidney Grice whipped off his pince-nez and said, 'That tray is worth more on the open market than you are.'

'Then perhaps it would like to run up and down with the tea things, make the beds and clean the hall,' I said. 'Perhaps it could answer the bell.'

'And sweep the stairs,' Molly prompted in a stage whisper.

Her employer seized the telegram and ripped it open. 'Tell the boy there is no reply.'

Molly put her hand to her mouth. 'Oh sorry, sir. I told him to go when he came. Do you want me to run after him and tell him not to wait?'

Her employer gazed fixedly at her. 'You have put the cause of female suffrage right back where it belongs,' he told her and she grinned again.

'Thank you, sir. I do my best.'

He opened his mouth but I broke in. 'You had better go now, Molly.' And she wandered uncertainly away.

'What do you make of this?' My guardian passed me the telegram.

I wiped my fingers on my napkin. 'It was sent from —'

'Clearly.' He pushed his plate away. 'But I refer to the content. What do you think it means?'

I read it.

MR GRICE YOU ARE LACKING VITAL INFORMA-
TION COME FACTORY THREE EXACTLY NO
LATER OR INDEED ANY EARLIER YOU SHALL
GET INSTRUCTIONS BY NEXT POST YOU MUST
OPEN LETTER UP IMMEDIATELY RECEIVED
KEY HAS BEEN ATTACHED TO NOTE LEFT

DOOR LOCKED SECURELY I SHALL NOT OPEN
SO NEED TO OPEN YOURSELF HOPE OBEY
ORDERS FROM PROMETHEUS PIGGETY ES-
QUIRE DONT FORGET KEY OR YOU REALLY
CANNOT MAKE AN ENTRY

I spooned some sugar into my tea. 'It is very jumbled but it would appear that Mr Piggety wants —'

He raised his hand. 'How can you possibly make any assumptions about what the odious Piggety does or does not want?'

'Well, his telegram —'

Sidney Grice slapped the table. 'Stop it, March. You are giving me a headache. If you received a telegram signed by the king of the moon would you unquestioningly accept that it came from his lunar majesty?'

'No, but —'

He clutched his forehead. 'No, but there are no *no buts.* The last thing one can do is assume that any telegram was written by the person it purports to be written by. That is part three of my sixteenth law. What is the most utterly dazzlingly manifest thing about this telegram? What is the hyena in the room?'

'Well, it is very long . . .' I began, and my guardian clapped his hands sarcastically.

'At last,' he said. 'At sixty-seven words it

344

is the third longest telegram I have ever received. Countries have declared war more tersely. What particular word makes it so singular?

'Esquire,' I said, and he threw up his arms.

'Precisely. On average I receive thirteen telegrams a day, which is . . . ?'

'Four thousand, seven hundred and forty-five a year,' I said, and was gratified to see an impressed eyebrow lifted. I did not tell him I knew the figure already because I had done my father's accounts and one of his tenants had paid thirteen pence rent a day.

'And this is the first time I have ever seen anyone use the title. Why pay an extra penny for an unnecessary frill? How would you paraphrase the message?'

'Well, to start with there is no need to use your name,' I said. *Have vital information stop come to factory three o'clock precisely stop will send key to get in.'*

'Which is fifty words less and four shillings and two pennies cheaper,' Sidney Grice said. 'Did Piggety strike you as a man with no regard for money?'

'I would have thought he was almost as careful as you,' I said.

Sidney Grice crushed his toast to powder. 'And what word did you use twice in your seventeen words that the alleged Piggety did not use even once?'

'*Stop,*' I said. 'Why would anyone be so extravagant with the words and not want to pay for punctuation?'

'I think we can assume — and I loathe to assume anything — that the cost was not a consideration.' He stirred the crumbs into his prune juice with a knife. 'For some reason stops would have interfered with the true import of the message. So who wrote it?'

'Either a lunatic or an inebriate,' I said as he pushed a piece of crust under the surface with the tip of his first finger.

'On the contrary.' He wiped his finger on his napkin. 'I would say it was composed by a highly organized mind. It conveys instructions but conceals a deeper meaning.' He held his spoon to the light. 'It is a riddle wrapped within a riddle.'

I lifted the teapot but it was empty. 'It came from the Copper Lane office. Shall I go and see if they remember who sent it?'

'Oh, they will remember.' He swirled his juice vigorously. 'No clerk would forget that message in a hurry, which leads us to conclude?'

'Whoever sent it wants to be remembered,' I said.

'Or?'

'Got somebody else to send it on his or her behalf.'

'Well done. I am slightly concerned about sending you to such an area unaccompanied, though.'

'I did not know you cared,' I said and his eyebrow fell.

'March, how could you doubt it? You know I shall always care.' His tones were tender. 'Think how my professional standing would suffer were I unable even to look after my ward.'

I got up from the table. 'And what will *you* do?'

He gave up on his breakfast and rose. 'I shall go to my study and cross-reference my files on matricide — that always relaxes me — while I ponder the implications of this loquacious telegram and await the prophesied arrival of the letter and key. Promise me, March. You will take a cab straight there, get it to wait and come straight home.'

'I shall be careful,' I said.

'That is not what I asked.'

'Goodbye, Mr G,' I said and went down into the hallway to turn the brass handle and run up the flag.

347

42
MOSS VELVET
AND BLACK SNOW

I put on my faithful moss velvet coat and a new Ardith bonnet with green trim and matching ribbon tie, and selected a parasol. I would not need the last item but, as my friend Harriet once told me, a bonnet is not a bonnet without one. A cab had already pulled up when I stepped out and the horse was trying to lower its head to the water running down the gutter, but the cabby kept pulling it up.

'Why will you not let him drink?' I asked as I clambered through the flaps.

'Thirsty 'orse works 'arder,' he said briefly, setting off at a trot before I was settled into my seat.

The air was grey that day with sour wisps of yellow streaming through it, and the soot hung in big black snowflakes, patting on to my sleeve and lapel. I tried to flick one off but only smudged it.

A gang of street urchins had spotted me

and were running after my hansom, chant-
ing,

'Siddie Grice Gower Streeter
'Ad a client couldn't keep 'er.
'Ad another didn't luv 'er.
Killed 'er daugh'er. Killed 'er muvver.'

Once I might have found them amusing,
but there was no humour in the deaths that
hovered around Sidney Grice and me. I
threw them some pennies. Not one of those
children would have had a meal half as
nutritious as the food I complained about.

We passed through Holborn and into
Newgate, once the site of one of seven gates
built by the Romans when London was a
walled city. Now its most impressive feature
was the forbidding massive-stoned structure
of the prison.

'Want to visit your dad?' the cabby called
down.

'At least I know who my father was,' I said
and he whipped the horse.

Cheapside and what Dickens described as
the busiest thoroughfare in the world was
bustling but strangely quiet. The atmosphere
had thickened and was sharp with coal
smoke. I could barely see the shops and of-
fices either side of us. Even the rumble of

carriage and cart wheels and clipping hooves of straining horses was muffled, and by the time we arrived in Wapping I could see almost nothing at all. The whole of the Thames seemed to be rising out of its basin and creeping over the city, gathering the filth from the air as it advanced.

We came to a stop. 'Four shillin's.'

'That seems rather a lot.'

'Four shillin's.'

I opened my purse. 'I should like to give you some beer money,' I said and was rewarded with a confusion of rotting teeth as I clambered out. 'But a thirsty man works 'arder.' And I pitched him two florins.

He wrenched the reins and swung round so sharply that I thought his cab might topple on to me, before I had the chance to ask him to stay.

I paused to get my bearings. The buildings were fuzzy in the diffuse light, their hazy sides scarcely distinguishable from the vapours they were jutting into, but I only had to turn to find that I was directly outside the telegraphy office. The fog had got in before me and the gaslights scarcely penetrated it as I made my way to the back.

'I received this telegram this morning.'

The woman behind the counter was writing in a long red book. 'You shouldn't 'ave done that.' She stopped writing. 'This is addressed to Mr Sidney Grice the detective and when he finds out 'e'll kill you just like 'e did all them others.'

She had a brown hat on that was much too small for her.

'I am Mr Grice's assistant,' I told her and she perked up, but almost immediately looked incredulous.

'Not 'er,' she said. 'Sidney Grice's assistant is tall and dark. I read it in *The Ashby Slashin's*. She's beautiful and mysterious, but you're like a free-quarters-drownded alley cat. No offence.'

A bored young man was sitting behind her, his finger static on a Morse key, a piece of fruit bread in his free hand.

'I must be his other assistant then,' I said. 'Did you send this telegram?'

'What if I did? I told 'im it was all wrong.'

'It was a man then?' I took the paper back.

'A mudlark, come in off the 'igh tide,' she said. ' 'E said 'e 'ad been told to make sure it went 'xactly as what it was written.'

'I always sends them 'xactly as they is written.' The young man sprayed crumbs over his desk.

'Did he say who sent him?'

'Did 'e 'eckers. And did I ask? Did I 'eckers.'

'What did he look like?'

'A mudlark.' She stretched to look over my shoulder and called, 'Next,' though the office was otherwise deserted.

There was a rapid series of clicks and the young man jumped to attention. He dropped the remnants of his bread and frantically riffled through the papers on his desk. 'My pencil. Where's my poxy pencil?'

'Behind your cruddin' ear,' the woman said without turning her head.

'Oh, so it is . . . Oh, sugar me, the lead's broken.' He rooted frantically through a drawer and the clicks stopped.

' 'Is brain's broken if you ask me.' The woman dipped a splayed nib into her ink pot.

'Oh, well,' he said. 'It was only about someone's mother dyin'. Nuffink you can do about that now.'

I waved the telegram under her nose. 'Do you have the original copy?'

The woman's lips pulled away from her like a braying donkey. ' 'Course I do,' she said. 'I frame every message to 'ang on the walls of my bleedin' palace.' She indicated the fireplace. 'Got to keep warm some'ow. Next.'

I took the hint and turned to go.

'Not even a tanner for my time,' she

grumbled to the young man as the clicker started again.

'And don't you go tryin' to fit us up for nuffink,' he shouted after me as I left. 'I got friends in 'igh places.'

'Monkeys in trees?' I asked politely as I went outside.

The fog had lifted a fraction and the ghostly crew of a spectral clipper filed down the alley towards the dock, the canvas of their duffel bags bulging over their shoulders. Not one man was speaking or looking anywhere but straight ahead to the cabin boy at the front carrying an oil lantern high on a forked stick. I tagged on behind and, where the bottom of the lane opened out, found myself on a quay a few yards from the looming outline of a long shed with a hexagonal tower on top.

43

MERMAIDS AND
THE MUFFLED MAN

I do not think I fully intended to go to Piggety's Cats. It was just that I thought I had
a better chance of finding a cab at a dock
than in the confusion of lanes and alleys
that led away from it. But now that I was
here it seemed a shame not to at least take
a look.

The shade of a gentleman was clambering
out of a blurred hansom at the foot of a
wharf. I hurried over.

'Will you wait while I visit that factory? I
shall pay you for your time.'

'All right.' The driver had leather gauntlets
on and a leather peaked cap, and was
wrapped in a long coat with a scarf around
his face.

'Promise?'

'I said *all right*.' He hauled out a huge fob
watch on an amulet-laden chain and set it
on his lap.

His horse looked well fed and groomed so

I decided I could trust him. I wound my way through a labyrinth of packing crates and between two hillocks of stacked sacks. Some girls were playing hopscotch. They threw their stones at the side of the shed and ran away as I slid my feet over slippery cobbles like a nervous ice skater until I got to the entrance. There I hesitated. I knew the telegram had forbidden Sidney Grice from calling before three o'clock, but there was no mention of me. I rapped and waited. Two dockers came by, rolling an enormous barrel up the slope. It was oozing black oil and glistening.

I knocked again but could not hear anything above the cacophony around me. A porter came by with a tray on his head and whistling 'My Mother Was a Mermaid in the Sea'. I put my ear to the door and thought I heard a noise — a creak? a cough? — I could not say what it was but it came from inside the building.

I put my hand to the door and despite Prometheus Piggety's verbose insistence in his telegram, it was unlocked. I pushed it open a foot and called out. 'Hello? Mr Piggety?' But there was no reply. I started forwards but then I hesitated. I knew Mr G would be angry when he found I had been interfering and also I had not really thought about what I was going to say. And then I definitely heard something. To this day I am not sure what. Perhaps it was a rustle or maybe the scrape of a boot on the metal platform, but I had a distinct impression that there was somebody behind that door, hiding from me, and suddenly I was frightened. I turned and rushed away, and when I checked over my shoulder that no one was following, I was almost certain that the door was closed.

'Gotcha!'

I was so busy looking back that I ran straight into a man but, instead of stepping aside, he clutched my wrist and held on tight. I looked up and it was the man in the green jacket, the one who had pulled a cudgel on us the last time we came.

'Let me go.' I took some satisfaction in noting that his nose was still bruised from our last encounter.

He grinned and his breath was like rotting meat. 'Fink you can make a dolly out of me, do you? Well, you won't slip me so easily this time, cod-face.'

'Let me go this instant.' But I knew that all my squirmings and protestations were useless.

'Well, you ain't much of a catch.' His lips were cracked and bleeding. 'And I am 'arf tempted to throw you back.'

I remembered something Inspector Pound had told me about the area and tried to straighten up and look him in his filmy eyes. 'Have you any idea who you are talking to? I am Mick McGregor's niece.'

The man tightened his grip. 'And what? Mick McGregor had a bi' ov a accident last week. Went for a swim and never came up for air. Favourite uncle was 'e? Seein' as he never 'ad no bruvvers or sisters.'

'The police know I am here,' I said.

'Good.' His saliva flecked my face. 'Then it won't take them long to fish you awt.' He had another look at me. 'Shame really, ugly bottle like you. Lay a bob to a wren you've never been kissed.'

'I have never been kissed by a stench-breathed mongrel,' I said, 'and I do not intend to start now.'

I thought about using my parasol again but he knocked it out of my grasp.

'Naughty.' He raised his hand to slap me with the back of it. I slumped as if in a swoon and, as the man leaned over to look at me, jumped straight up again. The top of my head crunched into his chin and cracked my teeth together. I yelped, he grunted, let go of me and staggered two steps back. I picked up my parasol and ran. I did not look to see if he was after me. I was quite good at running as a child, but I had not done much of it since and I was not constricted by several layers of feminine frippery then. I put everything I had into that race as I wound back between the cases. A young Chinaman in black robes and a coolie hat was carrying two baskets on a pole. I swerved to avoid him and nearly collided with a tin bath lying on its side, but just managed to clear it with a desperate leap.

I heard somebody clatter into it close behind and metal-studded boots on the cobbles. It was still quite a way to where the hansom had been parked, but when I lifted my head I could see it heading at a good pace towards me through the clouds. I put on a final spurt and jumped on to the board. A hand reached out from inside and I took it just as I felt my dress being grabbed and myself being dragged backwards. I kicked out and my boot made solid contact, but my assailant only swore and held on.

'Gerroff!' the cabby yelled and with one crack of his whip dealt with my attacker, and with another propelled his horse forward as I fell through the flaps and collapsed into my seat.

'Careful. You nearly shattered my flask.'

'What are you doing here?'

Sidney Grice tugged his coat out from under me as I straightened myself up. 'You did not seriously think I would let you wander around the docks by yourself?'

'Why did you not come sooner then?'

'We could not see what was going on in the fog. I was just about to get out and look for you when it lifted a little and Gerry saw you brawling with a ganger.'

The cabby pulled his scarf down and grinned broadly. 'I'll put a fiver on you against Gipsy James Mace any day, miss. You certainly got the better of Ted Gallagher there.'

'You know him?'

'Had him by the collar a few times, miss. Got him three years' hard labour once. There's a goodly few round here with grudges against me. That's why I cover my face.'

'Gerry used to be Police Sergeant Dawson,' my guardian told me.

We turned up an alley, the wheels nearly scraping the sides. 'Until I got a taste for the grog,' our driver said. 'I was captain of the Met Cricket Team too — miss that more than the work, I do. Mr Grice put in a word for me to get this job, though. He even paid for —'

'Your hat has not come very well out of

359

the fray,' Sidney Grice said loudly.

'Oh, my poor bonnet.' I took it off and saw the top had been completely crushed. I felt for a bruise and found a gratifyingly large one on my crown. The hansom stopped and we pulled out into a wider road.

An old lady was struggling with a wobbly pram full of rags. I leaned forward and skimmed her my hat and she caught it and grinned gummily. 'Bless yer, darlin',' she called and put it on her head.

'Looks better on her than it did on you,' my guardian said.

You would have disagreed with him about that. You always liked me in hats and almost fell out with Harry Baddington when he said that the one I wore to his brother's wedding made me look like a standard lamp. I told you to forget about it because he was your best friend, but you told me no, he was not, I was — and insisted he apologized. The silly thing was I caught sight of my reflection and thought he was probably right.

I wonder how you would have reacted to my fighting on the docks — probably a mixture of amusement and alarm but I like to think that part of you would have been proud of me.

'Does your head hurt very much?' Sidney Grice asked, and it was only then that I realized I was sighing.

44
THE NINTH SENSE

'*Smollet's whalebone corsets for the distin-guished gentleman,*' I read out. We were stuck behind an advertising van with its boards proclaiming in smaller print, *Unde-tectable Waist Trimming for Every Occasion.* Another van was trying to come down the road, extolling the virtues of *Dr Crambone's Liver Tonic — Never Suffer Biliousness Again,* and there was hardly space for one of them in the road already.

'So.' Sidney Grice pulled the cork out of his flask but, as always, did not have a spare cup to offer me a drink. 'What did you discover — apart from the gentle art of head-butting?'

My scalp was feeling quite tender now. 'The telegram was taken to the office by a river scavenger.' I rubbed my head gingerly. 'A boy. Other than that, they knew nothing about him and they burnt the original copy.'

'And then?' He tapped the cork back

into place.

I steeled myself. 'I went to Mr Piggety's factory.' I waited for the onslaught but my guardian only sipped his tea and said, 'I would have been astonished if you had not. So what happened?'

'I knocked,' I said, 'and when there was no answer I tried the handle and the door was not locked.'

His fingers blanched on his cup. 'And then?'

'Shift your frebbin' nag and your festerin' heap of scrap, you bloomin' grut,' Gerry Dawson bellowed, 'or I'll turn your sign to matchwood and stick the splinters up your mother's —'

'Ladies,' Sidney Grice called up.

'Nostrils,' the ex-sergeant muttered.

I said, 'I thought I heard somebody behind the door and I got frightened and ran away. I was probably just imagining it.'

'Not necessarily,' my guardian expounded. 'I am convinced there is something innate in man and many other creatures, which warns them of dangers they cannot detect by more recognized means — a ninth sense perhaps — and you were well advised to pay attention to it.'

I did not trouble to ask what the other extra senses were but said, 'I left the door open but when I looked back, it had been closed.'

Sidney Grice rested the flask on his knee and said, 'That is most intriguing. Either you were indulging in a bout of hyperthermic feminine hysteria or there was somebody behind that door and you were in graver danger than you realize.' He shuddered. 'If anything *had* happened to you, March, I might have blamed myself. But that would require a degree of self-criticism which is alien to my nature.'

'At flippin' last,' our driver shouted. Dr Crambone was reversing and Smollet's Corsets was forcing its way through the gap left on to King William Street, and we followed close on his heels before the Liver Tonic pushed its way back in. 'They likes to cause a jam so more people read their advertisements.'

'And hate their product,' I commented.

'You would have thought so,' Sidney Grice said, 'but when a Winston's Toothpowder board wedged in Mortimer Market for half a day, sales of their alarmingly corrosive dentifrice trebled for a week afterwards.'

We came to another halt.

'Hold on tight,' Gerry warned us, and my guardian hastily swallowed the last of his beverage just as we swung violently to the left again, one wheel mounting the kerb and flinging me over my guardian's lap.

'For goodness sake, man,' Sidney Grice shouted up. 'You will lose your licence.'

I disengaged myself just in time to see a very well-dressed lady and her three equally smartly attired children scatter like driven pheasants from a beater.

'Wanted to get home before Christmas, didn't you?' Gerry answered with a laugh, bumping us back on to the road.

A ginger cat shot out of the way as our horse sidestepped an eel stall and whinnied.

'Were it not for his promise, I would think he has been drinking again,' my guardian said. 'But Gerry is one of the few men I have ever met whose word I can rely on.'

'Are you not angry with me?' I asked and he straightened his collar.

'I myself was sorely tempted to do what you did, but there is no point in trying to sneak into a ball before the orchestra has started to play.'

'On the day I arrived in Gower Street you told me that you disliked metaphors,' I reminded him.

'And so I do.' He shook the last few drops out of his cup. 'But I find them useful devices for communicating with those of meaner mental capacities than my own.'

'By which you mean everybody.'

'It would be immodest of me to respond.'

Gerry started tapping his boots in a kind of dance on the roof.

'What about Chigorin?' I persisted.

'The Russian chess player? I imagine he could give me a game.'

Gerry was whistling tunefully.

'I have never met such an arrogant man in all my life,' I said and Sidney Grice showed polite interest.

'Really?' He put the cup back on his flask. 'I was not aware that you had met him.' And Gerry started singing 'Tell Me Ma' in a rich baritone.

'He is not even Irish.' My guardian rolled his eye.

'They pull my hair and they steal my comb,' Gerry sang and clicked his reins, and the horse shook its mane and lifted its head as it clipped along the side street.

After a late lunch I went to the hospital. There had been a fire in one of the operating theatres and they were dragging blackened equipment out into the corridor. The ether had leaked from an anaesthetic machine and an electric light had sparked.

'Was anyone hurt?' I asked a medical student who was helping to carry a half-incinerated table away.

'Just a nurse,' he told me. 'She won't live the night.'

They were wheeling her out as he spoke, a small charred figure hardly recognizable as a woman, and she let out a sob as she heard his words.

'He does not know what he is talking about,' I told her and her eyes swivelled towards me and she wheezed.

'I hope he's right,' she managed as they took her away.

Inspector Pound was conscious when I got to his bed. 'Miss Middleton, I believe I am indebted to you again.'

'If I ever need blood I shall know who to ask for it,' I said. 'At least I know we are compatible.'

He managed a smile. 'Oh, I already knew we were that.' And, before I could think of a response, he added, 'Sounds like I had a lucky escape. They were going to take me down to the operating theatre to clean up my wound today, but it's healing so well they decided not to bother.'

He was shifting constantly.

'Are you in much pain?'

'None at all.' His expression did not convince me. 'And how is Mr Grice?'

I took his hand and turned it to check his pulse.

'Struggling,' I said, and told him about the Last Death Club and the murders of its members.

'For the first time I am glad to be here,' he said when I had finished. 'I can imagine how my superiors would be on my back. How is Inspector Quigley dealing with it all?'

'By pretending that the murders are suicides or accidents.'

The inspector bristled. 'I sometimes wonder why that man became a policeman, other than his personal ambition . . . I'm sorry. I shouldn't have said that. No doubt he will get his promotion and I shall have to call him sir.'

'I should not have worried you,' I said.

'No.' He moved uncomfortably. 'I like to know what's happening on my patch.' For a moment he drifted but then he shook himself, as if out of a dream. 'It sounds like Miss McKay might be worth questioning again — an extremely unpleasant character if ever there was one. When I was a sergeant I arrested her for what I can only describe as a vile and violent attack on her house-keeper. The victim was anxious to testify and we had an independent witness in the cook. Miss McKay did not trouble to deny the offence and I was confident of a conviction and a stiff sentence. But I reckoned . . .' He looked blank for a moment, then forced himself awake. 'I reckoned without her father's influence and all charges were suddenly dropped, and — as I discovered later — this was by no means the first time it had happened.'

'But that is disgusting.' I felt his grip sharpen.

'I tendered my resignation.' He was fading. 'But they made hints about my prospects and I told myself I could do more good inside the force than . . .' We were still holding hands when he fell asleep.

I took some scissors out of my handbag and trimmed his moustaches, but it was more difficult than I expected and, if anything, they looked more ragged than before I had interfered. I put my scissors away, checked that no one was watching and kissed his forehead. One eye popped open and he mumbled, 'Water.'

And on the way out I came across the younger nurse. Her face was pink and she had been crying. 'Oh, miss, I have just heard some terrible news about Hilary Wilkinson.'

'Hilary?'

'The nurse who is usually with me.'

'Was that her in the fire?' She gnawed her lower lip but did not reply. 'I hope she will be all right,' I said.

'Oh, miss.' She burst into tears. 'I don't think she will.'

I took her hand. 'I am so sorry.'

'Oh blimey, here comes Matron. I'll be for it if she sees me like this.'

'Go into the ward and keep your back to her.'

Matron came marching down the corridor and her face darkened when she saw me.

'Flattery,' my father told me, 'is like make-up — cheap and false — but, if you must use it, lay it on thickly or people will see straight through it.'

'Might I have a have a word, Matron?'

'What is it now?'

'I have worked in several military hospitals,' I said, 'and we always prided ourselves on our efficiency.'

Her eyes glinted. 'What of it?'

'I just wanted to say that I have never come across a better run ward in my life.'

I cringed at my own insincerity and hoped she did not think I was mocking her, but Matron grunted and her face softened. 'I am glad you think so but, if you will excuse me, I must talk to Nurse Ramsey. I know she was very attached to Nurse Wilkinson.'

I froze. 'Was?'

Matron's mouth compressed as she controlled herself.

45
COAL DUST, FINGERPRINTS AND DEATH TRAPS

We were just picking at the remnants of some cold potatoes and re-boiled cabbage when Molly came in, sleeves rolled up and arms coated in flour. 'Special delivery, sir.' And Sidney Grice put down his fork to take a thick white envelope from the tray.

'Why is it special?' He held it by the corner.

She looked skywards for inspiration before deciding. 'I think it's because the boy said it was.'

'Was he a post-office messenger?' I asked

'No, miss. He was a ragamuffin — horrible he was, coughing and spitting. He —'

'Get out,' her employer said, and Molly went pink.

'But —'

'Now.'

Molly pouted. 'Yes, sir.'

'And no pouting,' he said without looking up as she left. 'Come, March. Let us go downstairs and examine this keenly anticipated correspondence in the heart and mind of this house, my study.'

We went down and stood behind his desk, and Sidney Grice shook the envelope. 'Feels and sounds like the key.' He held it up to the light. 'Looks like the outline of a key and therefore quite possibly a key. Plain white envelope with nothing written on it and no impression of anything having been written over it. No hallmark but not cheap paper. Four finger smudges and . . .' He perched his pince-nez on the tip of his nose. 'What do you make of this, March?'

I went to his side. 'They are a child's prints but the tips look clubbed.'

'What would cause that?' He brought out a pocket magnifying glass to look more closely.

'It can develop with lung diseases. I have seen it in people who work in mines or cotton mills, but never in a child.'

'What about soot?'

'He would have had to inhale a lot of it — a climbing boy could have.'

'An ex-climbing boy in this case,' Sidney Grice said. 'There is not a grain of soot on it, and even Molly would have noticed if he were a sweep's apprentice.'

'He is probably too ill to work. I have seen

four-year-olds sent up flues which are still hot from the fires and come down burnt all over and with seared lungs. And it is supposed to be illegal. Something should be done.'

'I seem to have installed a social reformer in the bosom of my home,' my guardian commented. 'Look at that. See how clear the print is? You can make out every whorl. When I have the time I shall make a study of the ridges on fingertips. I am half convinced that very few people share exactly the same patterns.' He opened the envelope carefully with a paperknife and sniffed the flap. 'This has been sealed within the last hour or so. I can smell the gum quite strongly and it is still tacky . . . what is this stuck to the glue?' He picked at it with a pair of tweezers. 'In that second drawer down you will find a sheet of black card . . . Put it on my blotter.' He laid his find carefully out, a long white strand.

'It looks very like a hair from one of Mr Piggety's cats,' I said. 'I am still finding them on my coat.'

'Then go and find another one,' he said, and I went into the hall and picked at my lapel. By the time I came back he had dragged the round table to the window and was setting up a microscope, twisting the mirror to catch the light. He took the hair from me, stretched it alongside the other between two glass slides and clipped them on to the stage. 'I have scratched the numbers one and two at the ends of the slides.' He peered down the eyepiece. 'So that even you will not confuse the specimens.' He fiddled with the focus and moved the slides side to side. 'Interesting.' He straightened up sharply. 'Now, you tell me what differences you can see.'

I adjusted the objective lens a fraction to sharpen the image and looked along the hairs. At two hundred magnification they had lost their smoothness and sprouted fibres all over. I touched the slide and the images jumped out of view. 'I cannot see any differences.'

'Look harder.'

I brought the hairs back over the hole in the stage.

'They are the same width and colour.'

'Try harder. Use your eyes.'

I tried again and rotated the slides a few degrees. 'They still look identical to me.' I gave up.

'Good,' Sidney Grice said. 'I could not see any differences either and if I cannot see something it cannot be seen. So what can we deduce from that?'

'That the hair in the envelope came from one of Piggety's cats,' I said.

'Nonsense.' He ran a hand over his head. 'All we can deduce is that the two hairs are indistinguishable under this magnification and so we cannot say with any reasonable certainty that they came from different types of cats, if indeed they *are* cats' hairs. If needs be I shall get Professor James Beart Simonds of the Royal Veterinary College to have a look at it. He was of great help in the Silver Beard goat-swapping scandal.'

We went back to the desk where he looked inside the envelope, turned it upside down and tapped it over the card. 'No dust.' He slipped a letter out, smelled it and held it to the light before opening it out on to his blotting paper. It was a sheet of double foolscap paper and had been folded three times. On the top side it bore a message using cuttings from a newspaper.

GRICE THIS KEY
OPENS
THE OUTER
DOOR
LOCK
TURN
ANTI CLOCKWISE TO
GAIN ENTRY PIG GETY

'The *Hackney Gazette* typeface,' Sidney Grice commented. 'It should be easy enough to find when they last printed *clockwise* as one word, especially as it first appeared in print only four years and twenty-nine weeks ago. And why the *anti* rather the more usual *counter*-clockwise?'

'This message is just as odd as the last one,' I said. 'I cannot make any sense of it. Why explain what the key does when you have already been advised that it was coming? And why tell you how to use it?'

He picked at the top corner of the Y. 'That which appears to be most stupid is sometimes the most clever,' he said.

I looked at the back of the paper. The gum had seeped through but it was otherwise unmarked. 'Also, you have both been reduced to just your surnames in this letter and Mr Piggety has lost his *esquire.*'

'The presence and absence of that word in the two communications is beyond question of immoderate significance.' He rubbed beneath his patch.

'Will you go?' I asked.

'Certainly. You look uneasy.'

'I know you will say —'

'You never know what I will say.'

I often did but I let that pass and restarted. 'I *suspect* you will say that I have been reading too many shockers but, if Mr Piggety is the murderer, it could be a trap.'

'One shocker is too many.' Sidney Grice looked at the reverse of the letter. 'But you may be right, March, and I certainly hope so. It is nearly six months since anybody thought it worth their while to lure me to my death and that was *such* an insultingly opaque attempt. A man can get discouraged so easily when nobody wants to kill him.'

'If you must go, why not go early and take him unawares?'

'Two reasons.' My guardian took the slides from the microscope and wrapped rubber bands round them. 'First, there is no point in trying to spring a trap before it is set. That is Grice's twelfth maxim.'

'And second?'

He looked at his watch. 'We have not yet had our postprandial cup of tea. Ring the bell, March, and I shall tell you the other thirty-nine maxims whilst we are biding our time.'

46
THE LONG ROWS OF DEATH

Sidney Grice tried the door.

'Well, it is locked now.' He slipped the key in, turned it easily and rotated the handle. 'Stand well back, March.' He stepped to one side. 'The last time I answered a cryptic summons, Princess Cristobel of Gladbach was waiting in the dark with a primed and loaded musket.' He swung the door open with his cane, took a small rectangular mirror on a stick out of his satchel and checked inside with it. 'Looks clear.' He folded the mirror away, poked his head round the frame and almost immediately recoiled. 'Handkerchief.' He clamped his over his nose and I followed suit.

The stench was even worse than before as we entered Mr Piggety's factory, and the heat hit us immediately. Sidney Grice put out his hand.

'Keep behind me.' I could hardly hear him above the crashing of planks being unloaded from a cargo ship outside.

We stepped on to the platform and looked down at the rows of cages.

'Hello,' he called and rattled the railings, but there was no reply. 'Hello,' he shouted.

We waited a moment before descending and it was immediately obvious that things had gone very wrong indeed. The first cage held about a dozen cats and all of them were dead. We went to the next cage and the same scene greeted us.

'Dear God,' I whispered. It was not until the fifth that I saw any sign of life, a tiny kitten lying on its side, panting weakly and with white-membraned eyes but, even as we watched, the breathing stopped. 'Oh, you poor little thing.'

'The water has been turned off,' my guardian said.

'And the heating up.'

The clatter of timber ceased and Sidney Grice touched my arm. 'Listen.' There was a shrill noise in the background. At first I thought it was a circular saw being used to cut the planks, but the noise was higher than that and changed pitch too much.

'The back room,' my guardian said. 'Wait here.' He ran jerkily between the long rows of death to the far end. There he paused and unsheathed his swordstick. I hurried after him and he rolled his eye. 'Canute had more luck in holding back the sea,' he said.

The sound was louder now and higher and fractured. I stood to one side.

I turned the handle and flung open the door. The room was unlit except through one sealed glass panel in the roof, and it took a while to adjust to the dark and the air heavy with big drops of water and to realize that what we had been listening to was a scream, and that the steam and the scream were both coming from one of the enamelled tubs. There was a tremendous splashing. Perhaps Mr Piggety was having a practice run with a sack full of stray cats. It was difficult to get close with boiling water spraying in every direction, but as we edged nearer I opened my parasol.

'Do *not* flap it.' Sidney Grice hung back.

'I shall try not to.' I held it before us as a shield. The splashing stopped and the scream was silenced, but the machinery still whirred as I peeked round the frilled edge of my parasol. It was then that I saw a head projecting from the bubbling surface of the water and, as I watched, the head turned and I found myself looking at a face. It was barely recognizable under a mask of swelling blisters, but I knew that low brow and flattened head.

Prometheus Piggety stared at me through the slits of his swollen scarlet eyelids. Time was petrified and no sound came now from his gaping mouth. Two ballooned hands broke through the surface, bound at the wrists, reaching out to me in supplication. But then the head went down, the mouth filling with scalding water, desperately trying to spit it out, but the water came over the nose and the tub became a frothing cauldron as the water closed over him.

I cried out something but I do not know what. I probably called to God again. But there was only Sidney Grice, clicking switches and pulling levers behind me. He managed to stop the motor and put it into reverse, and it was only then that I noticed the chains hanging loose into the tub. They straightened and tightened, and the motor whirred and strained before it stopped running. It had been strong enough to lower him but was not able to pull him out.

Sidney Grice ran round the tub and turned a horizontal brass wheel by its handle on top. There was a gurgling noise and the water began to fall, and all I could see was a scalded lump like something in a butcher's shop, lying in the bottom of the tub, trussed with silken cords tied in neat knots to a hook on the chain belt.

Sidney Grice re-sheathed his blade and used the cane to turn Prometheus Piggety's head up, but there was nothing distinguishable as a human face any more except the teeth, still gaping in wordless agony through a bloated fluid-filled purple sac. He withdrew his cane and a long strip of flesh came away with it.

'The gypsy was right about him dying in the bath before he was eighty,' I said.

'And Piggety was right about one thing too,' he observed bleakly. 'Writhing alive in boiling water does loosen the skin.'

47
TOUCHING THE STARS

There was vomit on the floor about two yards from the tub and Sidney Grice crouched to survey it.

'Mutton, roast potatoes, carrots and peas, and what looks like plum pudding.'

I turned away. 'Does it matter?' I was aware that my voice was trembling.

'All evidence matters. How important it is remains to be seen. Assuming he produced this, Piggety did not chew his food very thoroughly. Either this was his habit or he was in a hurry today.' He leaned over the pool and breathed in as one might with a rare truffle. 'No smell of wine, beer or spirits, so this was not some drunken escapade.' He took a cigar tube from his satchel and unscrewed the top to bring out a medical thermometer in cotton wool. He unwrapped it, shook the mercury into the bulb, checked the reading and inserted it into a big fatty lump of mutton. He brought out his hunter and flipped open the lid. 'When I was a child I had scarlet fever,' he told me, 'and was kept out of school for several weeks.'

'A sensible precaution,' I said, trying to block out the image of what lay in the tub behind me.

'I have to confess,' he continued, 'that, when the nurse used a thermometer, I deliberately tampered with the results.'

'You warmed it up to get more time off school,' I guessed and he frowned.

'Quite the reverse. I cooled it so as to be able to return to school. I was concerned that the masters were teaching my fellows without me there to correct them.'

'Your teachers must have loved you.' I spoke automatically, glad of anything to distract me.

'I can truthfully say that they did' — he clipped his watch shut — 'not.' He stooped. 'Vomit travels an interesting thermal voyage. The food may be at a higher or, with cooks like mine, lower, temperature than the body. It then reaches equilibrium with the stomach, which is two or three degrees above body temperature of ninety-eight point four. Once expelled it cools to room temperature, the time taken to do so depending on the temperature difference, the flow of air and the insulating properties of the substance ingested. This is at room temperature and therefore produced at least one hour ago.' He wiped the thermometer and put it away. 'What is that?'

There were a thousand stars sparkling on the wooden floor and I crouched to examine them. 'Powdered glass.'

'What sort of glass?'

'How many sorts of glass are there?' I put my finger out.

'Twenty-two. Do *not* touch it.' He came over. 'The glass of my eye is very different from that of a whisky tumbler, a house window, a church window, a pair of spectacles, et cetera, et cetera.' He bobbed down beside me and clipped his pince-nez on. 'Et cetera,' he said absently. 'Note the line here.' I could just make out what he meant — a faint arced impression. 'See how the glass on the concave side is much finer than that on the convex. What does that tell you?'

'The glass was broken and then crushed by something curved,' I suggested.

'Such as?'

'The heel of a boot.'

'Well done.' He brought out a six-inch steel rule and measured the line in both directions. 'Not Mr Piggety's boot. He had unusually large feet and this is small enough to be a woman's —'

'Primrose McKay,' I said. 'She would have enjoyed doing this.'

Sidney Grice put his head to one side briefly before he declared, 'The curve would indicate that the wearer was standing facing the pulley some three and a quarter feet away from it.' He took his rule and scraped the powder either side of the line into two envelopes, then folded and sealed them with four rubber bands, making notes on them with a stubby pencil. 'What are you looking at?'

I bent down. 'Just behind you. It looks like droplets of blood.'

He shuffled round. 'Good perception. They were not easily distinguishable in the shadows, though, of course, I would have observed them myself. Thirty-three drops, the largest being one eighth of an inch in an apparently random pattern over . . .' he held his ruler above them, 'an area of two foot four inches by one foot nine.' He dabbed a couple with his fingertip. 'And freshly clotted. Clearly from a minor haemorrhage and therefore of major importance. You may write this in your journal as the first clue you have ever discovered, though it will take my intelligence to calculate its significance.'

'Of course.' I spoke automatically.

'Right.' He steadied himself on the wall to get up. 'What now?' And with a shock I remembered.

'Those poor cats,' I said and ran back through.

'I have turned the hot water pipes off,' my guardian said, but the room was stifling and I hastily cupped my handkerchief over my nose again. 'If you try to find the tap which turns the water on, I will open the skylights.'

I ran up the aisle and found a tap, and the moment I turned it there was a clear hiss and water trickled into the bowls of every cage.

'I fear we are too late,' my guardian said.

'I am astonished that you care.'

'I have a degree of respect for cats,' my guardian said. 'They kill for food and they kill for pleasure. It is all the same to them and they make no attempt to wrap their cruelty in sentimental fabrics.'

'Good,' I said. 'Then if we find one alive —'

'No, March.'

'It would get rid of the mice.'

'It is just as likely to bring them into the house.'

I went up and down the aisles. One fluffy white ball was moving slowly, crawling towards the fresh water with sawdust in its

388

fur. It managed to raise its head and flop it over the rim but it seemed that the effort had been too much for it until I saw a pink tongue creep out, curl and scoop up a drink. Four more times it lapped before it struggled to its feet.

'I have a friend who wants a pet,' I said. 'I shall take her.'

'How do you know it is a female?'

There was a box with some straw in the corner and I placed her carefully in it.

'Because,' I said, 'she has spirit. Perhaps my friend will call her that.'

'Spirit,' Sidney Grice repeated thoughtfully. 'What a puerile name. Well . . .' He bent, reached into his satchel and crouched to pincer something on the floor with a short pair of tweezers. 'What have we here?'

I looked at the pallid soft squirming creature in his grasp. 'A maggot.' I recoiled.

'What a fine fat specimen he is too.' He popped it into a test tube.

I took a bowl of water to put in the box. 'What shall we do now?'

He recorked the tube. 'I shall summon the police. You shall go home. The cab is still outside.'

'But I might be able to help here.'

'Help who? Piggety is beyond help and I do not need any.' He touched my arm. 'Go home, March. I shall wait here. This is no place for anyone with human feelings.'

'And you?'

'Me?' He guided me up the steps. 'I am in my element. This is quite the finest murder I have witnessed in three years.'

'God help you,' I said.

'He is welcome to try.' We stepped outside and the stink of the cesspit suddenly smelled like fresh air.

48
Parasites, Monsters and Fat Hens

My guardian saw me across the jetty to our cab.

'You there,' he shouted at a small boy who was peering out from behind a capstan. 'I paid you to keep a lookout.'

The boy hobbled towards us, using a rough length of wood to support his bandy legs. 'Sorry, mister,' he said. 'We was doin' it like you said, three of us watchin' all the time, but then 'e came and chased us orf and we was too terrorized to 'ang abart.'

'Who chased you?' I said.

'The monster, miss. 'Orrible he was, like Frankunstein, and I ain't larkin'.'

'So why did you come back?' Sidney Grice raised his cane. 'Except for a well-earned thrashing?'

The boy dodged clumsily, almost slipping over on to the wet cobbles. 'I lorst a penny and I fought I might find it 'ere.'

'Here it is.' I reached into my purse. 'Only

it was a sixpence.' His hand was gloved in warts.

'Parasites, every one of them.' Sidney Grice checked his pockets as the boy scuttled off. 'Mind they do not bleed you dry as they suck the lifeblood of our nation.'

He helped me into the cab.

'I think we have a few crumbs to spare yet,' I said.

It was a long slow ride home, but I was scarcely aware of anything around me. All I could see through the fog was the torment of the frothing water and all I could hear were the screams and frantic splashes silenced at last by death.

I shook my head, but you cannot shake off memories like ants from an apple. They cling and burrow and they breed in your mind, and I sometimes think they poison it. I closed my eyes and put my thumbs over my ears and my face in my fingers, but the sights and sounds only grew more intense and I was not even aware we had stopped until the cabby leaned down and poked my shoulder with his whip handle.

'All right, miss? Or do you want to go round again? It's your dosh.'

I paid him and went up the steps over the cellar moat and into the house, where Molly was waving a feather duster around lethargically.

'Oh, miss, you look awful, even awfuler than what you usually does. You look like you've seen a phantagasm.'

'Worse than that, Molly,' I whispered. 'Much worse.'

I turned my back on her but she could see my face in the mirror. 'Don't cry, miss.' I spun back to her. 'Why not? Somebody ought to in this godforsaken house.' I brushed past her and ran upstairs, into my room, the only place I could call mine now, and even then only by invitation of a man I hardly knew.

I poured myself a gin and held it in my mouth but it could not wash away the taste and, when I swallowed, it could not warm me.

What would you have done? How could you have comforted me? This was a world more terrible than any battle you ever dreamed of. At least you would have known who you were fighting. At least you believed you would win and could dream of glory. Oh, Edward, I thank God you never had my dreams.

You would have held me, but you could not have helped. Nobody could help me now. We all make our own way into the next world and sometimes there is only the hope that it will be better, and the slippery rocks of faith to cling to.

I went into the bathroom and ripped off my clothes, and sat and waited for the tub to fill. But the rush of water and the rising steam frightened me and I turned off the taps and pulled out the plug and washed myself all over, standing at the sink, but the stench of death was too deep to scrub away and the towel did not seem able to get me dry. I took my bottle of Fougère perfume and put a drop on my face and another on my neck, and slopped it into my cupped hand and rubbed it over my untouched, untouchable body.

Back in my room I put on my black dress, the one Papa bought me to meet Princess Beatrice but which I wore instead to his funeral. I had another gin and went back into the corridor and up to the attic floor where only Molly lived. There was a skylight at the end which served as a fire escape. I hooked down the ladder and climbed on to the roof and sat on the wall, smoking a cigarette and watching the traffic, a line of omnibuses with loud young men on the top deck, throwing apple cores at each other and pedestrians, and the busy people marching past the vendors unheeding of their cries — *Pretty pins for the ladies, Buy my fat hens.* A knife grinder was dragging his treadle-stone along the side of the road. *Bring awt yer blades, yer scissors and yer axes.*

I stubbed out my cigarette in the wide, lead-lined gutter and wished I had brought my flask up with me, and that I was somewhere else, anywhere except this seething sulphurous city.

If there had been time to think it over I would probably have handled things better, but you had a regimental dinner so I did not see you that night and the next morning you were off on patrol. In the three weeks you were supposed to be away I would have cooled down. I would probably have discussed the letter with my father, but you came to the hospital just before muster to say goodbye.

I was busy and cross because pilfering was becoming a major problem and a consignment of bandages had disappeared. I went outside to meet you.

'I just came to say —'

But I cut you short. 'What?'

'Goodbye,' you said warily.

'Is that it?'

'Well . . . yes.'

'Goodbye then.'

You tried to kiss me but I twisted away.

'March, what is it?'

'I was hoping you would tell me that.'

You looked genuinely confused. 'I honestly do not know what you are talking about.' And you were not a good enough actor to have faked it.

'Your father,' I said, and the light dawned. It was one of the rare times I ever saw you angry, and the only time ever with me.

'You read my father's correspondence?'

And instantly I felt guilty. 'I could not help it.'

You raised your voice. 'You could not help opening my writing case, taking out his letter and reading it? Some things are private, March.'

'We do not have secrets from each other.'

Harry Baddington appeared, swaggering down the path towards us. 'Eddy,' he hollered. I hated him calling you that. 'The men are waiting.'

'I have to go. We will talk about it when I get home.' You leaned forward and I turned so that you pecked my cheek.

You stiffened. 'Goodbye, March.'

'Edward,' I called before you had gone three paces. I wanted to say I loved you and to take care, but I only said, 'Who is Hester Sandler?'

'We will talk when I return,' you replied firmly.

How fine you looked as you strode away, your polished boots kicking up the dust, your helmet white in the white sun and your sabre swinging by your side. I think I saw you as you rode off, but the sun and the dust and the tears were in my eyes.

49
THE SLEEP OF THE UNJUST

The sun was setting over the rooftops —
though I could hardly see it through the
tainted air, just the darkening and redden-
ing of the distance — before I clambered
down. I changed again into my old mau-
veine dress and went downstairs.

Sidney Grice sat upright in his armchair.
He had taken his eye out and was massag-
ing around it and wincing.

'I used to go on the roof,' he told me
without opening his eyes, 'and wonder at
this city of mine.'

'Yours?'

'Everything is mine in my world.' He
opened his eyes. 'Sit down, March.' His
socket was streaked violet and the patch lay
on his knee. He rubbed his good eye and
looked at me. 'No one should see what you
have seen today.'

'You cope.'

He wiped around his socket with the back

of his hand. 'If I do not cope nobody else will. Then who will stop these things happening?'

'I could say the same.' I fiddled with a button on my dress.

'But you are a young woman and women have finer feelings than men.'

'And my finer feelings tell me that I can help. Do you think you find murder more abominable than I do?'

'No but —'

'There are no *no buts,*' I reminded him. 'You will not push me out of the house quite as easily as that, Mr G.'

'I was not trying to evict you, merely holding the door open.'

'Then I suggest you close it before we both catch our deaths.'

Sidney Grice's mouth twitched slightly. 'Very well, March, but you must promise to tell me when you have had enough.'

'I will have had enough when there are no more crimes,' I said.

'Which will never happen.'

'Precisely.'

He replaced his patch and tied it behind his head. 'If only your mother could see you now.'

'Tell me about her.'

My guardian frowned. 'You have one failing in common, a sense of humour. She could light up a room with her wit — unfortunately. Otherwise there is no resemblance. You inherited your father's rugged facade but your mother was the loveliest of creatures.' He pinched the dimple in his chin. 'Or so they say.' He thinned his lips and stretched back to pull the bell. 'Quigley came and went. Accidental death, of course. According to our good inspector, Piggety must have been testing his own machinery and got entangled in the silk cords.'

'Nobody can accidentally entangle themselves in several neat knots,' I said.

'He knows that as well as you or I.' My guardian polished his fingernails on his trousers. 'I shall be glad when the promotions are decided next week. The man has never been much of a help, but now he is a positive obstruction.'

'How does he sleep at night?' I asked and Mr G regarded his fingertips.

'People talk about the sleep of the just.' He tugged his earlobe. 'But it is the wicked who have the best nights. Who have they to fear but themselves?' He crooked a finger. 'By the way, you left something at the factory.' He pointed to a tea chest on the floor by his desk.

I went over and something moved. 'Spirit!

How could I have forgotten you?' I bent down and lifted her out, and she opened her eyes and mewed silently.

'I hope your friend takes better care of it,' he said.

'Which friend?'

'The one you are giving it to.'

'Oh yes.'

'The only survivor,' he told me.

I stroked under her chin and Spirit nuzzled her nose into my palm.

You got a letter from your mother and you wept. There was no bad news, just family gossip and wishing you a happy Christmas. You made me swear not to tell anyone but there was no need. I would never have embarrassed you in front of your comrades. After all I never told how the brigadier cried when his pet canary died. He had just taught it to say 'God save the queen' when Dinah, my cat, got it. It was all my father could do to stop him executing her on the spot.

Three days later Dinah went missing and everyone, except the brigadier, made a search for her, but she seemed to have vanished from the face of the earth.

Six weeks later you brought me a cat, a lovely tortoiseshell with one black paw. You had purchased her from your *cha walla,* who told you he had heard of my loss and shipped it from England at great expense, and charged you accordingly.

'I know she can never replace Dinah,' you said, 'but I thought she looked quite similar.'

I picked her out of the basket and held her to me.

'You see. She likes you already,' you said.

'Oh, Edward, you pickle,' I said. 'This *is* Dinah.'

'Well, I'm fried.'

'You certainly have been,' I said and kissed you on the tip of your nose.

50
THREE-TOED SLOTHS AND CAPTAIN DUBOIS

'Let us imagine,' Sidney Grice said, settling into his armchair, 'what happened at that vile cat factory. And by *imagine,* I mean attempt to logically reconstruct what happened. It is not an invitation to unleash your lurid imagination. First of all, who sent the telegram?'

'Either Mr Piggety or the murderer.'

'And how will you find out which?'

'Me?'

'Yes. You are always whining in your diaries about me not giving you any responsibility.'

'Have you been reading my journal again?'

'Of course.'

'But I keep it hidden and the key is always on my person.'

'It is impossible to hide anything from me,' my guardian said. 'And as for locks . . .' He piffed. 'A three-toed sloth could open the average diary clasp with a parsnip.

Proceed.'

'My journals are personal.'

'Much too personal at times,' Sidney Grice said. 'Proceed.'

I let the matter drop. 'I have already asked the woman at the telegram office, as you know.'

'And how much did you give her?'

'Well, nothing.'

'Nothing?' He could not have been more astonished had I told him I was Cardinal Newman. 'Nobody with an income of below five hundred a year remembers anything for free. A telegrapher requires a shilling to recall facts as accurately as his or her primitive cranium permits. Railway porters' underdeveloped memories can be stimulated for one and sixpence and guards' for a florin. It is all in Beckham's *Financial Inducements of the Lower Orders,* though some of his figures are out of date. He lists three classes of our inferiors who will talk for a farthing, whereas I have never heard anything worth listening to for under a penny.' Molly came in with the tea tray. She was cleanly turned out and had not spilled a drop on the cloth. 'Bring a fresh pot in twenty-four minutes.'

'Certainly, sir.'

'She must be an identical twin,' I joked as

she left, and my guardian considered the remark.

'I hope not,' he said. 'Mercy — and never was a child so cruelly misnamed — awaits Her Majesty's pleasure in Broadmoor Criminal Lunatic Asylum, and will still be awaiting it on the day she expires.'

I put a strainer on his cup. 'What did she do?'

'Not a fraction of what she planned to do.'

I could see that he was not going to tell me any more, so I said, 'Are you suggesting that I return to the office and offer the desk clerk a bribe?'

'There is no point in striking when the iron is cold and has been taken away.' He levelled the surface of the sugar with the back of a spoon. 'I mention it only for future reference. So . . .' He eased the spoon in, taking great care not to disturb the smooth surface. 'We have two possibilities. First, Mr Piggety really did have information.'

'But why instruct us to wait until three o'clock when he described it as *vital*?'

'A moot point which leads us to suspect that the second possibility is more likely to be correct' — he plunged the spoon up to its hilt — 'that the murderer lured us there just in time to witness the crime, but too late to be able to prevent it.'

405

'How could somebody know this morning exactly what time he would die?' I asked and my guardian pursed his lips.

'How long do you think it would have taken those cats to die?'

'I am not sure.' I poured our teas. 'In that heat and with no water, perhaps two days.'

Sidney Grice straightened the tray. 'Captain François Dubois of the French Foreign Legion did some research on this topic during his country's typically inept intrusion into Mexico. He was concerned about the effects of heat and dehydration on his men, and experimented with dogs in cages in the full sun. He was astonished at how soon they succumbed, some as quickly as two hours. Now cats are hardier than their creepily sycophantic canine counterparts, plus it would take a long time for a room of that size to heat up, even with its insulation and instant hot water supply. According to my mercury thermometer, the water was two hundred and nine degrees Fahrenheit, the pipes were ten inches diameter and, since they go up and down all the rows, two hundred and forty-two feet long — the room must be . . .' he looked about him as if we were still in it, covering our noses from the stench of nearly five thousand dead cats, 'seven thousand, nine hundred cubic feet.

The room temperature was previously set at sixty-two degrees and rose to one hundred and four. So that would take . . . ?' He snapped his fingers at me.

'Four or five hours,' I hazarded.

'Not bad.' Sidney Grice looked mildly impressed. 'So, if we assume that the cats survived for another four or five hours in those conditions . . . ?' He pointed at me.

'We can estimate that the murderer went there some time between six and eight o'clock this morning,' I said. 'But why would he turn the heating up when —'

'Stop,' my guardian protested as if in pain. 'Three logical solecisms in twenty-three words and you have not even finished your sentence. It is more than the human frame can endure.'

'I was only making assumptions, as you have been doing,' I said and he winced.

'I have made twelve assumptions in four minutes, some of them unspoken. The difference being that I know these false friends for what they are, whereas you think of conjecture as fact. First, we cannot know that the murderer turned the heating up, second, we cannot know that it was turned up the moment the murderer arrived and, third, we do not know that the murderer is a man. However, for the sake of linguistic

407

brevity, we will agree to refer to the murderer as *he* for the time being.'

I spooned two sugars into my tea. 'The more I think about it, the more I am convinced we should be saying *she*.' I poured some milk and stirred. 'The cruelty of his death and the senseless killing of all those cats — it all reeks of Primrose McKay to me.'

'I hope so.' Mr G sneezed. 'It would be pleasant indeed to put that young lady into a condemned cell, but I shall stick with *he* for the time being.' He blew his nose. 'To continue — getting into the building was not necessarily a problem. He may have just knocked and been admitted. Perhaps Piggety knew or was expecting him. And, when he left, the killer locked up and posted me the key.'

'Mr Piggety only had one key,' I remembered.

'And, unless you are acquainted with Messrs Frankie Zammit or George Henderson, you cannot get a Williams-Hazard deadlock key made except by the manufacturers, and that is easily checked.'

'The key arrived here just after two and it takes a good half-hour to get here, so —' A thought struck me. 'The murderer was probably at his work when I arrived. But why did he not lock the door?'

Sidney Grice tasted his tea. 'There are two likely reasons. Either he was about to leave or he was waiting for you.'

'But why would he expect me to turn up?'

Mr G rotated his saucer. 'You have heard of Pandora?'

'Of course.' I reached for the milk jug. 'She was told not to look in a box, but she opened it and released chaos into the world.'

He turned the saucer back a fraction. 'Tell a woman not to do something and what will she do?'

'Very often the opposite,' I admitted.

He blew his nose. 'So tell a woman that she must on no account arrive before three?'

'And curiosity might get the better of her.' I splashed myself with the milk. 'But he would have had to hide behind that door for hours on the chance that I would turn up.'

He passed me a napkin to dab my sleeve. 'He may be a very patient man or more likely he had somebody alert him — an accomplice possibly.'

'The children,' I said. 'There were girls throwing stones against the wall. They could have been signalling that I was approaching . . . But why would he . . .' I put my hand to my mouth.

'There are two vats.' My guardian's face was sombre.

51
FLASH MOBSMEN AND ROYAL GARDEN PARTIES

It took a while for that thought to sink in and even then I could not imagine it — being stripped and trussed and suspended on that slow ride alongside Prometheus Piggety, watching each other's terror, feeling the first scalding splashes, hearing each other's desperate thrashings, knowing that all I could hope for was what I feared most — death.

I wondered if my guardian was as shocked as I by the thought of what I had escaped but he was humming lightly now, and tapping an irregular rhythm on his leg, and each of his eyes looked as dead as the other.

I stood up unsteadily and he rose from his chair, ready to catch me, but I would not swoon into his arms like the helpless school-girl he imagined me to be. He stepped forward but I held out my hand and sat back again with as much dignity as I could salvage.

'You look ill, March. Have you been eating enough vegetables?' He scrutinized me with concern. 'What is so amusing?'

'Enough?' I laughed louder than I intended. 'I have eaten nothing but wretched vegetables since I came here.'

My guardian said, 'Kindly moderate your language.'

'But they *are* wretched,' I insisted. 'They are miserable and soggy and cold. Besides, there is nothing wrong with the word.'

He puffed through his lips. 'You said it as if it were an expletive, and a lady should never say anything that sounds even remotely like an expletive. I had a cousin who once said *affable* in such a way that she was never invited to another royal garden party again.'

'Why are we discussing royal garden parties?'

Sidney Grice brushed an invisible speck from his right shoulder. 'Because it has stopped you shaking. Deliberate verbal distraction is an art usually only practised by flash mobsmen, Whig politicians and the better class of pickpockets, but it can be a useful technique. When Maximilian Hurst was preparing to assassinate me I initiated a conversation about the merits of electrical lighting, which I had to keep going for over an hour before the police arrived.'

'That would never have worked with a woman,' I said.

'Maximilian Hurst *was* a woman,' he told me, 'which was only apparent after she was executed by firing squad in Belarus.'

'Do you really think I would have been boiled alive?' For all his ramblings, I could not get the idea out of my head.

Mr G yawned. 'It is not unlikely that the murderer would have tried, but I would probably have saved you.'

'Only probably?'

'Most probably.'

I lifted the teapot lid and there was only a mound of soggy leaves. 'But why would anybody want to kill me?'

'To wound *me.*'

I was not in the mood to pursue that train of thought. 'So before eight o'clock this morning when the telegram was sent, the murderer had estimated the time of death,' I said. 'He must have been very confident that the chain belt would work, to go off and leave Mr Piggety unattended — and he knew exactly how long it would take. If he had called us too early we could have rescued Mr Piggety and he might have been able to identify his would-be killer.'

My guardian considered the matter, then

sprang up and went to his desk. It was littered with the day's envelopes. He took the bands off one and emptied the contents on to his blotter. I went over to look. It was a little heap of the glass fragments. Sidney Grice spread it out with the edge of a rule and set aside one of the larger pieces.

'Look at this.' He handed me his magnifying glass. 'There is a very slight but definite curve in it.'

He went back and emptied a second envelope of more finely powdered glass next to the first. 'You are a girl and therefore addicted to jigsaws —'

'I quite liked them when I *was* a girl,' I said, 'but I am a woman now.'

My guardian leaned back to look at me. He raised his pince-nez to his nose and let it fall on its string. 'A caterpillar may call itself a butterfly,' he said, 'but it has not the beauty and neither can it fly.' He placed the rule on his blotter. 'So, if you were to indulge in your juvenile passions and assemble these pieces as a disc, what diameter would you expect it to be?'

'It is difficult to say.'

'If it were an easy question, I should have asked Molly.'

'Two inches,' I guessed and he waved the rule in my face.

'What do I have on me that is glass and two inches in diameter?'

'Your eye,' I said, and he rolled his good one.

'My eye is not a flat disc and it is not that wide. I am not a horse. Think, girl. Clear out all that coagulated poetical flotsam with which you clog your brain and concentrate.'

'Your watch face.'

'At last.' He raked his hair back. 'So, armed with our conjectures, I think we can envision the series of events with a reasonable degree of confidence, but first, we have another urgent matter to attend to. That wastrel girl has not brought any more tea.'

He re-crossed the room and grasped the bell rope.

52
THE ETERNAL SCREAM

Sidney Grice still had his hand on the rope when the door flew open and Molly with it, her hat flapping and the tea spilling out of the spout as she rushed to put the tray down on the central table.

'Ever so sorry, Mr G,' she said. 'But —'

He jumped to his feet, tight with indignation. 'If you ever call me that again you will leave this house immediately.'

Molly drew back nervously. 'Sorry, sir, but I heard Miss Middleton call you that and I thought you liked it.'

'When you are my ward you may call me that, but not one particle of a second beforehand.'

Molly's eyes lit up. 'Oh, when shall that be, sir? Someday soon, I trust. Oh, I shall be fienderishly happy to stop this diresome work. The hours are so long and the pay so tiddlerish. Why, Miss Middleton and I will be like sisters. We shall comb each other's

416

hair and I shall call her *March.*'

'Oh, good grief.' Sidney Grice sat down.

'Mr Grice is not going to make you his ward, Molly,' I told her, and she jerked her head sideways as if she had been stung. 'He was just telling you not to call him that.'

'So he's —'

'I am afraid not,' I said and Molly ran her tongue around the inside of her cheek.

'Just as well.' She scratched her arm vigorously. 'I should have to stop cursing and stealing from the kitchen, and I enjoy both those things.' She cleared our tray and replaced it with the new one.

'Why were you so long?' her employer asked and Molly grimaced.

'Oh, sir, it was gruelsome. Cook got her ear caught in that automaticated potato masherer what you invented.'

'But how?' I asked.

'For once in my life I do not want to know.' Sidney Grice put his fingertips to his temples and whisked his hands apart.

'She was trying to hear if there was anything in there.'

'And was there?' I asked.

'Just her ear, miss,' she told me.

'Go away,' her employer said.

'What?' Molly screwed up her face and her apron. 'For ever?'

He half-stood. 'Y—'

'Just until you are called again,' I put in hurriedly. 'Is Cook all right?'

Molly wrinkled her nose. 'As right as a body can be with an ear and half a finger scrungulated.'

'What happened to her finger?'

'She was trying to get her ear back.'

'Does she need a doctor?'

'Yes,' Sidney Grice snapped. 'They both need an alienist.'

'A what, sir?'

'A man who thinks he can cure lunatics and is therefore more delusional than his patients,' he told her. 'Get out . . . Now . . . and do not even think about curtsying . . . Go.'

'Thank you, sir.' Molly froze mid-bob and left the room.

He looked at the tray. 'Give me two half-good reasons why you stopped me sacking that lumpen sluggard?'

'Molly may be scatter brained —'

'There is no *may be* about it.'

'But she is hard-working and loyal. She would die for you.'

He grunted. 'I wish she would get a move on.'

'And besides, nobody else would tolerate your behaviour.'

He tugged at his scarred earlobe. 'That is true. I once got through six servants in a week.'

I righted a tipped teacup and put it on the table. 'So what do you think happened at Mr Piggety's?'

'I can only make preternaturally intelligent guesses at present,' he said as I poured. 'Most probably,' he inspected his tea despondently, 'the murderer or murderers —'

'Why the plural?' I had an itch in the sole of my right foot.

'I will come to that, but I will stick to the masculine singular for now.' He sampled his tea. 'Actually, this is not too bad . . . The murderer comes to Piggety's Cat Factory. He gains entry without any force, so either Mr Piggety knew or was expecting him or the killer managed to talk his way in. They go through the cattery and into the boiling room.'

I tried to wriggle my toes around but the itch was getting worse.

'Could he have gone in through the skinning room?' I shuddered at the very idea of such a place.

Mr G crossed his legs. 'I looked around after you had gone. It has no means of access other than the door into the killing room.'

I pressed the sole of my boot on to the edge of the hearth and eased my foot up and down. 'So they go through to the boiling room. What then?'

'Mr Piggety undresses himself.' He curled his lips at the unpleasantness of the image. 'The clothes were not ripped off him — they have not been damaged. Indeed, they were neatly folded and his jacket was hung on a peg. So how do you make a man undress himself?'

'By seduction,' I suggested and he coloured.

'What a filthy idea, but one we must consider' — Mr G uncrossed his legs — 'and, I believe, dismiss. A man in what I must call *a state of excitement* does not lay out his attire as if it is on display in a draper's shop.'

The itch was driving me to distraction. 'At gunpoint.' I stamped my foot.

'Temper,' he said absently. 'Possibly, but then he would be even less concerned about sartorial matters.'

'I do not think he was overly concerned about them at the best of times.' I remembered Mr Piggety's shiny-elbowed coat, stained shirt and crumpled trousers.

'Besides which,' Sidney Grice took a sudden interest in the palm of his left hand, running a finger over the creases, 'you would have to put the gun down to tie him up, at which point he is going to struggle.'

'How do you know he did not?' I tickled my palm in the hope that creating another itch would get rid of the first, but my hand did not itch and my foot felt as though I were standing in an ants' nest.

'Because the knots were tied neatly and methodically, which is why we must consider the possibility of a second murderer — one to hold the gun and the other to truss their victim up. Which leads me to the rather alarming thought that these murders may involve at least three different felons — one poisoner for Horatio Green, for poisoners rarely resort to violent means, and two killers for Slab, Jackaman and Piggety.'

The silhouette of an omnibus crossed the room, its top passengers moving in a shadow-puppet display over his bookcase. 'And Braithwaite,' I suggested.

'Not my case.' He folded his arms.

I put the strainer back over my cup, but there was more tea in the tray than in the pot now. 'At this rate the murderers will outnumber the victims.' I got up to fetch a wooden rule from his desk.

'That is not unknown. Most of this peculiar nation murdered Charles I.'

'What if he were knocked out?' I suggested, and Sidney Grice smoothed his hair back.

'He could have been, but I doubt it. If you render a man unconscious with a blow to the head, you run the risk that he will not regain consciousness. He may even die and whoever killed Mr Piggety did not want him to die peacefully, otherwise he would have been tipped straight into the vat — whereas Mr Piggety knew exactly what was happening to him and probably for a number of hours. That is why he expelled his gastric contents.'

'But who would hate Mr Piggety so much as to kill him so cruelly?' I eased the rule down the side of my boot but could not get it to where it might have helped.

'Every man has his enemies. Possibly a cat-lover who knew what he was intending to do and thought to give him a taste of his own medicine. More likely, they did not hate him at all. I am increasingly convinced that the person the murderer really hates is' — he doodled with his forefinger in a puddle of tea — 'me.'

'Why are you taking it personally? The next victim might easily have been me.'

'I only take things personally when they are.' He eased his head back as if he had a stiff neck. 'And every step that has been taken seems calculated to wreck my career and therefore me, for no man is more than what he does and most people are a great deal less. What on earth are you doing?'

I pulled out the rule. 'I have an itch.'

My guardian looked revolted. 'Ladies,' he declared, '*never* itch.'

'How lucky we are.' I put the rule down with exaggerated care. 'So you think that somebody killed four men so brutally just to harm you?'

He took up the rule. 'It is a possibility that I must bear in mind.'

'But that is inhuman,' I said as my guardian measured his hand at several points.

'Unfortunately, it is all too human. I know of no beast whose savagery can even approach that of mankind, and Mr Piggety's death was one of the most ghastly it has ever been my privilege to witness.'

'You regard it as a cachet?'

'Death is a secretive fellow. It is always an honour to watch him at work.'

I closed my eyes. 'Then I have been privileged a great many times . . . if only I had realized.' I opened my eyes to see my guardian standing at my side and holding out his hand, and I reached up and he took mine awkwardly, like a bachelor uncle being given a baby and unsure what to do with it.

'The loss of loved ones is never a privilege,' he said, 'but to be with them when they are lost, is.'

'Not always,' I said.

'I know you had loved ones you would rather had not died, but would you want them to have died alone?' His voice was soft and his hand closed on mine, but I pulled away.

'I am sorry,' I whispered as I stood up to leave.

Sidney Grice winced and stepped aside, and I ran up the stairs, threw myself on to my bed and buried my face in my pillow to let the scream escape. But a scream is like an ocean; you can only drain it by creating another, and pain does not end just because you are weary of it.

What passed through your mind as I cradled your head that last time? Did your love turn all at once to a sense of betrayal? 'God bless you,' I said and I thought you nodded. You mouthed my name in flecks of your own blood.

My father stood beside me. 'Dear God in heaven, March.'

'Dead.' I mouthed the word as if not hearing it could make it less true. 'I have killed you.' My lips could not frame that sentence any more than my mind could reject it. I kept it, nurtured it and let it grow, four words which were my birth and became my life.

53
Rabbits and the Marquis de Sade

I washed my face in cold water with a rose-scented soap, smoked a cigarette out of the window, drank a large gin, sucked on a parma violet and was making my way down the stairs as my guardian came up them for dinner. He did not speak and neither did I.

We sat at opposite ends of the table, listening to the dumb waiter creak up from the kitchen. Mr G got up and brought out two plates, and put a dreary khaki slush in front of me.

'I fear you are too distressed to continue.' He returned to his seat. 'It cannot be easy being a member of the weaker sex.'

'I would not know,' I retorted, 'being a woman.' He looked puzzled. 'Anyway,' I continued, 'your concern is misplaced. Please go on with your reconstruction.'

And without the slightest pause he did so. 'Prometheus Piggety is trussed naked in silk cords and fastened to the first hook on the chain track. The killing tub is filled with boiling water and the engine started. This, I suspect, is when the drinking water in the cattery was turned off and the heating turned on.'

'The murderer would not have known how all the valves worked, so perhaps the cats' suffering was accidental,' I suggested with more hope than conviction.

'How did you know which tap turned on their water?' Sidney Grice polished his pince-nez.

'Because it was labelled,' I said.

'I rest my case.' He uncrossed his legs. 'We are not dealing with nice people, March. The suffering of creatures would have given them nothing but pleasure. I shall not soil my lips with the name of the French rascal whose practices they have adopted.'

'I am quite familiar with the story of the Marquis de Sade,' I said and my guardian drew back.

'How have the minds of the young become so polluted?'

'Why do men confuse innocence with ignorance?' I demanded and he wrinkled his brow.

'Because someone who is ignorant of a vice is not tempted to indulge in it.'

'But may be more easily lured into it,' I said.

'In my experience it is more often the women who do the luring,' he retorted. 'But, as always, your inanities are distracting me from the matter in hand.' He rubbed his left cheekbone. 'Where was I?'

'Turning the heating on,' I reminded him.

'Ah yes. Let me see.' Sidney Grice scribbled a few numbers on the tablecloth. 'There were twenty hooks on each chain. According to *Bridlington's Statistics,* the average fully grown cat weighs three pounds and two ounces, which would make a total load of somewhere in the region of one thousand ounces. Piggety must have weighed something like nine stone or two thousand, two hundred and forty ounces, which is more than twenty times the load that the system was designed to carry. Now, one of the many reasons that the electric motor will never replace steam is that it has a poor torque. For every ten per cent you increase the load, the motor will slow by twenty per cent. With the relatively large weight of Piggety, the progress would have been marvellously slow, but how do you calculate how slow it is?'

'You time it over a measured distance,' I said.

'Mr Piggety may have been an unpleasant man but he was no more asinine than average. He would have known what was happening to him. So what does he do?'

'He struggles and kicks out and knocks the watch that his murderer is timing him with on to the floor.'

'Or more likely he catches his persecutor on the nose — hence the blood droplets. The killer then drops the watch and accidentally steps on the glass.'

'So the murderer calculates when Mr Piggety will reach the tub, leaves him to his fate, locks up and sends you a telegram and the key,' I said. 'But why not send the telegram and key together by the same messenger?'

'He sends the telegram early to make sure I get it, and the key later so that I cannot enter the factory too soon and so that I have to stay here waiting for it.' Mr G tucked into his dinner.

'Is it not time we visited the last member of the club?' I proposed, and wondered what he had on his plate that warranted chewing.

'Ah yes, Mr Warrington Tusker Gallop.' He took a sip of water. 'We shall call upon Mr Gallop soon and unexpectedly, in order to catch him unawares at his place of business which is conveniently close by . . .' He winced.

'In Charlotte Street,' I put in as his fingers went to claw the air an inch from his face.

'Blast this thing.' He squeezed out his eye and cupped a hand over his socket.

'Perhaps if you left it out for a few days it might become less inflamed,' I said. 'Then I could help you make a fresh impression.'

My guardian put out his right hand. 'Stop,' he said. 'I can tolerate the pain but I could not bear it if I thought you cared.'

I did not know what to say. I wanted to reach out but Sidney Grice was, as always, unreachable.

Harry Baddington was devastated by your death. He was very supportive, but then he never knew that I had brought it about.

All of your things went into a packing case but Harry saved the writing box for me. Your father's letter was still in it and also one sheet of paper, a reply. I am sorry, Edward, it was wrong of me to read it but I had to know. There was no preamble. In an angry hand you had scrawled,

Dear Father
I have never understood why you and Mama pretend to think that I have

430

any kind of 'understanding' with Hester Sandler. Though she and I were childhood friends, we were never sweethearts and I have never given her any reason to think otherwise. If I danced with her at the last ball, it was because she was a friend and because you asked me not to leave her unattended at an event where she knew so few other people.

There was more in the same vein, but you never finished that letter. I tore it into little pieces along with your father's and put them in a kidney dish and set them alight, his disapproval and your last written words lost — like me — for ever.

54
BEEF TEA AND
THE HOSPITAL GHOST

Inspector pound was propped up on three pillows and listlessly sipping a mug of beef tea when I visited him the next morning, but his expression brightened when he noticed me and even more when I showed him the pies and bottles of ale I had brought along.

'My desk sergeant came this morning with a bag of tea. What on earth am I supposed to do with that here?' He coughed and clutched at his stomach. 'My constables clubbed together for a bag of apples. I hate apples at the best of times and these are crawling with worms. Which is' — he broke off with another fit of coughing — 'the closest you can get to fresh meat here.'

'Has your sister brought you nothing?'

From under his pillows he brought out a battered leather-bound copy of the King James Bible. 'It belonged to my father.'

'Do you read it?'

He covered his mouth in an attempt to smother another cough. 'Don't tell my men or I would never live it down, but I try to read a passage every day.'

The man in the next bed was winking at me. I tried to ignore him. 'I am not sure that Mr Grice believes in God.'

'I have come across so much evil in my profession that I cannot help but believe in the devil and, if he exists, how can there not be a God?' The inspector drained his mug. 'Mr Grice would find more answers in the Bible if he opened it occasionally.'

'I shall tell him you said that.' I put his mug on the side table.

'I would rather you did not.'

Matron came along. 'Mr Sweeney is much impressed by your fiancé's progress.' Inspector Pound hid his surprise at being so described with another cough. 'You must not tire him.'

'I shall only stay a moment,' I assured her, but when we looked back he had already fallen asleep. I stroked the hair off his forehead and bent to kiss his cheek. 'Goodbye, my dear.'

The matron ushered me away, but on the way out she added, 'He has recently been in correspondence with another surgeon in Edinburgh who has had great success with carbolic acid and is very much in favour of its use. My nurses may not thank you for drawing it to our attention for it stings their eyes abominably, but' — the sternness briefly vanished — 'I believe we have saved three lives this week.'

'Thank you,' I said, 'for saving his.'

She touched my arm. 'Do not thank me too soon. That cough of his may be consumptive and we cannot bathe his lungs in antiseptic.'

'I know you will do your best for him.'

I made my way back down the long white corridors and had just reached the stairwell when I saw her, a spectral figure walking through the night air towards me.

'March?'

I spun round.

'I thought that was you.'

'Oh, Dr Berry.'

She came close. 'Why, March, you look like you have seen a ghost.'

For one moment I thought I had. 'I am sorry. I was daydreaming.' And then I added clumsily, 'What are you doing here?'

She laughed as I struggled to collect myself. 'That is like me asking why you are at the scene of a crime. I work here — well, two sessions a week anyway. Not content with outraging all decent people by educating Jews, University College has taken to employing the occasional woman and I am one of the lucky few, albeit on a voluntary basis.'

I felt like hugging her but I took her hand. 'I have been visiting a friend of mine, Inspector Pound.' I told her about the attack on him and how I had brought it upon him.

'The blood transfusion,' she said. 'I heard about that. That was brave of you.'

'It was my fault he needed it.'

Dr Berry squeezed my hand. 'You must not blame yourself. I will take a look at him later — if I can sneak past Matron.'

'She is not such a dragon as she appears,' I said.

'In that case I shall go now.' She hesitated. 'May I visit you tomorrow evening?'

'Oh yes. I am sure Mr Grice will be pleased to see you — and I will too, of course.'

I felt a little happier as I went on my way.

Sidney Grice was pasting a cutting into a navy-blue scrapbook.

'An unusual case in the East End.' He squashed the air bubbles with a cylinder rule. 'A man with no arms was fished out of the Thames and his legs were shackled.'

'Chas.' I gripped my handbag and tried to stop shaking. 'Charles Sawyer.'

'An acquaintance of yours?' He closed the book and I nodded weakly. 'Well, you will be interested to learn,' Mr G continued, 'that he survived by hanging on to a mooring rope with his teeth until the river police hauled him out.'

'Oh thank God.'

'What a waste of public resources.' My guardian piffed. 'An armless man is nothing but a drain on society.'

'We could do with a few more drains like him.' I slumped in my chair. 'He saved me from the man who stabbed Inspector Pound.'

My guardian wrinkled his brow and opened his book to pencil a note under the cutting.

'Doubtless expecting a large reward,' he grumbled, 'like some red-haired man who came round claiming he had helped Pound. I told him to go to Marylebone Police Station if he wanted paying, but he did not seem very keen on the idea.'

'But I promised him. He was the barman at the Boar's Head who carried the inspector to hospital.'

'And how was I to know that?' he mumbled as he left the room. I took a look at what he had written.

Memoranda.

1. *Find and compensate red-headed man.*
2. *Bring would-be killers of* Charles Sawyer *to justice.*

And on his blotter I made out, *3 guineas a day + doctors' fees.*

55
CHOCOLATES AND SEAWEED

After lunch I walked to Huntley Street and the neat house with its green door, and waited for my three quick rings to be answered. A stray dog dragged itself to sit and whimper at me, though I had nothing to give it but a stroke.

The door was opened a crack and then fully by a slender middle-aged lady in a long red gown. 'Eve.' She threw out her arms. We all used false names in those days. An unofficial ladies' club was viewed with grave suspicion by the authorities and prurience by the masculine public.

'Hello, Violet.'

She shooed the dog away, shut it out and gave me a kiss, though her arms remained open.

'We haven't seen you for ages.' Her stiff black hair rasped my face. 'You are quite the celebrity since that murder trial.'

I winced. I never wanted to be well known

and certainly not for being associated with so many cruel deaths. I braced myself to peck her cheek. 'Is Harriet here?'

Violet had drenched herself in so much eau de cologne that my nose itched.

'I think she is playing Bezique with the Countess of Bromley.' The Countess owned a tobacco shop in Biggin Hill, her tiara was homemade and she had no more right to a title than I, but no one could begrudge it to a woman who had had fourteen children and lost them all in one winter. 'Why don't you step into my parlour and I will let her know you are here?'

I sat on the chintz sofa and picked up a copy of Myra's Journal of Dress and Fashion, and was dismayed to see that I needed an eighteen-inch waist to be able to wear anything remotely modern, when Harriet came in. I jumped up and ran into her embrace.

'March, I swear you look more the lady every time I see you. That dress — where did you get it? — could start a colonial war. I thought I turned a few heads in the ticket office at Rugby Station this morning, but I feel positively agricultural next to you in that mantel mirror.' She poured us both a generous Bombay while I lit two Virginians. 'Oh, that awful jumped-up woman. It is positively indecent to put that many aces in a pack. Rooked me for three shillings and sixpence, but don't tell Vi for goodness sake. Gambling on the premises — she'll have us out on the street before you can say chin chin.' She raised her glass.

'Cheerio,' I said and clinked hers, and we settled together on the sofa. 'I know you usually come on the first Tuesday of the month, so I was not sure I would find you here today.'

Harriet swallowed a mouthful of gin. 'Oh, you would find me here every Tuesday of late, and many a day between.'

'Does Mr Fitzpatrick not mind?'

Harriet put her head back and blew three perfect smoke rings. 'To tell you the truth, March, I do not think my husband would notice if I stayed here all year round — not until there was a crisis such as not being able to find his copy of *Wisden.* Do you know, March, I was trapped in the attic last month by a faulty door handle and I was up there all night — and it was the longest, coldest night since the Ice Age — bellowing like a regimental sergeant major and banging like a demented monkey on the floor with his Aunty Helen's bed brick until Sebastian, the youngest offspring and the only one who looks remotely like me, came to investigate and released me. I hurtled downstairs more encrusted in dust than a collier at the end of his shift and draped in more cobwebs than Miss Havisham's wedding cake, my hair hanging over my face like seaweed on the rock of the sirens, gibbering and in absolute floods of saline, and Charles tears himself away from his paper and kedgeree and says, "You really must have a word with the neighbours, Harry. Their builders kept me awake half the night with their hammering." And the really frightening thing, March, is that we share the same bed.'

She tossed back her drink and I refreshed both our glasses.

'Sometimes we do not notice things, but it does not mean we do not care.' I took her hand. 'My father once gave away my favourite chair and it was two days before —'

'That's it.' Harriet seized my words. 'That is exactly it. I am just a piece of furniture to him. I suppose I should be grateful he does not use me as a footstool. Do you know, March, that man pursued and I mean *pursued* me for two years. He sent me barrowloads of flowers and crates of chocolates and showered me with thoughtful gifts. He wrote me cleverly crafted poems and love letters that simply steamed with adoration.

441

He cajoled my mother and inveigled my sister into speaking on his behalf, and he positively hounded my father into nervous exhaustion for permission to press his pestering to its inevitable doom. He placed me in a shrine and as soon as I let him in, gave me a housekeeping book with a miserly allowance and disappeared into his study for the next quarter-century, reappearing only to work, eat and, very occasionally, have his not very wicked way with me.'

I laughed. 'Oh, Harriet, you are incorrigible, but it cannot really be that bad.'

'I have renovated, emery-papered and put French polish on it.' She leaned towards me. 'Listen to the awful voice of experience, March. Do you know why we have never had slaves in this country? Because we have ten million of them here already, only we call them *women.* If ever a man offers you a ring with one hand and a cup of hemlock with the other, take the poison. The result is the same but less protracted. Why, March, darling, what on earth is the matter? Here I am chattering like a squirrel and you look like you have seen an apparition.'

I had never told her about my engagement and I did not want to talk about Horatio Green. I had come to Huntley Street to escape such thoughts.

'I am just tired,' I said. 'Dear Harriet, you are my one haven of frivolity in this barbaric world.'

We finished our cigarettes.

'But how is life with the famous Sidney Grice?' she asked. 'If the press are to be believed, he has metamorphosed from the avenging angel into the angel of death.'

'He investigates murders,' I said. 'He does not commit them.'

We were quiet for a moment until Harriet perked up and said, 'Speaking of apparitions — as I was a moment ago — I could have sworn I saw one on Tuesday last week. I was rushing to get on my four thirty — the five fifteen is always packed to the gunnels especially in the smoking compartments — when I saw a very well-dressed lady getting off the train on the next platform, and for one moment I would have sworn it was her.'

'Who?' I asked, but somehow I knew what Harriet was going to say.

'That terrible woman, the murderess. I suppose, after what you told me, I must call her Eleanor Quarrel.' She ground her cigarette into the ashtray. 'It was probably what Charles always calls my overexcited imagination and I only got a glimpse, but she had a very distinctive profile — didn't she? —

and you know how you get a feeling. Even when I turned away it felt like she was looking at me. I have to say it sent shivers up and down my spine, but when I looked again she was gone — vanished. Perhaps she has come back to haunt us. Oh, and speaking of coming back to haunt people, one of our housemasters had a very unexpected and unwelcome visitor the other day.'

Her conversation darted to some divorce scandal in Rugby, but I found it difficult to pay attention. My mind was swirling with an image — Eleanor Quarrel rising rotting out of the water, knife in hand, ready to slaughter again.

56
THE FOX AND THE SPARROW

We had just finished what was an unusually tasty dinner of fried potatoes and boiled navy beans in a tomato purée when a telegram arrived for Sidney Grice.

'Good heavens.' A cord of vein engorged on his right temple. 'According to Dr Baldwin, my mother is dying and unlikely to last the night.' He drained his tumbler of water.

'Oh, I am sorry,' I said. 'Do you know what is wrong with her?'

He deposited his napkin on the floor. 'It appears she has taken an exorbitant quantity of heroin.'

'Oh dear.' I pushed my plate aside. 'What condition did she have to take it for?'

'Boredom.' He stood up. 'She has so little to do with her time since she came out of prison.'

I listened to him in disbelief. 'Your mother went to prison?'

'She was chairwoman of the Corporal Punishment Society.' He untied his patch. 'But she resigned when they refused to introduce branding of repeat pilferers.'

'I hope she is all right.' I tried to sound more sincere than I felt after that information and he contemplated me with disdain.

'Even with your ragged medical knowledge, I would have thought you would know that people who are dying are not *all right.*'

'I meant —'

'Did you, indeed?' He ran a hand over his brow. 'Well, really. This is most inconvenient.' He limped down the stairs to summon a cab. 'Try not to set fire to the cherry tree,' he said as he left and I went outside to light a cigarette.

I had hardly settled to enjoy it when Molly stumbled out.

'Oh, miss, I wish I could smoke cigarettes and —'

'Would you like one?'

Molly crossed her feet. 'Not for me, thank you, miss. I meant I wish I could smoke cigarettes and not worry about it being unladylike.' And she beamed as if expecting me to concur.

'Have you come to tell me something?' I asked, as patiently as I could, and leaned back to watch the machinery of her mind operate.

'There is a cabby at the door,' she told me at last.

'What does he want?'

'Funny you should ask that.' Molly reclined against the door frame. 'We had a bit of a chat and he wants to retire and buy a little public house by the sea. He wants a little vegetable plot and a little —'

'Why is he here?'

'He . . .' She wriggled her nose. 'He has a message to convoy.'

I stubbed out my cigarette, slipped it back into the case to hide the evidence and went to investigate. Gerry was standing on the top step when I opened the door.

'Miss Middleton.' He tipped his leather peaked cap. 'Molly tells me Mr Grice isn't here,' he said.

'Can I take a message?'

Gerry hesitated. 'While we were waiting for you at the docks we were talking about that McKay — excuse my language — bitch. I was on a case against her five or six years ago. I thought he might be interested to know that it looks like she is doing a flit. Her carriage is on Monday Row round the back of her place and the servants were packing all her worldly goods into it when I went by twenty minutes ago.'

447

I reached for my cloak. 'Take me there, Gerry.' But Gerry held up his hands.

'Not me, miss.'

'I will double your fare.'

Gerry turned his hands palms up. 'It isn't a question of the tin, miss. Old Pudding would kill me if I did.'

Despite my frustration I laughed. 'Why do you call him that?'

'G-rice Pudding,' Gerry explained. 'We all call him that on the ranks, only don't tell him for gawd's sake.' He looked abashed. 'I'm sorry, miss, but Mr Grice did me proud when I was chucked and he'd blow his boiler if I took you into danger.'

'I quite understand.' I hung my cloak up again. 'Thank you, Gerry.'

I waited two minutes, then turned the handle to raise the flag, and I was still turning it when there was a knock on the door.

'Sorry abart the smell,' the driver called as I climbed aboard his hansom and he swung up on top. 'Last gent 'ad four grey'ounds and they weren't particular where they did it. I swilled it awt but it do linger, it do.' It certainly did but I had come to accept that I was living in a city of stinks. I almost envied Mr G his blocked nose.

The streets were still busy, countless pleasure seekers heading for the West End. I would have loved to see *The Corsican Contessa* at the Criterion and I had heard some of the songs being bawled out by song-sheet sellers on the street, but my guardian would never have countenanced me attending such an establishment. I might have been in grave peril of enjoying myself.

Monday Row was a narrow street at right angles to Fitzroy Square. We went along slowly, our horse picking its way through the shadows. A solitary flame glowed in the distance.

'Stop here,' I called out in a stage whisper.

As my eyes became accustomed to the gloom I made out a covered four-wheeler with two horses in harness about thirty feet down the alley, in the glow of a lamp post, and the shape of a groom sitting up at the front. A doorway opened, casting a corridor of light on to the scene, and what looked like a woman and a girl came carrying a trunk out.

'Dunno what you're up to,' my driver said quietly. 'But best we go back now.' His horse shifted uneasily.

'I rarely do what is best,' I declared — how Mr G would have agreed with me there — and clambered down to walk towards the scene.

The road was cobbled unevenly, carpeted

with old straw and horse droppings, with wide gutters running along either side. I slithered and splashed through an unexpectedly deep puddle and the pair looked up. As I approached I saw that they were a man and a boy with aprons protecting their servants' uniforms. They balanced the chest on top of four tethering posts and rested their arms.

'Can I help you, miss?' the man enquired but even as he spoke I saw them — Thurston coming out of the door, carrying two bulging carpet bags, followed by Primrose McKay in a long fox-fur coat, lifting her skirts and exposing enough calf to have sent Mr G into an apoplexy.

'Miss Middleton,' she greeted me as she drew near. 'Is your master not with you?'

'I have no master,' I said, 'but Mr Grice has been called away on an urgent matter.'

'If you are touting for business you might do better outside King's Cross,' she advised, 'though you would be best to stand in the shadows.'

Thurston guffawed. 'With a sack over your head.'

'To avoid recognizing your mother?' I asked and he raised the back of his hand.

'It is all right, Thurston,' Primrose promised him. 'I shall let you hurt her very badly one day.'

'His very existence hurts me,' I murmured. 'Are you taking a holiday, Miss McKay?'

Primrose waved a bored hand. 'Life is a holiday for me, Miss Middleton.'

There was a scuttling in the gutter. A rat? I moved sideways.

'May I ask where you are going?'

The man and boy struggled to heave her trunk on to the already laden carriage roof.

'What an inquisitive child you are.' She clicked her tongue in reprimand. 'But I am afraid your curiosity will have to go unsatisfied.' She put the fingertips of her right hand together. 'Your master did not seem very impressed by my plan to sit it out and so I have devised another. It is also simple but even cleverer. Take a good look at me, Miss Middleton, and enjoy my gorgeousness. It may be the last you will see of it for quite some time; for tonight I am going' — she blew on her nails and her hand sprang open, revealing nothing inside — 'to disappear.'

'Disappearing is quite an easy trick,' I told her. 'The poor manage to do it all the time. You may find reappearing a little more difficult.'

The scuttling grew louder and she glanced

down. 'What is that?'

The boy darted over and went down on his haunches. 'A bird, miss.'

'Give it to me.' He scooped it up and she took it from him. 'A sparrow,' she said. 'It appears to be injured.' She cradled it in her right hand, its head poking between her circling thumb and first finger and its feet dangling out at the bottom. 'Poor little thing.' She blew it a kiss and the bird opened its beak, but the beak stayed open and the feet curled tight and it squeaked, and I saw that she was clenching her fist.

'Stop it,' I cried out but she only smiled sweetly, and its eyes bulged as her fingers blanched, and I heard a sickening crunching sound and a black liquid was expelled from the sparrow's mouth before its head flopped.

'There,' Primrose McKay opened her hand and let it fall back into the gutter.

'You disgust me,' I railed at her.

'Find me a rag,' she told the boy, 'to clean the blood and excrement from my hand. No, do not worry, I have one.' She reached out and wiped her palm down the front of my cloak. 'Why have you come, Miss Middleton?'

She walked past me to the open carriage door.

'I like to know what our suspects are up to,' I said.

'Suspect?' she repeated scornfully. 'Well, you may tell your master this, girl. When the Last Death Club closes its accounts there will only be one person left alive and that person will be me, and he may draw whatever conclusion he likes from that but he will never prove a thing.'

'But what can you possibly want the money for?' I asked and she put her head to one side.

'For the poor,' she replied. 'I shall take that seventy thousand pounds on to the street and burn it before their very eyes.'

Thurston closed the carriage door and laughed. He turned to me. 'She will kill them all,' he crowed, 'and not you nor your half-blind, dirt-digging cripple can do a thing about it.'

'I only pray that you are an accomplice,' I told him. 'Mr Grice would so love a double hanging.'

Thurston pushed his face close to mine and I forced myself not to flinch.

'One day' — he breathed whisky fumes over me — 'I will crush you just like that little bird in my bare hands.' He stepped into a pile of manure and shook his foot angrily.

'Be sure to clean yourself up,' I advised. 'You will want to look your best in the dock.'

Thurston scraped his boot on the kerb, strode past and climbed into the other side of the carriage. The groom cracked his whip and the horses set off much too fast for such ill-lit conditions.

I dashed back to my cab. 'Follow that coach.'

But the driver shook his head. 'Not likely, miss. That's Bloodthirsty Gates. I know 'im by reputation and that's as much as I wants to.'

He turned his horse and it headed eagerly from the shadows to the light.

The lights were on when I returned, and I looked into the study to find Mr G sorting through his filing cabinet.

'I have just found a case of murder with an icicle,' he told me happily.

'I thought you would be with your mother,' I said.

'Oh, that.' He slipped a newspaper cutting into a folder. 'Apparently she had a headache. She has never had one before and assumed the worst.' He printed a number on the cover. 'So it was all a false alarm . . .' he put the folder away, 'unfortunately.'

'You cannot mean that.'

'I most certainly do.' He took off his pince-nez. 'It was in Norway.'

I told him what had happened.

'And the point of chasing after her was . . . ?' he enquired politely.

'To see what she was up to.'

He ripped a page out of a journal. 'She was hardly likely to be *up to* anything with you peering over her shoulder. Really, March.' He tore the page in two, using his rule as a guide. 'I had four different drivers standing by to follow that woman before you alerted her.'

'Perhaps if you had told me —'

'What?' He slammed down his rule. 'You would not have gone charging round like a dragoon on manoeuvres?'

I was too tired to argue any more. 'She killed a bird,' I told him.

'Thank heavens for that.' He slid the drawer shut. 'By the look of your cloak I thought you had.'

57
PEBBLES AND
THE ICENI HORDES

Charlotte Street was ten minutes' walk or twenty minutes by cab on most days. We took a hansom.

'It is estimated,' Sidney Grice said, 'that the Iceni hordes rampaged through Londinium slaughtering the inhabitants at a rate of eight miles per hour. Today they would be lucky to get across Oxford Circus in an afternoon.'

We had been sitting for so long that he had drained his flask of tea while we were still within a few hundred yards of home. This seemed as good a time as any to broach the subject.

'Do you think it possible,' I hardly dared put the idea into words, 'that Eleanor Quarrel is still alive?'

I waited for my guardian to dismiss the idea contemptuously, but he only tapped the cork back into his insulated bottle and enquired, 'Why do you ask?'

'My friend Mrs Fitzpatrick, who knew Eleanor Quarrel quite well from the club in Huntley Street, thought she saw her, at Euston Station.'

A man was juggling three live hens. They flapped and squawked but he passed them hand to hand, high over his head, as easily as if they had been tennis balls.

'When?'

'Tuesday last week at about half past four.'

The man propelled all his hens in the air at once, but one launched itself in a clumsy falling flight and scuttled under a carriage with him scurrying after it.

'Did she speak to her?'

'No. She was alighting from a train as Harriet was boarding another, but she was convinced that Eleanor was looking at her. She thought it might be a ghost.'

Mr G snorted. 'If a fraction of sightings were proved true, you would never get a seat on a Metropolitan Line train for the number of shades already occupying them. Yes.'

'Yes, what?'

A policeman came by on foot, waving his arms and shouting at someone unseen to back up.

'Yes, I do think it possible that Eleanor Quarrel is still alive. The thought occurred to me the moment I read that the *Framling-*

ham Castle had gone down with all hands and passengers.' He put his flask back into his satchel. 'But I dismissed the idea as too optimistic.'

I shot him a glance. 'But you hated her. Why would you not want her to die?'

'Oh, I wanted her die but not like a bather who had got into difficulties.' Our cab jerked forwards. 'She should have choked and struggled on the end of a rope and I should have been there to watch. She should have been given to the anatomists to dissect. After Corder was hanged for the Red Barn Murder the surgeon tanned his skin for a book binding. Imagine having Mrs Quarrel's hide covering your written account of the case.'

'What a disgusting idea,' I said and he shrugged.

'What she did to the living was worse than anything that could be done to her dead.' He fastened his satchel straps.

'There are four reasonable explanations of what happened to Eleanor Quarrel. First, that she went down with the ship. Second, that she got off the ship, most likely with the pilot, before it went into the open sea. That is easily checked. Third, that she survived the shipwreck and was picked up by a passing vessel when the storm subsided, though this would probably have been widely reported.' We came to a standstill again. 'Fourth, that she was not on the ship when it sailed. Numbers one and four are the most credible events and, when you have a number of options, dismissing the likely ones does not make the unlikely ones any more likely. When this case is settled I shall devote some time to investigating further, but at present we have murderers to apprehend who are all too definitely alive. Let us deal with that first.'

A scrawny boy scrambled under our horse pursued by a skinny girl calling, 'Stop, thief.' They were both almost naked.

'What could she have had that would be worth stealing?' I wondered.

'Everyone has something,' Sidney Grice said, 'a coin or a cup of water, even an idea. Desperate men will fight over pebbles.'

Charlotte Street had developed in an ad hoc fashion but what it lacked in the uniform stylishness of Gower Street, it made up with dozens of different buildings ranging from the quirky to the imposing. The Prince of Wales Theatre stood on the corner, its once-grand facade more than a little tattered now.

'Clear off,' my guardian said to a respectably dressed lady rattling an orphans' charity box. Even by his own standards he was especially ratty that afternoon. 'You might as well throw your money down the drain,' he grunted as I gave her sixpence.

We passed the Sass Academy of Art as a wan young woman came out wrapped in a brown woollen coat, not long enough to hide her bare calves, and Sidney Grice turned away in a horror which I had never seen him display for a slaughtered body.

A police van went by with an old woman standing peering out. She had a clay pipe clenched between her gums and was gripping a bar with one hand and waving merrily to all and sundry with the other.

Gallop's Snuff Emporium had a small bow window crammed with glass jars and coloured pots piled so high that hardly any light filtered through or between them into the shop.

A small bent man stood side-on behind the counter, his head twisted at an odd angle towards us and his back hunched. He had a grey goatee dangling down his chest. 'Good morning, sir, miss.'

'Mr Gallop?' my guardian asked.

'Warrington Tusker Gallop it is, sir,' Mr Gallop confirmed cheerily. 'How may I be of —'

'Who is in the back room?' my guardian

demanded.

'Why, nobody.'

'Get down!' Sidney Grice shouted.

'I am not standing on —' Mr Gallop jerked his head away. 'Ouch.' His hand went to his neck.

There was a scuffling noise and I looked across just in time to see a thin tube being withdrawn from a knothole in a cream-painted door behind him. There were running footsteps and another door banged.

'Blowpipe,' my guardian said and scrambled over the counter, ignoring the pyramid of snuffboxes and row of ornamented humidors he scattered in his progress. 'Deal with him.' He jumped down, wrenched open the door and disappeared through it.

Mr Gallop put his hand to his neck. 'Oh dear,' he said and, before I could stop him, pulled out what looked like a bamboo meat skewer. His hand was covered in blood. 'Goodness, that stings.'

I lifted the flap and rushed round. There was a chair behind him and I guided him into it. I reached for my handkerchief to staunch the steady flow down his collar, but when I turned back Warrington Tusker Gallop was dead.

58
HUNTING MONKEYS

'Do not touch it.' Sidney Grice came back into the room. 'It will have been poisoned.' The skewer was still in the dead man's hand.

'But who?'

'He was out of the rear exit before I got into the room and he locked it from the outside. He could be halfway across the city by now.' My guardian put on his pince-nez and bent over. 'This dart has been hollowed out.' He clicked his tongue thoughtfully. 'I have seen blowpipes being used by tribes-men in the Amazon Basin to hunt monkeys and I have heard of them being used in tribal wars, but this is the first case I have ever come across in this country.'

'What a trophy for you,' I said acidly.

'Indeed.' His glass eye glowed red in the light through a jar as he went by the window, bolted the front door and pulled the blind down. I saw the mirror-image *closed* in black through the blue cloth. 'Come here.' I followed him to the doorway behind the counter and he held out an arm to halt me. 'Luckily, Mr Gallop was too mean to employ a cleaner.' The floor was thick with dust. 'What do you make of those?'

'Footprints and scuffmarks.'

'The footprints to the right near the wall are mine, but what do the scuffmarks tell you?' He pointed with his cane.

I looked at the long imprints. 'Something was dragged along the floor.'

'Nonsense.' His cane moved over the outlines. 'The curved front edge is a knee and the trail behind it is a trouser leg.'

'So we know we are dealing with a man.'

'Or a woman dressed as a man — but probably a man. See those?'

'A toe print in front of the knee and to the right of it, and another less distinct one behind the trouser mark.'

'I knew your eyes would be of some use to you one day.' He took hold of the jamb and leaned low into the room over the marks. 'The tip of my little finger to that of my thumb when I stretch my hand is exactly eight inches, so we are looking for a tall man with small feet.'

'Like the print at Piggety's in the crushed glass.'

'Possibly, though the heel shape is different over there, so if it is the same person he has changed his boots.' He looked up and round and pulled himself straight. 'I think we can disturb these now. Lift your skirts as much as is commensurate with decency and go in first.' He ushered me into a low-ceilinged storeroom, with sparsely used shelves on either side — a few old bottles, some rolls of cloth, some curling account books, all covered in grime and clothed in cobwebs. 'First impressions?'

'There is a strong smell in here — a sort of perfume.'

He breathed in through his nose. 'I can just about smell something. A scented snuff?'

'No. It is more like a toiletry but it is difficult to tell with the room being so musty — a sort of cologne, I think. Perhaps it was a woman after all.'

'Or a foreigner,' Mr G muttered. 'Now, let us see the room as the murderer must have.' He pulled the door to. 'Wait a moment for our eyes to adjust. What can you hear outside?'

I listened. 'Very little.' And waited for a sarcastic remark but he only said, 'That is because there is very little to hear — except the two dogs barking and the cries of a rag-man above the traffic.'

'I think I can hear the dogs and the man but I cannot hear the traffic.' Four circular cores and two slits of light came through the planks from the shop.

'That is because it is distant so the exit opens into a back alley.' He genuflected to position his knee over the imprint. 'See how much further back the toe is than mine.'

'A good two or three inches.'

'Also, if I were using a blowpipe, I would put it through this lower hole and look through the one above, but the killer used the two top holes. He must be at least five foot ten or eleven. I have a very good view of the shop from here but the side where Gallop stood is slightly obscured. The murderer could much more easily have fired at me or you, so he was clearly intent upon his victim.'

He brought a miniature safety lamp out of his satchel and lit it, the yellow glare momentarily blinding me. I shaded my eyes and turned to see an old packing crate.

'He must have sat on this.'

Sidney Grice came over to inspect it. 'And for quite a while, judging by the amount of shuffling about on the case and floor . . . and what do you make of those footprints?'

He bent over and held the lamp close, and I peered over his shoulder.

'The right foot is turned in a bit.'

'Good . . . and it has a less sharp outline, showing that it drags slightly. So he has a limp but not a bad one, more likely a sprained ankle than a game knee or hip.' He strode across to the back door. Hardly any light came in from the outside but a rectangle of day seeped underneath through a gap. 'What do you think happened?'

'The murderer entered through the back door.' He opened his mouth as I added hastily, 'Or else he was known to Mr Gallop and came in through the shop.'

'You must get out of the habit of saying things because you think I want you to say them. I could bring along Cook for that,' he said. 'Just look at the pattern of the prints.'

I followed them carefully with my eye. 'It was the back door.'

'But how did he gain access?'

'Perhaps it was not locked.'

He tutted. 'Who leaves an entrance unlocked in this metropolis? Use your eyes, girl.'

There were more marks on the floor in front of the back door, four of them with long straight edges overlapping. 'Newspaper,' I said. 'I have done it myself as a child. You slide the paper under the door, push the key out with a small length

466

of wire so that it falls on the paper, and pull the paper back.'

Sidney Grice rubbed his hands. 'At this rate I shall be able to leave the business to you and retire to my estate in Dorset by the end of the year. What next?'

'He went and sat on that box and then crept —'

'How do you know he crept?' He stroked a stain on the wall.

'Prints close together and very well delineated — small careful steps.'

'Then what?'

'He kneeled there, looking into the shop through a knothole, pushed his blowpipe through the other hole and fired at Mr Gallop. Either it was just Mr Gallop he intended to kill, or you alerted him and he panicked and ran.'

My guardian blew out his lamp and we went back into the shop where Warrington Tusker Gallop sat in his chair, his head still to one side. Sidney Grice went to him, tried to twist his head and pushed on his shoulders, and Mr Gallop tipped back. 'The spinal curvatures were certainly not feigned,' he said. 'So he could not have carried out the other murders himself or have been of much assistance in them.' He slid his lantern into an asbestos pouch to save his satchel from being scorched and took the dart with his tweezers from the dead man's loose grip. 'This is not from the Amazon. It has been sharpened with a cut-throat razor and the fletch is made from the feathers of a male *Turdus philomelos,* the song thrush. How did he die?'

The eyes were still open and fixed on me. 'Almost instantly, with no pain except from the actual wounding, and no fighting for breath or convulsions.'

He clicked his tongue. 'The tribesmen I came across use curare, which suffocates their prey. He would have died in a similar manner to Horatio Green if that had been used.' He dropped into a crouch and prodded the floors with his finger. 'Blood,' he remarked.

'Mr Gallop did bleed quite heavily when he pulled the dart out,' I informed him.

'Describe the bleeding.' He scrutinized the bare boards through his pince-nez.

'There was a gush and then a steady flow. So it did not hit an artery,' I told him.

'This blood is in droplets.' He jumped up and looked from side to side. 'Where did it come from?'

'Well, surely, Mr Gallop,' I said.

'Nonsense.' He wiped his finger on a cloth. 'I have told you before to look for patterns, whether it be fingermarks or pavements. The droplets form a flattened cone, the base being near Gallop's feet and the apex near the door into the storeroom.'

'So the murderer blew blood through the pipe,' I said and he looked at me questioningly. 'Perhaps he had a wound in his mouth or a severe chest condition such as consumption.'

'Perhaps,' my guardian conceded. He picked up a pot which had been smashed as he vaulted the counter, and sniffed the contents. 'Come,' Mr G said. 'I shall send a message to the inimitable Inspector Quigley from home.' He stopped on the threshold. 'I have had an important thought.'

'About the murderer?'

'Good heavens, no. But it occurs to me,' he pinched the dimple on his chin, 'that a little snuff, possibly a menthol mix, might help clear my nasal passages and restore my olfactory organs to their full and remarkable sensitivities.' He stepped outside. 'Though I shall have to seek another supplier now, of course.'

'How inconvenient.' The bell clinked weakly as I closed the door.

There was no shortage of cabs on the street, and a weak sun came through the clouds and filthy air as we clambered aboard.

'I had thought about visiting Lady Foskett today,' he said, 'but she will never see me at this hour.'

Our horse looked lively and a red plume waved merrily on its head.

'Would you like to know how Inspector Pound is progressing?'

'Not especially.'

A cart in front dropped a bundle of empty sacks, too late for us to avoid, and we bumped over it. Children were already scrambling for salvage.

'I saw Dr Berry this morning.'

'Oh, really?' He tightened a strap on his satchel.

'She said she would call on us this evening.'

'I will probably be out.' He polished the handle of his cane with his glove. 'I must have a second flask manufactured or I shall be forced to go without my tea on every return journey.'

But a moment later he was whistling between his teeth, something which might have been intended to be Beethoven's Fifth but may have been nothing at all.

59
Rubber Boots and Kisses

Dr Berry came in very wet.

'I thought I would be safe enough just walking from the hospital but Zeus was waiting behind a cloud with a gigantic bucket of water just for me.' She struggled out of her sopping cape and handed it to Molly. 'They have a very childish sense of humour, these Greek gods.'

'Like most men,' I said.

'Except Mr Grice.' Molly hung the cape on the coat stand, creating an instant puddle on the floor tiles. 'He is too clever to have a sense of humour at all.'

'I am afraid he is out at the moment but he should be back soon.' I directed Dr Berry to the study and into my armchair, pulling up a chair for myself from the table.

'Why do you not use the other armchair?'

'It belongs to Mr G.'

She furrowed her brow. 'He cannot be an easy man to live with.'

'He has his ways,' I said, 'but I am getting used to them. Did you see Inspector Pound?'

She looked very businesslike in a black coat and white blouse.

'He seems to be healing well. I have made him up a tonic.' She produced a brown bottle two thirds full of medicine. 'But please do not tell anybody. We doctors can be very possessive of our patients and if Mr Sweeney found out I was interfering . . . well, I am there under sufferance as it is.' She looked at me. 'You seem very agitated, March.'

'We witnessed another murder today.' I told her about Warrington Gallop. 'And now we only have two members left.'

'Goodness.' Dr Berry fingered her hair. 'I am getting very worried about you, March. This is no profession for a young girl.'

'I am not as young as I seem, Dr Berry.'

'Call me Dorna, and please do not be offended.'

I shifted in my chair to face her. 'You of all people should understand. You must have seen such horrors as I have, and I believe that I can help save lives by studying the forensic sciences, as surely as you can with the practice of medicine. I would prefer people not to be murdered just as you

would prefer your patients not to be mutilated in factories or ravaged by disease.'

'But you put yourself in such danger.' She
wiped her right eye.

'Why, Dorna, whatever is wrong.'

'Oh, March, I feel so vacuous.' She took a
handkerchief from her handbag. 'When you
first came to my house I thought Sidney
was one of the most objectionable men I
have ever met and I have come across many
in my battle for recognition.'

'But what has happened?'

She unfolded the handkerchief. 'As I got
to know him I began to see another side.'
She blew her nose. 'And I found myself
increasingly . . . attracted to him.'

'But, Dorna, that is lovely.'

'No, March. It is not.'

'But I am sure he has a good opinion of
you. You should have seen how angry he
was about those newspaper reports.' I
looked at the floor and Dorna touched my
hand.

'I admire Sidney enormously, March. He
is quite the cleverest man I have ever met.
Why, he knows more about some aspects of
medicine than I do, and I am so very fond
of him. But Sidney only loves three things
— his work —'

'You cannot blame him for that.'

'I do not blame him for anything.'

'And second?'

She crumpled her handkerchief into a ball. 'He could never love me as much as he loves his past.' She shuddered.

'I do not understand.'

Dr Berry stood up. 'There are things that you should know, March, but it is not for me to tell you.'

I stood too, and she put away the handkerchief and reached out her hand to stroke my cheek.

'What happened that was so terrible that I cannot be told?'

She put two fingers to my lips. 'Oh, dear, sweet March. You have such a heart. It is not only Sidney that I have come to care for.' Her left hand stroked my hair. 'Have you ever been kissed?'

'Yes, of course.'

'I mean really kissed, long and tenderly, like this?'

'Not for a long time,' I said and kissed her back.

Forgive me, Edward, but for one fragment of one second when I closed my eyes I could almost imagine it was you, somehow returned to me whole and beautiful and alive, and that all the pain and guilt and horror had been washed away.

I opened my eyes and it all flooded back.

'Oh, March.' Her face was flushed. 'Put your hand to me.'

'I do not —' She touched my mouth with her fingertips and took my right hand in her left, and placed it on her blouse.

'Feel how fast my heart beats for you.'

I felt the cotton and through it a pendant and a pulse, and her breath short on my cheek.

'Someone might come.'

Dorna sighed and pulled slowly away and pinched the bridge of her nose, pressing hard on the corners of her eyes.

'I have come to tell you that I might be going away, March. A permanent position has come up in Edinburgh and I shall not get such an opportunity again.'

'But when will you go?'

'At the end of the month, if I take it. They want me to start as soon as I can, so I may not see you again, March.'

I shuddered. 'The last woman who said goodbye to me like this was a murderess.'

She raised my jaw and looked deep into me. 'Make sure Inspector Pound gets his medicine.'

'What was the third thing Mr G loves?' I

asked, and her hand dropped from my face to the cameo brooch on her jacket.

'Why, you, of course.'

And I smiled unhappily. 'At best he tolerates me.'

'Oh, March.' She put a stray lock of hair behind my ear. 'He has such a good opinion of you, but he is afraid to make you swollen-headed. He loves you more than anyone.'

'Or anything?'

Her face fell. 'I did not say that.' She clipped her bag shut. 'Perhaps you could tell your guardian for me.'

'Surely you can wait and tell him yourself?'

'Tell me what?' I spun round to see my guardian coming into the room. 'Good evening, Dr Berry. I trust you are well.'

Dorna Berry flushed. 'Oh, I did not hear you.'

'I did not mean to startle you, but Molly already had the front door open to polish it and I was trying out my new boots.' I looked down and saw that his feet were clad in two clumsy black lumps. 'They are made of rubber,' he said, 'which means that no cattle have to be slaughtered and skinned to provide them. They also have the advantage of being completely waterproof and, as I have just demonstrated, much quieter than the leather and nails that one is accustomed to clack around in.'

'Excuse me.' I brushed past them both and went upstairs for a gin. I could not flood away the memory of what had just happened, or my disgust with myself, but I could wash away the taste.

I was not trying to replace you — why would I want to and how on earth could I? But I had such a hunger for love. It comes so rarely in this world that, for a broken instant, I thought I had glimpsed it.

I smoked a cigarette. It was my last one and the tobacconist would close soon, but I dare not go down. I could not see her and I was frightened to see him. He might have looked human.

60
WORD GAMES
AND PICKLED LEGS

It was a chilly night but Sidney Grice rarely felt the cold. We sat either side of the unlit fire, which only served to cool us with the draught from the chimney.

'My father used to say one sack of coal will keep you warm all year,' he reminisced. 'Whenever it is chilly, you go down to the cellar for it and, by the time you have lugged it up the steps, you are warm enough to take it down again.'

'Why do you speak of your father in the past tense?'

My guardian rubbed his shoulder. 'I have not communicated with him for nine years and three weeks.'

I wrapped a shawl around me. 'But whyever not?'

'We are not worthy of each other.' He folded his arms. 'What were you asking Dr Berry to tell me when I arrived?'

'She said nothing?'

'Nothing of any great import.'

'I think she had some news, but it is not for me to tell it.' I pulled my shawl tighter. 'I was thinking about those messages claiming to be from Mr Piggety.'

'And what conclusion did you arrive at?'

'It may be nothing . . .'

'Almost certainly.' He picked a speck from his lapel.

'But it struck me that they both read like a children's word game.'

'How so?' A lump of soot fell and burst on to the hearth.

'Well, I cannot remember exactly what they said . . .'

'I have them here.' We went to his desk where the telegram was folded inside Mc-Hugh's *Explosive Devices, Their Construction and Concealment and Divers Means of Discovering Their Whereabouts and Thereafter Rendering Them Impotent*. 'It is patently a code but I find myself as yet unable to break it.'

He flattened the paper out.

MR GRICE YOU ARE LACKING VITAL INFORMATION COME FACTORY THREE EXACTLY NO LATER OR INDEED ANY EARLIER YOU SHALL GET INSTRUCTIONS BY NEXT POST YOU MUST

OPEN LETTER UP IMMEDIATELY RE-
CEIVED KEY HAS BEEN ATTACHED TO
NOTE LEFT DOOR LOCKED SECURELY
I SHALL NOT OPEN SO NEED TO OPEN
YOURSELF HOPE OBEY ORDERS
FROM PROMETHEUS PIGGETY ES-
QUIRE DONT FORGET KEY OR YOU
REALLY CANNOT MAKE AN ENTRY.

'We used to write messages where the first letter of every word made up other words.'

He grunted and began to print in a hand so small I could hardly read it.

MGYALVICFTENLOIAEYSGIBNPYMOLUI-
RKHBATNLDLSISNOSNTOYHOOFPPED-
FKOYRCMAE

'That does not appear to make much sense.'
'What if we reverse it?' I suggested. 'EAMCR . . . No, that does not work. Sometimes we would use the letter before or after in the alphabet.'

He printed out DZLBQ and then FBNDS.

'It could be two or more letters in either direction.' He tried a few combinations, and as he did so I looked again at the first letters, and then it sprang out at me.

'My life,' I said and he looked down.

'Of course. What a dullard you have been. It uses the first letters of alternate words.' He wrote them down.

MY LIFE LIES IN YOUR HANDS SO NO HOPE FOR ME

'Now the letter that came with the key said . . .' He had it inside a copy of *Exchange and Mart*.

GRICE THIS KEY
OPENS
THE OUTER
DOOR
LOCK
TURN
ANTI CLOCKWISE TO
GAIN ENTRY PIG GETY

Sidney Grice wrinkled his brow briefly and printed GKT.

'No, that is no use.'

'Try starting with the second word.'

'I was about to.' He wrote TOOLATE. 'Too late.' He cricked his neck to look back and up at me. 'They are toying with me, March. Do you still think I am imagining it?'

We went back to our chairs.

'Is that all it is?' I asked. 'A game?'

My guardian closed his eyes and from his heavy regular chest movements I might have thought that he was asleep, except for the two halfpennies clicking around in his left hand while his right hand massaged his brow. I watched him for twenty minutes while my mind whirled in its search for a solution. Then, without opening his eyes, he spun the coins high in the air, caught them and announced, 'I requested another interview with Baroness Foskett this morning but she refuses to see me.'

'I do not think she believes she is in danger,' I said.

'Who' — my guardian opened his eyes — 'is in danger from whom?'

We heard a thump and turned to see the window splotted with horse manure. 'Botheration.' He blinked and his socket welled with blood. 'A cat-o'-ten-tails would be too good for them.'

61
MACBETH AND
THE GUINEA PRIZE

Sidney Grice was usually a dapper dresser but that evening he had excelled himself — white tie and tails and a long black cloak lined in red silk.

'Are you going to the opera?' I asked and his face darkened.

'Almost as bad.' He selected a cane. 'Dorna has invited me to the theatre — some Shakespearean tripe — and she had already obtained the tickets so I did not see how I could get out of it. And you know how I hate to offend people.'

'You would rather kill yourself,' I said.

'And deprive the world of my genius? Never.' He swapped his cane for another.

'Which play are you going to see?'

He frimped up his bow in the mirror. 'Oh, *Hamlet* or something equally dreary — *Macbeth,* I think.'

'Actually, I was thinking about that quotation . . .'

'Yes, yes.' He polished the nap on his top hat. 'We can discuss your opinions on henpecked Celtic regicides when we are stranded on a desert island and have dredged every other topic of conversation to the apogee of exhaustion. Where is my cab? I shall be even later than I hoped.'

'Yes, but speaking of *Hamlet,* when —'

'*Macbeth,* March. Do pay attention.' There were four sharp raps on the door and Sidney Grice threw it open. 'At last.'

A cabby stood on the steps in a short woollen jacket and scuffed bowler. He put his arm over his eyes. 'Cripes, Mr Grice, you quite bedazzled me. Goin' to arrest the queen, are we?'

'I do not know where *you* are going,' my guardian said, 'but *I* am going to witness the murder of a Highland king.'

'Blimey. Can't you put a stop to it?'

My guardian shivered. 'I am two hundred and seventy-six years too late, I fear.'

'I wasn't that slow in coming,' the driver protested. 'Oh, and the men wanted me to ask — does the guinea prize still hold?'

'Until further notice.'

'How will we know the other one?'

'She has a large brown birthmark on the left of her face.'

'So does my greyhound,' the cabby

grumbled and went back to his cab.

'Do not wait up.' Sidney Grice went down the steps. 'I shall be too depressed for conversation.'

'She got it wrong,' I called after him, and he turned reluctantly.

'Who got what wrong?'

'The baroness. She said *How weary, flat, stale and unprofitable seem to me all the uses of this world,*' I recited. 'But she should have said, *How weary, stale, flat, et cetera.* I do not suppose it matters.'

My guardian's cheek ticked. 'You knew that the first time we saw her?'

'Well, I noticed, but it did not seem important.'

'*Important?*' The wind whipped at his cloak, wrapping it around his legs. 'All clues are important.'

'I did not know it was a clue.'

'For gawdsake,' the cabby complained from his high seat.

'Of course you did not.' He fought to untangle his legs and keep his hat on at the same time. 'That is why you will never be a detective.'

I took two steps back and slammed the door as hard as I could.

'I do that,' Molly said, running up to see what was happening. 'When you are both out and clients call. *Stop botherating him,* I say. *He's got too much to worry about already.*'

'I would advise you not to tell Mr Grice that,' I said and Molly screwed up her nose while she thought about it.

'I will take your advise,' she decided at last and went back down the basement stairs.

I ran upstairs to bring Spirit down and we played with the tassels on a cushion until she grew tired and fell asleep on it, and I tried to read Jane Austen, but it was all simpering girls whose only ambition was to marry. The next thing I knew Sidney Grice was shaking my shoulder.

'Are you awake?'

'Very nearly.' My first thought was to hide Spirit, but she was already standing on her hind legs and trying to claw the hem of his cloak. Somewhat to my surprise, he ignored her.

'You should not sleep upright. It drains blood from the brain.'

He laid his hat on the table.

'I am sorry I did not mention Baroness Foskett's misquotation sooner,' I said and he piffed.

'Perhaps it means nothing.' My guardian unclipped his cloak. 'Perhaps it means everything. I shall find out which.'

'Do you think she was telling us something?'

He puffed. 'I am not even sure she is mentally continent.'

'So how was the play?'

'Unutterably tedious,' he said. 'The only saving grace is that we missed the beginning because Dorna could not find her glove.'

'At least *Macbeth* is one of the shorter plays,' I consoled him. 'You did not have to sit through *Hamlet*. That is a much longer play, though you might have found the murder more . . .'

Mr G looked at me closely. 'More what?'

'Unusual,' I whispered.

'When you have ceased exhibiting a hitherto unsuspected talent for imitating alabaster statues, perhaps you would like to tell me what you are talking about.'

'Dear God,' I said. 'How could I have been so stupid?'

'I have often asked myself that.'

'Do you know how Hamlet's father was killed?'

'I was not engaged on that case but I suspect you would like to tell me, preferably before I am too decrepit to care.'

'By poison,' I said, 'through his ear.'

Mr G's face tightened. 'You knew that?'

'Of course I did. I have just told you so.'

He took off his scarf. 'And yet you did not tell me?'

'You hate it when I talk about poetry or plays. Besides, it may not really be —'

Sidney Grice flung his cloak and scarf on to the back of his chair and Spirit darted under his desk. 'What affliction did Green suffer from — apart from obnoxiousness and toothache?'

'Earache.' I sat up. 'Do you really think somebody could have put cyanide in his ear?'

'No.' Sidney Grice looked absently at Spirit as she came out with a ball of paper. 'I think that *Mr Green* put cyanide into Mr Green's ear. Remember he had the vicar with the same ailment to whom he showed his medicine? Remember the boys who came into his shop? I remarked that it was an intriguing incident at the time. The only reason a street creature would ransack a shop and not steal anything is because he was under strict instruction and being paid already. The murderer did not want to risk any of them being apprehended with stolen goods. A captured minion points a finger, no matter how vaguely, towards his master.'

'Speaking of fingers,' I said. 'What has happened to yours?'

The top of his right first finger had a cratered ulcer with dead white edges. He looked down as if interested to find it in that condition. 'Oh that. I burnt it. Where was I? Oh yes. What could be easier than to slip a poisoned capsule into his pill box in the confusion?'

'But how could anyone know which one he would use the next day?'

'Simplicity itself. The capsules are made of soft wax. You lightly press them so that they stick together and place the poisoned one on top.' He rang for tea. 'I called in at St Agatha's Rectory on the way back from a nightcap with Dr Berry.'

'I bet they were pleased to see you. It is well after midnight.'

'Well, you would lose your wager.' He sat on the arm of his chair. 'They were most irate and informed me that I shall fare badly on Judgement Day. But, more relevantly, they were adamant that a Reverend Golding did not and never has resided there.'

I thought about it. 'But if a capsule of prussic acid leaked into Mr Green's ear surely he would have been in agony.'

'I shall verify the point, though rather more articulately, with Dorna, but it is probable that Horatio Green had been using oil of cloves for years in his ear, and that you could smell this rather than his dental treatment.'

'I could also smell nitrous oxide,' I said more snappily than I had intended. I knew it was unreasonable but I disliked the thought of him discussing our case with another woman, but he resumed, seemingly unaware. 'In which case the oil would have corroded most of the nerve endings in his ear and Eustachian tube long ago. Also, he had probably administered laudanum to himself before his trip to the late and unlamented Silas Braithwaite, to assuage his anxiety and relieve his pain. On top of this, I believe, some dentists get their patients to rinse with a solution of cocaine for its analgesic effects, so he would not have felt anything much until the acid drained into the back of his throat and down his oesophagus.' He sat on his scarf in the chair. 'I am still not sure if the murderer could know that the capsule would melt while Green was here or if it was pure luck,' he pondered as Spirit, ignoring my warning signals, jumped up beside him.

I clicked my fingers and he winced. 'When you told Mr Green to stop talking twaddle,' I recalled, 'I think he was trying to tell you that he inserted the capsules after breakfast so . . .'

Sidney Grice tickled Spirit's ear. 'The first cup of tea he had after that would have been hot enough to melt the wax.' He dangled his watch on its chain for Spirit to toy with. 'And, unusually, the pot was steaming that morning.'

'So, if you had not interrupted —'

'What a charming creature,' Mr G interrupted and allowed himself a tiny smile. 'Get rid of it.'

62

STALLIONS, STICKS
AND SANDWICHES

I went back to my room and lay on the bed, and looked at the spidery cracks radiating from an old lamp hook in the ceiling, much too tired to even think about sleep.

You rode a black stallion. It reared and I was afraid it would throw you or bring its great metalled hoofs crashing on my head, but you laughed and steadied it and reached down to pull me up, lifting me as if I weighed nothing, almost floating me into the saddle behind you, and I put my arms round your waist and my face against your broad back. I could feel your sword handle dig into my thigh and the roughness of your woollen tunic damp on my cheek, and I could smell it too, like freshly scythed hay. Your horse reared again but I was safe now. I held on tight and knew that you would never let me fall. But even in my happiness I knew that I would betray

492

you and that any moment you would turn,
a faceless horror, towards me and that the
nightmare would start all over again because the nightmare was always true, but
the stirrup was very tight on my boot and
it was tugging quite hard. I called out.

'Edward!'
But Molly was shaking my foot and say-
ing, 'Wake up, miss, or his nibs will go
without you.'
I stretched. 'Go?'
'Without you,' she repeated.
I forced my eyes open. 'Go where?'
'Baryness Fostick.'
I sat up. 'Give me five minutes and do *not*
let him go without me. Hang on to his
ankles if necessary.'
Molly looked doubtful. 'I'm not sure he
would like that, miss.'
I climbed off the bed. 'Just tell him I am
coming.'
Sidney Grice was winding down the flag
and Molly was dashing along the hall with
his flask as I trotted down the stairs. He
looked up at me. 'March.' He had reinserted
his eye and his face was fresh and clear. 'I
thought you were planning on spending the
whole day in bed.'
'What time is it?' I glanced at the clock as

I reached the bottom step. 'Why, it is very nearly seven o'clock.'

He took out his watch. 'Six forty-eight and fifteen seconds.'

'Have you eaten?'

He dabbed his lips as if expecting to find crumbs. 'I made do with toast and prune juice and a very good pot of tea, but there was no time for eggs, I am afraid.'

I grabbed my coat. 'But I have had nothing.'

He looked along his cane. 'You have only yourself to blame, if you must slumber your life away.' He dropped his stick back into the rack and chose another, swishing it, handle down as if rehearsing a golf shot.

'I have had less than three hours' sleep.'

'Three hours!' Molly hugged herself. 'What luxurousness. He had me up half the night boiling kettles and making bread sandwiches.'

Sidney Grice hummed atonally as he slipped his arms into his Ulster.

'But we always breakfast at eight.' I grabbed my cloak and shook myself awake. 'Has something happened?'

'There was a possible sighting at about six o'clock.' He selected a bowler.

'Primrose McKay?' I fastened the clasp and he nodded.

'The driver could not be sure, but he thought he spotted her going north from Richmond.'

'Do you think she could be heading for Kew?'

He smacked some dust off the rim with his gloves. 'What I think is irrelevant. It is what might happen that matters.' His face was grim. 'Presumably the baroness is taking my telegraphed report seriously, for she has agreed to see us immediately.'

There was a hammering on the door and Molly opened it to a corpulent blotchy-faced cabby in a long coachman's coat. 'Did you want this cab today or next year?'

'That is a fatuous question if you care to consider it, which I do not,' my guardian told him. 'If you are quite ready, Miss Middleton . . .' He slipped the flask into his satchel. 'You may sate your epicurean excesses when we return. In the meantime, we have a murderer to catch.'

Cutteridge was waiting for us and we were much in need of his lantern for, though the sun had risen to the left of us as we travelled through the city, there was another pea-souper and even the snarls of the mastiffs were dampened in the choking air.

'They have been very restless,' he said,

'especially as you instructed me not to feed them, sir.'

'They will be fed soon enough.' Sidney Grice lit his safety lantern. 'How quiet it is. The whole world might be listening to us.'

We made our way slowly along the path, Cutteridge leading and my guardian to the rear, following the paraffin glares and placing our feet carefully into the shadows.

'I saw a dead adder there last time,' I said and Sidney Grice stopped.

'How did it die?'

'I do not know. It was rotten and its head had been chewed off.'

'Dear God,' he said softly as we reached the gravelled clearing.

Mordent House was half-hidden from us that morning, lost in the heavy fog and only breaking through it into darkness. At the top of the steps Cutteridge paused. 'Have you come to save her ladyship, sir?'

My guardian took off his hat. 'If the baroness can be saved then I shall do it this day, but I fear I may be too late.'

The old butler looked alarmed.

'Has anybody else called?' I questioned him. 'A lady with long golden hair and a mark on her face?'

'No one, miss.' He glanced anxiously at Sidney Grice.

'Is there any way she could have got past you?' I asked as we entered the hall. It was gloomier than I had ever known it.

'Not whilst I have life,' Cutteridge vowed, and we stood in the dank oppressiveness, listening to him make his way up the crooked stairs as the house groaned forbiddingly.

Mr G went to the window, pulled back the curtain and crouched as if to peer out of the lower pane. 'Not only has the lacewing been removed but the entire web has been replaced.'

'What an astonishing turn of events.'

'Do you not understand?' He traced the web with his finger. 'I said *replaced* not *rebuilt*. This web was constructed by a different spider — the same species but with structurally sound legs.'

'Perhaps its leg healed,' I suggested as he scrabbled about in the dust on the floor. 'It might have just sprained it sliding down the banister with a tray of drinks.'

'No. Here it is.' He held up the squashed remains for my inspection.

'I did not realize you were so fond of it.'

But Sidney Grice was not listening. He had shuffled back to the window and was busily pulling the web apart. 'Dear God,' he said again as he crammed his pince-nez on to his nose. 'I fear the murderer is already in the house.'

He let the mildewed satin flop back over the glass and got to his feet.

'Then we must go upstairs immediately.'

Mr G stood and stared out into the garden. 'On the contrary, we must wait.'

'For what?' I thought about my own question. 'But surely the baroness could not have killed them?'

'I have been a fool, March.' He spun round, his lantern almost going out. 'Baroness Foskett is the kindest, most gentle woman I have ever met.'

I coughed. 'That is not the Baroness Foskett I know.'

He turned his back on me. 'Then perhaps you do not know her at all.'

'Perhaps you are seeing her as she was,' I challenged him. 'Perhaps she became embittered by her bereavements.'

He banged his cane on the floor, the impact travelling through the empty hall and passageways, to the masked ceiling and through the faded rooms. 'Lady Foskett's heart was broken by the disappearance of her son and her husband's death, but she turned to good works. She spent her fortune on the charities that you only witter about and, when her fortune was gone, she wrapped herself in mourning so deep that the eye of man could not penetrate it.'

'But why are we discussing this rather than trying to protect her?'

'The numbers are against us,' my guardian said.

Cutteridge returned. 'Her ladyship will see you now, sir, miss.' And my guardian sighed. 'Oh, Cutteridge, good and faithful, I only hope that you are telling the truth.'

The old man stiffened. 'I would never lie to you, sir.'

And Sidney Grice patted his arm just once. 'And I have never doubted your integrity.'

'I must ask you to put your light out, sir.'

Mr G did as he was bidden and slipped it into its pouch before we crept, well apart and close to the wall, up the swaying staircase, not able even to see the floor of the great hall so far below us, while the corridor was filled with a blackness so heavy that Cutteridge's lantern, as he placed it on the boards, could scarcely break through it.

My guardian stopped and crouched so suddenly that I almost toppled over him.

'Fun,' he whispered.

'What is?'

Cutteridge knocked once before pushing the door open to reveal the room, wavering in the candlelight, with the gauze box and the two chairs to which he directed us.

'Sidney,' the speaking horn hissed. 'To what do we owe this allegedly urgent intrusion?'

'The time has come,' my guardian said. 'This great dynasty is swaying on its rotten foundations and is about to come crashing down.'

'Are you presuming to threaten me, you ill-bred —'

'The Grices go back a thousand years,' Sidney Grice interrupted, 'and, should I choose to continue the line, it will survive another millennium. The Fosketts are drowning in their own filth.'

'How dare you —'

'I cannot hear you.'

'I said —'

'I heard what was said,' my guardian broke in. 'Loud and clear. But I cannot hear the voice behind it.'

The smell of incense was even stronger today.

'I do not know what you mean.'

Sidney Grice leaned forward. 'When somebody talks through a speaking tube you hear their voice *and* the magnified sound. I can only hear the sound.'

'You are not making yourself clear.' There

was a long pause. 'My acid-corroded vocal cords are very weak.'

'Fifteen point two-two-five-nine-six-six,' my guardian said.

'What are you talking about?' The voice shook a little.

'The logarithm of today's date to the first six decimal points. You must have got up very early to have scratched that on the window, Baroness' — his tone became mocking — 'Lady . . . Parthena . . . Foskett.' And as he spoke Sidney Grice undid the straps of his satchel.

'Mr Grice,' Cutteridge said, 'I must ask you not to address her ladyship so disrespectfully.'

'Nor shall I.' There was a slight scuffling noise and Sidney Grice sprang up. Cutteridge snatched the air behind his shoulder, flinging the chair aside as my guardian rushed for the gauze box.

'Save me, Cutteridge.'

Sidney Grice whipped round and I saw in the candlelight that he had his revolver in his hand. 'Stand where you are.'

Cutteridge stopped in his tracks. 'I do not know why you are doing this, sir — I can only assume that you have gone quite mad. But you must know that the threat of death will not deter me from doing my duty.'

Sidney Grice took two steps back and the old servant took two forward. My guardian took aim. 'Do not make me do it, Cutteridge.' And Cutteridge regarded him wonderingly. 'I pushed you on a swing, Master Sidney. I gave you rides on my shoulders.'

'Oh, for heaven's sake,' my guardian said and tossed the gun on the floor. I leaped off my chair but Cutteridge was at it first. It looked so small in his great left fist, that tiny metal bringer of death.

'Move away, please, sir.' He raised the gun and my guardian took one more step back. He was level with the box now. 'Move away.'

'Shoot him, Cutteridge,' the metal voice commanded. 'He will kill me if he can.'

My guardian reached out slowly and grasped the curtain as the major-domo pulled back the hammer. I ran at Cutteridge but he flung me aside with his right arm. 'Please excuse me, miss.'

'Have a care. I am not wearing any protective clothing,' Sidney Grice told him and I thought I saw him tremble. And the gun was pointing straight at my guardian when Cutteridge pulled the trigger.

The flash almost blinded me, but I still saw the impact on Sidney Grice's coat, directly over his heart, and his hand jump convulsively to the hole. And the explosion all but burst my eardrums, but I still heard the curtain rip in his clenched fist and the crash as he toppled over on to the table, sending it flying, and the candle snuffing out mid-air. And I still heard the thin cackle through the speaking trumpet, drowned out by the scream that came from me.

63
THE DARKNESS

The darkness was complete.

'You have killed him!'

From behind and above me. 'I did my duty. He understood that.'

'Oh dear God!' I crawled towards where I saw my guardian fall and felt the tumbled table. 'Get a light. He may still be alive.'

'I fear not, miss. I have always been an excellent shot.'

'Get a light!'

There was a scratching and the flare of a Lucifer was thrown up on Cutteridge's gaunt face as he stooped for the candle and lit it shakily.

'My lady . . .' He stopped in confusion, shielding the dancing flame with a cupped hand.

The gauze had been torn away and Baroness Foskett sat in her high-backed chair perfectly still, her long black dress arranged carefully over the dais, her jaw hanging in a frozen laugh.

'Get the lantern.'

'Right away, miss.'

The candle blew out as he opened the door. I reached Mr G. 'Do not dare to be dead, you miserable old devil,' I whimpered as Cutteridge returned, turning up the wick on his lantern. My guardian was waxen and his eyes were closed. I slid his sleeve up to feel for a pulse.

'Oh, my lady,' Cutteridge whispered as I unbuttoned my guardian's waistcoat.

'Ouch,' Sidney Grice said, coming up on one elbow and rubbing his chest.

'How on earth . . . ?' I released his wrist.

'It was a blank, but the impact of the wadding had quite a punch.' He scrambled to his feet and checked himself. 'It has torn my favourite Ulster.' He shook himself down and patted his trousers.

I dusted my dress. 'A good job you were wearing it.' And we turned to look at the box.

'My lady,' Cutteridge gasped.

The baroness's hair was fastened back by a silver comb, her hands resting on the arms of her throne, her fingers bare except for one gold band on the left, her eyes unblinking and membranous white, her head thrown back a little. Her skin was grey, blotched with maroon and splattered with dark streaks, a grotesque, shrivelled distortion, white teeth bared in silent mirthlessness.

'Is her ladyship . . .' Cutteridge could not bring himself to finish.

'Dead,' Sidney Grice said. 'And for quite some time. She is starting to mummify.'

'That perfume,' I said. 'It is myrrh.'

Sidney Grice looked at me. 'You smelled it before and did not mention it?'

'I assumed you —'

'You knew I was incapacitated by a cold. If I had known . . . Dash it all, Miss Middleton. I would have thought even you would know it is used to preserve bodies.'

Cutteridge set the lantern down heavily on the floor. 'But . . .'

'The speaking trumpet is connected to this brass pipe.' My guardian indicated with his cane. 'Which goes under the chair and back through that hole in the panelling. Why do you knock before you enter, Cutteridge?'

Cutteridge looked confused. 'Her ladyship instructed me to do so, sir.'

'Servants never knock,' I remembered. 'Not unless the occupant of the room wants some warning to be ready.'

Sidney Grice raised his voice. 'You might as well join us now, Rupert.' And almost

506

immediately a panel in the wall at the back of the box hinged open, and out stepped a man. He was tall with faded and thinning red hair, and had to lower his head slightly to go under the lintel.

'Hello, Sidney.' The voice was husky and quite faint. 'I could never stop myself scratching those numbers. It drove my father almost into a frenzy.'

'We thought you had been eaten by cannibals,' I said.

'If only I had,' he responded. 'Something far worse than that feeds on me now. Oh, Sidney, you have no idea what it was like out there.'

'I have a very good idea,' my guardian said. 'I went looking for you.'

'You knew I was alive?'

'No.' Mr G gazed at him. 'I intended to bring your body home, and I believed I was getting close before I was stricken by malaria and shipped back against my will.'

'Malaria? Oh, fortunate man,' Rupert cried derisively. 'You deserved far worse than that, Sidney. It was because of you I journeyed to that unutterable pit of Hades in the first place. I had everything — a title, wealth — I was one of the most eligible bachelors on the kingdom and you destroyed it all by convincing me that it might all turn to dust.' A brown liquid trickled down Rupert's chin. 'I went looking for God. I thought I could find him by spreading his word.'

'And did you?' I asked and a great sigh came from him.

'I lost him — or rather he lost me — and you cannot be lost by something which does not exist. It was in God's abandonment of me that I found him for certain.'

'That is the biggest perversion of logical syllogism —' my guardian began but Rupert doubled up in spasms of coughing.

'Shut your mouth,' Rupert screeched when he had recovered sufficiently. 'I hate you.'

Mr G flinched. 'It is not my fault that there is no proof for you to cling to.'

Do not ask for proof. It shall not be given, Rupert quoted.

'I should be out of a job if that were the case,' Sidney Grice said wryly, and Rupert caught his breath.

'Very well then, how about this for evidence?' He raised his head. At first I thought it must be a trick of the light, but his skin was as white as bone and his nose had been eroded so that the turbinate bones were clearly visible through the few shreds of skin remaining. His left lower eyelid was

508

gone too, exposing a raw eyeball.

'*Cochliomyia,*' Sidney Grice said in shock and Rupert laughed hollowly.

'Well diagnosed, Sidney. Most people would think I was a leper and, in every other sense of the word, I am. As it is, I am a modern-day Herod, rich and powerful and being eaten by worms, blowfly maggots burrowing into my putrefying flesh.'

'Can nothing be done?' I asked and he grinned gruesomely.

'When it began I was told it was just a question of picking them out with tweezers. They come up for air sometimes and then you grab them, but they are too numerous for that — and to think it all started with an insect bite. Then the doctors tried surgery, cutting them out of me, but the new wounds only helped them burrow deeper. I have bathed in mercury and been soaked in paraffin. I have been cupped and bled and burnt. The most expensive doctors in England were as effective as the witch doctors' charms I endured in that accursed place. They are inside me now. They burrow into my gut and hatch out in my lungs. I cough them up in gouts of foaming blood. They are destroying my face. I was such a handsome fellow once, was I not, Sidney?'

My guardian did not respond, but Rupert

509

clutched his own head and cried out, 'They are in my brain. I can feel them — loathsome.' He fought for air. 'My mother hid me away and this house became my prison, with Cutteridge the jailor. She could not let the world see what the last Baron Foskett had become and I had no wish to be gawked at by society, pitied and repellent, and with no hope of carrying on our ancient line unless a remedy could be found. She nursed me. Every penny she had went on quack treatments and tricksters. She gave eight thousand pounds to a man who had cured a maharaja and brought him along to show us, but they both turned out to be shipping clerks from Southampton. The Foskett fortune went to swindlers and cranks.'

Sidney Grice said, 'And so you formed this murderous society.'

'It was not meant to be murderous,' Rupert said. 'You were supposed to prevent that.'

'Oh, Rupert.' My guardian straightened his cuffs. 'Every step of the way was calculated to destroy me.'

Rupert coughed. 'I know nothing of that. The only crime that I have committed was to cover up my mother's death. If it were known that she had passed away, then the prize would have gone to one of the other members.' Rupert pinched at his face and tugged and held out a squirming, hook-headed, bloated maggot for our inspection before tossing it away. 'You see what lives in my flesh. My mother tended to me. She spent hours with needles, digging these disgusting creatures out of me, but they were too many for her and they burrowed too deep. I thought that she was safe so long as none of the flies hatched — they do not live long in this climate — but some survived and she got bitten. She did not notice until it was too late. I tried to help. Can you imagine it, Sidney — the last surviving members of one of the greatest families in England sitting picking at each other like monkeys in a cage? In the end she was blind, clawing at her eyes as they tunnelled behind. We called in Dr Simmons. He had treated the family for years and at least we knew he would be discreet, but he was hopeless. He injected caustic soda under her skin and into her stomach. She died horribly, Sidney, beside herself in agony. I could have killed the man but he saved me the trouble and killed himself with his glut-tony, and here I was, penniless and alone save for Cutteridge.'

'And so you set up the speaking tube to

make it appear that the baroness was still alive,' I said.

Cutteridge was staring at the shrivelled remains of his mistress. 'So I have been serving a ghost.'

Rupert cackled. 'I thought about tying wires to her wrists to make them move, but I was worried you might spot them.'

Cutteridge picked up a long pole from the dais floor. 'And may I ask what this boat hook is for, sir?'

'I tried to turn her head with it when they first visited but it made too much of a clatter.'

Cutteridge exhaled heavily.

'But how would you claim the money?' I asked.

'Once the other members had expired I intended to get Dr Simmons to explain that he had been treating me secretly, and to certify that my mother's heart had failed, but then he died.'

'How inconsiderate of him,' my guardian said. 'But what good would money be to you in your condition?'

'It will buy me a cure. There *is* a cure now, Sidney, but it is expensive.'

'False cures invariably cost more than real ones.' Mr G peered at his old friend. 'Step forward, Rupert.'

'What?'

'Just one step for the lady . . . Thank you. I see you still drag your foot a little from the broken ankle.'

'What of it?'

'You are wearing a lot of cologne,' I remarked.

'It masks the stench of my decay, and it might even kill a few of the worms.' Rupert had a hole through his hand, an unholy stigmata. 'It deters the blighters from coming to the surface at any rate.'

'That could be why we did not find any in Mr Gallop's storeroom,' I said, and he eyed me sadly.

'Plus I wore a balaclava helmet to attract less attention.' He wheezed in a laugh that I had come to think of as his mother's. 'And to think at one time I craved it. You have no idea how hard I tried to impress you, Sidney.'

'I saw them use blowpipes when I went to look for you,' Sidney Grice said. 'There were footprints in Warrington Gallop's storeroom showing his killer to be a tall man with small feet and a slight limp.'

'Do you really think that any jury will convict an aristocrat of murder on such a sketchy conglomeration of evidence?' Rupert said.

'I have much more evidence than that,' Sidney Grice told him. 'Show me your watch, Rupert.'

But Rupert laughed. 'I have no idea what you are talking about, but how do you think you can even get out of here, Sidney?' he challenged. 'I released the dogs the moment you came in the house.'

Cutteridge cleared his throat. 'I feel it my duty to inform you that I bolted the cage gate this morning. The catch is rusty and I did not want any mishaps while we had visitors.'

'Gerry will be cross,' my guardian said. 'He could have had an extra hour in bed.'

Rupert coughed a spray of black blood into his clawed, torn hand.

'That is why we saw blood droplets on the floor in Mr Gallop's shop,' I realized.

'Precisely.' Mr G wiped his face. 'But tell me, Rupert, how did you plan to divide the money?'

Rupert blinked, but his upper eyelids had been too badly chewed to meet the lowers. 'Divide?'

'You do not think I believe that you alone committed all those crimes?' Sidney Grice poked a finger through the hole in his coat.

'We were to be married.' Rupert smiled ruefully and behind the ravages of his

514

disease I glimpsed the remnants of a shy young man in love, but my guardian flapped his hand in contempt.

'Do you really imagine you would survive twenty-four hours after whatever mockery of a wedding you entered into?'

'She loves me.' Rupert wiped his nose with the back of his sleeve and looked down, as if suddenly realizing the implausibility of his words.

Sidney Grice's face was ashen. 'You are going to hang, Rupert, and your lovely partner in crime will hang with you.'

'I am afraid I cannot allow that, sir.' Cutteridge licked his dry lips. 'I am sure you have not forgotten that you are not the only one who carries a gun, but mine is loaded with bullets.' He brought a revolver out of his inner pocket and Sidney Grice took a step towards him. 'You know I will use it, sir.'

Sidney Grice froze.

'Will you kill me too?' I asked, stepping in front of my guardian.

'Get out of the way, March,' Sidney Grice commanded.

'No.'

'I cannot but salute your loyalty and sacrifice, Miss Middleton,' Cutteridge said, 'for they are qualities which I have always sought to cultivate. And your guardian is the man I admire above all others, but you must realize that my first loyalty is to the house I have served as my father served, since childhood.'

'And you would murder innocent people for this vile creature?' I asked.

'When Baron Rupert was but five years old I dived into the stormy seas at Calais to save him, though I could not swim.' Cutteridge swallowed. 'I shall do my duty to the end, miss.'

'And so shall I.' I straightened my body in an attempt to stop it from shaking.

'Why are you protecting this man, March?' Rupert sneered.

'March, please . . .' Sidney Grice spoke urgently.

'Because he protects me.'

'Please stand to one side, miss.' Cutteridge steadied the gun with his right hand.

'He is all I have,' I burst out and my guardian took hold of my shoulders.

64
THE WEB AND THE CAGE

'You will never get out of London, let alone England,' Sidney Grice told him, and the old servant frowned thinly.

'Be that as it may, sir, I cannot let the last Baron Foskett hang like a common felon.' His hand did not waver and he did not take his eyes off us as he backed away.

'Got you this time, Sidney,' Rupert crowed, stepping off the dais. Close up, I could see writhing under the blackened skin of his cheek. 'You always thought you were cleverer than me.'

'I,' my guardian corrected him. 'Cleverer than *I*. You are using *than* as a conjunction not a preposition. If you are going to make an ass of yourself, you might as well do it grammatically.'

Rupert scrunched his body in a paroxysm of pique. 'You —'

'That aside,' Mr G continued, 'I have always had a very high opinion of your intelligence.' And Rupert exposed more stumps of teeth in what might have been a vestigial smile before my guardian added, 'for a non-Grice.'

Rupert emitted a cry of rage. 'I had you in my sights, Sidney. I should have put a dart in you while I could.'

'Just out of interest,' Sidney Grice said, 'am I correct in assuming that you used viper venom and that you hollowed the dart out to carry a larger dose?'

'The dead adder,' I recalled.

'Which you omitted to mention to me at the time.'

'I see what you are doing.' Rupert spat some blood into a sodden handkerchief. 'You are trying to distract me, but it will do you no good.' He turned to face Cutteridge. 'They will raise the alarm if we leave them. Get rid of them, Cutteridge. Shoot them in the stomachs so they die slowly.'

The old retainer frowned. 'Do you remember when you were six, sir? You used the Devlin Plate as a toboggan and dented it, and I took the blame, though your grandfather laid into me with his riding crop. I have always done everything in my power to protect you and, if I could take your place, I would willingly do so, but this is beyond my powers now.' He cleared his throat. 'And I must do what I can for the family.' Cutteridge swallowed. 'I am so sorry.' His arm jerked up as he raised the pole and thrust the boating hook squelching into his master's shoulder. Rupert instinctively pulled away and howled. 'You will find it hurts a great deal less if do not struggle, my lord.'

Rupert forced himself to hold still. 'Cutteridge, what are you doing?'

'You made a puppet show of my mistress, the finest woman who ever graced this world, Lady Parthena the Dowager Baroness Foskett. You have desecrated her body.'

'She was *my* mother,' Rupert sneered, 'not yours.'

Cutteridge twisted the pole and Rupert shrieked, clutching at his shoulder.

'You might be best not to encourage me to hurt you as much as you deserve,' Cutteridge said. 'Please pick up the lantern, my lord. We shall be needing it.'

Rupert bent gingerly and did as he was told, and Cutteridge backed out of the room, leading Rupert like a bull by its ring.

We waited, craning our ears. I heard the stairs creak and Rupert yelp in pain and Cutteridge saying, 'I am so sorry, sir, but if you keep up, it will be less painful.'

'Stay here,' Sidney Grice whispered and rolled his eye when he saw that I would not.

'Keep behind me then.'

He brought out his safety lantern and lit it, and I looked back at Baroness Foskett as we quit the room. Was this husk really all that was left of the beautiful, wealthy, intelligent woman whose portrait graced the ballroom, who had lost the man she loved and died nursing her monstrous son? The long, lovely hands that must have cosseted her child were leathery claws now.

Mr G picked up his gun and slipped it into his pocket.

'Why did you throw it down?'

'I knew that Cutteridge would be prepared to shoot me if he thought he was protecting his mistress.' We crossed the corridor. 'And I preferred him do it with a blank rather than his own gun.'

'Do you not have any live bullets?'

'Yes, but I shall not shoot Cutteridge.'

'Because he spared our lives?'

My guardian piffed. 'I thought you would have known by now that gratitude is alien to my nature.' There was light coming into the hall when we peered over the banister rail. 'But I have never yet killed an innocent man on purpose.'

'The front door is open,' I said, the stairs swaying alarmingly as we set off down them.

'But they did not go out through it. The

cobweb in that archway is ripped.' He raced into the passageway. A rotting velvet curtain had been tied back with what was probably once a golden cord, and it fell to dusty scraps when my shoulder brushed against it.

'Where does this go?'

'To the servants' quarters.' He was running now, his body dipping with his shortened leg and, with the lantern in front of him, I could hardly see to keep up. The passage sloped down, yard after yard, windowless and airless. 'More torn webs.'

There was a light in the distance and we raced towards it, almost tumbling as we emerged into an old kitchen dominated by a long, central pine table and a huge cooking range, copper pans resting empty upon it.

I touched the back of a chair. It had a streak of fresh blood on it. 'They must have come through here,' I said.

'You astonish me.' An open side door led into another corridor. 'As I recall from when I played here, this wing is more of a maze than Hampton Court.'

We ran along to a flight of stone steps going down and he held out his lantern. 'They did not take this way. The steps are littered with dead beetles and not one of them has

521

been crushed.'

'What —'

'Listen.' Sidney Grice cocked his head and I heard the dogs, their barks hurtling down the passages.

'Something has agitated them,' I said. 'Where is that draught coming from?' He licked his finger and held it up. 'I have never found that works,' I said.

'This way.' My guardian darted to the left. 'The back way is open.'

The barking was nearer and wilder.

The corridor was lit by the day now and a breeze blew along it from outside, carrying the fresh air and the yips of the dogs and a cry that pierced through it all. Sidney Grice broke into a run, drawing his revolver from his pocket as he went, with me close at his heels, out into a courtyard garden, the raised squares of what must have been herb beds overflowing with nettles. The side gate was ajar and, as we rushed round the beds towards it, there was a rattling and clatter and the squeal of rusty wheels.

'Cutteridge. Listen to me. I am Baron Foskett, the master you are sworn to serve.'

We rushed through the gate on to a stone path. 'This way.' My guardian slithered on the wet moss as he swung to the left and round the corner. The clattering was louder now and the barks more frantic.

Rupert stood trapped in an iron-barred run, leading from the dog pound to the garden and gated at either end. He was stooping, the boat hook still jutting from his shoulder and dangling into the ground. Behind him, yapping wildly and throwing their solid bodies at the inner gate, was a pack of huge black mastiffs, teeth bared as they snarled and snapped at the barrier separating them from him.

'I swore to serve your father and your mother,' Cutteridge declared and I looked over to see him standing to one side, turning a corroded metal wheel, and I saw that it was pulling on a wire and that the wire was connected to a heavy bolt which was sliding steadily backwards on the inner gate.

'And, for your mother's sake, I was of service to you, but no man could command my obedience when he has turned my lady into an obscenity.'

The bolt stuck but the old man strained one last quarter-turn and it clunked fully back. And as the gate flew open under the weight of the slavering animals, Rupert turned and flung himself helplessly on to the outer gate, but the first dog was on him the moment he touched the lock. He wrenched at the handle but it would not give and the whole pack tore in behind, ripping at his legs and flailing arms.

'Sidney!' he begged. 'Save me.' And I saw that my guardian was slipping a bullet into the chamber of his revolver and walking forward, taking careful aim, from two feet away.

Rupert fell to his knees and the biggest mastiff leaped over the others, scrambling across their backs as they battled for a share of their quarry. There, at the top of the seething pile, it steadied itself, snuffled at Rupert's hair and licked his ear three times before curling back its lips to take his cheek between its front teeth and tear it away. Sidney Grice took one more step so that the barrel of his gun was between the bars and Rupert's bloodied hand came through and clutched at his trouser leg. Three of Rupert's fingers were missing. One of the mastiffs rammed its jaws out, gripping the hem of Sidney Grice's coat, and he tried to yank away.

'Let go, you filthy animal.' He levelled the gun again and fired, and after the detonation there was a stillness such as I have never witnessed before. The dogs froze in their attack and a black hole appeared in the middle of Rupert's forehead, and it seemed an age before his skull broke.

The silence shattered and a dog behind him yelped and fell back. The rest looked up and then down and set again about their prey, snapping their bloody jaws, squabbling with each other for a portion of his worm-riddled flesh.

Sidney Grice raised his gun again, slowly exhaled and lowered it, uncocking the hammer in one practised movement.

'Filthy animal,' he repeated as he turned away. 'And so the last Baron Foskett dies just as the first, torn apart by a pack of dogs,' my guardian mused aloud and bowed his head. 'Come, March.'

I looked around. 'But where is Cutteridge?'

'He has gone back in and bolted the door but there is a shortcut to the front.'

Our way was tangled with brambles but Sidney Grice scarcely seemed to notice as he trampled round the side of the house, the thorns ripping at his clothes and mine.

'Why did the *Hamlet* quotation matter?' I asked.

He snapped a sapling that blocked our way. 'The baroness was a respected Shakespearean scholar. She would never have got it wrong by mistake, so either she was trying to tell us something or —'

'It was not her.'

'Precisely. Rupert was taunting me.'

Several times I had to stop to wrench my torn dress free, but he marched determinedly ahead until we came out on the gravelled clearing. Sidney Grice put his gun into his satchel.

'The door is still open,' I said. 'Do you think —' But my question was drowned out by a loud hammering.

We ran up the steps and inside, just in time to see the great staircase tipping away from the wall and hanging for a moment before, with a great groan, it collapsed then crashed into the hall, no more than a pile of splintered timber now, and Cutteridge at the top with an axe dangling in his left hand, clouds of dust billowing up around him and the lantern at his feet.

'He did not deserve to be put out of his misery,' he shouted. 'He should have lived to see his rotten heart torn from his breast.'

'Come down, Cutteridge,' my guardian called. 'I shall not tell the police what you have done.'

And Cutteridge tilted his head to one side. 'You were always an honourable boy,' he said, 'and you are a true gentleman, sir, but my mistress needs me one last time. I cannot let her be burnt alone.'

'Burnt?' I queried and Cutteridge bowed.

'I am sorry to have manhandled and threatened you, miss.'

The dust was still rising when he swung the axe back and with hardly a glance let it swing forwards again, sending the lamp flying from the edge of the top step, arcing brightly through the gloom as it fell, smashing into the wreckage and spraying oil in every direction. For a moment it looked like the light had been extinguished, but then a hub of blue appeared and a dozen spokes of yellow ran outwards in every direction, and three more up the wall, where the shards of shattered oak dangled from ancient fixings. The wood was dry and burst into flames like seasoned kindling and soon there was a huge bonfire blazing in the hall. The paintings blistered and the wall hangings smoked and ignited.

Cutteridge stood for a moment peering down at his work.

'Please do not risk your lives by trying to come up the back stairs,' he called. 'I have secured the doors at the top.'

'Go to a window,' I shouted above the crackle of fire. 'You can easily climb down the ivy.' And Cutteridge put a handkerchief over his mouth and nose.

'My place is here,' he said. 'Please excuse my not showing you out. The key for the gate is in the left lodge. Goodbye, sir, miss, and God bless you both.'

The smoke was thick now and it was difficult to see exactly when Cutteridge disappeared, but the ceiling had already taken and the floor was hot beneath our feet as we went out through the front door. We stepped back on the gravel and looked up. The flames were visible through the shattering first-floor windows and as we backed slowly up the path, transfixed by the sight of Mordent House ablaze, we heard it — muffled but unmistakeable — the single shot of a gun.

We made our way to the gatehouse and found the key, and put it in the lock as Cutteridge had done so many times before.

'Shall we call the firefighters?' I suggested.

'What for?' His eye was out and the socket oozing, and his right eye was trickling too. His gaze was fixed on the conflagration. There was a deafening crash and then another and the very building shuddered. He spun round and slashed his stick into a pillar. Again and again he smashed it into the old bricks. The cane cracked and twisted, its steel core bending under the fury of his blows. 'Damn you to eternal damnation!' He raised his arm once more and flung the shattered cane into the undergrowth. It hit a branch and tumbled into the bushes as he turned to me, his face contorted in a strange terrible passion. 'Nothing . . .' He fought to control himself. '*Nothing* can save the House of Foskett now.'

65
SOGGY MESSAGES
AND THE ST LEGER

We were quiet for most of the way back, our heads down against the wind and drizzle.

'I was supposed to be calling on Dr Berry at half past,' Mr G said, flipping open his hunter, 'but I am not my usual effervescent self. I shall send her a message from home.'

A thought struck me. 'What did you mean about Gerry being disappointed?'

He glanced across. 'I anticipated Rupert releasing the dogs, for he must have known that he was close to being exposed, and arranged with Gerry to use his cricketing skills and toss four dozen poisoned lamb chops over the wall and deep into the grounds. What I did not foresee — for, near miraculous though my powers are, I am not a soothsayer — was Cutteridge's locking the gates of the pound.'

We rounded a sharp corner and I fell heavily against him. I was not sure where we were now. A gas pipe explosion had closed three streets to traffic.

'I am sorry you have lost your friend.' I pulled myself up.

'As I have told you repeatedly, I have no friends.' The corners of his mouth pulled down. 'How could I, being such a *miserable old devil*?'

I laughed involuntarily. 'I am sorry about that.' And he patted my hand.

'I lost Rupert nineteen years ago.' He inspected the torn hem of his Ulster. 'What you saw today was the corruption of a man, not the person I knew.'

'Do you think it possible that he was right and that the maggots *were* in his brain?'

Sidney Grice pulled on a loose thread. 'I think it unlikely. It is too pretty an explanation of what destroyed him and I dislike prettiness in all its manifestations. You cannot trust anything which is appealing if its appeal is the only reason to trust it.'

'So how will we find Miss McKay?'

'We have no need to.' The thread was unravelling. 'There is no one left to kill and if she does not come forward she cannot claim her prize. She will know as well as you or I that we have very little evidence against her.'

I looked out at the ragged people trudg-

531

ing along the drab streets or standing list-lessly on corners or sitting on steps. What could they hope for other than sustenance and shelter to keep their souls trapped a little longer in their malformed bodies?

'I lost something else today,' my guardian said suddenly.

'Your faith in God?' I asked and he humphed. 'In human nature?'

'I have never had any faith in that.'

'Yourself?'

'How could I possibly doubt myself?' He snapped the thread. 'No, March. I am not sure what I have lost or where it has gone, but I doubt that I shall ever find it again and I shall always be the poorer for it.'

'Surely not a feeling?' I said, but he was looking out of his window.

I recognized the Edgware Road, and was turning to look at a new hat shop when the hatch shot open and the cabby appeared, his long, lank black hair hanging over his face.

'Before I forget,' he said. 'Joe Dubbins said to let you know 'e picked one of 'em up this mornin'.'

Sidney Grice cricked his head back. 'Which one?'

The driver screwed up his mouth and eyes. 'The one wiv the stained face,' he said.

'Primrose McKay,' I interjected.

'What time and where did he take her?' Mr G demanded.

The hair flopped side to side. 'Dunnow 'cause 'e writ it down and I missed my book learnin' thru 'avin' a kidley fever when I was a pup.'

'Give it to me, man.' My guardian put a finger to his eye, and the driver leaned so far forward that I feared he would fall through as I stood unsteadily to take a folded note from his gloved grasp.

'This is sopping.' It was disintegrating in my hand.

'Swap places and see 'ow dry your pockets is,' the driver challenged me as Sidney Grice tried to unstick and unfold the offering.

'Ridiculous,' he grumbled. 'How can anyone be expected to read that?' He fished out his pince-nez as I leaned over. 'Dash it, the lenses are steamed up.'

'Bryanston,' I said. 'It says Bryanston.'

He polished his pince-nez with a handkerchief and took another look. 'Dr Berry's house.'

'Why would she go there?' I asked, but the thought was already in my head and my guardian pursed his lips.

'Dorna is the only person who can definitely link McKay to the site of a crime.'

'Tavistock Square.' I hardly dared express my conclusion. 'So with Dorna out of the way —'

Sidney Grice jumped up and banged on the roof. 'Bryanston Mews and quick about it.'

'Make your mind up, guv.'

'A sovereign if you make it before the hour is done,' I called.

'Of your money, not mine,' Sidney Grice muttered. And the horse's head turned to the right and all of a sudden we were on one wheel and almost overbalancing, and I was flung across my guardian. 'Mind my flask, March.'

An omnibus was coming straight at us but we just managed to get in front of it.

'Who d'you fink you are? Fred fleckin' Archer?' the omnibus driver bellowed, hauling hard on his reins.

Our driver laughed. 'Wouldn't be sitting on this ole dustcart if I was.' He looked down at my companion. 'You follow the gee-gees, squire?'

Our left wheel came down with a bump, the horse straightened and lifted its head, and set off back down the road.

'I can think of little more tedious.' Sidney Grice unclipped his satchel to check the contents.

'I did get five to two on Silvio at the St Leger,' I told him, and my guardian glared at me.

'You are talking like a flash mobsman.'

I did not dare tell him I got the tip from a barman at The Bull, and we swung sharply across the road again — nearly upsetting a gig this time — and down Bryanston Road into the mews.

The church bell was striking as we pulled up, our horse tossing its head proudly as if it had just crossed the finishing line first at Doncaster.

'I do not imagine Dr Berry is in any real danger,' I said, a little battered, as our driver pulled open the flap. We were a short way down the street from the house as a coal wagon was blocking the way.

'Perhaps not.' Sidney Grice helped me out. 'But —' He gripped my arm and I stepped forward to get a better look.

The door to the house was ajar and, as we hurried towards it, I saw a woman. She was lying face down on the floor in the hall.

66
THE POKER AND THE CLEAVER

Sidney Grice let go of my arm and ran. I rooted around my purse, passed the payment up to the cabby and followed. He was already at the front step and signalled for me to stand clear. For once I obeyed, and watched as he stepped back and pushed the door fully open.

'It is just a servant,' he called and stepped inside. 'All clear.' I hurried in to find him crouched over the prone body of a housemaid. 'See to her.' He stood up and called out, 'Hello? Dorna?' Then he rushed into the consulting room.

I kneeled beside the maid. Her hand was hot with a gold cross on a snapped chain wrapped around her fingers, but I could find no signs of life. Her face was towards me, eyes open and still shining, and mouth agape, showing her small grey teeth. I brushed her eyelid but it did not react. A pool of blood, still wet, had oozed from the back of her head but I could not see any wounds beneath her smashed-in stained hat and thick black hair.

'Just a servant,' I whispered as I closed her eyes.

There was a poker lying nearby and I rose to look at it. It was bent near the end and caked in blood with a clump of hair.

My guardian came back into the hall. 'She is not in there and there are no messages on her desk.' He looked about. 'Good. You have not disturbed anything — except her eyes.'

'She cannot have been dead for very long.'

'And a probable weapon conveniently on display.' He closed the front door and another door slammed. 'What the . . .' We set off down the hall, past the stairs and through an open doorway into the back of the house.

The door ahead was closed and Sidney Grice flung it open to reveal a kitchen, small with a central scrubbed table. The moment he did so, we heard a crash and turned to see Dr Berry, hanging by her neck from the ceiling next to a pine dresser.

'Dorna!' I exclaimed.

She had her hands clutching at the noose and her eyes were strained unnaturally wide, turned towards me in desperation, and her pupils were pinpoints. A wooden stool lay

537

upturned beneath her. Sidney Grice snatched it up and scrambled on to it, grabbing a high cupboard door for support. Dorna's feet were in an open cutlery drawer. He bent his knees, put his arms round her waist and straightened up to slacken the rope.

'Untie it,' he commanded. My eye followed the rope from her neck up to a butcher's hook on the ceiling, where it looped through and then down at about thirty degrees from the vertical to an iron ring on the wall by the back door. 'Hurry, March.'

I ran across and tore at the knot. 'It is too tight.'

Dorna was making choking sounds and her face was dark, and I could see my guardian was having trouble holding her and balancing on the stool, which was wobbling beneath him. I snatched a meat cleaver from a rack and slashed at the knot three times as hard as I could, impacting into the whitewashed wall, and ripped the last few frayed strands apart. The rope fell loosely away and I dashed back to steady the stool.

Dorna Berry's eyes were closed as we lowered her to the floor, and she was not breathing, but her fingers between the noose and her chin had taken most of the pressure, and the moment we loosened the rope she shuddered and inhaled noisily.

'You are safe now,' he said, raising her head to take the rope from under it.

Dorna's limbs jerked. 'Thank God,' she gasped hoarsely. 'Thank God you came.'

67
THE POKER AND THE ROPE

In a few minutes Dorna was recovered enough to sit up and, shortly afterwards, to be helped on to a chair. I filled a glass of water, but, when she took it from me, she was shaking so badly that she could not drink.

'I really thought . . .' She rubbed her throat gingerly. 'I really thought . . .' She broke down in tears.

'Try not to speak,' I said, but my guardian batted my words away.

'Try to if you can.' He steadied her hand and she managed a sip of water.

'If you had not come when you did . . .' She sobbed again and I took her hand. 'I am sorry.'

'What happened?' Sidney Grice pulled up the stool and sat beside her.

'I hardly know,' she wept, cradling the air around her face with open fingers. 'Somebody came to the door.'

'Was it a ring or a knock?'

She swallowed painfully. 'What? . . . A ring, I think . . . Yes, just one ring. Emily answered the door.'

'Where is your usual maid?' I enquired.

'Jane had yesterday off and a half day today. Emily came from an agency. I have used her a few times in the past.'

'Did you see her go to answer the call?' my guardian rattled off.

'No. I was in my consulting room with the door closed, but I heard her footfalls in the hall and the front door open, and she told somebody to wait. Then —'

'How many people?' he asked abruptly and she put a hand to her brow.

'For heaven's sake,' I said. 'Dorna has just escaped death.'

'And her memory of it will never be fresher,' he snapped, but added to her more tenderly, 'If you can manage, it will help enormously.'

'I will try.' Dorna Berry worried at her forehead in quick little pinches. 'I could not tell at that stage because I did not hear any voices except Emily's saying, *Please wait here.* Then there was a sound, a loud thud, and she cried out — no words — just a cry of surprise or pain, and then a crash as if she had fallen over, and three more thuds. I

541

heard them all separately but in rapid succession, the sort of speed that one might . . .' she hinged her hand down to cover her eye, 'beat a carpet.'

I took her left hand in both of mine. 'Are you sure you can go on?'

Her right hand fell on to mine. 'If it helps to catch them . . .'

'Them?' He pounced and she nodded twice.

'I went out and saw her.' Her grip spasmed. 'That woman — the one I saw in the square. I am sure it was her — the one with the birthmark.' She touched her cheek silently.

'Primrose McKay,' I said and she nodded again.

'Just her?' my guardian asked.

'At first. Then I saw Emily. She was lying face down towards the front door and it was open, and the McKay woman was standing just behind her with a poker in her hand, raised' — she held out her fist — 'like a weapon.'

'Where could the poker have come from?' I asked. There was no fireplace in the hall. Dorna unclenched her fist.

'Jane kept it in the umbrella stand . . .' She laughed ironically. 'For our protection as we were frightened, after I saw that

542

woman in Tavistock Square, that she might come for me.'

Sidney Grice caught his eye. 'You never told me.'

She started to rock to and fro. 'I thought you would tell me not to be silly. How could she even know who I am or where I live?'

My guardian touched her shoulder. 'She would have known where *I* live and seen us together. All the world knows where I reside and it would have been a simple matter to have tracked my movements. I am sorry if I led them to you.' Something in his apology sounded hollow. Perhaps it was just that I was unused to hearing him use the word *sorry.* 'What happened next?'

'I stepped into the hall.'

'That was brave of you,' I said and she crinkled her brow.

'Brave or stupid? I think I did not really believe what I was seeing. It was like one of those bad melodramas that my foster parents put me in as the village beauty.' She smiled tightly. 'And that was when I was attacked — a man grabbed me.'

'Thurston Gates —' I began but Mr G hushed me.

'Continue,' he instructed and Mary struggled on.

'He must have been standing behind the

door. He got me in a bear hug and lifted me off the ground as easily as I might pick up a pillow. I tried to scream but he clamped his hand over my mouth. I tried to hit him but he did not seem to notice, and then that woman came towards me and raised the poker and I thought . . .' She put her knuckles to her teeth and tears sprang in her eyes. 'I thought that she would dash my brains out and the first thing I thought about' — she coughed — 'was that I might never see you again.'

'That would have been one blessing for you.' Sidney Grice polished his eye with a square of blue cotton, but Dorna shook her head.

'It was the one thing I could not bear.' She put her hand on his. 'I have seen death so often that I believed I was not afraid of it . . . He carried me here, down the hall. I kicked and tried to bite his fingers but he held my jaw so tightly. No matter how I struggled, I was no more than a child in his grasp. He pinched my nostrils and I could not breathe, and before I knew it I was standing on a stool while he tied a rope to that ring on the wall.'

'Where did they get the rope from?' I asked and she flared up.

'How should I know? They probably

brought it with them.' She forced herself to calm down. 'He slipped the noose over my head and tightened it and' — she closed her eyes — 'kicked the stool away. I only fell a few inches. Either they miscalculated or they wanted me to die slowly. I clutched at the rope and tried to loosen it around my neck.'

'I wonder why they did not tie your hands,' I said.

'Perhaps to prolong the struggle even more.' Sidney Grice prised his eyelids apart and forced his glass eye into its raw socket. He drew a sharp breath but waved away my concern to ask, 'What next?'

'She stood there watching me. Dear Lord, Sidney, the look of pleasure on her face. I have never seen such undisguised evil.' Dorna took a deep breath. 'Then you arrived. They glanced at each other, shrugged and walked very calmly out into the garden. She looked back at me and she was still smiling, almost serene. She blew me a kiss and left . . . I could not hear any voices then. And I thought whoever had come in might have run off, on seeing Emily, to find a policeman. And I could be left here to die.' She pulled the collar of her dress as if re-enacting her words. 'The drawer was partly open and I managed to pull it out with my feet and stand in it to support myself.'

I gave her my handkerchief. 'That showed great presence of mind.'

'But I could not get my fingers out from under the rope and I was choking and . . .' She burst into tears. 'Nobody came and I was choking.'

'I think you have had enough,' I said and my guardian concurred.

'Would you like a proper drink?' I asked and she managed a half-smile.

'There is some sherry in that cupboard. Cook was going to make a trifle.'

'Where is Cook?' Sidney Grice stood up and Dorna looked about her as he went to the back door.

'Oh, you don't think . . . ?' Dorna began as he went outside.

He kneeled over the prone form.

'Dead,' he said as he returned, 'in the rose bed — attacked from behind, almost certainly with the cleaver which is lodged in her occiput.'

'Sweet heaven,' Dorna whispered. 'Will it never end?'

'Yes.' My guardian closed the door. 'It will all end today. Stay with Dorna, March, whilst I go next door and summon help.'

68
THE STAKING OF LIVES

I sat with Dorna Berry sipping sherry and saying little, while Sidney Grice examined the bodies. He paced round the hall and spent a long time in the garden, apparently taking soil samples and measuring footprints, before rejoining us in the kitchen.

The police came, two constables, a grey-haired sergeant and Inspector Quigley.

'Do not leave me,' Dorna begged and I put my hand on her shoulder.

'Well, you *have* excelled yourself today,' I heard Quigley say as my guardian went to meet them. 'Two brutal murders for the price of one and very nearly a third.'

Dorna buried her face in her hands.

Mr G tucked his thumbs into his waistcoat pocket. 'You seem to forget that whilst I am under no obligation to protect these people, Inspector, you have a sworn duty to do so.' He lowered his voice but it was still clear. 'These women were not clients of mine and

I am only here as a courtesy to Dr Berry.'

I walked across and shut the door but could still hear the muffled voices coming from the hallway, intermittently raised as Sidney Grice and the inspector debated heatedly. There was silence for a while and they must have gone out of the front and through the side gate, for I heard them again in the garden, their voices getting angrier, until the back door flew open and they all marched into the kitchen.

Quigley picked up the noose from the dresser and held it out to Dorna. 'Show me how it fits round your neck.' But I snatched it from him and shouted, 'Leave her alone. Can you not see she is in a severe state of shock?'

Quigley coloured indignantly. 'I have to question her.'

'Of course,' Mr G agreed. 'But not today.'

'She will come to the station tomorrow then.'

Dorna buried her face in her hands while the constables poked about, opening and shutting drawers but showing little interest in what they contained. The sergeant lifted the kettle from the side of the range. 'Any chance of a cuppa?' he asked hopefully.

'None at all,' I told him, and the constables grunted in disappointment as they all trudged back into the hall.

'I will have these corpses taken to the morgue,' Quigley announced.

He put on his bowler hat and patted it down, and, bidding us a crisp goodbye, marched out of the house. The constables took the bodies on blankets into the back of a black van and rode off with the sergeant.

'Is it all right to clear up?' I asked, and Mr G shrugged and went back to Dorna. I found a mop and bucket to wash the hall floor and, once the bloodstains were gone, he brought Dorna through to her consulting room.

Jane, the maid, returned and I sat her down in the back parlour and explained what had happened, but there was nothing I could say to lessen the horror of events. She swayed in her seat and for a moment I thought she would vomit but she steadied herself, though her face was white as candle wax.

'Oh, miss, if it had not been my half day . . .' She did not need to complete her words for us both to know what she had escaped.

I poured her a sherry and for once I did not have another. Sidney Grice came in. 'Ah, Jane, I have convinced your mistress that she needs to eat. She thinks she can manage a ham sandwich.' I glared at him and he returned my look. 'Yes, I know what you are thinking, Miss Middleton, but this is no time for me to preach a civilized diet to her.'

'No.' I stood up. 'Nor any time for you to consider Jane's feelings.'

'Oh.' He waved airily. 'There will never be a time for that. It is inconvenient enough having to be so attentive to my own servants. I will have three peeled raw carrots.'

He wandered away.

'I will make it,' I said, 'if you tell me where the meat safe is.'

But Jane struggled to her feet. 'No, miss. I can't sit back and watch you work. It wouldn't be right.'

'If you feel unable to continue, I can contact the agency,' I offered, but she set her expression.

'My place is with my mistress.'

I tried to help by cutting some bread but Jane put my rough blocks to one side, trimmed the loaf and cut four perfect thin slices.

'And we will take coffee.' My guardian reappeared. 'I have tried to persuade Dr Berry to stay in Gower Street for a few days but she is determined to remain here.'

'Will you and I stay to protect her?' I

asked and he flicked his hair back with a jerk of the neck.

'She is adamant that we shall not.'

Jane hung on to the tabletop and I stood by ready to catch her.

'But what if they return, sir?'

'I have given your mistress my word, and you have it too, that they will not,' Sidney Grice told her.

Jane straightened up and let go of the table. 'You are a gentleman, Mr Grice, and your word is good enough for me.'

My guardian crossed the room to view his reflection in the polished base of a hanging saucepan. 'Rest assured.' He tidied his cravat. 'I will stake your life on it.'

69

SALT AND THE SPITEFUL SON

I stayed with Jane while she prepared the sandwiches, carrots and coffee, and I double-checked, at her request, that the back door was secured before she took the tray into the front room.

Dorna seemed much cheered. She stood up and embraced Jane and whispered something to her, but Jane said, 'You took me in when no one else would give me an interview. I shall not desert you now, miss.'

Dorna kissed her cheek and took her hands. 'I shall not forget this, Jane.'

'I require salt,' my guardian said, and after her maid had gone, Dorna explained, 'It is a sordid story but all too common I am afraid. The oldest son of her household tried to take advantage of her and, when she spurned him, told his mother that it had been the other way round. Jane was dismissed without a reference and her ex-mistress was vindictive enough to put word about that she had behaved improperly with several guests. After a month of being offered nothing other than virtual prostitution she tried to gas herself, but was rescued and given three months in prison for attempted suicide. After that her position was hopeless.'

'It was good of you to take her on,' I said.

'Or naive,' my guardian grunted, but she addressed me unabashed. 'Sidney has been telling me about *your* morning. It seems we have all had lucky escapes today and we must thank God that none of us was harmed.'

We sat in three padded upright chairs round a low, rectangular table, Dr Berry pulling her chair quite close to his. The rubber plant behind them was wilting and the leaves were yellowed.

'I fear I have been more than a little harmed,' he said. 'I was not paid to protect members of the society, but that is generally assumed to be the case and every person in it met an untimely and violent end. And, if Primrose McKay is hanged, nobody will benefit from their deaths except me. Who is to say that I did not kill the others for personal profit?'

'Why, that is nonsense,' I said. 'I was with you all the time.'

'But you would scarcely be credited as an independent witness,' he pointed out.

'Help yourself to milk and sugar, March.' Dorna poured coffee from a tall pot into three dark pink cups with silver rims. 'But surely, Sidney, there will be no doubt as to Miss McKay's guilt. I may not have had a good view of her in the dentist's window but I certainly had a very good look at her today.'

Sidney Grice cleared his throat. 'Unfortunately, it is your word against hers and I have no doubt that she could buy herself a dozen witnesses, all of good standing, who would swear that she was with them in Penzance from dawn to dusk to dawn again every day this week.'

'But there was that gold cross on the chain,' Dorna reminded him. 'You told me she liked wearing those.'

I picked up the clawed tongs. 'I do not remember that.'

'Have a sandwich, March.' My guardian thrust the plate under my chin. 'She will argue that the cross could have been anybody's. No, Dorna, what we must do is build a body of proof against her in which your evidence is but the keystone that supports our case.'

'But how can we do that?' Dorna was

calmer by the minute.

'Let us reason this thing backwards for a moment.' He meditated as Jane came in with his salt. 'I have long been convinced that at least two people were involved in all the killings, except that of Warrington Gallop. If we accept that premise for the time being and that Rupert was one of the murderers, who else — other than the youthful Primrose McKay — could have been involved?'

'Cutteridge could have assisted, especially if he thought that Baroness Foskett was instructing him,' I said, but he held up his hand.

'Cutteridge had not left Mordent House in years. He did not know that Trivet's Tea Shop was demolished eight years ago, and the leaves around the main gate had fallen weeks ago but not been trodden on until we made our first visit. I remarked that they were interesting at the time and I need not remind March how scornful she was.' He took the salt cellar and blew down the hole.

'No, you need not,' I agreed, 'though you have just done so.'

He scratched the back of his hand.

'What about that cat man you told me of — Mr Piggety,' Dorna suggested. 'Could he not have acted with Rupert until Rupert killed him?'

'Which might explain why Rupert committed the last crime alone,' I said, but he shook his head.

'Two people were needed to kill Piggety.'

I took three lumps of sugar. 'What will happen to the money if Miss McKay is executed?'

'A moot point,' he said. 'I suspect the fight for it will go through the courts for years, every distant relative coming forward with a claim, but there is no one who can reasonably expect to inherit everything. The constitution of the society obliged their solicitor to draw up a list of all legal claimants in the unlikely eventuality of the last two members dying simultaneously, and it is a tortuous forest of family trees indeed.' He picked up his coffee and swirled it round. 'What I often do when faced with these conundrums is try to reconstruct the sequence of events in my imagination. I have used March for this in the past but she is pretty hopeless at it.'

'Thank you,' I said and he waved my words aside.

'You are the fourth most intelligent woman I have ever met, Dorna, so perhaps you could assist me this time.'

'Where do I come on your list?' I asked

and he blinked.

'You are not on it,' he said, and Dr Berry reached over and rested her hand on his.

'I will do whatever I can to help,' she said.

'I know you will.' He stroked her fingers.

I gazed at them. 'Would you like me to leave?'

'Oh, March,' my guardian said, 'I can see that you are irrationally insulted, but you must allow Dorna to be the murderer just this once.'

70
PLAYING IN THE GARDEN

Dorna laughed in a way that would not have seemed possible half an hour previously. 'You make it sound like a game.'

'Life *is* a game,' Sidney Grice said, 'and it always ends in tears.'

'Perhaps this one will end happily.' She tried to force a smile. 'And you must feel free to join in, March.'

'Thank you, but I would rather go outside and play,' I retorted.

'Sulking is one of her less attractive qualities' — he held his coffee under his nose and savoured the aroma — 'but preferable to her clumsy attempts at humour.'

'Do not be so hard on March,' Dorna said and sat forward, her green eyes sparkling. 'So how shall we start?'

'Let us begin with the second murder, the man who died in my study, the chemist Horatio Green.' He sipped his beverage and rolled it around his mouth before swallowing. 'How did you kill him?'

Dorna wrinkled her brow. 'I believe you told me he was poisoned with prussic acid.'

'Indeed he was, in one of the wax capsules which he inserted into his ear, but how was it replaced?'

'I do not know, dear.'

Though I knew Dorna was fond of Sidney Grice, I had never imagined her ever calling him *dear*. It seemed an affront to his pomposity, rather like addressing Her Majesty as *ducks*. He appeared to be happy enough with the epithet, though.

'By the man claiming to be Reverend Golding,' I said before they started cooing. 'When the urchins wrecked Mr Green's shop.'

'Who better to impersonate a man of the cloth than another man of the cloth?' He took his hands from hers and unclipped the lid of his snuffbox. 'Remember, March, how Green told us that the vicar picked things up and gave them to him to put away. Perhaps the vicar could not reach the shelves himself.'

'And Reverend Jackaman was a very small man,' I said. 'So whilst they were doing that, his alleged daughter put the poisoned capsule in his pill box. But who was his daughter?'

'Who indeed?' My guardian took a pinch of snuff. 'Jackaman had no children.'

'So let us assume that I — Primrose McKay — am posing as the daughter,' Dorna said. 'But if Reverend Jackaman were the murderer, who murdered him?'

'I was nonplussed by this for a long time.' He wriggled his nose. 'First, I could not understand why he would have done it. The simple explanation is that he hoped to get rid of one of the other members of the society, but how did such a ruthless killer become such an easy victim?' Sidney Grice put another pinch of snuff to his right nostril. 'But then I thought, what if Enoch Jackaman did not know he was helping to kill Mr Green and thought he was merely assisting in a schoolboy jape, perhaps in revenge for a trick that Horatio Green, a notorious practical joker, had played on Miss McKay.'

'Reverend Jackaman did not seem like a prankster,' I pointed out. 'And why did he not go to the police when he realized the consequences of his actions?'

'Who would have believed him against the delightful and powerful Primrose?' Sidney Grice produced a large blue handkerchief with white polka dots. 'The mistake I made was in wondering what Jackaman had to gain by his actions. What I should have been wondering was what he had to lose.'

'Blackmail,' I said.

'Precisely.' He turned to Dr Berry. 'Do you have any observations about that?'

She unfolded a napkin. 'Perhaps I tempted him into improper behaviour — got him to write me a letter, for example. The consequences of that being made public could be ruinous to a clergyman.'

'I can think of no more seductive a temptress.' He dusted his upper lip.

'I feel a little queasy,' I said.

'Is the coffee too strong?' Dorna enquired.

'Not the coffee.' I took another sip to remove the taste in my mouth. 'So Primrose has lured the reverend into a compromising situation and tricked him into helping her with a murder. What next?'

He folded his handkerchief and tucked it away. 'Let us proceed to the third death, that of Silas Braithwaite.'

'The dentist?' Dorna asked. 'I believe you told me he was not even a member of the society.'

'He perplexed me the most,' Sidney Grice said, 'especially as his death was probably suicide.'

'I thought that you said it was an accidental death,' I objected and he tutted.

561

'I said it *could* have been accidental. He was not killed by Jenny, his Salopian maid. You would need a cool head to carry out a crime like that, but the moment I put her coolness to the test she fainted. I would have been moderately satisfied with the misadventure theory, especially as I was not investigating his death,' he turned the tray and pulled it towards him slightly so that it was exactly in the middle of the table, 'until you, Dorna, spotted Primrose in his house. Let us imagine that Silas Braithwaite had been involved in the murder of the taxidermist Edwin Slab and that he was also acting under duress. Perhaps pressure was being applied to make him commit another murder. There are two kinds of blackmailers. The most common are after a reward, sometimes — how shall I put this? — personal services, but more often money, and they usually increase their demands until they have drained their victims' finances. The cleverer blackmailers operate what I describe in my paper — *A Brief History of Felonious Extortion Techniques in Modern Society* — as a *cascade.* The victim is first caught in or enticed into committing a small offence. It may not even be illegal, but its exposure could be highly embarrassing and socially ruinous. He or she is then coerced by threats of exposure to commit an act which *is* illegal. From then on, the victim is trapped in a descending spiral of offences. The more he does, the more he is compelled to do and, once he has been implicated in murder, why then his very life is in the extortionist's hands. Handing over all his money would be the least of his problems. You, Dorna —'

'In my role as Primrose,' she put in.

'I thought we had established that.' I was getting a little impatient with her coyness.

Sidney Grice continued as if neither of us had spoken. 'Persuaded Silas Braithwaite to take part in the murder of Edwin Slab. The chances are that he did not know what he was letting himself in for until it was too late, but somebody held Mr Slab whilst he was injected.'

'Perhaps Primrose told Silas Braithwaite that she was just going to give Mr Slab a sedative while she hunted for incriminating letters,' I suggested.

'Which would tie in with my observation that the study had been searched.' He rolled his carrots around the plate before selecting the most symmetrical of them.

'They then go back to the workroom where Silas is horrified to find that Mr Slab has suffered a fatal seizure,' I said. 'So he

563

helps to tip Mr Slab into the tank of form-aldehyde in the belief that it will make the death look accidental, not realizing that it will do the exact opposite as the lungs will not inhale any liquid.'

'And Primrose makes certain that foul play will be suspected by leaving the syringe on the floor and moving the ladder from the tank' — he dipped his carrot into the salt — 'little knowing that Rosie Flower, the senile housekeeper, will supervise the most thorough destruction of evidence I have ever seen.'

'If I had not had my suspicions, they might have got away with it,' Dorna said.

Mr G straightened his back. 'It is unlikely any murderer could escape my investigations.'

'And Silas Braithwaite is so appalled at what he has done, or so frightened of being made to commit another murder, that he kills himself,' I suggested.

'This is all guesswork.' Dorna finished her coffee. 'What makes you think that Silas Braithwaite was involved at all?'

'His trousers.' Mr G waved his carrot as if conducting the conversation. 'First, they had been splashed with a bleach which smelled very like formaldehyde, though I did not know the significance at the time.'

'But why did he not change them?' I said.

'Because, as Jenny his maid told us — if you were listening and not daydreaming about wandering lonely as a cloud or some such nonsense — his other clothes were at the laundry, which was holding them in lieu of payment.'

'And second?'

'When I picked at them I found traces of a fine white powder, which Dr Manderson of the University College chemistry department analysed as hydrated potassium aluminium sulphate, otherwise known as alum, which is used by taxidermists to tan animal hides.'

'It is also used by unscrupulous millers to adulterate flour and Jenny's father was a miller.' Even as I pointed that out I knew it was a meaningless coincidence.

He clicked his tongue. 'I am afraid that March tends to say the first thing that flits through her head.'

'There was a sack of white powder on the floor of the workroom where he died,' I remembered, and was rewarded with, 'Well done, you have finally bleated out something relevant.'

Dorna put her cup down heavily. 'She is hardly more than a child. Do you have to be so rude to her?'

'No, but I choose to be,' he said. 'She is little enough use as it is without making her any more swollen-headed.'

I was not sure whether his intentional or her unintentional insult wounded me more, but something jogged in my mind, though I could not think what it was.

'But who rang the bell that Rosie Flowers answered before she found Mr Slab's body?' I asked.

'Why, I did, to vex Sidney.' Dorna smiled. 'You know how he hates being teased.'

Mr G tisked. 'It is a pointless exercise, like trying to teach the French to cook.'

Dorna and I looked at each other and raised our eyes, while he smoothed a crease out of the tray cloth.

'A few days after Mr Braithwaite died, I believe you saw somebody in his house,' I said.

'Perhaps it was a patient seeking to destroy any connection with him,' Dorna suggested, 'to avoid any taint of scandal.'

'Or you looking for a suicide note implicating you in the crime,' I said.

'Me?' Dorna queried. 'Goodness, I *have* been busy.' She touched her blouse and I remembered the time when we had been alone in my guardian's study. 'Perhaps it was his shade.'

'Please do not start seeing them,' Mr G beseeched. 'March has friends who see them everywhere.'

'And for a moment I thought I saw the ghost of Eleanor Quarrel in the hospital once,' I admitted, and Dorna shivered.

'Well, I hope she does not reappear. I think I have seen enough murderesses for one day.'

'Be careful, March.' My guardian handed me his napkin. 'You have spilled your coffee.'

71

GAS LEAKS AND CRUMBS

Dorna passed me two napkins.

'I hope I did not get any on the rug.' I mopped my dress.

'Do not worry.' She refilled all our cups.

'Shall we continue?' Sidney Grice looked at his watch.

'Where were we?' Dorna asked.

'Well, so far,' I counted them off on my fingers, 'you have killed Edwin Slab with the aid of Silas Braithwaite, Horatio Green assisted by Reverend Jackaman, driven Silas Braithwaite to suicide and searched his house.'

Dorna laughed a little too loudly. 'It seems quite a hectic life being a murderess.'

He huffed. 'Do try to take this seriously.'

She trembled and I stood to put my shawl around her. 'If I did that I should have to take to my bed for a year.' Her voice became shaky again.

'Can you go on?' I sat down and she nodded silently.

My guardian bit off the tip of his carrot. 'Let us consider the peculiarly cruel death of the diminutive Reverend Enoch Jackaman.'

'Well,' Dorna shook herself, 'you told me how he died but did I kill him by myself or with yet another accomplice?'

'One moment.' We watched in silence as he re-dipped his carrot and nibbled it slowly. 'Delicious.' He dabbed his lips. 'And all the way from Lincolnshire, if I am not mistaken.' He put the carrot down. 'Here is where you strike a bit of luck. You find a man who is greedy, lacks any kind of compassion and is not in the least bit squeamish.'

'Prometheus Piggety,' I said.

'The cat man?' Dorna lowered a lump of sugar into her coffee and opened the tongs to let it sink.

'The very same.' He twisted his chain and let the watch spin round. 'I cannot imagine that he would have needed much persuasion to participate in a murder that was very much to his advantage. If he could dispose of the vicar and Warrington Gallop, there would only be Miss McKay and Baroness Foskett left. Whoever won the duel between Prometheus and Primrose could probably

anticipate waiting for the baroness to predecease him or her naturally. After all, she was
an old woman and to kill her would have
made the survivor the only suspect.'

'So how do we dispose of the vicar?'
Dorna stirred her beverage and clinked the
spoon dry.

'You make him sound like a waste
product,' I objected.

'Perhaps that is all he was — to Mr
Piggety,' she said despondently.

'The greatest problem is getting into the
church,' Sidney Grice said. 'The front door
is locked but the back door lock was faulty
and could not be used. This would not have
worried Jackaman overly as it led into a
high-walled garden with a securely bolted
solid gate, leading on to Mulberry Street,
and the only other entrance was through
the rectory, which was also locked, with his
trusted housekeeper inside. But she is the
weakest point of his defences. It takes a rare
level of expertise to break into a house from
the front on a busy street unobserved in
broad daylight — I have only managed it
twice myself. But servants are almost invariably dull-witted. Why else would they be
servants?'

'Perhaps they have not had our
advantages,' I suggested.

A furniture van paused outside the window, cutting the daylight, and then reversed.

'Indeed they have not,' he agreed, 'our greatest advantage being our superior minds. Remember I found that cloth cap? Piggety, wearing an old coat with the collar up and the cap low over his face —'

'He must have bought them from that road digger with red hair,' I interrupted. 'I said at the time that the —'

'Piggety rings the rectory doorbell,' Mr G carried on tetchily, 'and tells the housekeeper that there is a gas leak from the roadworks. She must evacuate the house immediately, taking the cook and maids with her, to the safety of nearby St Michael's Church until she is told it is safe to return.'

'She must have been told that her employer had already gone or she would not have left without him,' I speculated.

'Of course,' he said. 'Now, where was I? Piggety tells her he must come into the house to secure the gas supply. She goes out and leaves him to it. He lets you in. You both exit the rectory into the garden, enter St Jerome's through the back and perform the deed — whilst we are helpless to assist on the other side of the church door. You put a noose over Jackaman's neck, lead him to the screen, nail him to it, pierce his scalp with a crown of needles, and finally his side with a spar of wood from the smashed crucifix.'

Dorna swallowed. 'I have seen some terrible injuries in my profession but they were all industrial or road accidents. I have never heard of anything so cruel as that.'

Sidney Grice touched her arm. 'Would you like to stop?'

'Not if I can be of any help. This woman must be brought to justice.' She looked down. 'And who is to say she will not make another attempt to kill me?'

My guardian raised her chin and held her gaze. 'I guarantee it.' And she forced a small smile.

'How did they get out?' I asked.

'Piggety went through the back gate.' Mr G selected another carrot, leaving his half-eaten one aside. 'He threw his bloodstained overclothes into the bushes and went out on to Mulberry Street where, if he was noticed, no one would think it worth mentioning as he has a stall there, selling . . .' He pointed at me with the carrot.

'Clockwork mice and dogs,' I said.

'Just so. He would not have run the stall himself but no doubt he visited it often. He was not a man to leave his employees unsupervised. Remember he told us that he

572

would not trust a boiler man to work unattended.'

'So how did Primrose leave?' Dorna asked. 'Presumably she was somebody who might stand out in a toy market.'

'Through the rectory,' I said, 'either after we had gone or when we went into the church.'

'But what grounds do you have for suspecting Mr Piggety?' she asked.

'They are threefold.' Mr G swung his watch like a mesmerist. 'First, there is a limited number of suspects and he is one of them; second, I took a sample of mud from the floor of St Jerome's. It had an elongated moulded shape and I intended to keep it in case it fitted the defect in a suspect's boot, but it dried and crumbled in the envelope so that when I came to re-examine it I found a small white hair imbedded inside.'

'Like the cat hairs?' I asked.

'Very like,' he confirmed. 'Third, I was so intent on examining the torn page of the Bible which was forced into the vicar's mouth that I paid insufficient attention to the book from which it was torn. On scrutinizing it later, I found a number of what at first appeared to be bloody fingermarks, but there was an odd bluish tinge to them.'

'And Mr Piggety suffered with coloured

sweat,' I recalled as he put his watch away.

'*Chromhidrosis,*' he confirmed.

'I told you there were still answers to be found in the Bible,' I reminded him.

'You cannot pretend that is what you had in mind.' He nibbled the tip of his carrot.

'*The Lord works in mysterious ways,*' Dorna quoted. 'This coffee is cold. Let me ring for some more.' She got up and went to the bell pull. 'Oh, March.' She was a little drawn now. 'I would not have your job for all the tea in China.'

'Imagine you could cut cancer out of your patients,' I posited. 'The process might be painful and gory, but you do it to save lives. I hope to save lives by ridding the world of something just as insidious as cancer, the calculating murderer.'

'Why, March,' my guardian crooned, 'you almost make it sound worthwhile.'

72
FOUR MINUTES AND
FORTY-EIGHT SECONDS

Jane came and cleared the tray.

'Are you all right?' Dorna asked and Jane's head went back.

'Yes, thank you, ma'am.' She was clearly close to tears.

'I know this has been a great shock,' her mistress commiserated. 'Would you like me to request a police guard?'

Jane looked at my guardian, who said firmly, 'There is no need.'

There was an uncomfortable silence until Dorna said, 'Then you shall sleep with me tonight.'

'Thank you, ma'am.'

'Why do you not come to Gower Street?' I urged. 'I am sure we can fit you both in.'

'That is a kind offer but I hope you will be the first to agree that, just because we are women, we are not helpless,' Dorna retorted.

'But I am frightened for you,' I burst out

and Jane looked at us all.

'Bring a fresh tray,' Dorna told her.

'Yes, ma'am.' She bobbed and left.

Sidney Grice stretched his arms up as if about to dive. 'There is something quite addictive about sleep. Hardly a night goes by without me craving it in one form or another and I had none last night. However . . .' He lowered his arms and rotated his shoulders. 'Since you are not helpless, let us consider the penultimate murder.'

Dorna held her head. 'Remind me, dear.'

'Mr Piggety,' I said. 'I suppose there was some kind of natural justice in what happened to him since he intended to do the same to thousands of innocent animals but, even if he did kill Reverend Jackaman, I would not wish that death on any man.'

'The manner of his death was exceedingly unpleasant,' my guardian conceded, 'and the greatest proof yet that the deaths were planned in such a way as to taunt me.'

'The coded messages seemed to serve little other purpose,' I said, 'except to make sure we arrived at the right time. Do you think Rupert wrote them?"

'Probably.' He rested his right heel on the toe of his left foot. 'Whilst few men could equal the last Baron Foskett's numerical prowess, his lyrical skills were rather more limited, which is why I was so slow decoding them.' He waggled his right foot from side to side. 'I was looking for something clever, but they were so elementary that even March was able to work them out.'

'*Even?*' I seethed.

'Sulk later,' he told me.

'Do not worry, I will.'

Dorna rubbed her neck uneasily. 'So presumably I was responsible for killing Mr Piggety too.' A strand of hair fell forwards from behind her ear but she let it stay. 'Did I have an accomplice? Thurston Gates, perhaps?'

But Mr G shook his head. 'Rupert,' he said.

'How can you be sure?' I asked, and Sidney Grice looked at the carrot in his grasp as if surprised to find it there.

'Quite simply, because he was seen, or rather he deliberately showed himself.'

'To the boys who were supposed to be keeping watch,' I remembered. 'He frightened them off by pretending to be a monster.'

'And there were few men more monstrous than Rupert in their appearance.' He put the carrot on to the table as if it were an exhibit.

'Or in their actions,' I said.

My guardian tugged at his earlobe. 'And, whilst he was sending the boys packing, you, Dorna, were bribing a gaggle of gutter girls to warn if anybody else came near.'

'Which they did when I turned up,' I said.

'By yourself?' Dorna looked alarmed. 'You did not let March go by herself?'

My guardian put his third finger to his eye and rotated it a fraction. 'First, I forbade her to go but, as I am sure you are aware, March may not have much of a mind but it is very definitely her own.'

'Why are you always so rude about me?' I asked.

'I cannot be blamed if the truth offends you.' He twisted his eye a little the other way.

'Sidney would not tell a lie to save his own mother,' Dorna said.

'And she would be the first to condemn me if I did. Second, I took the precaution of waiting nearby with a cab and a burly ex-policeman.' Jane returned with another tray of coffee and a plate of shortbread. 'Four minutes and forty-eight seconds,' he observed when she had gone. 'We are lucky if Molly brings our tea in twice that time, no matter how much I shout at her.'

'Perhaps your shouting flusters her,' Dorna suggested.

'Nonsense.' He coaxed his lower right eyelid up. 'She likes being bullied.'

'I think she probably does,' I agreed.

'In that case I shall stop it immediately,' he said. 'Happy servants are lazy servants. Where was I?'

Dorna touched the coffee pot but did not pour. 'You were about to tell me how I killed Mr Piggety.'

'Simple enough.' He drummed his finger-tips on the arm of his chair. 'You rang the doorbell. He was either expecting you on some pretext or you bluffed your way in. Either way you go down to his killing room. One of you points a gun at Piggety and tells him to undress. The other binds him — probably not Rupert, who was hopeless at knots as a youth — fixes him to a hook, turns on the hot water supply and starts the motor. You time his progress for a while. He kicks out wildly and knocks the watch out of Rupert's hands, smashes it and one of you steps on the broken glass. At some point March turns up, probably as you are about to leave, since the building is unlocked. She takes fright, runs away and becomes embroiled in a pugilistic match on the docks. You write a telegram and give it to a street urchin to deliver. Later you send the letter and key with another boy. You pay well and

579

scare them to be sure they carry out your instructions.'

I tested the pot but it was so hot that I decided to leave it. 'How can we be sure the monster was Rupert? There is no shortage of men who look like ghouls in this city.'

He scratched his cheek. 'Would you say Piggety was neat in his person?'

'No. He had a scruffy air about him.'

'What man carefully folds his clothes when he is being forced to undress, let alone a man who has little interest in sartorial matters already. Rupert, however, was an obsessive man. Apart from being driven to write numbers he was compulsively tidy. He could not have abided seeing a messy heap of clothing and would have had to rearrange them. Also . . .' He stood and took out his hunter. 'Knock this out of my hands — and that is not an invitation to perform an act of violence.'

I got up and swiped his watch from his grasp. It fell six inches, swinging on its chain, and he flipped it open.

'Undamaged,' I said. 'So why did the murderer's watch get smashed on the floor?'

'Rupert could not tolerate chains.' He clipped the lid shut. 'They hang untidily and clink, and he drove himself to distraction forever trying to straighten the links.'

Mr G put his watch away. 'In the end he decided to forgo the chain and so, if the watch was knocked out of his hand, it would have fallen to the ground. I asked to see his watch — which used to be his father's — and was about to press the matter when Cutteridge intervened. Also, I found this.' He picked his satchel from the floor and delved inside to produce a test tube.

'The maggot,' I recalled.

'And not just any old maggot, of which there is no shortage is this hub of empire, but a specimen of *Cochliomyia*. They are not native to our shores, but by this stage Rupert was shedding them liberally.'

'And the last murder?' Dorna asked.

'Warrington Gallop, the snuff seller,' I said.

'Gallop was killed by Rupert alone.' Sidney Grice put the test tube away. 'There was only one set of footprints in the room from which the dart was fired and they were those of a man with a slight limp who exhaled blood. The type of dart used is typical of the region where he was disseminating his Christian doctrines and I do not doubt that, if Mordent House had not been razed to the ground, we would have discovered his blowpipe. Rupert could not bear to throw anything away. He saved every finger-

and toenail clipping from the age of four —
all these and many other things in labelled
boxes. He loved organizing his files.'

'I cannot think why he was your friend.' I
helped myself to a biscuit.

'Everyone who has ever pretended to be
my friend has betrayed me.'

Dorna reached across. 'Poor Sidney, but
surely . . .' she said, and he smiled wryly.

'All of them,' he said, 'without exception.'

73
THE ASHES OF
MORDENT HOUSE

Dorna went red. 'But I have never —'

He silenced her with a glare. 'I would be more flattered by your concern if I did not know you have deceived me already.' And she looked at him blankly.

'But what —' I began.

'I tried to get a copy of your nib made by Harrington's,' he butted in, 'but they told me there was no need to put in a special order.' He reached inside his coat and scattered a dozen nibs on the table. 'They already make them.'

Dr Berry picked one up. 'They are very like mine.'

'Identical,' he said and she grimaced.

'Oh, Sidney,' she said, 'you were so over-bearing and dismissive of my status when we met. The only thing you admired was my pen so when you asked who designed it, I unthinkingly blurted out that I had. It was a harmless deception.'

'That is an oxymoron,' he said. 'All un-truths harm somebody, if only the people who cheapen themselves by spawning them.'

I am sorry I deceived you. It was almost a joke when I started.

'Everybody tells fibs,' she said and he humphed.

'I do not.'

'You told a mob they had cut your eye out once,' I reminded him.

'No, I did not. I told them it was an of-fence to do so.'

'I am sorry. It was stupid of me.' Dorna blushed.

My guardian leaned forward and scooped the nibs off the table with the side of his hand into his other palm. 'If that were your only deception I could probably forgive you. After all, it is not unknown for March to treat the truth as a toy to be broken and thrown away whenever she is bored with it.'

'Perhaps I can redeem myself by pouring the coffee,' I said.

'You may pour but it will not redeem you,' he told me as I picked up the pot.

'I am sorry,' Dorna Berry said in the awkward silence. 'I hope that we can still be friends.'

Sidney Grice watched her closely. 'If only your other lies were so easily discounted.'

And Dorna bristled. 'What lies? I have never —'

'You told me your parents were actors but I have consulted Jonathon Furbish, the foremost theatrical historian in Europe, and he could find no trace of them.'

'Then tell him to look harder. They worked under the stage name of Marlowe, after the playwright.'

'When and where were you born?' he fired off.

'Paris, April the first, 1850. I would imagine that all the records were destroyed in the crushing of the commune.'

He blinked. 'How convenient.'

'Yes, it is, because I generally add a few years to my age to give me more gravitas.'

'We are both guilty of that offence,' I told her.

Dorna dabbed her mouth with a little triangular napkin. 'Now, if you will forgive my playful deception over the nibs, I will consider forgiving your unwarranted attack on my parentage.'

Sidney Grice puffed his lips and exhaled. 'You have a capacity for rebuttal which would do you credit in the Oxford Union.' He surveyed her coolly. 'Why did you not tell me you were Rupert Foskett's medical attendant?'

She held out her cup for me to refill. 'I did not know you had any interest in Baron Foskett until today.'

'I do find it a little odd that you did not mention it while we were discussing him just now,' I said and she looked at me sadly.

'Oh, March, do not let living with him make you as cynical as he is. First of all, I did not wish to interrupt your story and, second, there is the question of professional ethics. I am obliged to keep the details of my patients confidential. The Hippocratic Oath says —'

'All that may come to my knowledge in the exercise of my profession or in daily commerce with men, which ought not to be spread abroad, I will keep secret and will never reveal,' Sidney Grice quoted. 'The case of Harkness versus the Crown established that this duty expires with the patient, and you are presumably well aware of this since you exhibited no such reticence when it came to discussing Edwin Slab with us.'

'I would have told you, had you given me a chance,' she snapped. 'Anyway, how did you know?'

'I use my eye,' he told her. 'And I saw an imprint in the dust at Mordent House when

Cutteridge set his lamp down at the top of the stairs. Four clusters of berries in the corners of a rectangle, the same design you have on the feet of your case. I believe you told me it was *fun.*'

'And so it seemed,' she said. 'Perhaps you would like to recite the names of all your clients for me now so that, if we have anyone else in common, *I* can accuse *you* of withholding information.'

Sidney Grice drank thoughtfully. 'I have accused you of no such thing,' he said, 'yet.' He took a longer drink. 'What concerns me more, though, Dr Berry —'

'Dr Berry? Since when have we become so formal?'

He replaced his cup as if it were a delicate artefact. 'I am always formal when I interview suspects.'

'That is rather harsh,' I said, and Dorna Berry's cup rattled in the saucer as she struggled to put it down. 'Interview? Suspects?' You have gone too far this time, *Mr* Grice.' She rose from her chair. 'I am afraid I must ask you to leave my house.'

My guardian laughed flatly. 'That is the last thing you need be afraid of,' he said. 'If you choose not to talk to me I shall be forced to divulge my concerns to Inspector Quigley, who will no doubt wish to discuss the issues with you at great length in the comfort of Marylebone Police Station.'

She froze. 'Are you threatening me?'

He smiled briefly. 'Of course.'

Dr Berry sat down gracefully. 'Very well. Let us get this over with and then you may quit my house' — her voice trembled — 'never to return.'

Sidney Grice leaned back. 'I am not overly concerned with your having been Rupert's physician.' He crossed his legs. 'For there is no doubt he was in need of medical assistance, though it might have been better for him had you consulted Professor Stockton who is the foremost expert in tropical parasitology and, as I am sure you are aware, lives less than two hundred yards from here.'

'Baron Rupert forbade me to discuss his case with anyone,' she said.

'But he told us that his doctor had sought every expert's opinion,' I recalled.

'He was confused,' she said.

'What concerns me more . . .' my guardian produced his snuffbox, 'is the fact that you must also have been attending his mother, the baroness.'

'What of it?' She smoothed her dress.

'At what stage did you inform Cutteridge that she was dead?'

She flushed. 'Since when does a doctor discuss her patients with their servants?'

'Since when does a doctor allow the servants to believe that they are receiving instructions from their dead mistress and allow that deception to carry on for weeks on end?' I asked and she turned on me.

'Oh, how you have changed. The last time we met it was all affection, but how you snap at my heels now. My first duty was to my living patient, Rupert.'

'Concealing a death is a serious crime,' Sidney Grice said, 'particularly for somebody in your profession.'

'I wrote a death certificate. It is probably in the ashes of Mordent House.'

'Your answers are very neat,' Mr G said sharply and she looked hurt.

'That is because they are true.' She peered across the corner of the table at him. 'Your socket is still oozing. You must let me clean it up before you go.'

He closed both eyes and rubbed his good one. 'Oh, Dorna,' he said. 'Why did it have to be you?'

She put her cup down and reached across to touch his wrist and he opened his eyes and looked at her.

'And why did it have to be *you*?' she asked, and he raised his left hand and let it fall on hers and his fingers curled inwards to give it a little squeeze.

'I am tired of these games,' he said and she smiled encouragingly.

'So am I, dear. Tell me what you know.'

74
Shellfish and the Foskett Thumb

'It is a simple tale,' Sidney Grice said, 'though not a happy one and largely inspired by shellfish — the countless millions that petrify into limestone and one bad oyster. The Honourable Rupert Foskett had a crisis of religious faith, which began when I was able to demonstrate that many things he had accepted as true were in fact unprovable. Doubt is common enough since the geologists started chipping at limestone and finding fossils, and his beliefs were undermined further when historians had the temerity to study the Bible in a rational way.

'Rupert found the possibility of mortality impossible to accept and decided to immerse himself in missionary work, presumably in the hope that, if he could convince others that the gospels were gospel truths, he could convince himself in the process, and so he set off for the tropics. At first things went well. He wrote letters to his

591

parents and to me that were full of hope and enthusiasm. He contracted jungle fever but recovered quickly. He was going to move deeper inland to convert natives who had never even seen a white man, let alone heard of Jesus the Christ, and then the letters stopped.

'Nobody was overly concerned at first. The chain of mail delivery was long and tortuous. A runner might get killed or simply not bother to carry out his task; a canoe might overturn; countless letters are eaten by rats before they reach the coast; but the weeks turned into months and two years went by without word.

'At the request of the family and because of my own friendship with Rupert, I went in search of him. It was not easy. The crossing was appalling, and, when the ship reached port, the heat and humidity were almost intolerable. However, I assembled a team of porters and a guide, and went into the jungle. The trail was overgrown and, to make matters worse, I was struck by a particularly virulent form of malaria. Apparently, I was raving like a madman for a while.'

'Only a while?' I queried, but he ploughed on regardless.

'When I was recovered sufficiently we

pressed on, crossing rivers and tangled ravines, until eventually we came to a squalid village in a clearing where I was told that Rupert had been roasted alive and eaten. I was given to believe that human flesh tastes very like pork and have been unable to tolerate the smell of it since.'

'Is that why you became a vegetarian?' I asked.

'One of the nine reasons,' he concurred. 'In this fetid settlement I was shown an item which I recognized as Rupert's signet ring and a thumb bone which I was assured was his. I did not doubt it as it had an extra spur of bone, which was a characteristic peculiar to the male line of the Fosketts. I purchased them both — they are presently in the family crypt — and set off for England, arriving, after another awful voyage, almost a year to the day after I had set off.'

He picked up a finger of shortbread. 'However, as we are all aware, I had been deceived. And here I am obliged to conjecture a little — during my outward voyage Rupert came secretly back to Mordent House, riddled with blowfly and wasted by fevers. His parents could not bear for the world to know that their fine son, the last of a long and noble line, was no more than food for maggots and so they hid him away.

Their only dishonesty would have been to charter a clipper to overtake my ship, carrying the bone taken from an ancestor's coffin and Rupert's ring, and bribe the natives to say that he was dead.'

'But why did they not tell you the truth, Sidney?' Dorna asked. 'The Fosketts must have known they could trust you.'

'That was exactly why. They knew I could be trusted never to tell a lie, and their whole lives had become founded in deception.' Mr G snapped his shortcake in two, spraying crumbs over himself and the table. 'Baron Reginald Foskett had a weak heart — it came from taking exercise as a child — and he died soon after his son's return. His wife, who adored him, was devastated but determined to do everything she could for her son. She called on every so-called expert she could find. They took her money and left her son to rot, and in the end her care of him was so unstinting that she came under attack herself. Dr Simmons, the family physician, was worse than useless. One might — as Rupert did — argue that he hastened her ladyship's death with his incompetence, and that it was more agonizing than it would have been if he had left her alone. Let us return to shellfish.

'Dr Simmons was a glutton with a particular predilection for oysters. He ate them with such a passion that he did not pause to check if they were fresh or not, and died of food poisoning. His practice is taken over by an ambitious young doctor by the name of Berry. She is only too pleased to have a baroness on her books, though she is sworn to secrecy about Baron Rupert. There is little she can do, but she has a reassuring manner and gives Rupert hope. There is a cure for his condition but the drugs required are rare and very expensive, she tells him. What fortune the Fosketts have left is tied up in their property, but Dr Berry comes up with a plan to make money. All they have to do is form a last death club and ensure that the other members die before the baroness. The baroness would then die of her infestation and Rupert would come forward and claim his inheritance.'

'But how would he explain where he has been?' I asked.

'By telling the truth. No crime has been committed in keeping him hidden. There was no attempt to have Rupert's death registered or to make any insurance claims. He was not hiding from debtors or a fugitive from justice.' He rattled his halfpennies in his left hand. 'His illness was a shame upon the family. It made the last of the line unmarriageable, but once he has his inheritance he can be cured. And who better to marry than the beautiful young woman who rid him of his affliction, the woman he loves and who he believes loves him — Dr Berry.'

Dorna raised her eyebrows. 'Why, Sidney, you are wasted in detection with such a talent for romantic gothic horror stories.'

'A good detective needs an imagination' — he flung his halfpennies in the air and caught them with a downward scoop — 'but only for imagining the truth. Bear with me a little longer. I have almost finished. At some point Baroness Foskett dies. This is most unfortunate for, if she is not the last survivor of the club, the winnings will go to the unpleasant Piggety or the crook-backed Mr Gallop, or whoever else is still alive at the time. Luckily for our conspirators, Lady Foskett is a recluse. Who is to know that she has died other than her last surviving retainer? All Rupert has to do is embalm her in spices. Perhaps he sought the help of Edwin Slab, though that would have made him more vulnerable to exposure. It is an easy matter then to sit her in a curtained chamber and fake her hoarse whisper through a speaking trumpet. At the rate the members are dying, the deception need not be maintained for long. Once the last member has been disposed of, it is merely a question of forging the baroness's signature on the society's contract to claim the prize and, after a suitable interval, declaring her dead.'

'This is a very silly game,' Dorna said. 'I do not wish to play it any more. I shall get Jane to see you out.' She rose but my guardian caught hold of her by the arm. 'Your blotting paper,' he said. 'It is smudged with the ink of eight letters and a death certificate.'

Dorna flapped her hand. 'What of it?'

'Oh, Dorna,' he said softly, 'the certificate is for Baroness Lady Parthena Foskett and it is dated today.'

'Rupert sent me a message that his mother had died. I was in no doubt as to the cause and quite happily filled out a form. I planned to visit Mordent House later today.'

'But she died weeks ago,' I objected.

'I had not seen her for weeks.'

'When did you last visit the house?' Mr G challenged.

'I do not know . . . about a month ago. It was —'

'Yesterday,' he said, 'at a quarter past three.'

Dorna paled. 'You were having me followed?'

'There was no need.' He let go of her arm. 'I put out word that any driver who reported where he had taken you or Primrose McKay would be paid a guinea.'

'There you have it. They would say they took me anywhere for a guinea.'

'Another driver reported picking you up there just over an hour later.'

'They were in collusion to earn two guineas between them. Who would take the word of a common cabby?'

Sidney Grice stood to face her. 'The second driver was a Mr Gerry Dawson. He was in the area because I planned to visit Lady Foskett that afternoon and I wanted him to deal with the dogs if necessary, but we were delayed by the murder of Warrington Gallop and Gerry was just about to leave when he picked up a fare — you.'

'Gerry is a retired policeman,' I informed her, 'and his word will carry some weight in court.'

Dorna touched her forehead. 'I remember. I did visit yesterday but only to attend to Rupert. He told me his mother was asleep and did not wish to be disturbed.'

Sidney Grice raised an eyebrow. 'You are quick on your feet, my dear. Be careful you do not trip yourself up.'

Dorna laughed scornfully. 'What evidence

do you have? The imprint of my case on a floor which has gone up in flames? Blotting paper, which I have explained? The fact that I visited my patient? The hearsay of a dead, worm-riddled mad baron? Juries do not like to convict beautiful women of murder and, as you said yourself, I *am* beautiful.' She ran her fingers under his chin. 'Nobody can resist my charms.' She turned to me. 'Can they, March?' She blew me a little kiss.

Swollen-headed, I thought. And then I remembered when she had first used those words — in my guardian's study. 'Whose ring do you have around your neck?' I got up to look her in the eye.

'What?'

'When you kissed me —'

'When *I* kissed *you*?'

'When we kissed —' I restarted.

'What the devil has been going on?' My guardian stared at us both and we all sat down.

'I felt a ring on a chain,' I continued. 'It was an odd shape — like an animal.'

'I do not know what you are talking about.'

'Show us the ring, Dr Berry,' Sidney Grice said. 'Or I shall summon the police to search you by force.'

Dorna's eyes filled with tears. 'You would not humiliate me so.'

'There are three women in my household,' he said. 'If I paid any attention to weeping I should be immured in a mental asylum by now.'

Dorna reached under her collar and produced a fine-linked gold chain.

'A jackal,' he said. 'The insignia of the Fosketts.'

'Rupert asked me to look after it,' she protested. 'He suspected Cutteridge of pilfering.'

'He prised it off his dead mother's finger,' Mr G said.

'I do not know where he got it from.'

Sidney Grice looked about him as if for inspiration.

'The tonic,' I remembered. 'You made up a tonic for Inspector Pound but I have not given it to him yet.'

'And what will we find when it is analysed?' Mr G asked and she jumped up.

'Damn you,' she said. 'Damn you and your meddling girl.' She darted sideways towards the door but we were both there before her.

'Oh, Dorna,' Sidney Grice said gently. 'It is *you* who is damned.'

75
THE ECONOMICS OF HOPE

'Shall we sit down again?' Sidney Grice turned their two chairs so that they were facing each other, and guided Dorna Berry back into hers. He sat opposite her and took her hands. 'Why Inspector Pound?' he asked.

Dorna shivered. 'Can you not guess?'

'It is apparent that you have a grudge against me — though I do not know why yet. Presumably you have some grievance against the police too, though I do not believe you have a criminal record.'

'I had a perfect plan,' she said. 'I would have been rich and titled. I would not have had to tolerate Rupert for long. The maggots had entered his body cavity and it was only a matter of time before they fed off his vital organs.'

'Did you care for him at all?' I asked and she snorted.

'He was a self-pitying, obsessional child.

He would talk for hours about numbers.'

'He was a mathematical genius,' my guardian said, 'on the verge of disproving Pythagoras' Theorem before he decided to squander his life on religion.'

'And Lord, how he hated you, Sidney, for making him doubt it. Hour after hour he would pour bile upon your name. He told me he had almost spared Warrington Gallop and used his dart on you, but he knew how angry I would be and how desperately he needed that money.'

'For a cure that does not exist,' I said.

'*I* was his cure.' She raised her head. 'I gave him something he had never had before — hope.'

'False hope,' I insisted.

'I gave him something to live for.'

'You gave him something to kill for,' Sidney Grice said, 'and something to die for and, ultimately, you made him more corrupt than those filthy worms had done in all those years.'

'You did not do this for yourself,' I said.

'Now you are talking nonsense. I do not know why you involve that stupid little slut in your enquiries, Sidney. No wonder your reputation has suffered so much since she arrived.'

Sidney Grice sat watching me. 'Go on,' he said.

'Have you ever told Dr Berry about Eleanor Quarrel?' I asked.

'Never,' he said. 'It is not a case I am proud of.'

'Neither have I,' I told him. 'And yet . . .'

'I read about her.' Dorna pulled her hands away.

'Where?' he demanded and she struggled for words.

'Eleanor Quarrel has never been mentioned in any newspapers,' I said. 'She was never convicted of any crimes and we did not know her real name until after she disappeared.'

'Until she died fleeing you.' She swept her arm to indicate us both and I stood up.

'What lovely green eyes you have,' I said and she looked deep into mine, and at that moment I knew. 'Oh, Dorna, did you really do it all to avenge your mother?'

'Can you think of a better reason?' She jumped up to face me. 'Mrs Marlowe was a dull-witted, vain dipsomaniac and I hated her. I had no parents and then my real mother found me about a year ago. She was beautiful and clever and witty, and we were just getting to really know each other when you took her away from me.'

'She died fleeing justice,' my guardian said.

'Justice?' she echoed bitterly. 'What justice did she ever have? For pity's sake, she was sent to prison for defending herself from a policeman's advances when she was hardly more than a child.'

'She probably encouraged him,' Sidney Grice said and I rounded on him.

'That is a filthy thing to say.'

Dorna shushed me. 'All men are vile, March — however they choose to present themselves.'

'I believe Inspector Pound to be a good man at heart, but you set fire to the operating theatre and tried to kill him,' I said and she looked at me with disdain.

'Now you are being ridiculous. Even if I did you cannot prove it.'

'Carry on.' Sidney Grice leaned back in his chair and surveyed her.

'But I qualified and found employment and my private practice was expanding, and when my mother turned up I was so happy. I loved her from the first and she loved me.'

'She never loved anyone,' I said, 'and no more do you.'

She eyed me with contempt. 'You know nothing about love.'

I let that pass.

'But surely when you found out what she had done —' Mr G began.

'*What* had she done?' she shouted. 'Other than be an innocent pawn in a sordid affair! She told me that you hated her for exposing you as a fraud, an incompetent who sent an innocent man to his death, and that you and the police were trying to destroy her. The day I heard that she had died I made a vow: I would destroy you all, and what better way to do it than make myself rich in the process. I assumed that Pound would be involved in the case too, but he avoided that by being put on another investigation.' She smiled grimly. 'Imagine my joy when he fell into my hands, utterly helpless. I could have smothered him where he lay and no one would have suspected me, but why should I let him die peacefully in his sleep when he could die painfully and at your hand, dear March?'

'Do you really hate us that much?' I asked.

'As a matter of a fact I have become quite fond of you both over the last few weeks, but by then the wheels were set in motion.' She looked around the room. 'Oh, March, if you had truly known her as I did. We were so alike. I do not mean in appearance — she told me I looked like my father.'

'Did she tell you who your father was?' I asked.

'He was a captain in the Guards who was going to marry her when she came of age, but then he was sent abroad and died.'

'Dear Dorna,' Sidney Grice said. 'How like a small child you are to believe that.'

She turned on him furiously. 'What now? Are you going to tell me he was a corporal or a private? I do not care what he was.'

'Dorna.' I went over and touched her shoulder, but she brushed me away. 'Your father was your grandfather.'

She flinched. 'You are talking nonsense.'

'I wish I was.'

She stood up, grasping the chair to steady herself. 'No wonder she never told me his name. Oh, my poor mother . . . She was *thirteen*.' She cradled her mouth in her free hand.

My guardian took her elbow. 'Sit down please, Dorna.'

She obeyed meekly, and suddenly she looked very small and vulnerable. I went over and crouched before her. 'I have something else to tell you.'

She looked confused. 'Have you found him? I do not want to meet him if you have.'

'No,' I said. 'Your father died a long time ago but your mother is *not* dead.'

Her face twisted into one contorted word, so tangled with hate that I had difficulty understanding it. 'Liar!' She leaped up to stand over me.

I spoke slowly as I rose. 'A friend of mine, a lady who knew your mother quite well, saw her a few days ago boarding a train at Euston.'

Dorna looked at me blankly. 'But I have avenged her.'

'And now she might as well have died for you shall never see her again,' Sidney Grice said. 'She has abandoned you, Dorna.'

And she covered her face and for a while we were silent and, when she took her hands away, her expression was calm again. She unclipped her bag and brought out a scent bottle.

'Was that how you were going to destroy me — getting me to kill the inspector?' I asked, and she put her head to one side.

'That and this.' She pulled out the stopper. 'Though I planned to do it at night when you could not see me.'

'Perfume?' I said as her hand went back. Sidney Grice was watching her with interest but made no effort to intervene.

'Sulphuric acid.' Her hand darted forward, dashing it into my face.

I screamed and clutched my face, curled

over, but I was too late. I felt it splash into my eyes with the first throw and over my hands, cheeks and neck with each succeeding cast.

76
THE FREQUENCY OF UNVOICED WONDERMENT

Sidney Grice sprang to his feet and pulled my fingers away.

'Take this.' He pressed something into my palm. 'It is all right. Open your eyes.'

I forced myself to do so and found that I could perfectly well see the white handkerchief he had given to me.

'It does not sting.' I fought down my panic.

'But I filled it myself.' Dorna sniffed the empty bottle in wonder.

I dabbed myself dry.

'So you did,' he said. 'But last night when we went to the play — and you only took me there to mock me — I hid your glove and when you went to help Emily find another, I looked in your handbag.

'My suspicions were aroused when I saw a bottle of Fougère. I do not know which perfume you wear — for I have yet to study the subject in depth — but March uses

Fougère and your scent is very different. I shook the bottle and touched the rim.' He held up his finger, the tip still raw. 'If there had not been a carafe of water on your desk to plunge my digit into, I could have lost the end of it. I thought perhaps you carried it for self-defence as you go into some very shady corners, but then I saw the little handgun and I decided that was security enough. So, to play it safe, I poured the acid into your plant pot and rinsed and refilled the bottle from the carafe.'

'I wondered what had happened to that rubber tree,' I said.

'Unvoiced wonderment is rare in the young,' he said, 'but almost always welcome. I also took the bullets out of your rather lovely little revolver while I was at it. I am never happy socializing with anyone who possesses the means of killing me.'

'Oh, Sidney,' she protested. 'How could you ever think I truly meant to harm you?'

He reinserted his eye. 'Apart from the particularly cruel murders you have committed or your attempts to destroy my reputation, my ward and my police colleague — I cannot imagine what makes me so suspicious of your intentions.'

'But you will not hand me over to the police,' she said, 'after everything we have been to each other.'

'Oh, Dorna.' Sidney Grice ran his fingers through his hair. 'It was all built on nibs and lies.'

77

CLOCKS AND
THE ATOMS OF DECENCY

There was little to say after that. Mr G rang for Jane and Dorna put her hand up.

'I am still mistress here.' And when Jane came, Dorna instructed her to fetch the police without saying why.

'Inspector Quigley of Marylebone Police Station,' my guardian told the young constable who marched in ten minutes later. 'Mr Sidney Grice requires him at his earliest convenience.'

For half an hour or more we sat, listening to the clocks tick and chime. I hardly dared look at my companions but whenever I did Dorna's eyes were downcast, whilst Sidney Grice was gazing at her with a peculiar intentness. In the end I could stand that and the silence no longer.

'But why did you kill Emily and your cook and pretend to hang yourself?' I asked.

'Did I?' Her face was a mask.

'Partly because they were witnesses to the

charade Dr Berry had planned and partly to cast more victims at Miss McKay's door,' my guardian answered. 'If there is an atom of decency in all of this, she did at least wait until it was Jane's day off and kill a virtual stranger instead.'

Dorna Berry shrugged. 'Perhaps it just happened to be Jane's day off.'

'Not an atom then.' He pinched his ear lobe. 'The murders of the servants and the fake hanging were all designed to put a noose round Primrose McKay's neck when she came out of hiding to claim her winnings. It would have been your word against hers and she had every motive for all the killings whereas you, apparently, had none.'

I clicked my fingers to his obvious disapproval. 'But what about Thurston, her manservant?'

'If you were a man, which you very nearly are in some ways,' my guardian brought out his Mordan mechanical pencil, 'who would you rather have as a mistress, the hypochondriac and dangerously sadistic heiress to a failing business . . . ?'

'Failing?' I queried and he waved the pencil at me.

'I have advised you before to read the business pages. McKay Sausages has taken a tumble with the deteriorating quality of

613

their product since death wrenched Mr McKay's hand from the tiller eight years ago. Coupled with his daughter's unwise forays into the equine world — and I am surprised you did not look into that aspect of her affairs, Miss Middleton, eighty-four horses which she would have been better putting into her product — she is on the brink of bankruptcy. Why, even that figurine of a mandarin was a cheap fake. She put the original pair up for auction along with a number of valuable paintings last year. She needed the money. Why else do you think she joined the society? And Thurston could choose between her and an alluring young doctor who was about to acquire one of the oldest titles in the country.'

'What a filthy mind you have,' Dorna told him bitterly.

'The world I deal with is filthy but I remain pure,' he responded. 'In case you are interested, you made three major mistakes this morning.'

She leaned back in her chair and closed her eyes. 'My only mistake was in trusting you. It is that McKay trollop who should be facing these accusations, not me.'

Sidney Grice turned the pencil between his fingers as if he were rolling a cigarette. 'First, the noose — luckily, March had to cut it so I could judge the length of the rope to the inch. It was much too short. If you had stood on the stool it would have been above your head. It was only when you climbed into the drawer that you could put it round your neck.'

'He lifted me up.'

'You told us he kicked the stool from under you,' I reminded her and she breathed out slowly.

'I was confused. I wonder how clearly you would remember things when you have seen your maid horribly killed and almost been murdered yourself.'

'The knot was quite interesting, as knots very often are.' Sidney Grice lowered the pencil to point it like a rapier towards her. 'A reverse reef knot.'

She looked at him coldly. 'What of it?'

'The same sort of knot was also used to tie up Piggety.'

'And?' She yawned ostentatiously.

'And is otherwise known as a surgeon's knot.'

'I am a physician, not a surgeon.'

'Even I know how to tie a suture,' I said and she eyed me sourly.

'Lastly' — my guardian lowered the pencil — 'the gold cross on the snapped chain in the hall. Primrose McKay never wore one.'

Dorna opened her eyes. 'But you told me she did.'

'I never lie.' He looked at her with his pencil at arm's length, as if about to start a portrait. 'I merely asked a few days ago if March had mentioned that Miss McKay liked wearing little gold crosses on chains, and then by some strange coincidence one appears in Emily's dead grasp. It was one clue too many, Dr Berry, and perhaps the final nail in the scaffold.'

Quigley came at last and Mr G spoke to him in the hall before ushering him into the room.

'At this gentleman's request I shall not manacle you,' the inspector told her.

'This is an outrage,' Dorna protested, but followed him to the door without resisting.

'Take a good look, Dr Berry,' Sidney Grice said. 'You shall never know these comforts again.'

She forced a tense smile. 'Oh, I shall be back,' she vowed, but Sidney Grice demurred.

'Dear Doctor' — he crunched on his last piece of carrot — 'the last person you shall see is the man who is about to choke you to death for a fee of two guineas.'

She spun away and let Inspector Quigley lead her out and into a Black Maria.

'You see,' my guardian told me, 'I said you must allow Dorna to be the murderer.' He clambered aboard the van. 'I shall send you a cab.'

'Not yet,' I said, turning back to the house. 'Somebody has to talk to Jane.'

It was almost midnight before Sidney Grice returned, grey with exhaustion.

'I shall not talk about it tonight.' He took two sniffs of snuff and threw back his head with his eyes closed. At last he bowed his head and I watched him for a while, staring into the open snuffbox as if waiting for something to happen. 'You should go to bed.'

'We both should.'

My guardian patted my shoulder awkwardly and I thought he shivered.

And, as I lay in bed that night looking out into the starless sky, I thought about that shadow on my guardian's face. The sadness had been there since the day I met Sidney Grice and it was never to go away.

When I returned to the hospital the next day, the screens were pulled round Inspector Pound's bed and my first thought was that something dreadful had happened, but the nurse told me that he had visitors and was playing cards, and they did not want Matron to see.

'He must be feeling better,' I said and, as I neared the end of the ward, I heard a stranger chuckle and say, 'Got you that time, Baker.'

Somebody else grunted and said, 'No sign of your fiancée today, Pound?'

'Miss Middleton isn't actually my fiancée.' The inspector's voice was weak. 'It was just something she told Matron so she could visit me.'

And someone else laughed but this time with a hard edge. 'Give him some credit, pal. He's not that desperate.' And the men roared in mirth and one of them leaned back, and the screen parted and I saw Inspector Pound propped up in bed. He was not laughing but he was not speaking, and at that moment he glanced up and our eyes met.

I spun round as if he had struck me and I almost wished he had.

'That was quick,' the nurse said.

'I just remembered something,' I said.

I lifted my skirt — how my guardian would have fussed about that — and ran.

78
THE TRIAL

The trial of Dr Dorna Berry was not a prolonged affair. There were so few witnesses left. Sidney Grice and I told the court what we knew and Inspector Quigley turned up to pick what scratchings of glory he could from the case. My guardian had briefed the prosecuting counsel well. Valiantly though the defence tried to shift all the blame on to Baron Rupert Foskett, they could not make a convincing account of it.

Dorna was demure and her replies were quick and seductive, but they were crushed under the weight of evidence against her.

The only time she seemed about to break down was when it was revealed that Rupert's cousin, the Earl of Bocking, had recently died childless, leaving him all his estate via the baroness. Had Dorna been content with merely seducing and marrying Rupert, she would have come into two titles and a considerable fortune.

The jury deliberated for a long time, doubtless desperate in their attempts to believe her. As Dorna Berry had said, nobody wanted to sentence a beautiful woman to death. The judge, however, showed no such reluctance.

There was none of the crowing triumphalism that I had witnessed in Sidney Grice when he had seen William Ashby condemned. He sat throughout, rattling his halfpennies and ignoring the attentions of the press. I had thought Waterloo Trumpington might be there but apparently he had been sent to report on a gasworks explosion in Derbyshire.

'I have an appointment with the patent office,' Sidney Grice told me in a strange monotone. 'A fraudulent American is claiming to have invented the Grice-ophone before me — some stupid device with wax cylinders.'

He saw me to a cab and wandered away, deep in thought. I got the driver to drop me off at Tavistock Square and sat watching Silas Braithwaite's empty house. Once I thought I saw a woman in the waiting-room window and an insane thought shot through me that Dorna might have been telling the truth, and that she had seen somebody in there. But the figure moved and I saw that it was just the reflection of a dray driver.

I walked slowly back to 125 Gower Street, paying little attention to my surroundings or the masses of people bustling by.

Molly admitted me and took one look at my face. 'Oh, miss,' she said in dismay as she took my cloak and hat. She touched my arm.

'Thank you, Molly,' I said and trudged upstairs to my bottle of oblivion.

Not an hour goes by without me thinking of him repeatedly. Edward, so young and brave and caring and foolish. Dear God, how we loved.

He did not put me on a pedestal; he put me in his eyes and — for all my plainness — I saw myself in them as more lovely than is humanly possible.

But Edward was not handsome. He was beautiful. He blushed when I told him that but it was true. He was so very beautiful.

He was a subaltern in India. There had been some trouble in the area and he went on patrol, him and eleven others. I thought he was safe, miles away, but we had had that argument and he wanted to see me. So he persuaded his commanding officer to let him join the group that was coming to our camp . . . They were ambushed. Four of them died on the spot and four were seriously wounded, but their comrades managed to fight their way through and get them home.

The normal practice was for the officers to be dealt with before the men but I had persuaded my father, who was the camp surgeon, to allow me to triage casualties so that those who would benefit the most received treatment first.

His face had been blown off by a musket shot at close range. I thought he was a hopeless case and that we would be better treating his juniors. I left him for the padre, so disfigured that I did not know him. He was unrecognizable, my father said, but it was always with me, the thought — if I had truly loved, I would have known him through a mountain. And a voice in the night whispered to me, 'You knew it was him all along and did not want him when he was no longer pretty.'

'Liar!' I screamed. 'You damnable, sick, perverted liar.' And I woke up drenched with my father shaking my shoulder. He hugged me for the first time and I sobbed until I thought I could sob no more. How very wrong I was. But then I was born wrong.

79
THE CORRIDORS OF PERDITION

Dorna Berry was simply attired in a black dress with a white lace trim. Her hair was neatly tied back and at first sight she looked so cheerful and relaxed that we might have been meeting for afternoon tea in Hyde Park, but there was nothing elegant about her surroundings: a stone sepulchre, dripping condensation, and lit only by a high, barred window and the traces of day seeping past the silhouette of the warder standing in the open doorway.

'March' — her voice was acrid with irony — 'how lovely.' She gestured to the bed and we sat side by side a foot or two apart and, as we turned to each other, I saw that her complexion was grey and her eyes darkly ringed.

I hesitated. 'I was not sure you would want to see me.'

'I have nothing else to occupy my time.' Her left fingers tremored in her lap. 'And I am curious as to why you wanted to come.'

'To see if there is anything you need.'

She twitched in grisly amusement. 'A ticket to America might be nice.'

I watched her fingers. 'Is there anything you need that I can get you?'

'No. Is that all?'

There was a tic in her right cheek. It crawled under her skin like one of Rupert's maggots. I shuddered and burst out with, 'Oh, Dorna, why did you have to do it?'

She inhaled sharply. 'I came from nothing, March, and I was no one. The Marlowes dragged me round the fleapits and louse-riddled hostelries of every decaying principality in Europe. Before I could even speak they had me on the stage. I hated it and I hated them. My earliest memories are of being exhibited like a prize pig, being laughed at when I tripped and hit my head, being booed when I forgot my lines or derided when the Marlowes made me sing.'

Her arm shook. 'I lost count of the times we sneaked out of inns before dawn because we could not pay bills, or were put into prison for debts. I was reared in a morass but I scrambled my way out of it by my own determination. I fought tooth and nail for my professional qualifications and even then I was spurned. Only one hospital would employ me occasionally and then only because I worked for free.'

She quivered. 'And then I saw my chance to escape and rise above them all. Rupert fell in love with me. Imagine it, March. I could have been a baroness. Who knows what suitors I would have attracted? And then my mother found me. The club was her idea.'

'It would be,' I said.

'When I heard that she had died it felt like everything that I wished for had lost its savour. It was Rupert who suggested bringing Sidney Grice into the club. Why not make our fortunes and be avenged at the same time? He hated Sidney for destroying what is most precious in any man — the sure and certain hope of immortality — but it is always a mistake to mix business with pleasure.'

'Pleasure?' I whispered and her expression lit up.

'You have no idea, March, how exquisite is the joy of taking a life slowly and deliberately, the power and pitilessness of it.'

I leaned away from her.

'You are a monster.'

But she smiled gently. 'You are the monster, March — putting human suffering under the microscope, glorying in every detail and then pretending to be shocked. We are not so very different, you and I.'

'No,' I protested. 'I tried to stop what you did.'

'Did you really?' Her voice was low and mocking. 'Well, perhaps you should have tried harder. We scattered clues like rice at a wedding. Or did you merely follow what we did with a horrible fascination?'

'No. I wept for those poor men.'

'Poor men?' she repeated. 'Those *poor men* who so willingly killed for profit and jostled with each other to be seduced.'

'How could you give yourself so cheaply?' I asked and she chuckled.

'I never gave myself to any man,' she told me. 'A hungry man who smells dinner is much more obliging than a man who has eaten and will very often move on.'

'That is disgusting.'

'Oh, March,' she said softly, 'I know the passion of your kisses.'

The warder coughed, either in embarrassment or to remind us he was there.

'Why did you tell me and not Mr Grice that you were going to Edinburgh?' I asked as she picked a stray hair from my cheek.

'So that you would not be suspicious if I went away. Things were coming to a head and I could see that Sidney was starting to pull the strands together. I did not tell him because he would have asked probing questions whereas you, March, you are a trusting child.'

'And yet you would have thrown acid in my face.'

She snorted. 'It might have been an improvement.'

'I would never have been as ugly as you have become,' I retorted and the warder stepped forward.

'No fighting, ladies.'

Dorna laughed. 'Why, my visitor and I have been doing battle since the day we met.'

'And all the time I thought you were my friend.'

'The murderer and the detective have one thing in common,' she told me. 'They have no friends. There are only victims or prospective victims.'

I shivered. 'When I saw you in the glass at the hospital I thought you were your mother's ghost.'

Dorna's eyelid quivered. 'Even my mother is not her own ghost yet.' The tic shot up her cheek, twisting it sideways. 'And now I shall never see her again. She can hardly visit me here.'

'Oh, Dorna,' I said, 'surely you set out to

cure, not to kill?'

'And you?' She clenched her left fist in her right. 'What did you set out to do?'

'To love and be loved.'

Dorna put her head back and sucked in the thick, moist air. 'That is too much to hope for, March.'

'It is the hope that keeps me alive.' I stood up. 'I shall pray for you, Dorna.'

She lowered her head very slowly. 'Do not waste your words. It is too late for me and it was always too late for Sidney Grice. Pray for yourself, March, while there is still somebody to pray for.'

I started to go.

'They will not hang me,' she cried with sudden fire. 'I am too beautiful. Can you imagine it? I hear there are petitions to the Home Secretary. He owes favours to Sidney and Sidney will speak up for me. I shall pick ochre until my nails are torn from their roots. I may be transported, but in the end I shall be reprieved and survive to start again.'

'Again?' I could hardly speak the word.

'March.' Dorna pressed something into my hand. 'Give him this.'

I did not need to ask who she meant. The warder looked at what she had given me but I had no reason to. I felt the hard metal and it bit into me.

The warder turned sideways to let me pass.

'I cared for you, Dorna. I cared so much,' I just managed before the door clanged. 'We both did.' And the lock clashed and I walked in a dream down the corridors of perdition, through the gates which would never open for Dorna Berry again and into the explosion of life which was condemned to be extinguished in her.

80
EIGHT MINUTES

Sidney Grice was invited to the execution and attended with some alacrity, always keen to see his work completed, but he was quiet when he returned.

'I never saw a woman face death with greater courage.' He massaged his eye. 'From her demeanour she might have been promenading along the Strand. They went to bind her ankles but she waved them away, saying, *I shall not run off.* She caught sight of me in the audience and called out *I . . .*' Here his voice faltered a little. '*I loved you.* A damnable lie, of course . . . Then they put the hood over her head and the noose round her neck. I had had a word with the executioner and persuaded him to try a long drop to break her neck instantly but, as he pulled the lever, Dorna jumped sideways, presumably to try to make sure of it.' He stopped, mouthed something silently and cleared his throat. 'But her foot caught on the edge of the platform and the fall broke her leg — I heard it snap — and it slowed her enough to be sure that she struggled for eight long minutes in agony.'

He shivered and did not raise any objections when I went to light the fire except to say, 'Molly should do that.'

'I like to do it.' I poured his tea and brought out my father's hip flask and held it out, but he put his hand over his cup.

'Just a spoonful. Just this once,' I said, but he kept his hand in place.

He drank slowly and in silence, the fire glinting in the jackal ring on his watch chain.

'Did you love her very much?' I asked and he peered at me as if I were a new species.

'What on earth would I want to do that for?' He took out his eye and the socket was raw with inflammation.

'People cannot choose whom they love.'

'Then why do they bother doing it? Is it, by any chance, because they are witless and undisciplined?' He swilled the last of his tea, staring deep into the dregs. 'There is a decanter in the sideboard. I keep it for over-excited clients.'

I got it out with two tumblers and poured us each a generous measure of brandy.

'You seemed very fond of her.'

'I was gaining her confidence.' He raised

the glass in an unspoken toast. 'How could you think I would love a woman who committed such crimes?' He put on his black eye patch. 'For heaven's sake, March — she preferred coffee to tea.' His face froze and his lips struggled with each other, but even his silence could not muffle the howling of his soul.

'She was so lovely,' I said and the very life seemed to dwindle in him.

'Quicklime.' He looked around the room. 'She is in quicklime now.'

He put the tumbler to his mouth but, in a sudden movement, hurled it smashing into the fireplace.

81
WITCHCRAFT, TEA AND CRUMPETS

Two days after the hanging a black carriage with curtained windows pulled up outside 125 Gower Street. It was the same frog-like equerry my guardian had sent away in such a pique only a few weeks ago.

I offered him a seat but again he preferred to remain standing, while Sidney Grice stayed in his chair, his feet crossed on the table.

'My master has asked me to extend his warmest gratitude to you, Mr Grice, and this small reward.' He handed my guardian a little velvet-covered box. 'The photograph was exactly where you said it would be.' The equerry smiled. 'In another age you might have been burnt for witchcraft. In these more enlightened times, we stand in awe of your genius and my master requests that you accept the appointment as his official private detective.'

'*Personal*,' Sidney Grice grunted. 'Tell

your master I shall be happy to be of service — if I have no other pressing business.' And when we were alone he flipped open the lid and I glanced over. It was the largest ruby I had ever seen.

'But how did you know where it would be?' I asked and he twisted his lips wryly.

'My remark was meant to be ironic because that is exactly where I found a compromising letter at the end of last year. I did not think even he would be such a dunderhead as to use the same hiding place or to forget for a second time that he had done so.'

We had tea, crumpets, muffins and fruit cake that afternoon, with our chairs pulled close to the glowing fire. This was the nearest thing to luxury I had known since I arrived.

'I am still not clear —'

'You will never be that.'

I let the insult pass. 'Are the New Chartists really such a threat?'

Sidney Grice stretched lavishly. 'The New Chartists are an unimaginative invention of our very good friend, Inspector Quigley. He planned to arrest a few would-be rabble-rousers, have them deported and announce that he had saved the empire.'

'Was Inspector Pound trying to infiltrate

their organization then?' I hoped he would not be involved in such a shabby plot.

My guardian yawned. 'Pound had real criminals to tackle. There were reliable rumours of a planned assault on Coutts Bank and he was trying to get into the gang.'

'And I ruined it for him.'

Mr G selected a muffin carefully, though they all looked the same to me. 'On the contrary, the gang thought they had been infiltrated and, with the attempted murder of a police officer over their heads, fled to Canada and Australia where their violent ways will be properly appreciated.' He nibbled his dry muffin. 'So it would seem that your clog-footed intervention did the inspector's job for him.'

'I do not suppose he will thank me.' I saw his look of disgust as I spread the butter on my crumpet and said, 'I did not know you had had malaria.'

'I still get occasional bouts. That is one reason I lock myself away.'

I cut my crumpet in half. 'Next time I will look after you.'

'I do not need any fuss.'

'Perhaps I need to.'

He massaged his brow. 'I will think about it.'

'And, while you are thinking about it, we

will get that eye cleaned up.'

He wiped his fingers. 'Yes, Nurse.'

'That is better. Now, would you like the last slice of cake?'

'No,' Sidney Grice said. 'Let us share — and then we have work to do.'

'We?' I cut it in two and he raised an eyebrow.

'You cannot spend your entire life lounging about and preening yourself if you are to be London's first female personal detective.'

'Do you think I could?'

Sidney Grice leaned back and surveyed me lazily. 'Time will tell,' he said with something very nearly like a smile.

POSTSCRIPT

Primrose McKay did not reappear until after the hanging, though she did write a letter asking if she could attend. Sidney Grice got his three thousand pounds for every murder and the rest of the fortune was hers. Much good did it do her. With breathtaking misjudgement she married her footman, the notorious Thurston Gates, and had her neck broken in an unwitnessed riding accident within the month.

The affair of the Fosketts was over and the discreet recognition of Sidney Grice in royal circles was of enormous help in restoring his professional pride and standing, but there was one affair which did not seem likely to be resolved — until I received a letter.

I went back to University College Hospital that evening and I had not even reached Liston Ward when I saw him — Inspector Pound, leaning lightly on the arm of Nurse

Ramsey and heavily on a walking stick.

'Should you be out of bed?' I asked. He still looked haggard. His suit hung loosely on his frame and he wore a shirt open at the top with no collar.

'No, he should not.' She tried to sound cross as she steadied him. 'You can use this side room — only don't be too long or I'll be in trouble.'

She sat him on a wooden chair and left us alone together.

'You look so much better,' I said.

'Now that my moustaches have recovered.' He smiled.

'I am sorry about that.'

We fell into an awkward silence, but he broke it with, 'They want to move me into a private cottage hospital in Dorset. They think the fresh air might do me good, but I'm not sure my lungs would know what to do with it.'

I looked up. 'But can you afford it?' And he shook his head.

'At three guineas a day plus doctors' fees? I'm on the wrong side of the law for that,' he observed wryly. 'It appears that a gentleman who wishes to remain anonymous offered to foot the bill, but I like to know who I am in debt to.'

I could make a very good guess but I only

said, 'I am glad I shall still be able to visit you.'

'I should miss that,' he admitted and a shaft of pain shot up the side of his face.

'Can I get you anything?'

The inspector shook his head and cleared his throat. 'I believe you may have overheard my colleagues.' He struggled for words.

'I was with the army,' I reminded him. 'I know how men talk.' I took a slow breath. 'But it was not what I heard that hurt me.'

Inspector Pound's gaze fell away and he rubbed the stubble on his chin. 'If I had said anything, they would have mocked you and I could not face that.'

'So I am to believe that you did not defend me in order to defend me?' My voice shook.

His hand went to the back of his neck. 'I was weak and I am sorry for that.'

I remembered a letter and a man striding away through the dust, taking my last chance to forgive him.

'You have been staring at death,' I said.

'That is no excuse.' The inspector coughed from deep in his chest. 'The next time I see them I shall tell them exactly how I feel.'

'I would rather you told me.'

He flopped his arms. 'You are a remarkable woman and I have come to respect and . . . admire you.' He put his palm gingerly over his wound. 'Miss Middleton . . .'

'Call me March.'

'March' — he looked at his hands — 'there is a favour I need to ask of you.'

'I shall do my best.'

'I know that.' He shifted uncomfortably. 'I have my mother's wedding ring around my neck and it is my fear that I shall be robbed of it whilst I am asleep. So many people come and go in the ward.'

I chewed my lower lip. 'Why not ask your sister?'

He fiddled with his jacket buttons. 'I would never get it back. Lucinda is of the opinion that it would be best sold to improve our situation.'

'Not when it means so much,' I said.

'It means a great deal to me.' He reached under his shirt and pulled out a black cord with a plain gold band round it. 'I wonder . . .' he looked into my eyes and I saw that his were dark blue, 'if you would consent to' — he cleared his throat again — 'wear it for me?'

He looked down.

'Around my neck?' I asked and he looked at me again, and all at once his face was alive.

'For the time being,' he said.

'Put it on for me.' I leaned over him and he slipped the cord over my head, and my hair brushed against his.

Inspector Pound shivered. 'How lovely you are,' he whispered. 'Have you ever been kissed?' I closed my eyes and when I opened them I was happy to find myself held closely in his.

There were two letters on the desk for me when I returned, one from Mr Warwick, the land agent, saying he had found a tenant for the Grange. I was glad that the house would be looked after but I hated the idea of strangers living there.

The other was in a plain brown, badly creased and grubby envelope with no stamp upon it. The handwriting was small and fluid, and I hardly dared recognize it as I ripped the flap open and sat in my usual chair.

Mr G was buried behind a newspaper and grunted absently to acknowledge my presence.

My Dear March,
I know that I have no right to address you thus but I cannot call you anything else for I have truly come to love you in

the short time we had.

I cannot ask you to think well of me, but only to believe that I spent my whole life seeking to heal before I met that woman. Perhaps you were lucky never to have known your mother for it was meeting mine that set me on this terrible course.

I make no excuses and ask no forgiveness, but if anybody can bring Eleanor Quarrel to justice I truly believe it is you.

I do not add 'and your guardian' for, if I have one wish before they take me from here into the executioner's shed, it is that you see him for what he is.

This is the last letter I shall ever write, the last there shall ever be of me, and I shall not waste it in idle words.

Be strong, March, as I tried to be: be true as I know you are and I once was: but most of all guard your heart.

I am afraid for you, March. You must leave that house. Leave it today or Sidney Grice will destroy you, just as he destroyed me and just as surely as he murdered your mother.

I shall bear you in my last breath.

Ever yours
Dorna.

I stared at the letter and reread it twice.

'Oh, Dorna,' I whispered and let the paper fall. It seemed to hang a while before it sailed, swishing from side to side across the hearth and settling face up upon the glowing coals. The middle blackened and the edges curled and it rose a little before falling back, the paper as black as the words upon it, and the flames crept yellow around it, shot red through it with white wisps and then blue rising high into shadows flickering over the dark tragedy of the accursed House of Foskett.

I had destroyed the letter but those words could never be erased: 'Just as surely as he murdered your mother.'

Sidney Grice lowered his newspaper.

'Is everything all right?' he said.

ABOUT THE AUTHOR

M. R. C. Kasasian is the author of *The Mangle Street Murders* and *The Curse of the House of Foskett.* He lives with his wife in England.